Savannah
to
Sweetwater

The Long Journey Home

By Doris Staton English

Doris S English

Sweetwater Legacy Series Book One

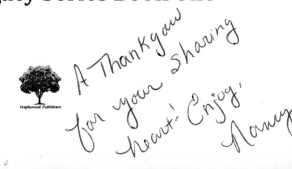

A Thankyou for your sharing heart. Enjoy! Nancy

Sweetwater Legacy Series
Savannah to Sweetwater
Copyright 2012 © Doris Staton English

Published by Maplewood Publishers
Atlanta, Georgia
Cover Art by David Wall
Photography by Dawn Bloye

ISBN: 978-0-9856132-0-4

Dedication

This book is dedicated to the love of my life and the finest man I have ever known, my husband, Bob. Without his encouragement, this book would have never become a reality.

Acknowledgements

Also I would like to acknowledge my deep appreciation and indebtedness to my daughter, Donna and her husband Mel for the tireless hours that they spent formatting, editing, and proofing. I would like to thank my sister, Judy for her energies and giftedness in promotion and marketing.

I want to thank my daughters Debbie and her husband Allen, Dawn and her husband, Kevin for their support and belief in me along the way.

I am blessed beyond measure with a family so loving and giving and it was with them on a family picnic at Sweetwater Park on a Mothers' Day that the idea for this series was born.

. . . They could not drink of the waters of Marah for they were bitter. . .
Exodus 15:23 _{KJV}

ONE

Rachel clutched the ship's railing and looked westward across the endless miles of slate gray water. Somewhere beyond that churning sea was home. It was 1859 and she had been away too long. She pulled her cashmere shawl close around her because the breeze had a biting edge for so late in April. Sea spray stung her face, leaving a salty taste on her lips, but she hardly noticed. Her mind traipsed on beyond the sullen ocean to the red clay hills and pine forested glades of North Georgia.

She moved toward the bow of the ship. Her hands gripped the slippery railing while her feet maneuvered carefully across the rough fir planking, wet from the ocean's spray. The three tall masts that towered above her with their billowing sails popping in the stiff breeze creaked and groaned with every roll and pitch of the barkentine. It cut through the choppy waters, its destination the sandy bluffs of Savannah.

The ship was a frenzy of activity. The smell of sweat, tar and sea filled her nostrils as some sailors vigorously scrubbed the teak decks while others, suspended high above her, repaired tattered sails ripped by ferocious winds that had blown them off course. Even in this cool breeze their sun bronzed torsos, stripped to the waist, gleamed with the perspiration of hard labor. Her very presence interrupted the rhythm of their work as the sailors paused to cast furtive glances at the beautiful woman. Their wistful eyes conveyed a hunger for the sight and touch of a woman. Even in one brief glance, they seemed to drink in her beauty. Tall and slender with lithe movements and regal bearing, she wore a grim mourning garb of black but it did little to disguise the curvaceous young body beneath it. The heavy broadcloth strained across her delicate shoulders and high full bust as it tapered down to a tiny waist. Her skin was creamy ivory, her cheeks flushed with youth and good health. Her long luxurious auburn tresses were swept up beneath her bonnet while tendrils escaped here and there framing her face and caressing her neck, yet her eyes dominated her face. Large and wide-set they were the color of an angry sea, deep green with flecks of golden brown and gray, framed with long, thick lashes like delicate black lace.

Despite her beauty and presence among so many men, Rachel had endured the rigorous journey thus far without any unwelcome advances from the men—officers or crew. Perhaps it was her queenly grace that evoked a sense of awe and reverence or maybe it was the captain's stern warning. Her presence remained a mystery; save for the captain and all he knew was he had orders to take her to Savannah unharmed. In the past the captain had resisted having women passengers on his cargo ship, but this time he'd had his orders and so here she was.

Rachel arrived safely at the bow of the ship, oblivious to the furtive eyes that followed her movement. It was one of the few times she had ventured this far from her cabin. Aunt Letty had warned her to stay out of sight, which she had except for once each day when Captain Smythe escorted her around the deck. She usually could not bear to stay cooped up for any length of time, but she hadn't missed her daily rides. She had not thought about Philip very often.

She looked up at the gulls screeching overhead as they wheeled and dived into the briny water. The sun hid somewhere up above the heavy, low hanging clouds and the world looked gray and dismal. Or was it her inner turmoil that made it appear so? "Oh, Papa, how can I bear it? What happened? Perhaps if I'd been home. . . ."

"Excuse me, Ma'am, but the captain said I should stand here with you. What were you saying?"

Startled, Rachel turned to meet the steady gaze of John Davids, the first mate. Captain Smythe had told her it was his first voyage with him. She shook her head slightly and replied, "Oh, nothing, just thinking out loud. Am I not supposed to be here?"

"It would be better if you were not alone, the sea's rough today, and you do provide an attractive, but dangerous diversion for the men." He answered with a smile that dimpled one cheek.

Rachel arched one eyebrow quizzically, "Dangerous diversion?"

Davids' face flushed beneath his bronze tan, "The men, they we've been at sea a long time."

"My arrival detained you," she acknowledged with a nod, "But why did you wait for me? Surely there were other scheduled packets for Savannah leaving later in the month?"

"None of them were Mr. Meredith's ships."

"Mr. Meredith?" She puzzled at the strange name.

"This is his ship and he arranged your passage." Davids remarked as if that were explanation enough.

"You must mean Mr. Wilkie; I do not know a Mr. Meredith." Rachel protested.

"Well, he must know you, our captain has never had more explicit orders concerning cargo or passenger," he added, flashing a smile which revealed even white teeth.

Rachel thought for a moment then shrugged her shoulders, "Perhaps he is an acquaintance of my father's, or Uncle Randall."

"Uncle Randall?" Davids prompted.

A sad smile parted her lips slightly, "Yes, Randall Wilkie. He's not really my uncle, just a very close friend of my parents, and our family attorney. He is the one who sent for me. I can't imagine what Mr. Meredith has to do with my passage."

"Perhaps he was acting on Mr. Wilkie's behalf."

She dismissed the mystery with a wave of the hand, "I suppose. Anyway the delay could not have been helped." Sadness touched her eyes as she added, "I came as soon as I received word of my father's death."

"I'm sorry to hear about your father; however, your presence aboard has made this trip more interesting. First voyage I've taken with a woman on board; we are ill equipped to fit female or even male passengers comfortably."

Rachel arched one dark brow; "I was quite comfortable."

Davids laughed nervously, his flush deepening "Well, you see eh . . . . "

Rachel blushed and dropped her eyes, "I—I had the captain's quarters."

"That's true."

"It seems I have really put your captain at an inconvenience."

"He was glad to do it for Mr. Meredith. Anyway you didn't delay us that long; the storm was the real culprit. Let me compliment you on how you weathered it. I didn't hear one scream of panic and that was a storm to scare an experienced sailor."

"Maybe I didn't know enough to be afraid."

"Miss Gregory," he continued, "Anyone would have been afraid in that blow."

"Thank you, Mr. Davids, but what would screaming and fainting accomplish? Your attentions needed to be elsewhere not in coddling a woman's whims."

The tall young man looked at her seriously for a long moment, his dark eyes losing their merry twinkle as he studied her face, then with a slight bow, "Your courage and discipline amaze me. I had heard about the beauty of Southern women, but I didn't know their fragile loveliness concealed such strength."

"Thank you, sir, and I had heard how gallant the British officers are. Where is your home?"

"Cornwall. You ever been in Cornwall, Ma'am?"

"No, never have, I'd hoped to some day."

"You have family there?"

"No, a friend of mine."

"Their name? I might know them."

"Philip Duval."

"Sir Philip? A powerful man around Cornwall, but a just landlord, I hope his son will continue his honest dealings with his tenants and the village."

"It is his son with whom I'm acquainted. And I'm sure he has the same high character as his father." She retorted shortly.

"Oh. The young Sir Philip. I only know of him, never met him personally. He doesn't spend much time on his estate, but then his father is in control. Seems I heard he spends most of his time traveling abroad. Many of the noblemen only visit their estates now and then; many make their homes in London and leave the running of their estates to an overseer. If I had land holdings, I'd ne'er see it in the hands of others to care for."

"I am sure Sir Philip has good reason for his long absences," she commented stiffly.

"Tis said that Sir Philip rules with an iron hand. Perhaps his son doesn't enjoy his home very much."

Rachel turned from Davids and peered into the rolling swells beyond the ship, "Why did you take to the seas?" She asked, closing the conversation about Philip and the regrets it might stir up.

"It would be easier to explain if you'd ever been to Cornwall. It is the tail of England, splendid and detached. The air smells of tar and rope and you're never far from the pounding surf and salty wind; to live there, you either love the sea or hate it, I loved it, anyway I'm a second son."

"So you intend to make your fortune at sea, Mr. Davids?" Rachel probed, relieved that the conversation turned from Philip and the bittersweet memories hiding in a heart already heavy with remorse.

"Yes, and then I may settle here where there is opportunity for every son."

His wistful tone pierced through Rachel's preoccupation and for the first time in weeks a smile toyed with the sorrow in her green eyes. She changed the subject, "How far are we from port?"

"Tomorrow late. If the day were clearer, you could see land from here."

"Georgia." She responded softly to herself.

"Ma'am?"

"Georgia, I haven't been home in a long time."

"What part of Georgia?"

"North Georgia, just above Atlanta." She answered barely above a whisper, a longing in her eyes.

"You've still a long journey to go, Ma'am," he observed.

"Yes, the longest of my life," she responded softly to herself rather than to him.

"Your family will be meeting you at the dock?"

"Not exactly. The only family I have left is my aunt and she is in France." Rachel replied her voice sharpened. "I was at her home when I received word about my father."

"I'm surprised that you would, or your aunt would allow you to attempt such a trip alone."

"I had no choice. My father's estate has to be settled. I told you that our attorney sent for me." Rachel answered brusquely, impatient with his meddling.

"Your close family friend, Mr.?" Davids continued ignoring her impatience.

"Yes, yes, Randall Wilkie."

"He is meeting you in Savannah?"

"How would he know when I would arrive? But I'm sure he would do his best to meet me or have someone here from home. At any rate I'm sure he has made suitable accommodations for me."

"Still, a woman alone on so long a journey . . . ."

A cool smile teased Rachel's lips as she raised one eyebrow, "Sir, I have just made a 5000 mile journey across a raging sea."

Davids tried to hide his smile, "Not quite that many miles."

"Well, it seemed so, as far off our course as we were blown. My point is that I have been a woman alone on a ship full of men for many days."

Nodding he reminded, "Under the captain's strict care. There is a difference."

"Nevertheless, I must go." Rachel concluded firmly, echoing the words she had spoken to her aunt during their last heated argument.

Seared into her memory was the anger on her aunt's, aristocratic features as she shouted, "Rachel, I forbid you to go. Philip is about to propose."

Rachel had whirled from her packing her face ashen. "How did you know about Philip?"

"I made it my business to know. Did you think you were riding out by yourself every day and I knew nothing of your activities? Don't be foolish. When I found out it was Sir Philip you were meeting, I told my servant to watch you from afar. Knowing your independence, I knew you would stop seeing him if you knew I approved." She shrilled, refinement abandoned.

"You mean if you started your usual matchmaking tactics? You've done nothing but humiliate me since I've been here. I didn't even tell Philip that you were my aunt. He thought I was visiting a farm family in the village." Rachel trembled recalling the scene and the anger that had boiled in her threatening to erupt.

Aunt Letty pursed her lips, satisfaction gleaming in her small hazel eyes, "So I discovered; however now he is well aware of who you are. I was expecting a proper suit for your hand any day. Don't you realize that you'll ruin all of my efforts if you return now?"

"Your efforts, Aunt Letty?"

"Of course, my efforts. What else would have brought him to the altar?"

"If it were not his love for me, I wouldn't want him."

"Perhaps he loves you but you don't understand the nobility. Appearances are very important to them. He would never allow his future wife to travel unescorted anywhere. Why it's unheard of, his father would immediately stop the wedding. If you go, he'll never marry you."

"How can I stay? You read the letter."

"Yes—I read the letter! Who does this Mr. Wilkie think he is anyway, demanding that you come home?"

"He's our family's dearest friend." Rachel defended, a lump catching in her throat as she thought of the slender sandy-haired man who had adored her growing up.

"Some friend! It appears to me if he cared for you, he'd handle the affairs himself and send you your money. You need a substantial dowry. Philip Duval is not just an ordinary catch, you know."

Humiliation burned Rachel's cheeks as she remembered, "Catch?" She croaked. "Am I some kind of bait with a dowry to lure him?"

Letty had cackled, "Don't be so naive, Rachel. How did you think you'd ever get them to the altar if you didn't use a little woman's wiles? That's just the way it's done."

"That's not the way I do it." Rachel all but shouted.

"You will if you make a proper match."

"Then I guess there'll be no proper match for me." Rachel turned her back to her aunt, before she could see the threatening tears.

Letty had moved toward her then. As she put a hand on Rachel's arm, her voice softened, trying to persuade, "Rachel, my dear, you must think this thing through. I'm the only family you have left. There's no one waiting for you in America, except this Wilkie and he's nothing more than a neighbor."

"You don't understand, Aunt Letty. Uncle Randall is like family." Rachel defended, trying to calm her pounding heart.

"That may be, but you've got to think of your future now. Post him and tell him to see to the running of the plantation and mill himself. Have him forward the funds to you. As wealthy as your father was, there should be ample compensation in it for him. Better yet, suggest he sell the whole business and send you the money so we can invest over here in your new home."

"New home?" The realization of never seeing her father or the plantation had descended on Rachel piercing her like a dagger, "You mean, never go back?"

"Of course, look at me; do I miss that innocuous life? Certainly not! How could it ever compare with life here in Europe—the arts, the fashion, gifted conversation, politics, all the finer things? That back woods culture is not the thing for you or me, we're much too refined." Letty lifted her brows, a knowing look in her eyes. "Really, Rachel, don't act so foolishly. Besides it was what your father wanted.

"What did my father want?" Rachel's eyes narrowed, suspicion in them.

"He wanted me to arrange a suitable marriage for you over here." Letty crossed her arms in front of her, determined to hold her ground.

"You're lying to me Aunt Letty. My father was expecting me to come home, to be the mistress at Sweetwater. And that is exactly what I am going to do."

"Grow up, Rachel! It is just not feminine to be so headstrong. Your father spoiled you and should have reined you in a long time ago. You will have a very difficult time finding anyone to marry you until you change that independent spirit." Letty pointed her finger in Rachel's face.

"I'm not trying to find anyone to marry me. If I find someone I love then I'll consider it but I won't marry anyone that would change me. As for Philip, if he won't marry me because I traveled alone to America, then so be it, I will marry no man who would seek to rule me."

"You would walk away and leave Philip Duval?" Letty's face paled, her eyes round with disbelief.

"After what you just told me, I understand why I haven't seen him in weeks." A mirthless chuckle rolled in her throat. "Marriage to Philip is out of question. There's nothing to keep me here any longer. I leave for Bristol at daybreak."

The boatswain's shrill whistle startled Rachel back into the present. The sailors had begun to scurry around in renewed vigor as a sailor called out from high on the crow's nest, "Land ahoy." And Rachel's heart lurched.

Rachel Gregory stood quietly in the shadows looking out across the river toward the teeming waterfront. Even from here the clop, clop of the horses pulling heavy wagons over the cobblestones bounced across the water.

The Sea Maiden waited in a slip on Hutchinson Island for her turn to dock, Savannah was a busy port. Ships from all over the world docked bringing merchandise to be exchanged for cotton, rice and indigo raised on the verdant South Carolina and Georgia plantations. This was the first time Rachel had been to Savannah since she was a girl. She shuddered as she recalled that one last trip here after the death of her mother.

When she was a child, she made several trips with her parents. Her father came to deal with the brokers directly about buying his goods, cotton grown on his plantation and yarn produced in his small mill.

Warm memories of that visit rippled lightly through the Rachel's mind. She smiled as she recalled her petite, dark haired mother gazing up in rapt adoration into the face of the tall slender, man with red gold hair. Even as a young child she had recognized the love between her parents was rare and glorious.

Her heart constricted and the warm memories faded when she recalled the bitter dregs of loneliness and despair that had beset her father after the fever had taken his beloved Anna.

She shuddered as she remembered the dark nights when she had pulled pillows over her head to shut out his cries of agony which pierced the night. At first young Rachel trembled with fear as she heard him curse the God whom Anna had served so faithfully. One night she watched in horror as he set fire to the chapel he had built for her mother. But gradually Rachel, too, had turned away, refusing to consider the God who required her mother's life. Thoughts rushed in to touch a part of her she had locked away many years before. The feelings and questions even now were too painful to consider. Suddenly a strange longing filled her being, almost suffocating her. She willed her mind away from the doubts that darkened her soul. She would think of other things, her future, a new beginning. Sweetwater, she uttered the word quietly, reverently like a prayer.

Unwanted tears welled up in her eyes. How many years had it been since she had felt the solid earth of home? Too many to think about . . . a girl had left for school, a young woman of nineteen had left from Virginia for Europe with only two brief visits in the interim. She shook her head. Had she only seen her father three times in all those years, twice at Sweetwater and then when he saw her off after her graduation?

Vivid images of his bloated face, reddened eyes, and stooped body invaded her memory, and she wondered that she never, before this moment, had considered how quickly he changed after her mother's death. With the callous disregard of youth she had taken it as a natural effect of time and the aging process. Startled, she realized he had been in his early forties—still a young man! Did loneliness and grief accelerate his deterioration or was he, even then, suffering from some dark, unknown malady? If she had been there to care for him, to keep him company . . . but then Aunt Letty was right, he was the one who had insisted she go. Was her aunt also correct in saying that he wanted her to stay away, marry, and not come back?

A chill ran through her settling in her bones in the warm afternoon sun as she contemplated the very thought. She shaded her eyes and looked westward, her mind out distancing her vision to the quiet lane lined with towering maple trees, and a large white house beckoning her home.

"Unthinkable! Never return to Sweetwater? I'd rather die than to live anywhere else!"

Startled, Rachel dropped her hand to look around; the last thought was voiced aloud. No one had heard her deepest longing and she moved forward. Perhaps someone in that crowd waited for her, to take her home after all those years.

"Miss Gregory," Rachel turned her head toward the voice that called her name. It was the captain. She saw him making his way between the scurrying sailors who secured the ship.

"Ma'am if you would be so kind as to wait for a few minutes, I will escort you over to the offices of Meredith Mercantile."

"Sir?" A frown darkened Rachel's face as her aloneness hit her full force. Perhaps not even the familiar face of Randall Wilkie would be there to meet her. Hoping for a miracle, she asked, "Is my attorney meeting me there? Or someone from home?"

"No ma'am, since the storm delayed us, he had no way of knowing the exact time we would arrive therefore, my instructions were to take you to Mr. Meredith's offices where they will make all the necessary arrangements for your journey home."

"I really don't understand, Captain Smythe. What has Mr. Meredith to do with my affairs? I thought my father's attorney was responsible for getting me home."

"I can't answer that, Miss Gregory. I only know Mr. Meredith is my employer; and my most prominent order and pleasant duty is to deliver a certain Miss Rachel Gregory safe and secure to 234 Bay Street."

Rachel stood on deck in the bright spring sunshine, her dark bonnet protecting her face from the harsh light. She looked down at the milling masses before her. The wharf teemed with men in varying shades of color who hurried to and fro. Slaves sang as they unloaded sugar and rum brought by ships from the Caribbean. Occasionally their ebony faces, streaked with perspiration would part in a brilliant smile at a comment from one of their co-workers.

Strong muscular, white men were among the workers, some with conspicuous hair of red, marking them as Irishmen. Although some had recently arrived from the Emerald Isle, the Savannah Irish population had been a source of controversy since Oglethorpe sent the first load of indentured servants in the 1700's. People who had desired to implement slave trade in the rich agricultural region maligned the hard working fair, skinned immigrants. But the Irish had stayed and their presence had proven no hindrance to the slave trade. Now white and black worked the waterfront, loading wagons with fine furniture of rich walnut and mahogany made by the craftsmen of England and bound for the opulent plantations near Savannah.

Horses pulled wagons equipped with runners like sleds down the steep ramps leading from Bay Street to the docks below. They were filled with raw materials grown on the plantations nearby and further inland, to be unloaded into these same ships for the return trip to Europe. Thus was the cycle that kept the trade in the port city lively and profitable.

The busy harbor seemed oblivious to the great political debates going on from the mid-west to the halls of Congress. Few knew or cared about the gathering political storm. To them life was busy, productive and would always be thus. But the sands of time were running out for traditional life in the South.

Rachel, who had been away so long, was blissfully unaware of the gathering tempest that would forever alter her life. She watched the scene before her for several minutes, her mind more on what awaited her than the collage before her. Finally, anticipation made her restless and she began to pace up and down the deck. She had been on board ship for a long time and away from the touch of the Georgia soil beneath her feet even longer.

She anxiously watched the sun as it approached the trees on the bluff that towered above her. She turned to find the captain and saw that he was in deep conversation with two men who had boarded a few minutes before. Now they seemed to be in some dispute and were ripping open boxes of cargo, inspecting them.

Finally Rachel's impatience overwhelmed her. Tying the ribbons of her wide brimmed black straw hat, she lifted her valise in one small gloved hand and stepped gingerly toward the gangplank.

Arriving at the edge of the narrow bridge of weathered planks, she paused to look back at the captain. He, along with his first mate who had now joined him, was still deeply engrossed with the two men. She lifted her skirt slightly and walked down the plank that spanned the distance between ship and shore.

For the first time in many days Rachel felt the firm earth beneath her feet, and it felt strange. Several yards down the wharf, she had to pause to regain her land legs. As she did, she looked around her trying to decide which way she should venture. The captain had told her she was to go to the offices of Meredith Mercantile. She scanned the horizon above her and in the distance saw a sign identifying her destination. For a moment she felt overwhelmed as she looked upwards.

Maneuvering down the rough street toward the distant ramp while carrying her small valise, proved a greater undertaking than she had anticipated. She took a few steps toward the steep incline and felt the rough cobblestones piercing through her delicate slippers. She hesitated for a moment and looked back toward the ship, undecided, then squaring her small shoulders and lifting her chin, she forged deliberately ahead.

It was not long before Rachel's foolishness and the Captain's wisdom became apparent. While she wrestled with her physical discomforts, she failed to notice three men who stood in the shadows observing her departure along the wharf with interest. After she had walked far enough to leave the protection of the ship and the captain, the men left their place of concealment to follow her.

Rachel stopped and placed her baggage on the street. The late afternoon sun beamed down heating the heavy broadcloth of her long black dress. As it clung to her, beads of perspiration glistened on her forehead and curled her hair in damp ringlets on her neck and around her face.

Vainly Rachel searched for a passenger vehicle for hire. No help was in sight; only loaded wagons rumbled to and from the docks. With a deep sigh she picked up her valise once again and walked closer to the sheds lining the wharf. Here in the shade she gained a brief respite from the heat and her pace quickened.

Just as she approached the end of the buildings and the final incline that led up to the bluff housing the offices she sought, she realized that she had left behind most of the bustling activity that hampered her progress. The cool shade and the nearing of her destination gave her a new burst of energy, so she picked up her tempo. Only one group of deserted sheds remained before the road led upwards. She stopped to rest briefly in the shade of the last building.

The three men, who had been stealthily following from a distance, increased their speed and surrounded her as she paused to catch her breath.

"Well! Missy, now what's a loverly little gal like you doin' all by herself on a hot day like this?"

"Yeah, seems you otta' go inside to rest yourself a bit," drawled one of the men as he reached out a filthy hand to grab her arm.

Rachel stared wide eyed, at the men. One of them, tall and unshaven, smiled a broken toothed grin at her while his shorter, muscular partner looked her up and down with a leering snarl, his thick lips parted slightly showing uneven yellow teeth, tobacco stained and decaying. The third man was medium height and thin, his wiry hair partially concealed by a faded red, cotton bandana tied about his head and his face had an unhealthy yellowish pallor.

Rachel jerked her arm from the tall man who held it, "Get away from me, before I call for assistance."

The short muscular man spoke in a drunken lisp," Miss High and Mighty who do you plan to call? There ain't nobody around to help wimmen who want to walk on these docks alone. You wanna li'l excitement, eh? We're just the ones to give you that, Missy."

By this time the men had backed Rachel into the edge of the shed, the thin one reached out to grab her just as she swung her valise and hit him in the face. He bellowed in pain, dropping his hand and putting it to his eye. His two partners shoved him aside while one grabbed her arms and pinned them behind her as the other bent over her and took her face in his hand. Rachel squirmed and twisted her arms to no avail, then dropping her chin; she opened her mouth and sank her teeth into her assailant's dirty hand. Salt and grit filled her mouth as another howl of pain from the wounded man echoed in the deserted building.

The man grasping her arms jerked her hat off. Then, catching her hair; pulled her head back as long auburn curls cascaded wildly down her back. A scream of fear and anger unleashed from Rachel as blackness engulfed her.

Two

Rachel shook her head as the biting fumes of ammonia burned her nostrils and deposited a bitter taste in her mouth, jolting her back into the world of consciousness. Her eyes flew open and encountered two almond shaped ones, jade green with amber lights peering directly into hers.

"She's with us now, Mr. Andrew." Hands withdrew the ammonia and the eyes took on a soft lilting voice tinged with a West Indies rhythm. Rachel warily raised herself on one elbow. She tried to access her situation, but her attention riveted to the face and form of the exquisitely beautiful woman with golden skin bending over her.

The young woman's dress was vivid magenta chintz and fashioned in the newest style. It dipped discreetly at the bodice where a costly cameo nestled at the base of her slender, shapely neck. Fitting the upper part of her body like a glove, the dress accented her tiny waist. Yards of fabric billowed around her where she knelt on the cobblestones beside Rachel. From the cultured tone of her voice to the elegance of her attire, her presence bespoke wealth and refinement; yet, Rachel puzzled, she was a woman of color.

As a lifetime can pass in an instant, Rachel received these sights and sounds, greeting her on a sun warmed Savannah dock even while she struggled to get her bearings. Her memory teased her brain, trying to recall something fearful and painful agony that remained just beyond its grasp. Even where she was and why she lay prostrate on the hard stones jabbing her back, remained a mystery.

Finally she turned her head from the woman, desperation winning out over curiosity. When she did, her eyes rested on a motley crew of three standing in the darkening shadows of an abandoned shed. Suddenly the memory of leering yellow smiles and fetid breath invaded her senses.

With the lithe grace of a doe, she jerked erect and bounded to her feet, flight her only thought. Strong arms captured her as she turned and rushed headlong into a tall stranger standing behind her and blocking her exit. Like a cornered animal, her eyes widened with fear but her small chin lifted defiantly as she pushed against the strong arms gripping her like a vise. He loosened his hold and she broke free, stepping back, determination to resist written in every tense line of her body.

Her disheveled auburn tresses fell in abundant masses across her shoulders and down to her waist while her eyes blazed like fiery emeralds. Her face was smudged, her arm bare where the sleeve of her black dress lay limply, torn during her melee with the three ruffians. Her appearance offered a rude contrast to the carefully coiffured and immaculately dressed young woman standing beside her, but pride crowned her bearing to complete a picture of savage beauty that Andrew Meredith would take to his grave.

He'd decided to come to the dock in person when he saw his ship finally arrive, days later than expected. A good thing he had or Miss Gregory would have been shark bait. He had dreaded this duty. Attending to a young woman without family could be a tedious business, one he hadn't relished. In a moment of weakness he'd made a promise to a dying man, but he was a man who kept his word, so here he was. He'd brought Daphne, fully expecting to turn the burden over to her. He didn't need to further complicate his life with the care of some clinging, vaporous spinster, but this girl was no shrinking violet.

Meredith masked his surprise and admiration with a hint of arrogance. Amusement played in the warm brown eyes that captured and held hers as he responded, quietly; "Don't be afraid, you're safe now."

Rachel squared her shoulders and, with the queenly grace of a woman at court, demanded, "And who, sir, are you?"

A humorless smile touched his lips beneath the neatly trimmed, dark mustache. He answered crisply, his voice lacked the soft slur of a southern drawl, "I'm Andrew Meredith, Miss Gregory."

"Meredith? I've heard your name before." She frowned and confusion cooled the fiery eyes to softly glowing embers as her thoughts ran to and fro, searching.

"You were a passenger on my ship."

"Oh, that Mr. Meredith." her eyes narrowed, soft glow extinguished as her memory found firm footing. "Exactly what do you want with me?"

Meredith's mouth, quirked in suppressed amusement. "I want nothing more from you than to see that you are safely and comfortably accommodated for the night or as long as it takes until you can return home."

Suddenly an enchanting half smile curved her full lips revealing a dimple, her tense shoulders relaxed slightly while bewilderment replaced defiance in her eyes. "I'm confused Mr. Meredith. I hear your name wherever I turn. It seems you've taken charge of my life, yet I don't even know you."

Meredith's countenance softened, his voice not so crisp, "Perhaps it does appear so, but my only concern is to see you safely home."

"Did Uncle, er, Mr. Wilkie send you? Do you work for him?" She asked, an urgency to understand pressed her.

"No, on the contrary, Mr. Wilkie works for me. It was my idea to send for you."

"Then you were a friend of my father's?" This time hope fired her emerald eyes.

"No. A business associate."

The light in Rachel's green eyes dimmed as painful memories and questions misted them. The reality of her situation, a woman alone in a port city, 300 miles from home, struggled with recollections from the past that intruded, hampering her judgment and reasoning. The last remnants of determination slipped from her face. Vulnerability washed her features and for a moment she looked younger than her twenty-three years.

A movement behind her brought her attention back to the present and the three men standing in the shadows. Anger coursed through her and she turned to her benefactor, "And who are these men? Do they work for you also?"

Annoyance pricked Meredith's cool facade, "No, of course not."

"Then why haven't you called the authorities and had them arrested?" Frustration and bewilderment raised her voice.

"I don't need to. First they are going to apologize to you, and then I will tend to them."

"I don't want an apology, I want them off the streets," involuntarily she shuddered.

"Don't worry I'll see to that, too."

Rachel's eyes widened, surprise and curiosity struggling with the anger in them, "Who are you to take the law into your own hands?"

"Sometimes other means can prove more effective than calling the authorities."

Rachel didn't respond, but lifting a questioning eyebrow, turned her attention to the three misfits in question. Meredith looked toward them as they stared back at him fear blazing in their eyes. Evidently they knew something she didn't. The men shifted uncomfortably as the warm brown eyes, which held theirs, turned cold black.

Andrew Meredith nodded his head toward them and the tall thin one dropped his head.

"Miss, we're powerful sorry, we didn't mean nothin'. We wouldn't hurt cha none, just havin' a little fun," he looked up, dread heavy in his eyes as he added with a shudder, "we'd never bothered ya if we'd knowd you wuz Mr. Meredith's friend."

Intrigue outweighing her revulsion, Rachel responded in clipped tones, "What does that have to do with it?"

"Well nothin' really, cept'n we'd had a leetle too much ale and nice wimmen don't usually walk alone on the waterfront, especially friends of Mr. Meredith." His two companions looked up, as if hopeful that their friend could win them some clemency. Anger once again flushed the face of the beautiful Rachel, dashing their fragile hope.

Before she could retort Meredith spoke tersely to the three, "My man is waiting over there by the ship; present yourselves to him."

The men turned and looked toward a tall clipper resting in the gentle swells at the end of the wharf. A man nearly seven feet tall and black as coal stood facing them. Startling white teeth parted his face in an impish grin and a huge gold earring hung prominently from his left ear. With a shudder the thugs hesitated until Andrew Meredith asked quietly, "Shall he come for you?"

The men scurried away, terror darkening their eyes.

Meredith turned to Rachel after the men were out of ear shot and stated in crisp, no nonsense tones, "You were supposed to wait for Captain Smythe to escort you to my office. Didn't he inform you of my instructions?"

"Yes he did, but the captain told me that he was extremely busy, and I felt that I'd already caused him too much inconvenience so I didn't wait."

Rachel saw Meredith's jaw tighten. Was it annoyance with her or the captain? "That was part of his job." He spoke softly, but his intent was clear, his orders were to be followed explicitly.

Rachel defended, "Don't blame the captain; he had a large cargo to attend. It wasn't as if he didn't want to escort me. I didn't want to wait."

"Miss Gregory, you're mistaken, I understand precisely. The captain's priorities went amiss. You were his first responsibility, one he was well paid for."

Rachel stared at him a moment, her eyes probing his. "It appears, Mr. Meredith, that we are back where we started. I'm having a difficult time understanding your involvement in my life. I don't know you. You weren't a friend of my father's, and you don't work for Mr. Wilkie so why have you taken charge of me?"

"If this afternoon is any example, you need someone in charge. Had you followed my instructions, those men wouldn't have bothered you. They were right, ladies don't walk on the waterfront alone," he responded, ignoring her question.

"Some ladies are alone in the world, Mr. Meredith. What are they supposed to do?" Rachel asked. Her defiance aroused once again.

"Accept the help they are offered," he answered curtly.

"I'm sorry but I'd rather take care of myself."

"Like this afternoon?" Amusement replaced annoyance in his eyes.

For the first time in weeks a smile parted her full lips, warming her eyes as she graciously acknowledged, "It seems I've been most ungrateful, would you accept my apology for causing you so much inconvenience? I really do appreciate your coming to my rescue. No telling what would have happened. . ."

"What would have happened to you wouldn't do for discussion in mixed company. Ultimately you would have ended up in the river." His brow furrowed as he answered matter of factly, then he chuckled, his smile dispersing the last remnants of sternness in his face, "You seemed to be holding your own, right up until the last. I'm sure those three will think twice before they try that again, but all the same I'm glad Daphne and I arrived when we did."

"Daphne?" She asked turning toward Meredith's beautiful companion.

"Yes, ma'am. I'm Daphne DeLucie. I work for Mr. Meredith." While her tone was properly respectful, her eyes challenged Rachel's, declaring an equality that went beyond the color of her skin.

Andrew Meredith noted the exchange with a wry smile. "Miss Gregory, my carriage is back down the wharf, if you'd like to wait?"

Rachel interrupted, "No, I'll walk with you."

Andrew chuckled, "I don't think you'll have any more trouble, I'll leave Daphne with you."

"I don't think she would be much help." The very idea that this slip of a woman could defend her irritated Rachel.

"No one will bother Daphne."

"I thought you said I had invited disaster, why would it be any different with the two of us?" Rachel persisted.

"Everyone knows Daphne, and they know me. You'll be quite safe." Meredith's answer, cool and deliberate; his face closed.

Rachel raised her eyebrows and said softly, "I see."

"I doubt it." His curt reply startled Rachel.

"I still would prefer to walk with you to the carriage, that is if it's acceptable for a lady to walk, escorted, down the dock." A cool smile curved her lips but her eyes dared.

With a curt half bow, he responded, "As you wish, shall we go? I have much work ahead of me tonight."

"Where are we going?"

"To Balmara, my home."

"I beg your pardon?" Rachel paused mid step; her brows drew together. Even for her liberated views, she found his answer disturbing.

"To my home. Did you have other plans?"

"Yes, I planned to stay at one of the local hotels."

"Your plans have been changed." His answer gave no room for disagreement.

A surge of blood pounded Rachel's head, flushing her face. "And what right do you have to change my plans?"

"The right of responsibility, Miss Gregory."

His cool assumption fired Rachel's independent spirit and she retorted, "I would have been fine. I can usually take care of myself. "

"Really?" He gave her a long sideways glance.

The memory of the afternoon's events brought a deep flush to Rachel's face; her self assurance wavered as she questioned, "What responsibility?"

"To see you safely home to Sweetwater."

The mention of her home brought a longing within Rachel that momentarily quelled the tide of anger and confusion churning inside her and she answered docilely, "I stayed at the Pavilion once with my father, and it was quite nice."

"Just the same I don't think it would be a good idea this time, since you are alone without the protection of an escort or comfort of a traveling companion." A strange compassion softened his face, his words gentled, his voice persuaded, " I'd prefer that you are in my home where your needs can be attended."

"I just meant, after all your inconvenience this afternoon, I wouldn't want to be an imposition on you and your wife with an unexpected guest."

"I'm not married and you aren't unexpected. In fact, we've been expecting you for days. On the contrary, it will be a pleasure, not an imposition." He turned his head and looked directly into her eyes, a slight smile curving one corner of his mouth.

"Then of course I couldn't possibly accept your invitation, sir." Rachel averted her gaze, suddenly uncomfortably aware of her disheveled appearance in the presence of the handsome stranger's bold look.

Andrew Meredith threw back his head and laughed, "Miss Gregory, your sense of propriety surprises me. You sailed all the way from Bristol, the only woman on board a ship filled with sailors, walked unescorted down the Savannah waterfront; yet, you don't want to come to my home? You have nothing to fear from me."

Rachel narrowed her eyes and lifted her head, dishevelment forgotten, "Not fear, Mr. Meredith, good manners."

Amusement still played in his face, his mouth twitching with suppressed laughter, as he nodded his head and remarked, "Well in that case, be assured, my servants have prepared for you, and in case you're worried about your good name, my Aunt and young niece live there and will provide all the chaperone you or society would need or deem proper. Shall we go?"

The retort on the tip of Rachel's tongue died without utterance as they reached a trim, new barouche attended by two matched grays.

A driver dressed in a deep burgundy cutaway with gold braid decorating his shoulders and sleeves perched high in the driver's seat and held the reins lightly in his hands. When he saw the trio approaching, he bounded down, "Thank the Lord, Mr. Drew, you're back." His curious dark eyes briefly touched Rachel, and when he encountered her disarray, dropped them respectfully.

Andrew chuckled, "You were worried about me, Elijah?"

The small, wizened ebony face creased in a brilliant smile, "Naw, sir, you know better'n that, Mr. Drew. I' was worried about the young lady. I'm mighty thankful to see her safe."

"Well, we arrived just in time. I'm going to implement more security on these docks, especially when my ships are in."

Elijah nodded in agreement, "It just don't do the way rif raff's a botherin' decent folk now a days. By the way I didn' see no baggage and ain' see no cap'n."

"Never mind, I'll send it on when it comes, Captain Smythe should be awaiting me in my office now. Please take Miss Gregory and Daphne home."

Gratefully Rachel took the arm Meredith offered and climbed into the carriage. She sank into the seat, thankful for the respite from the uneven cobblestones and the leering stares of strangers.

The desire for a bath, a change of clothes and a comfortable bed outweighed her objections to Andrew Meredith's aggressive protection. She sighed. For the moment she remained content to let him make the decisions. There would be time enough to face the inevitable decisions that awaited her. It relieved some of her anxiety that by going straight to Meredith's home she would avoid an encounter with Captain Smythe. Once again her impulsive habits had landed her in an embarrassing predicament and had caused others distress. Even if the good captain had been well paid, she appreciated his kindness and protection. Now she had earned for him the ire of Andrew Meredith which, even in her brief encounter, she sensed was not something to take lightly.

Rachel watched in wonder as Andrew Meredith handed Daphne into the opposite seat with the same deference and respect he had given her.

Now looking at Daphne, he spoke with a warm smile, "I believe our original choice of the east room for Miss Gregory will be best. It's cool and she might like the view from the alcove."

"And you?" A questioning smile touched her lips while her golden eyes remained cool, guarded.

Meredith beamed her, a warm, somewhat intimate smile, his eyes reassuring, "I'm going to walk back to the office, I may not be in at all tonight, I've so many things to take care of, but I'll try."

Rachel noticed Daphne's lips tighten slightly before she replied evenly, "Very well, I will attend to it just as you wish."

"You always do," he replied softly, something akin to affection warming his eyes.

Despite Rachel's weariness, she noted the exchange between the two and it puzzled her, leaving her vaguely uncomfortable. The Southern heritage, which flowed through her blood, left her with an innate sense of superiority. Not that she recognized her prejudice or ever considered it, but rather that she was simply white and Southern. Now here, for the first time, she encountered a white man treating a woman of color as an equal and it disturbed her.

Meredith turned to Rachel and with a formal half bow; he said politely, almost stiffly, "I hope an evening of rest will restore your energies. It may be tomorrow evening before I see you again. Then I will be able to tell you how and when you can leave for home. I'm sorry about the delay, but because the ship was so late, the plans I had made for your trip home had to be changed. Until your arrival I didn't know how to make alternate ones."

"Thank you, Mr. Meredith, I shall look forward to hearing from you and thank you for your hospitality, for everything. You've been more than kind. I hope I can repay you some way."

His face relaxed with a genuine smile, "You can, by arriving safely to your home."

"You've assumed too much responsibility for me."

"That's something for me to decide." Then the smile left and a frown creased his forehead, "I desire only your welfare, which is my only motivation and goal."

"I'm having a great deal of trouble understanding your concern, but it seems I have no other choice at the moment except to accept your invitation."

"Very well, then I'll see you later." Turning to the driver, he instructed, "Take the ladies on to Balmara, Elijah. Zooto will follow in the wagon with the baggage."

Rachel looked at Daphne, "Zooto?"

Her lips parted in a cool smile, "The man at the ship. He is Mr. Andrew's what do you say—uh, man with a strong arm."

Rachel nodded, puzzled even more.

The carriage lurched back and forth over the rough cobblestones that paved the ramp like street leading to Bay Street. The stones had been used to ballast empty ships coming to Savannah from all over the world in order to fill their holds with precious cargo of rice, indigo and cotton, grown on the plantations surrounding the port city and further inland even as far inland as Rachel's own Sweetwater.

The smart barouche pulled into Bay Street and drove past the Factor's Walk where deals of commerce were made between plantation owner and tradesman. Some of the plantation owners had their own offices, making their own deals.

Her father had two factors. At first he dealt with one in Charleston because of Anna, Rachel's mother. She had been born there and most of her family lived there yet. But over the years for shipping convenience, he began diverting some of his produce to Savannah. Finally in the years just before Rachel left for school, he'd built a small factory on Sweetwater Creek in Campbell County, which turned the cotton they grew into thread and fabric. It had proved a thriving business because it enabled his neighbors to send their goods on to the port cities ready to make the trip abroad, resulting in greater profits for the community and the individual producer.

He had kept it a small operation compared to the Sweetwater Manufacturing Company built by Governor McDonald in 1849. Two years ago her father had written that McDonald was expanding the mill at factory shoals on Sweetwater Creek, and had changed its name to New Manchester Manufacturing Company. She was glad her father had not seemed unduly threatened by the increased competition. He had felt the surrounding farms and counties provided enough business for both mills. In the past the two owners had shared a congenial cooperative relationship.

When Rachel was a child, she had loved the trips to Charleston with her father. While he huddled with his factor, she watched out the windows, mesmerized by the sights and sounds of the big harbor; thrilled with the romance of the tall sailing ships, dreaming of the lands and people they had visited.

After her dad would finish his business, they would go to her mother's ancestral home on the Battery where her lovely dark haired mother would be waiting.

After his wife's death, Adam Gregory channeled all his business to Savannah and sold his plantation interest in Charleston. He never returned to the lovely South Carolina city, the memories were too painful.

Daphne stirred and nodded toward one of the buildings facing them and spoke, startling Rachel from her somber reverie. As if answering an unasked question, her lilting dialect explained, "Mr. Meredith has his office there."

Rachel leaned over and peered out to get a better view of the building that was obviously a source of pride to the young woman. The building was elegant, even prestigious, but no more so than the other structures. The accommodations, unless more elaborate within, were what one would expect of any successful businessman.

"He has living quarters upstairs. Before he built Balmara, he lived there when he came to town."

"When he came to town?" Rachel questioned, her curiosity pricked.

"He's not from Savannah. He has a factor here, but he owns shipping and ship building companies in Boston. He's a very busy man."

"Hmm. Seems he'd be too busy to look after me," Rachel responded.

Daphne held her gaze, and then nodded her head. "He is."

Rachel didn't miss the message Daphne conveyed. Anger and discomfort stung Rachel's senses provoking her to retort, "And what business would that be of yours?"

A slow smile spread across Daphne's face, "Mr. Meredith is my business. I look after him."

Rachel arched an eyebrow, "Really?"

Daphne laughed exulting in her own private joke. Then she paused to explain, "No wife, no housekeeper, no close family except his aging Aunt Matilda and his young niece Laura, who live here. Neither of them is interested in Mr. Meredith's business so he employs me to look after his household."

"Employs or owns?" Rachel's gaze challenged.

"Employs. I am a free woman."

"How?"

Mr. Meredith set me free."

"Why?"

"Because he wanted to." She replied curtly, then turned her face from her white charge and stared at the passing traffic, not willing to volunteer any further information to this unwelcome intruder.

An uneasy silence filled the carriage and Rachel turned her attention to the passing street. She hoped to see someone, something that would be familiar, something to give her a taste of home, something to assuage the loneliness that engulfed her.

A house here and there looked vaguely familiar and her mind turned backwards to the last time she had been in Savannah. As a youth, she had accompanied her father on one of his rare trips to the port city.

As time passed he had made fewer and fewer trips to Savannah, leaving more of his decisions to his factor most of the time. If he was needed, he sent Mr. Wilkie in his place. Only once after her mother died, had he brought Rachel with him. Before his sister in law had left for Europe, she had told him Rachel needed a broader social experience. She felt that an introduction to the more genteel coastal society might curb Rachel's free spirit and her inordinate attachment to rural life.

Grudgingly Adam Gregory had promised to take Rachel to Savannah on his next trip (Charleston was out of the question, he had shouted to his sister in law, his face red and his breath tinged with brandy.) And he had kept his word. Rachel had been excited about the trip for no other reason than because her beloved father was taking her. Her constant companion after her mother's death had been Aunt Letty continually monitoring every word, movement and gesture in the light of lady like behavior.

She had her corseted and laced until she could hardly breathe, and only by the most devious cunning could Rachel slip away with a sack of crisp, juicy apples and a beloved book to her hideaway in the pine and maple tree forest surrounding Sweetwater Manor. When she felt especially brave she would range further and hide under the old oak "hanging tree" not far from the river. A place of fear and superstition for the slaves, even Agatha, her personal maid since she was born, hesitated to follow her there. She closed her eyes and remembered the stolen moments when she would rush to the crest of the hill to gaze at the river meandering below her. She could almost feel the brisk spring breeze as it had blown her thick auburn tresses loosed from their staid constraints.

Afterwards she would curl up on the ground beneath the thick canopy of leaves and bite into a crisp, juicy apple as she studied the gnarled branches of the ancient tree, imagining the unknown events that had named the tree.

Somehow Aunt Letty would always find her and bring her back for more French lessons with her waist and hair once more restrained as a proper lady's should be. She loved Aunt Letty but she was glad to see her go. She'd hoped things would be as they once were. But as time can only move forward, Rachel found life had unalterably changed, never to return to the simple joys she had known and loved as a girl. But even now, as a woman her heart yearned to return.

Suddenly she recognized the home of Andrew Low. What an exciting night she had spent in that home. Her father had confided to her that Mr. Low was one of the richest men in the English speaking world. His wealth had made little impression on the young Rachel, but his guest of honor had. William Makepeace Thackeray was on a lecture tour and was a houseguest. What a thrill to meet the man who had written Vanity Fair!

Now she recognized another home, that of her father's factor, Jules Green. Her heart beat faster, warm memories bathed her face erasing some of the tension and fatigue. It was in that imposing Greek revival house where they had attended a lovely dance. Rachel remembered the billowing white dress with the dainty green ribbons she had worn. She hadn't understood the tears in her father's eyes as she came down the stairs to take his arm that night. She was too bemused with what the looking glass had told her. And with the blasé of youth, she had soon forgotten him in the excitement of the evening. It was her first important ball and she'd been too busy dancing with the young Savannah blades to take notice of her father. He stayed outside or near the punch bowl most of the night, never dancing, refusing to take part in the festivities.

Although young, she had been the belle of the ball. Her first taste of the pleasures of growing up, gave her food for thought. Maybe Aunt Letty wasn't completely wrong after all.

Her first ball proved to be the last she attended in the old port city because her father cut their visit short and left for home the next morning. Their visit had only lasted two weeks. The burden of his daughter's social training proved too much without his beloved Anna beside him. Every party and dance became a tragic reminder of his loss.

The next year he sent her to Virginia to school. He hoped she could learn there what proved too painful for him to provide and she did. She was skillful in all the social graces but the years at Miss Winter's Academy for Girls never extinguished her love for the red clay hills and the green pine forests of her beloved Sweetwater. It still drove her. From Bristol, across miles of turbulent seas to the teeming waterfront of Savannah, she had come with one desire driving her, to see and feel, to taste and experience Sweetwater. Her heart raced and her throat tightened—so near yet so far. When, how long would it be before she could run free across the meadow, into the woods and drink from the cold sweet spring where in the distance she could hear the roar of Sweetwater Creek as it emptied into the Chattahoochee?

Once again Daphne's lilting voice broke the silence that divided them like a curtain inside the small carriage.

"You have visited Savannah before?" Daphne questioned, her keen eyes observing Rachel closely.

Rachel flushed in the darkening carriage. Could Daphne sense the turmoil, the heartbreak, the longing? Was her face transparent? She fought with her emotions, close them down, protected her vulnerability. Fatigue defeated her, and with a sigh she raised her hand in a helpless gesture, "Yes, many years ago."

Daphne's intent gaze wavered, softness crept in and fired the amber lights in her eyes, and she observed softly, "An unhappy memory?"

"No, more like bittersweet. I was so young, I didn't understand. When you are older, so many things you would change." Rachel eyes held Daphne's, daring her to take advantage of her vulnerability.

She responded with a sad smile, laced with understanding, "Youth is foolish, but if we learn from the mistakes we have strong building blocks for the future."

Rachel cast a tired, grateful glance toward her companion and the two wary combatants laid down their defenses briefly in acknowledgment of a shared moment of understanding.

THREE

The deep purple of the eastern sky was overtaking the pink and golden sunset when the barouche turned into a long drive lined with massive live oaks. Their long branches met overhead forming a thick canopy where gray bearded moss draped the limbs and hung down like wisps of fog in the deepening shadows. Rachel shifted in her seat to get a better view of the house at the end of the drive.

Curiosity about Andrew Meredith's home momentarily dulled the aches and pains plaguing her. Would it be large with the opulence of the newer Savannah homes she had noticed on her long drive from River street or more tasteful, perhaps small with an understated elegance? She envisioned it smaller because, just from those brief moments with Mr. Meredith, she felt opulence would not be his style.

Her eyes widened in amazement as a large house loomed before her framed by the tall trees encircling it. Already candles twinkled like so many diamonds inside the dim windows as the last light of day outlined a Greek revival house nestled in the bend of a brooding river. Neither small nor opulent, but rather grand and elegant it reigned in splendor in the darkening evening shadows. The lines of the mansion blended so well into contours of the landscape that it seemed to spring from the earth itself. It bespoke of wealth and good taste, yet the whole impressive setting seemed out of character for the man whom she had met this afternoon. Yet why would she feel thus? Her encounter had been brief, but intuitively she knew that this man knew who he was and exerted no effort to please or impress others. A strange warmth touched her and somehow she felt reassured. For a brief mysterious moment she felt secure for the first time since she heard of her father's death and it comforted her.

A hundred feet or so in front of the house the drive curved to the right making a circle bringing the passengers to wide, marble steps descending from a broad portico with Ionic columns.

Two figures detached themselves from the shadows, but only one descended the broad steps. The other, a woman waited where she was. The carriage hid the man from Rachel's view as he reached ground level, but Daphne peered out the window waiting for his outstretched hand to open the carriage door.

Elijah called a greeting to the two as he jumped down from the driver's seat. Rachel saw Daphne purse her lips, her smooth brow wrinkled in an impatient frown as the one who was out of Rachel's view paused to answer the driver.

She could not make out the conversation, their voices had dropped but from Daphne's expression, something displeased her. Then the carriage door flew open and a tall, muscular man the color of creamed coffee, stood silhouetted in the lingering light of day. He looked into the carriage his eyes only brushing Rachel's before resting on Daphne. Hazel eyes, both sensitive and intelligent, glowed as they fastened on the beautiful woman, compelling her to look at him.

Fascinated, Rachel pushed her fatigue to the back of her mind and even Andrew Meredith was forgotten for the moment as she watched the two. He reached inside to offer Daphne his hand, never taking his eyes from hers. That he loved her was unmistakable, but Rachel read more in those glowing eyes, a jealous possessiveness and a hunger unrequited.

Daphne paused for a moment and returned his gaze. Her eyes, cold and hard, held his as she drew her lips together in a thin line; her body tense, rejecting. A slight knowing smile met her silent rebuff, curling one corner of his mouth and his eyes challenged hers with some secret triumph known only to him. Rachel shivered in the warm spring air as Daphne took his hand and stepped outside. When she finally spoke to him it was softly and in French. He merely nodded and turned from her belatedly to walk slowly and deliberately to the other side of the carriage where Rachel awaited.

His look, curious and appraising, met Rachel's squarely before dropping in the respectful, submissive gesture of a servant. Weariness settled on her again as she rounded the carriage and looked to the top of the long set of steps where Daphne stood waiting with an older woman.

Calling to Rachel, she explained, "I have asked Louisa to hold supper for an hour in order to give you time to refresh yourself."

Rachel nodded her head in a weary acknowledgment, grateful for the delay. Although her stomach growled from a light lunch and no afternoon tea, her aching body cried out for rest and a refreshing bath.

Obviously the small dark woman with drooping shoulders and graying hair was Louisa. Dressed in a bright calico, with a snow white apron over it, she studied Rachel with open inquisitiveness as she opened the massive carved oak door and Rachel stepped into a hall ablaze in light.

Louisa called to a girl standing just inside the door, and turning to Rachel explained, her old dark face wrinkled in a pleasant smile, willing her eyes away from Rachel's disheveled appearance "Leona will be your maid while you are here. I have instructed her to draw you a hot bath immediately as Daphne said you have had a hard day and would want one. Since your bags have not arrived, I will send up some clothes for you to wear to supper."

Rachel inclined her head and then objected, "That will not be necessary. If I might have a bite in my room, surely my luggage will arrive shortly."

"I am not sure when they will be here, but Miss Matilda is expecting to meet you at supper."

Rachel looked at her, brow wrinkled.

Louisa explained, "Miss Matilda, Mr. Andrew's aunt. She is taking a nap right now but she asked to meet you."

Rachel nodded her head wearily, the last thing she wanted to do tonight was to have to entertain some stranger, and wearing borrowed clothing at that. But they had offered her the hospitality of a place to stay; how could she be so rude as to refuse to have supper in the dining room.

"Very good, Ma'am. Now, Leona will show you to your room." Louisa responded as she nodded toward a magnificent spiral staircase which cantilevered upward for three floors with no central support newel.

Rachel walked to the steps and gazed upward, charmed at the exquisite beauty of the ascending stairway. Wearily she climbed the stairs, which swept her above the blazing candles in the hall below. From a beveled glass skylight in the ceiling above, she could make out the last brush strokes of golden pink streaking the sky.

Rachel followed Leona into a large bedroom where a gentle breeze stirred the lace curtains draping two windows that reached almost from floor to ceiling. A hint of lavender fragranced the air and a massive bed of intricately carved walnut graced the room. Strategically placed in the center to catch the gentle breezes, it boasted a delicate crochet coverlet with a matching canopy above it. A mosquito netting was attached to the tall four posts of the bed to protect its occupant from unwanted pests the gentle river wind might bring inside.

From the bed one had a perfect view of the river whose black surface swallowed the streaks of gold from the last remnants of day.

Her heart fluttered, was this by design or merely coincidence? The bed was almost a replica of her own bed at Sweetwater. From her bedroom windows she could see the distinct waters of the Chattahoochee, so different from the dark, mysterious water that lay before her. Meredith had specifically instructed Daphne to give her this room, yet how could he have known? Had he been to Sweetwater, perhaps stayed in her very room? Whatever the answer, her heart raced all the harder, the yearning for home overwhelming.

Leona spoke, her soft southern dialect proving a pleasant homecoming to Rachel's ears, "I will brang the water; the bath is through those doors." She pointed toward a pair of narrow doors at the far end of the room, some twenty feet away.

Rachel walked over to the doors and opened them; inside was a small room containing a large copper tub. A floor to ceiling walnut mirror graced the wall behind the tub. On the opposite wall a washstand with pitcher, bowl and towel stood in readiness along with another mirror whose glass could be adjusted to give full view to the mirror behind. Two lamp stands provided soft light and perfect illumination for completing one's dressing.

A blush tinted Rachel's features as she stepped inside the small chamber and caught sight of her disheveled appearance. For a moment she forgot Leona's presence in the room behind her as she leaned forward into the mirror and gingerly rubbed the smudges on her face. Her auburn tresses cascaded wildly down her back and across her shoulders where one was bare from her torn sleeve. She jerked it up, trying to cover her bare arm, only to hear a rip as the entire sleeve came loose from its moorings and slid useless to her wrist.

Thorough humiliation washed over Rachel as she remembered the amused gaze of Andrew Meredith taking her in from head to toe. No wonder Daphne treated her with contempt; she looked like a ragamuffin. Helpless to salvage her dress and a thorough bath the only answer to her hair and dirt, Rachel backed out of the cubicle and away from the mirrors and their humiliating images. Lifting her chin, she gazed into Leona's eyes, daring the young servant to acknowledge in glance or gesture that anything was amiss. Rachel clothed embarrassment with arrogance as she crisply commanded, "Yes, bring warm water immediately and see if my trunks have arrived."

With downcast eyes so Rachel could not see the amused curiosity in them, she murmured respectfully, "Right away Ma'am. But I know fer shore yore clothes ain't come yet, but don't cha worry none; I'll get that water and Louisa will find ya some clothes then you'll feel better right soon."

Before Rachel deemed it possible, Leona had returned. Two husky male house servants followed her with oversized, steaming kettles of water attached to their shoulders with harnesses. Bustling with importance, Leona briskly instructed them to pour the kettles into the tub. Reaching in to test the temperature with her elbow, she approved and announced they need not bring any more water just yet.

Not eager to endure anymore curious stares, Rachel retired to the tall windows facing the river and waited quietly until Leona pronounced her bath ready.

Steam from the tub filled the small alcove and spilled out into the bedroom, and with it the fragrance of lilacs permeated the air. Rachel moved woodenly toward the small room, reluctant to have this strange girl help her disrobe.

The bright young woman seemed to sense Rachel's reluctance and chirped, "Miss Rachel, let me unhook those back fasteners fer ya and while ya get out of yore clothes, I'll just turn yore bed down for ya. Then when you is in the tub, I'll come get the pins out'n yore hair. By then you're gonna be feeling like a different person. After that I'll go find them clothes Louisa wuz gettin' ya. Them ya got on ain't good for nothin' but the rag heap."

"Where is Louise going to find clothes to fit me?" Rachel asked, frowning.

Pleasant laughter bubbled from Leona, "Don't you worry none bout that, Louisa is in charge of the sewing room, she know how to fit ya."

"But who . . .?" Rachel left the question unfinished. The only explanation was slave clothing. How could she meet Andrew Meredith's aunt wearing the homespun garments of a common slave? The irony of her situation brought a tired smile to her face and she shrugged resignedly. Well at least maybe she would be fully clothed, which was some improvement over her current state.

Rachel stepped out of her dusty, torn garments and into the inviting warmth of the tub. The tub was large and deep, the water rose up around her like a silken embrace, enveloping even her shoulders. Thick bubbles covered the surface and some of them tickled her nose as they escaped upward, released by her movement. Stretching full length in the tub, she leaned her head back against the rounded lip of the tub and closed her eyes. For the first time in many weeks, she felt some of the tension ease from her. Her eyes grew heavy as she battled with sleep, yet not willing to disturb this sense of euphoria. Leona's voice startled her and she realized she must have dozed off. "Miss Rachel, I'm ready to take the pins outta yore hair, now." Quickly the pert little woman had the few remaining pins from Rachel's hair, "Now then ya just ease yore head back into those bubbles and raze it up. But be keerful ya don't get none in yore eyes cause it'll burn lik pure fire."

Rachel closed her eyes and obediently dipped her head backwards, immersing her mass of auburn curls into the lilac scented foam. The clean, fragrant water caressed her scalp, floating away the accumulated grime of weeks aboard ship and the dust of a Savannah dock.

Leona broke into her reverie, "O.K. Miss Rachel, let Leona scrub dat head good and then when ya finish the rest of yore bath, I'll go fetch some fresh water."

Rachel lifted her head from the water and tilting it back, Leona applied a thick liquid into the thick tresses, then vigorously lathered the silken mass, scrubbing it skillfully and thoroughly. After the servant finished, she pressed the excess water and lather from her hair and left it in a foamy topknot remarking, "I bet yore mamma used to do yore hair like that when ya wuz a li'l gal."

A grateful smile brightened Rachel's face, "As a matter of fact she did. Now how are we ever going to get all this soap out?"

Leona cackled, "Don't ya worry 'bout that none. Mr. Andrew has fixed up this here place real fine. I'm goin' git some more water and yore clothes, ya finish up now and I'll be back quick as a wink."

Rachel nodded and soon, true to her word, Leona returned, carrying a strange half moon shaped copper tub. She called back over her shoulder to someone beyond Rachel's view, "Josiah, jest set them kettles down out there and I'll git 'em in a minute."

Leona attached the smaller tub to the larger tub, directly behind Rachel's head. The curve of the two tubs fit exactly with the lip of the larger tub curving over into the smaller. After securing the tubs, the young woman left, returning with two medium sized kettles, "Miss Rachel, hold yore head back over the edge here and I'll pour this kettle of water through yore hair."

Soon the servant girl had Rachel's hair rinsed and wrapped turban style in a snow white towel, "Now I'll empty this li'l tub and bring ya more fresh water to finish yore bath."

She returned with two larger kettles of water, "Now there's a stopper in the bottom of that tub yore in. All ya have to do is pull it and this here soapy water will go out, then you can rinse off with these kettles."

Rachel looked puzzled, "Where will the water go?"

Leona chuckled, "I tol' ya Mr. Andrew wuz smart. It goes through a pipe in the floor to a room with big buckets underneath. All the upstairs baths are fixed so they can drain into the buckets in the room below here. When they is full up, Josiah takes the buckets out and empties them. Nows ya best hurry if'n we gonna have time to fix that hair of yor'n."

Impressed with the ingenuity and convenience she had just experienced, Rachel grudgingly admitted to herself that Europe or even her beloved Sweetwater trailed behind the luxurious innovations of Andrew Meredith. What kind of man was this, inventive, successful and obviously accustomed to being in control?

Rachel finished quickly, and donned a dressing gown placed neatly on the stool beside the tub. Stepping into the bedroom, her eyes widened in surprise as she saw a fresh wardrobe laid out ready for her on the bed.

Puzzled she fingered undergarments made of finely woven, handkerchief linen, and apparently in her size. Beside them lay an emerald green silk dress in the latest style. Fine ivory lace graced the modest neckline and matching satin slippers proclaimed this was no servant's outfit, but rather a fashionable dinner outfit made for a woman of substance. But—who? Was it Daphne's? Rachel frowned with distaste at the thought of having to wear a servant's clothes.

But deeper consideration forced Rachel to admit she couldn't wear Daphne's clothes. Daphne was petite in frame, Rachel, tall and willowy. Then, who—?

Rachel sighed and began to dress. Her fingers caressed the undergarments, their snow-white appearance proclaimed them new and never worn by another. Her woman's heart admired the fine workmanship and the delicate lace and with a pang realized that her own wardrobe was sadly lacking. In fact she had never owned garments as delicate as these. The finely woven fabric felt whisper light against her skin where it settled on her body, perfectly molding her every feminine curve as if patterned for her body alone.

Hesitating to don the lovely dress with her hair still wet, she put her dressing gown back on just as Leona knocked and entered the room with a tray.

"Miss Rachel, Daphne said ya probably' need a bite to eat, since supper done been pushed back for another two hours."

Rachel looked gratefully at the tray. Her stomach gave a hungry lurch at the aroma of freshly baked biscuits and tea. Lunch had been shipboard fare and many hours before. Maybe a bite to eat would energize her. "Thank you, Leona, I believe I could use a little nourishment, it has been a long time since I ate."

The servant set the tray down on a small, walnut gate leg table placed in front of the windows. Pulling up a chair, she motioned Rachel to have a seat, "Whilst ya eat I'll take a towel to yore hair and see'n if we can't get some of that water outta it. It won't be dry before supper, but if'n it ain't dripping I can fix it real pretty."

Rachel cast a doubtful eye at the optimism of the girl, but without comment she sat down and relished the light flaky biscuits as they practically melted in her mouth.

When Rachel had devoured the last remnants of her food, Leona removed the turban that bound her locks and vigorously toweled the thick mass of hair. She bit her bottom lip, suppressing a yelp of discomfort. Then when it seemed as if Leona would pull her head off, the young servant put the towel down and gently massaged her scalp. By this time her hair tumbled around her shoulders in a cloud of tangled profusion. How would they ever bring order to that nest of tangles?

Leona smiled reassuringly as if she recognized Rachel's apprehension, then she reached into the pocket of her snow-white apron and brought out a round bottle with a clear liquid in it. When she uncorked it, a hint of citrus escaped into the room.

Rachel raised one eyebrow, inquisitive yet unwilling to ask.

Leona laughed, simply explaining, "I calls it, hair magic." She poured a little of the thick substance into the palm of her hand. Rubbing both hands together, she massaged it into Rachel's damp hair for several minutes. Afterwards she combed her hair with ease, the tangles seeming to evaporate easily with each sweep of the wide toothed comb.

"What did you put in my hair?" Amazed, Rachel questioned, her curiosity overcoming her cool aloofness.

"I don't rightly know, but it's some oil that Mr. Drew gets for Miz Matilda when his ships come in from the East. It's good stuff. I see it bout work wonders with Miss Laura's hair."

"Miss Laura?"

"Yes, that be Mr. Andrew's niece. She's got a head full of hair just like you has, cepting it's yaller like the color of corn silk afore the ears get ripe. Fact is, she's bout yore size. Those be her clothes yore wearin.'"

"Won't she object? These seem to be brand new." Rachel asked.

"No ma'am. She won't even know. She's fifteen and ain't interested in no kinds of clothes. She just likes to read and roam about the plantation. Miz Matilda cries her eyes out cuz that girl ain't interested in boys and such. Mr. Andrew just laughs and claims she'll grow out of it. He finally giv in to Miz Ttilda and promised that Mis Laura could have a grown up wardrobe, so he turned Louisa loose. She mighty handy in the clothing room, and was powerful glad to get to work with something besides that dull ole homespun. The only time she gets to strut her stuff is when Daphne wants something. Miz Matilda don't hardly need nothing. Anyways she just wants them old blues and black stuff, and that ain't no fun for Louisa. What a pity all those purty clothes going to waste. Miz Laura said she wuzn't wearing none of them clothes cause it would make her sick to be all corseted up. 'Course when Miz Tilde done saw them dresses, she said they wuzn't fitin' for a young Missy like Miss Laura, they be too ole lookin', so she ordered a dressmaker from Savannah. Louisa wuz mighty downcast 'bout nobody gonna wear her clothes she done made. She's got a smile on her face tonight. She knows ya goin' to do justis to them things."

Rachel raised a brow, a smile threatening, "Where is Miss Laura now?"

"She be up in Virginia visiting some of Miz Matilda's folk. That's one reason Miz Matilda n'sist on seeing ya tonight, she be lonely, but wouldn't admit missing that high strung miss. She done got her aunt so upset, Mr. Andrew had to send her off for a little while."

"Why?"

"Cause she done told her aunt she ain't gonna be all corseted up for nobody not even for them new Savannah clothes." Leona explained a broad grin of indulgence on her face.

"Will Mr. Meredith make her wear the clothes?"

"No'm I don' speck so."

"Why?" asked Rachel, her curiosity peaked that Andrew Meredith would be amenable to his niece's unrealistic preferences.

"Cause she's the apple of his eye and besides I 'spect he don't want her growin' up afore she has to."

"Whose child is she?" Rachel inquired boldly.

"She is his youngest brother's child. He done up and disappeared when Miz Laura was a leetle tyke so she been with Miz Matilda all these years. When Mr. Andrew brought 'em to live with him she was a sickly child. That's why they had to move from Boston. That cold weather up there didn' suit Miz Matilda or Miss Laura none. Sure does keep Mr. Andrew busy shufflin' off between Boston and Savannah. But then agin I guess he's used to it." Leona sighed, considering the hectic lifestyle of Andrew Meredith.

"Is her health better now?" Rachel probed, unwilling to end the conversation her curiosity sparked, her fatigue forgotten.

"It am better, but sometimes these cold, damp winters goes against her and she gets sick. So does Miz Matilda, but then she be awful frail. You'll see at supper," Leona responded.

"What about Daphne? Does she really run the household?"

Leona's open face closed as she explained, "Yes ma'am. Miz Matilda ain't able, and running a plantation is a big job."

Rachel persisted, "Who is she? She said she was free."

"She is. Her name is Daphne DuLucie and that's all I knows."

"Don't tell me that," Rachel insisted, "I know all about plantation grapevines. Now tell me who is she really?"

"I told you, I don't know and I don't wanna know. The last person who asked too many questions about that business left here for parts unknown. I like it here with Mr. Andrew sos I jest keep my mouth shut, do my job best I can and ask no questions. Now then if'n we is gonna get that hair presentable, we'd better quit this talkin' and get to fixin.'" Leona finished with a laugh, effectively diverting anymore probing by this beautiful white stranger.

Suddenly confident in the girl's abilities, Rachel submitted herself to her skilled hands as curiosity and a strange sense of exhilaration took hold of her.

Finally Leona motioned toward the dress and observed, "I think we need to put it on now so as not to mess up yore hair. I ain' quite got the finishin' touches on it yet sos we can slip it right over yore head."

With dress in place and fastened, Leona finished Rachel's hair and led her into the bath alcove to peer into the softly lighted mirrors. What Rachel saw bewitched her. Gone was the bedraggled ragamuffin of a few hours earlier and in her place stood one who would rival any beauty on the continent.

The deep green of her dress captured the emerald fire in her eyes while the cut of the dress emphasized her soft feminine curves as it accented her tall, regal bearing. Leona had caught her hair in an upsweep with soft curls caressing one side of her neck, while damp tendrils escaped here and there to frame her face, leaving her with a softness that displayed an enchanting feminine vulnerability.

To say Leona was an artist seemed an understatement. Rachel only knew that all Aunt Letty's couturiers in France and England had failed to achieve what Leona had for this simple plantation dinner for two women.

Rachel drew her breath in sharply and Leona's countenance fell, "You don' lik Leona's fixin'?"

Rachel smiled reassuringly, "Oh, yes, it looks quite nice. It's just that I'm in mourning."

A broad smile beamed Leona's face, "Oh, don't you never mind, Miss Rachel, the good Lord knows ya can't help not having any clothes with ya. Anyhows that green is near 'bout black. Course it do set them fires aburnin' in yore eyes."

An uncertain smile touched Rachel's full lips but didn't quite make it to her eyes as the heartache she had pushed aside these past few hours rushed in to greet her. "I'll soon have my clothes, I'm sure."

"Yes'm and until then, I so wish Mr. Andrew could see you now. Bet he wouldn' even recognize ya."

Rachel laughed. "Would anyone? I'm hardly sure I would recognize myself. What a sight I was. However, I've no interest in bothering Mr. Meredith further, as Daphne pointed out—he is a very busy man."

"Daphne, hmmp, she well knows ain't no man too busy to eye a purty lady. That's one enjoyment the Good Lord gives them all whether they be young or old, black or white." Leona commented with a knowing cackle.

Rachel's cheeks grew hot as a blush tinged her face. She was unaccustomed to carrying on such informal and intimate conversations with servants, except for her beloved Agatha and that had been many years ago. Since then anyone she deemed beneath her socially, she treated with an aloof politeness. She wondered what manner of household this was. A woman of color was the apparent mistress of the plantation, servants spoke freely to their superiors and an adolescent girl refused to grow up, all under the authority of a seemingly domineering man. Despite her preoccupation with her own predicament, the whole set up intrigued her.

"How much longer until supper, Leona?" Rachel asked turning

48

the conversation to safer ground.

"In 'bout an hour. You have time to catch a wink or two. If'n ya muss yore hair, I'll come straighten it out. Now ya lay down 'n I'll go help Liza with Miz 'Tilde."

A loud commotion in the yard below her windows awakened Rachel with a start. Her exhaustion had been so complete that she had fallen into a sleep so deep that for a moment she found it difficult to recall where she was or why.

The soft netting draped around her bed swayed softly in the slight breeze coming in from the windows and touched her arm, startling her. She jerked her arm away, crossing both in a tense position as she searched the semi darkened room for something familiar.

Across the room, she spotted the bath alcove, double doors flung wide and awash in soft candlelight, and reflected back into the room by mirrors. Lilac softly fragranced the room and suddenly reality crashed in. She was in Andrew Meredith's home awaiting a late supper with his aunt, and she had dropped off for a brief nap. Bolting upright, she called out to Leona. Had she overslept? Was supper over? Had she insulted her hostess? All these questions deluged her mind as she groped for the satin slippers that had been by the bed when she took her rest.

The room remained silent and no Leona answered. Rushing to the window, she peered out and could see the obscure outline of several men in the dark, some had lanterns but she could not see their faces. Shouts further out in the darkness, indicated activity toward the river and then the lanterns moved away from the house and toward the river where other lanterns came into view.

From the shouting, Rachel surmised that a boat or ferry had docked somewhere beyond the view of this room, and then a door slammed somewhere beneath her and she heard muffled voices and scurrying feet. Then a soft knock at her door and Leona called her name.

"Miss Rachel, supper be ready in jus a few minutes, do ya need me to fix yore hair?"

"No, I'm just fine. I'll be down shortly." Rachel answered from the mirrored alcove. Her hair was still in place and her dress wrinkle free. She must have slept without moving. Feeling refreshed from her nap, she heard her stomach rumble as hunger issued its command in anticipation to an authentic southern plantation meal. Even though it would be the tidewater variety, nostalgia and hunger proved more powerful for the moment than the melancholy thoughts of her past and uncertain future. Suddenly she realized she was looking forward to the meal and meeting Aunt Matilda, with the exception of Daphne she had not even spoken to a woman in days.

Leona had whetted her curiosity about the family. With the resiliency of youth and a healthy body, she put her problems in abeyance for the moment, exchanged them for a strange kind of exhilaration.

Opening the door, she peered out hesitantly. When she encountered no one, she pushed the door wider and stepped out into the broad hall ablaze with light. She turned to her left and walked slowly toward where the hall gave way to an open balcony whose walnut spindled railing led to the grand stair case and its downward sweep. When she reached the balcony she paused and looked downward.

Louisa and Josiah rushed around beneath her in frenzy, just as the ornate front door opened and Andrew Meredith stepped through. Surprise washed her features and involuntarily she glanced down at her dress, her hands pressing away imaginary wrinkles, then a knowing half smile touched her lips and she moved toward the staircase, arriving at the top, just as he looked up from below.

Their eyes collided, and astonishment flared in his. Rachel slowly and deliberately moved toward him, drawn by a primeval woman's awareness that for this brief moment she was in control.

FOUR

Like players in a predestined drama where time and space recede leaving the two major characters on stage alone, all activities ceased, all others forgotten, Andrew Meredith stood transfixed while Rachel came toward him. As if paralyzed by some strange emotion, he seemed unable to tear his eyes away from the apparition descending his staircase. Beauty so graced her bearing that he felt a reverent awe before her, something altogether foreign to this self contained man. His breath caught in an inaudible gasp, before he came to himself. Then with a slight shake of his head, will brought emotions under control and the brief instant was gone as if it had never happened. But it had and Andrew Meredith would never recover.

His lips smiled a greeting, while asking with an affected amusement in his voice, "Miss Gregory, I presume?"

Looking boldly into his warm brown eyes, hers dancing with green fire, Rachel declared, "The very same."

He extended his hand and taking hers, tucked it into his arm and led her toward the dining room. A genuine smile now warmed his whole countenance making him seem years younger and more approachable. He looked directly into her eyes and protested, "Not possibly."

Rachel looked up provocatively through long dark lashes and insisted, an enchanting half smile parting her full pink lips. "Most assuredly. Tidied up a bit, I grant you."

He laughed with abandon, obviously enjoying the repartee, "More than a little, I'd say."

This time a becoming pink flushed Rachel's face, "I did want to make a good impression on my hostess. By the way, what are you doing here? I thought only the ladies would be dining tonight."

He smiled down at her, mischief dancing in his eyes, "Could be I wanted another look at the little wild cat I rescued this afternoon, to see what I might be letting myself in for."

"Could be, but I doubt it. Daphne told me that you are a busy man, too busy to be concerned with me it seems." Rachel raised one brow.

"I do have a rather full plate but, after I left you, I met some of my neighbors and they wanted to drop by after dinner for a brief meeting, but I also came bearing unpleasant news. There was an accident at the dock today and some cargo fell into the river. Your trunk was dropped overboard—."

"My what?" Rachel gasped in disbelief.

"I know it's hard to believe, that's why Josiah didn't deliver it. I found Captain Smythe waiting in my office with the news. Seems it was one of those freak accidents. Of course the company will replace what you lost."

"But I won't have any clothing—."

"You look lovely in what you have on." His smile somehow made the compliment intimate.

She blushed and spoke more sharply than she intended, "As you well know, this isn't mine."

"It looks made for you. Didn't Louisa attend to your needs this afternoon?"

"Well, yes, but one green taffeta dress is hardly adequate."

"I assure you there is an ample supply of everything you need," he insisted.

"You don't understand. I'm in mourning." Rachel protested.

"Then Louisa will make you what you need," he answered matter of factly.

"But that will take weeks!" She exclaimed.

"Probably, but you're welcome to be our guest during that time."

"Mr. Meredith, I want to go home," Rachel pleaded, her eyes filled with longing.

Meredith's face softened at the pleading in her eyes, and spoke gently, "I know, Miss Gregory, and you shall. Suppose you take the clothing already made and Louisa can make what you need. We will see that it is sent to you as soon as possible. Given the circumstances anyone would understand your failure to wear black."

"People won't know the circumstances."

Meredith laughed aloud, and then observed, "After this afternoon, I find it hard to believe that you would allow society to dictate your conduct, much less your wardrobe, Miss Gregory."

Rachel smiled a reluctant half-smile, "How could you judge my actions and attitudes by one brief encounter?"

"'T'was purely the nature of the encounter."

"Be that as it may, that doesn't bring my trunk back, now does it?" She replied primly, her full lips drawn together in a thin line.

He sobered as he looked down and straight into her eyes, "No, and the good Captain did not escape a stern reprimand for his carelessness. However, part of his neglect was due to his discovery that you had left the ship. When he went to look for you, the unloading went unsupervised."

Rachel flinched, "Oh, I am sorry that I have caused the good captain so much anguish."

"Quite so. He was justly agitated. He knew how much importance I had placed on your safe arrival into my care."

"Why?"

"An agreement that I made with your father."

"My father? You were a friend of my father's?" Hope fired her green eyes.

"Not exactly, we were business associates and had a mutual friend, Wilkie."

"What agreement, Mr. Meredith?"

"That I would see that you came home safely, in the event you wanted to come home."

"And here I am. I'm safe, but my clothes aren't"

"Did you have anything in your luggage that can't be replaced?"

"No, not really. What few treasures I possess were in my valise. My father kept Mother's jewelry except for this pendant," She lifted a filigree gold locket inset with emeralds and diamonds, nestling in the hollow of her neck. "He gave this to her on their wedding day and I always wear it, no matter what the occasion."

He leaned toward her, his eyes on the exquisite pendant in her hand, and a faint fragrance of lilacs from her hair filled his nostrils, confusing his emotions and delaying his response. Then he observed his voice quiet and husky, "He had impeccable taste. There were other pieces?"

"Yes, many. Father enjoyed buying beautiful gifts for my mother. After she died, it seemed he could not part with them. I begged him for this one and he finally relented."

"Perhaps he was saving them until you were older and could appreciate were them."

"I'm sure you are right. Youth can be callous and unappreciative."

Meredith nodded his head in agreement, something akin to pain touched his eyes, "But life has a way of teaching us what's really important and with that lesson inevitably comes a sense of gratitude."

Rachel hesitated a moment before responding, trying to decipher the strange moment of vulnerability revealed in his eyes, then stated, "You've learned that lesson."

He laughed a short bitter laugh, dispelling the softness. "I've learned to be grateful for whatever life has to offer, for there are lessons to be learned in the good and the bad experiences of life."

"It's hard to believe that you've ever had any bad experiences if one judges your obvious wealth and accomplishments," Rachel observed thoughtfully.

"Both came as a direct result of the bad experiences. You have two choices when difficult times come. You can let the difficulties defeat you or you can learn and benefit from them."

"Obviously you've learned."

"Still learning, Miss Gregory. Life is a process, not an accomplishment. Now, back to your immediate problem. Louisa will attend to your wardrobe and you can order anything you want. They can be shipped later. I've booked you on a train leaving for Macon next week. Because of the accident, I felt you would need a few extra days to complete your shopping."

"That's very thoughtful, but I want to go home as soon as possible."

"I've still a few details to work out as to who will accompany you home. You cannot travel unescorted." Meredith explained.

"Surely, I won't—."

"Yes, you will," Meredith replied, "Now come meet Aunt 'Tilde. I know she's dying of curiosity. This will be a real treat for her. She has been looking forward to your arrival. I hope you have tales to tell her about life abroad. All her life she has wanted to go."

"Why didn't she?"

"Because she always had someone else's needs to care for. First my brother and me after my mother died and then my niece. By the time she came to live with me, her health was too frail."

Meredith and Rachel turned the corner and approached the large dining room, ablaze with lights. A petite, silver-haired lady sat at one end of a massive mahogany dining table, her head barely reaching the back of the ornately carved chair. Lively brown eyes fixed on Rachel as Meredith escorted her across the room, her hand still captured in the bend of his arm. A fact Matilda Burnes' sharp eye noted, as well as the unusual flush of pleasure that warmed her nephew's countenance.

When Andrew introduced Rachel, Matilda held out her hand and remarked with an engaging smile, "Welcome, my dear. You should have come sooner. It's been a long time since I've heard my Drew laugh like that. What a pleasant sound, a house filled with laughter."

"Why, thank you. It's a pleasure to be in such a lovely house and to be treated so hospitably." Rachel found to her amazement that she meant it. Looking into alert, wise eyes made her feel as if she were almost home.

"I've been looking forward to meeting you, my dear and hearing all about your adventures," Matilda responded.

Rachel smiled, "I've had a few more than I bargained for, but I'll be glad to share them with you. At least the ones you haven't already heard about."

Andrew interrupted, "She'll be eager to hear about all. Have a seat next to Aunt 'Tilde and I'm going to move my plate across from yours since it will be just the three of us."

Aunt Matilda rang a small crystal bell beside her plate and the servants began serving an elaborate meal of seafood delicacies. Dinner proved a delightful time of repartee between guest and hostess as Matilda plied her with questions about life abroad.

As they finished the last of their fruit dessert and coffee, Josiah entered the dining room to announce visitors. Aunt Matilda raised an inquisitive eyebrow toward Andrew as he directed the servant to show the guests into his study.

"Drew, have they come to harangue you about politics again?"

He smiled, his eyes warmed by affection as he looked at his aunt, "Probably, they are trying to convince me to get involved in the coming crisis. Up until now I've tried to stay out of Georgia politics, but with the political climate in Washington like it is, I'm afraid my days of observing are over."

"I hate to see you add any more responsibilities to the ones you have now. A man just has so much time, you know."

"I know but this slavery question is volatile and has been for years. The issue is going to have to be settled. And if sane heads don't decide it then we'll have a war, we came close to it in 1850. Already the state is becoming divided, people choosing sides. I imagine that's what Noah and William have come for. They want to know where I stand."

Matilda searched Andrew's face before asking quietly "Where do you stand, Drew?""

He sighed before answering, "That's a big question, Aunt 'Tilde. I'm not on the side of the "fire-eaters", but I'm not an abolitionist either. I guess I'm somewhere in the middle."

Matilda's brown eyes darkened, "Me thinks, my dear, that this is one issue on which you can't straddle the fence. I know you must have a strong opinion one way or the other.

Meredith tweaked her under the chin and his mouth parted in a grim smile, "You are my conscience, Matilda Burnes. I'm afraid it would be very inconvenient to get off the fence right now."

"You mean it might mean making a choice between what is right and what is expedient?" Matilda's eyes fastened on her nephew; the love and affection in them softened the mild rebuke.

Rachel watched the exchange between nephew and aunt. Expecting a sharp denial from Meredith, she was surprised when he merely chuckled and said, "Maybe. But I hardly think either answer is expedient. What I must come to terms with is what I am sure is right and what my course of action will be."

Rachel looked steadily at her host, a frown wrinkled her brow, "What do you mean the slavery issue is going to have to be settled. How can it be or why does it need to be?"

Drew turned to Rachel his dark eyes hooded, "Many people, even slave owners, feel that it is wrong to own slaves. Congress was fighting over that issue long before you ever left for Europe."

"Perhaps, but I guess I just wasn't attuned to politics."

"I'm sure and a grave error," Meredith observed, dryly.

"How was I supposed to know about it when our curriculum was limited to the social graces that were supposed to make us into marriageable women?" Bitterness tinged Rachel's voice.

"In my opinion any man worth his salt would appreciate a wife who is well educated in every area as well as the social graces."

"Obviously you are in the minority, Mr. Meredith," Rachel defended softly.

A smile softened Andrew's countenance as he answered half-apologetically, "You're quite right. Not a single Female Academy has asked me to sit on its board. But the fact is, I feel that our nation is destined for some dark years and men will not be the only ones to suffer hardships. Sometimes being adequately informed helps one to endure them."

"If what you say is true, you would find me a ready student if you'd care to inform me. Let me warn you in advance, I may not agree with your opinions because no one makes up my mind for me." Rachel commented with a toss of her head.

Meredith eyes narrowed slightly before he lifted his head and gave a full-throated laugh and replied, "I believe that."

She knew his mind had flashed back to the Savannah dock and the memory of a disheveled waif brawling in the afternoon shadows.

Rachel blushed, and rushed on to deter his wandering mind from her humiliation, "I mean—,I hardly think you or anyone can convince me that slavery is wrong or that the rest of the nation has any right to interfere with something that is vital to Georgia."

"It isn't just Georgia, it's a power struggle in Washington between the abolitionists and those supporting slavery. Both groups want to decide national policy. Each new state that's admitted into the union threatens that delicate balance of power. If we get a President who favors abolition, many in the South threaten secession from the Union. Secession will mean war." he explained.

"Why? If we can't agree on something as vital to our survival as slavery, then don't we have the right to withdraw from the Union?" Rachel insisted, warming to the debate. "What about our rights, our sovereignty as a state? Shouldn't we decide what's best for Georgia?"

"That question is being argued across the south. Greater minds than mine are grappling with the answer. Meanwhile if you'll excuse me, I must greet my guests. Perhaps we can talk more about the issues before you return home."

———————

Andrew Meredith entered his cherry paneled study. Shelves of soft leather bound books lined the side walls from floor to ceiling. Their covers engraved in gold, reflected the soft light from the sconces placed strategically between each wall of shelves. A pleasant aroma of citrus and coffee permeated the room, giving an inaudible welcome to all that entered.

More than any room in the house the library reflected the personality of its owner. Tall ceilings added to the ambience of spaciousness. During the day light infused the room from broad, floor to ceiling windows forming twin alcoves on opposite ends. His finely crafted cherry desk resided in one alcove. A stack of neatly arranged papers beside a quill pen proclaimed it a functional working area.

Hidden behind one of the wooden wall panels, a spiral staircase led to Meredith's bedroom directly above which was the same size as his study below. This wing was on the opposite end of the house from the room that Rachel occupied. However, the same view of lush lawn and meticulously attended gardens dropping off to the banks of the slow moving river beyond greeted Andrew Meredith each time he worked at his desk or occupied the room above.

Tonight Andrew Meredith was oblivious to his pleasant surroundings. His mind was set on the encounter that awaited him. What would his response be? Matilda was right; soon he would have to take a stand, but where? The questions nettled his soul.

Pausing at the door, he observed the three men who were just finishing desert and coffee that Josiah had served them. William Walton, his rotund affable neighbor and Dr. Noah Adams, Drew's personal physician, were engaged in an animated conversation with a tall thin stranger whose back was toward him. From the flush on William's face and the whine in Noah's voice, it was evident that the conversation was not pleasant. Drew took a deep breath and let it out slowly before speaking.

Walking over to his three guests who sat in soft leather chairs adjacent to the now empty fireplace, he observed, "I see Josiah brought you some refreshment. Sorry that I was delayed, but we have a house guest."

William Walton wiped his face and hands on a snow white linen napkin then patted his ample mid-drift and replied, "Your hospitality made the wait most pleasant, Meredith. In fact, I would give you a good profit for that cook of yours."

"William, the last thing you need is a better cook," chuckled a red-haired balding man with long sideburns and whiskers that curled, embracing a face with a laughing mouth and dancing eyes.

Meredith smiled as he offered his hand to his neighbor, Walton. Turning his head to speak to the red-haired man, genuine affection warmed his eyes as he observed, "Doc, I thought you put William on a diet for that gout of his."

"Did my best, Meredith. But your man isn't helping much when you tempt us with food fit for the gods." Doc Adams, the local physician, retorted, before nodding toward the third man, "Drew, this is my cousin, Charles Johnson, who has a plantation upriver from Charleston."

Andrew reached out, offering his hand to a thin faced man with dark, somber eyes and thin lips drawn in a disapproving line, "Welcome to Georgia, Mr. Johnson. What brings you to our part of the country? "

"To visit plantation owners and other business men hoping to raise an awareness of the need for cooperation between states."

"Oh, really? And what might that be?"

"State sovereignty. Our rights are eroding and if we don't take a stand now, it'll be too late," Johnson barked.

"What does Georgia have to do with the state sovereignty of South Carolina, Mr. Johnson? Wouldn't you be better served to pursue your goal in your own state?"

A frown creased Johnson's forehead, his lips pressed even more tightly together, if possible, "South Carolina is not the problem. We are willing to pay the ultimate price to defend what is ours. The problem rests with states like Georgia and Virginia who don't seem to understand that our way of life can only be preserved by fighting for it."

"You are here to start a fight?" Andrew questioned softly, his eyes hooded as he took a seat by his visitor.

Out of the corner of his eye he could see Noah Adams squirming in his chair. William pulled out a large, linen handkerchief and began to fan himself.

"If it takes it," Johnson said, his eyes narrowed to little more than horizontal slits.

"Why would you do that?" Meredith probed.

"If you don't know what's going on around you, Mr. Meredith, then you have buried your head in the sand. The South is in a struggle for her life, and I believe before another year is out we'll be forced into secession," Johnson bellowed in exasperation.

Andrew Meredith's eyes narrowed. The pleasant light in them turned wary. His jaw tightened while his voice answered amiably, "I fervently hope not, Mr. Johnson. A confrontation seems inevitable but I hope that we can come to a peaceful settlement, another compromise that will satisfy both factions."

Johnson's face reddened. "The North is going to try to take our property away from us, you just wait and see. The only way the South can win is to secede. Then they'll listen to us and if they won't, we'll have our own country, a Confederacy of southern states who recognizes the sovereignty of each state."

"It'll never happen. If the South secedes there will be a war." Andrew disagreed.

"And we'll teach those abolitionists a lesson." His thin lips tightened, the veins in his neck bulged.

"I'm afraid not, sir. The South could never win a war with the North." Meredith's voice came soft and smooth but his eyes were hard like flint.

"That's heresy. You're a traitor to the very cause that's made you wealthy" Johnson accused, civility thrown to the winds.

"Now, Charles, settle down, we told you that's no way to bring a peaceful resolution to anything," Walton pled.

"We might as well tell it like it is. You told me that Meredith might be sympathetic to our cause, but I can tell this trip was a waste of time. He enjoys the lifestyle but is not willing to defend it." Johnson judged. His bulging eyes seemed ready to pop out of his head as beads of perspiration dampened his thin freckled face.

Meredith arched an eyebrow toward his friends who dropped their gaze, not willing to meet his eyes. Then he asked, "Cause? I don't believe I understand."

"Secession! I believe that we must organize. There is no doubt what South Carolina will do, but I must make sure that Georgia and other questionable states come on board. The only way to achieve that is a strong organization so that when the showdown comes, we'll be ready to move. If the South is to have any bargaining power we must be united in purpose and action. We must form a strong confederacy." Johnson pounded the library table, bouncing the leather bound books.

"And what does this have to do with me?" Meredith pursed his lips, only the drumming of his fingers on the table by his side betrayed his apparent calmness.

"We need money and manpower and men who can persuade other men to join us. William and Doc said you would be a good choice as a spokesperson, but I disagree. I've checked up on you. You still have holdings in the North and I feel that has tainted your loyalty." Johnson's lips curled in disgust.

"Charles, you don't insult a man in his own home. Give Andrew a chance to respond," Walton exclaimed, his face growing dangerously red.

"William, just settle down you'll get that blood pressure too high. Charles, we didn't bring you here to insult our friend. Now you just pipe down and let him talk." Turning to Andrew, Doc Adams smiled apologetically, "Sorry Andrew, Charles is a little overwrought tonight. I see it was not a good time to bring him. He just got word from his plantation that his neighbors foiled a slave uprising, and he is distraught over the safety of his own family."

"I understand, Johnson. I hope your family is safe. Perhaps you should continue your mission at another time when you're not so overwrought." Andrew suggested evenly.

"I will not go home until I have some commitments from Georgia." Johnson responded.

"I see. Well you won't get a commitment out of me, Mr. Johnson. I don't believe that secession is our answer. I think it would be more advantageous to work and organize for the presidential election next year. If we can get a man in office who is more sympathetic to the South's predicament, maybe we can work out another compromise until the issue can be settled."

"That's a waste of time. Secession is our only option. We need a solution, not a compromise. We've already seen that compromises don't work," Johnson railed, a green maniacal fire in his eyes.

Meredith took a deep breath and quietly explained, "Secession is not an acceptable option for me. I love the South, I enjoy our way of life, but change is inevitable and we must find a way to accept it. Slavery will have to end someday whether we secede or not."

"Why do you say that, sir?"

"Because there must be a better way than owning people."

"My slaves are better off than the poor workers up north."

"That may be, but when a man is in bondage his soul yearns to be free." Meredith explained softly.

"That's abolitionist propaganda. You talk to any of my slaves. They're happy, just like family."

"And you are distraught over this black 'family' revolting and doing harm to your loved ones while you are away?" Drew pointed out with a sigh, weariness suddenly drooping his eyes.

"Well, sir, your neighbors were misled about where your loyalties lie." Johnson all but shouted.

"My loyalties are not in question. Southern born and bred, I love the South, but she's not perfect. We both agree that we have a serious problem, we just see the solution differently."

"What's your solution? Set the slaves free?" Johnson sneered.

"Ultimately. I know that it would be an economic disaster to free the slaves at once, but somehow we need to work out a plan of gradual emancipation. I believe that a share cropping or fee basis could be worked out to the advantage of both landowner and laborer."

"You know those slaves won't work if you don't have someone

driving 'em."

"I disagree. Incentive can be more powerful than any whip." A hard edge now tinged Meredith's voice.

William Walton interrupted, "Andrew, what if Charles is right and it comes down to secession. What will you do then?"

"I'll support my state, but until then I commit all my efforts to averting secession and arriving at a peaceful solution."

Doc Adams asked, "Why are you so opposed to secession, Andrew? Seems to me that's the best solution. We go our way and they go theirs. That way we preserve our way of life."

Andrew Meredith turned to his friend, with compassion and affection warming his brown eyes, "Noah, the North will never allow us to secede without a fight and there is no way we can win against them."

Johnson interrupted, "The north could never whip our boys, we came up shooting and our cause is just!"

Meredith faced his opponent, "Perhaps you are right, our boys would be better fighters, better with guns, more motivated. But in order to fight and win, those boys need to have guns with which to fight and ammunition to arm them. We don't have the factories to produce implements of war. Ours is an agrarian society with a few textile mills. Secession will mean a blood bath on our land and a war we cannot win. When it's over life as we know it will never exist again and the slaves will be free. Wouldn't it be better to work for a peaceful solution to the slavery issue?" A pleading tone softened the edge to his voice; sadness dulled his brown eyes.

"You are unnecessarily pessimistic, Mr. Meredith, because you are an abolitionist at heart," Johnson accused.

Drew shook his head sadly and rose, hoping to bring the unpleasant conversation to a peaceful end. "No, Mr. Johnson, I travel extensively and I know the strength of the industrial North and we're no match. All we're going to do is sacrifice our finest young men for a lost cause."

Charles Johnson jumped to his feet, his large eyes bulged with emotion, his face pale, and "We'll go, sir, before I make a regretful response in a man's own home. If you were in South Carolina, you would be looking down the barrel of my pistol come dawn."

"I'm sorry that two men who obviously both love our Southern heritage cannot disagree on solutions in a peaceful manner."

Walton and Adams stood eyes downcast and jaws clinched.

Andrew turned to his neighbors and asked, "Have I insulted you also?"

William Walton shaking his head sadly followed Charles Johnson out of the room. Noah Adams waited and when they were alone said, "You haven't offended me, Andrew, in fact you gave me food for thought. I've always respected your judgment. I feel it in my bones, troublesome times are coming, Take care, my friend, I fear your strong principles will cause you much pain and sorrow before these issues are resolved."

A chill of apprehension swept through Drew's body as he watched his friend move out the door and away from him. Andrew had made his decision; the encounter with Johnson had settled the issue for him.

Later that night in the quiet sanctuary of his bedroom a strange urgency compelled him. In a split second he decided who would accompany Rachel to the red hills she called home. He would. Johnson had issued a call to arms. Now Andrew Meredith stood ready to oppose him with every ounce of his energy. But first he must test the political climate of Georgia. In hoping the problems would cure themselves, he had ignored the truth too long. Now he must act quickly, but not before he had studied the opposition.

The trip to north Georgia would be his first endeavor. How and whom he would contact once he arrived was still a big question. Then a brief smile eased his taunt features as the gravelly voice of a portly college friend boomed down the corridor of his memory and he remembered the outspoken editor had located in Marietta as editor of a local weekly. Meredith knew he would be the source he needed.

Satisfied, he made his plans. He realized it would be several days before he could leave, his business would dictate that and then he would have to order a private car for the trip north. Since Daphne would need to accompany him to provide a companion for the Gregory girl, a private car would circumvent any unpleasant encounters. He would delay the trip until one was available. And then there was the question of Rachel's clothes which proved an unfortunate delay. A slight smile once again tugged at the tension on his face as the memory of her dazzling beauty descending the stairs in Laura's rejected finery flooded his mind. Well, maybe, the loss of her luggage was not such a tragedy after all. Remembering the turmoil that she had left in her wake, his smile broadened despite his heavy heart. Not knowing if he'd be able to arrange his affairs by Rachel's scheduled departure; he decided to keep his travel plans to himself. No need to give that little miss any prior warning; as long as she was in his care, she would do as he thought best. After that he didn't know who would look after her. Involuntarily icy fingers of dread for her future clutched his heart.

FIVE

Rachel awakened before the dawn came, her insides churning with anticipation. Today her unexpected visit in the Meredith mansion would end. She thought back over the days she had spent here and then in Andrew's townhouse on her shopping trip. Their hospitality overwhelmed her. Never had she felt more welcome, not even at Aunt Letty's. Aunt Matilda had encouraged her free reign of Meredith's home, insisting it was her nephew's wishes. Every morning when the sun was still low on the horizon and the day was new, she visited the stables, selecting a beautiful mount, a different one each day, and rode across the fields and meadows. One morning, she rode the dikes and observed the rice fields, on another she explored the pastures and barns where Meredith raised fine horses imported from England. The last morning before she and Daphne had left for her shopping trip, she rode across the fields, recently tilled and awaiting seeds that would bring in a crop of Sea Island cotton. Although the earth turned up was dark, rich loam so different from the clay of Sweetwater, the waiting furrows reminded her of home and aroused the latent homesickness she had pushed aside all week.

Now in Savannah, a train waited to carry her home. Home. The word sounded strange. A place she had yearned for; yet, now anxiety tinged her excitement. Questions buffeted her within. The thought of Sweetwater without Papa brought tears to her eyes. How would she manage without him? How could she roam the hills and valleys, sit at the large dining table with his place at the head of the table, empty?

And then there were practical things to consider. Could she run a plantation, what about the mill? She had heard of women who did it, women with absentee or ne'er do well husbands, but at least they have someone to consult. Then, too, she'd been away from plantation life for a long while and she was little more than a child when she left. What did she know about the work that loomed ahead of her? She shuddered.

On and on the onslaught of self-doubt bombarded Rachel in those moments of deepest darkness just before the new light of day dispels the doubts and fears that bind the night.

Finally streaks of pink and gold brightened the horizon, filtering a soft light into her room. With the day, her hope renewed and her usual confidence returned. If other women could do it, she too—would be up to the challenge!

She could always count on "Uncle" Randall, who had always been more like family than attorney. He'd always been available when her family needed him, and she knew how much he loved her. He called her the child he'd never had. Her mind detoured for a moment, musing, wondering why he'd never married. He had celebrated every holiday with them and then when her mother died, even in her own misery she had noticed the pain and sorrow in his. Yes, Randall Wilkie would be there for her as he had been for her father and mother. Then there was Andrew Meredith . . . .

The thought of Andrew turned her full mouth upward in a half-smile. What an enigma he was. Apparently eager to divest himself of an unwanted responsibility, he had turned her over to Daphne at the first possible moment. Yet, he arrived home for supper that first evening unexpected, and proved an impeccable host. With efficiency and concern he had anticipated her every need and attempted to meet it. His concern for her welfare seemed to far exceed the parameters of a reluctant promise to a dying man. He seemed genuinely to care. Encouragement warmed Rachel's heart.

Rachel didn't yet know who would be escorting her home or if she would see Meredith before she left. Perhaps they had shared their last moments together. Somehow her heart refused to acknowledge such a possibility.

She knew he had business interests in the northern part of the state. She reasoned that their paths were sure to cross from time to time and when they did—? When she considered his strength, confidence in her own ability to cope blossomed.

From the opposite end of the house, Andrew Meredith faced the same glorious dawn that wafted through Rachel's window. He, too, had been awake for hours and had soundlessly descended the stairway into his library in order to meet the day in his favorite place. The visit from his neighbors and their guest had provoked his decision to get involved. He had experienced an impatience to begin his journey of discovery. However, it was not the unsettling events of that night or his decision that filled his mind as fingers of pink and gold caressed the horizon before him.

Unwillingly his mind filled with thoughts of the beautiful Rachel and the dawning of a new day did nothing to dispel his troubled mind.

He understood better than she did, the almost impossible task facing her. Somehow his involvement in her life had taken on a dimension he had neither planned nor desired. He had promised a dying man safe passage home for an unknown daughter. It was a promise that seemed simple enough to take care of, one that he had planned to delegate to another, someone in his vast number of employees, which would require no personal involvement. He had enough women to look after.

For years there had been Daphne and her welfare to consider. Now he had Aunt Matilda and Laura. His troubled countenance lightened when he thought of her and a chuckle warmed the room as he thought of her conflict with their aunt. She was his brother's child, but the image of his sister whom he had loved so dearly. Pain, dagger sharp and quick, pierced him as he remembered the heartache of his loss. The dreaded summer fever that plagued the South Carolina coast had taken her when she was Laura's age.

Without warning a longing to see his niece swept over him. She had brought much needed laughter to his existence. She forced him to take a little time to experience a few of the joys in life.

He admitted to himself that without Aunt Matilda and Laura to look after, his life would have been bleak consisting only of harsh lines and challenges. One provided the lightness, the other gentleness and stability. Both lavished love on him. Yes, he needed them for balance as much as they needed him for survival.

His sister's death had severed the last tie he had to a life that had offered little but heartache and pain. When the inevitable conflict with his father finally exploded, he left without a backward glance. There was nothing left to hold him on their small South Carolina plantation. His mother had long been dead, his brother left the year before and with his sister gone he had no reason to stay.

Meredith's eyes narrowed, remembering. Unwanted thoughts and emotions locked away for years clamored for admittance. He shook his head trying to dispel memories of screams in the night and his father's fury as Andrew confronted him and tried to intervene.

At sixteen he had been large for his age yet no match for the towering, giant who was his father. He could still remember the beating. The pain of those wounds had long since healed, but the words were forever etched in his mind. Accusations that he would never be a real man because he was weak and unmanly rang through his memory. Shouts that he would never succeed in life because he lacked the drive and the lust for life rang through the corridors of his memory.

A bitter chuckle parted the early morning air as he looked around him. This room alone proclaimed his father wrong. The sweet taste of success had been his. His fingers caressed the smooth, hand-rubbed mahogany tabletop beside him. The finest craftsmen in England and America built it, as the rest of the furnishings in this house, to his specifications. Pain washed his features in the waiting shadows as he acknowledged a hidden truth to himself alone. This whole palatial estate was a monument proclaiming his father wrong. Only one among many of his vast holdings, it was worth many times over the wealth his father had amassed and lost during his lifetime.

And suddenly all his achievements, the house, his wealth, seemed little more than ashes in the wind. For what were possessions without someone with to share them and life with no goal beyond achieving wealth? Unless his heart had a cause to stir it, would the world be any different because he had walked its dusty paths? Emptiness strummed Andrew Meredith's heart strings in the quiet shadows of the morning, leaving a longing in his soul that nudged him a step further toward self discovery. Oh yes, he needed Aunt Tilde and Laura, but were they enough?

Then unbidden Rachel Gregory's face invaded his mind, the fire in her emerald eyes challenging him. But what about her? From the moment she arrived, she had disrupted his life. Her very presence disturbed his equilibrium, evoking strange emotions within him. Emotions he had tried to deny, refusing to explore yet he could not shake the feeling that because of her his life stood on the brink of upheaval.

The aroma of coffee wafted beneath Rachel's door, and she turned her head just as Leona opened it and stepped into the room carrying a tray of pastries along with a pot of the steaming beverage into the room.

"Miss Rachel, yore breakfast gonna be light this mo'ning. Mr. Andrew done sent word downstairs that ya'll gotta hurry if'n you catch that early train. Yo miss it and ya have to wait til next week. Now you get up and drank yore coffee while I fix yo hair. I done got all yo thangs packed up and ready to go. Mr. Andrew, he don' like to wait fo nobody. When he say frog you best leap."

Rachel smiled at the sprite servant and her description of Andrew Meredith. Then her brow creased in bewilderment as she observed, "Mr. Meredith surely doesn't have to see me off. He's been too kind already."

"See yo off? Why, Chile, he's a goin' wit you. Daphne, she be goin' too. Why we been scurryin' 'round since before daybreak tryin to get yo and her ready."

"Mr. Meredith and Daphne both?"

"Ye'sum. He done decided, according to Miz Tilde to take a business trip up country and Daphne's goin' so's people won't talk." Leona answered as she bustled importantly around the room.

"Must have been a sudden decision. I thought I was to leave tomorrow."

"Sudden or not, tha's the way 'tis. Course how come you be aknowin' anyhow since you and Daphne coming' in from shopping in Savannah last night so late? Now what in de wuld cud take three whole days? Now why you two spend so long down there when I had packing' to do for you?" Leona scolded, clearly agitated at the possibility of displeasing Meredith.

"It just took that long. Anyway I didn't realize there was such a hurry." Rachel argued.

"You come on an' git up, so's you'll make it. Here's yore wrapper. Oh, me." Leona moaned as a voice from down the hall called her name, "I hear Miz Tilde calling. I be back quick as I can. Meanwhile you git to eatin' or you might have to leave hungry. That Mr. Andrew don' wait fer no dawdlers. When he be ready to leaves, he leaves. If'n you ain't ready, you left."

Rachel lingered a moment longer in the semi-light of her room, thinking about the trip awaiting her and the week that had passed. What a surprise! Andrew Meredith would accompany her home and Daphne would go along to protect her reputation. She almost laughed aloud, as if her reputation needed rescuing. If her trip so far had not destroyed it, she saw little reason for worrying about the rest of it. But Andrew Meredith had insisted and she was learning one thing, if he decreed anything, it happened.

She slowly stretched her arms above her head, then her whole body, luxuriating in the soft feather bed and smooth sheets beneath her. A slight lingering fragrance of lilacs from her bath the night before kissed the room. The breeze from the river stirred the curtains bringing in the morning sounds of activity that announced a new day.

The aroma from her breakfast tray set her taste buds watering as anticipation propelled her from the bed and to the table placed strategically next to the open window. Thus Leona found her up and eating when she scurried back into the room, a lovely traveling suit in her arms.

"Miss Rachel, I pressed this suit fer ya. I thought it would be comfortable fer yore long trip."

Rachel nodded as she took a large gulp of warm coffee. Her eyes glanced, then lingered on the garments Leona laid carefully on the unmade bed.

Rachel had been without any new clothes for a long time. While in Europe she'd had to make do with what she had and, at times, borrowing from her aunt. Aunt Letty had complained about her father's penury, but Rachel had defended him by saying she really didn't care about such things. She hadn't until now. But what woman could resist such finely tailored clothes? She felt a twinge of guilt. She shouldn't indulge. She was still in mourning. Yet, she had nothing suitable; it was at the bottom of the Savannah River. She walked over to the bed and with her finger gently traced the embroidered swirls on the dove gray jacket bodice. Her heart fluttered in anticipation.

For three days, she and Daphne shopped for her intimate needs and ordered shoes and hats to be made and sent later. The shopping had taken longer than they expected so they had spent two nights in Meredith's townhouse. He had been "upriver" on business so she and Daphne had occupied the simple townhouse with only the servants in residence.

She shivered as she remembered the large amount of money spent, but Daphne had tersely insisted. Mr. Andrew instructed her to buy generously without consideration of the funds spent. After all, it was the negligence of his captain who caused her loss and inconvenience.

Rachel protested that they were replacing much more than she had lost, but Daphne turned a deaf ear to her protestations. Whatever her private opinions were, Mr. Meredith's instructions were her command.

A knock on the open door and Matilda Burnes' soft voice interrupted Rachel's reverie. A smile of welcome warmed Rachel's face.

"My dear, I was afraid Andrew would not give us time for a decent farewell," the older woman explained as she bustled into the room, her brown eyes merry. "I'm so glad he is escorting you home."

"It's so kind of him, but I fear that I have disrupted his life unmercifully. I really don't need him to escort me. I could manage just fine, I'm sure," protested Rachel.

"Nonsense, my dear. It would not do for a young woman like you to travel all the way to Atlanta alone. Why you have to stop over in Macon and no telling what you'd encounter. Anyway, Drew needs to make this trip."

"Unexpected business problems?"

"No, my dear. His guests the evening you arrived forced my nephew to face a problem he's ignored too long. Now he's committed to finding the best solution."

"Miss Rachel, I better fix yore hair right now or you ain't goin' nowhere with Mr. Andrew," Leona interrupted.

Matilda laughed and motioned Rachel toward Leona. "We'll talk while you get ready."

Leona replied, "Well, Miz 'Tilde, ya'll get yore talkin' started and I'll be back in a jiffy with the rest of Miz Rachel's clothes."

And the two women did. One, lovely and strong, listened intently to the older whose bent frame housed a fragile beauty, which came from a lifetime of devotion to others. Rachel learned much more than her expected itinerary. Aunt Matilda allowed her a glance into a wise heart, one that yearned for a more complete happiness for her nephew.

Rachel was to puzzle later why Matilda Burnes would convey to a stranger the intimate longings of her heart. However, for the moment, only fascination held Rachel in its sway.

It seemed that Matilda's challenge to Andrew the night she had arrived hit its mark. She told Rachel he planned to accompany her for political reasons.

There would be an overnight stop in Macon at a plantation where he would meet and discuss political issues with his friends. In Atlanta and Marietta he planned more visits. The older woman smiled. It seemed that when her nephew made up his mind, he pursued his goal with vigor.

Rachel admired that in a man or in anyone for that matter. She recognized the same strong will and determination coursing through her veins. She shivered as the thought occurred to her what the outcome would be if the two of them collided in cross purpose, then shrugged dismissing the likelihood and turned her full attention to her hostess.

Matilda confessed that she felt Andrew Meredith lacked true happiness and contentment. How could that be, Rachel protested. Matilda's eyes misted when she observed that accomplishments and riches in the world could prove empty without anyone to share them.

"But he has you and his niece," Rachel reminded.

Matilda patted her hand, "My dear, my remaining days are few upon this earth and someday Laura will find someone who will give her a life away from Drew. When that happens, I fear he will find life barren and lonely."

"Why Andrew Meredith seems the most complete and self-sufficient man I've ever encountered," Rachel exclaimed.

"Only on the surface, dear. The pursuit of wealth without a life's mission and a family to share it leaves a person unfulfilled. I'm convinced there is a place in his heart that remains empty."

"He certainly disguises it." Rachel retorted, unconvinced as her thoughts captured images of the handsome, self-confident man.

"Not disguise, rather denial."

"But why?"

"Fear, I think." Matilda answered softly, her bright blue eyes taking on a faraway look, her mind returning to some distant past that held the answers to the enigma of Andrew Meredith.

Rachel chuckled; rejecting the notion Andrew Meredith was afraid of anything, "Andrew Meredith afraid?"

"Only of himself, to get in touch with his needs. Sometimes fear forces us to ignore the heart's yearnings. It is especially true if our heart carries scars from past experiences. In Andrew's case, I think it was a case of self-preservation. "Sometimes we fill our lives with busy activity in order to bury past hurts, we push our real needs aside, denying their existence."

"Then how do they ever get met?" Rachel asked.

"The good Lord has a way of allowing circumstances to awaken our longings. Then we are in a position to accept what He has in mind for us. It's part of a completion process. "

"I don't think I understand, `completion' process."

"All of life, He is changing us into who He wants us to be. It's a lot easier if we cooperate," Matilda laughed.

"You sound as if you've experienced this."

"Oh I have. Still am as a matter of fact. I learn new things every day, about myself, about others and how we relate to each other. You know it's a process, we never quite arrive. As for a love that completed my heart, oh, yes, I experienced that blessing. Although our lives together lasted only a few years, they were wonderful."

"But you never re-married."

"I never even considered it. When you've had the best, second best just won't do. It wouldn't have been fair to another, I'd have always compared them with Matthew and no one could have measured up. Anyway God had another plan for me. When my sister died, He gave me Andrew and Jacob to care for, and my singleness made that possible."

"The loneliness and sorrow must be painful."

"No, my dear. The memories of that love warm the cold evenings along with the blessed assurance that someday we will be united where there is no death or parting."

Matilda noticed tears brighten Rachel's eyes, threatening, and she added, "My dear don't sorrow for me. I gave my whole heart to Matthew, living everyday as if it would be our last and when the end came, I had no regrets to tarnish my memories."

Rachel turned from her before the older woman could see the

regret and guilt clouding her eyes as the memory of her father rushed in to haunt her.

Leona opened the door, destroying the intimacy of the moment and providing a welcome distraction for Rachel. The conversation turned to pleasantries concerning the physical aspects of the trip, giving Rachel time to recover her composure.

Before it seemed possible, Leona achieved the miraculous. Rachel was dressed and ready to go a half-hour ahead of time. She descended the long stairway for the last time, her gloved hands caressing the smooth patina of the aged walnut. As she walked, she puzzled over the things Matilda Burnes had said to her. Absorbed in the mysteries of her host that Matilda had unveiled, she reached the bottom of the staircase and turned toward the open doorway. With her head down, she failed to see Andrew standing directly in her path. That is until she collided with him full force.

Her eyes, wide and startled, looked up into his, quiet and amused, as she fell into his open arms. He held her a moment longer than was necessary to keep her from falling and her heart raced. He smelled of wood smoke and his dark frock coat scratched her face as she lingered there willingly.

His arms offered a momentary haven. His broad shoulders buffered her from the world and its frightening decisions. His whole being transmitted vitality and strength, and something more. Just like that, an indefinable yearning flared inside Rachel.

She regained her balance, if not her composure, and reluctantly pushed against the hard, muscular arms tensed beneath the black frock coat. He let her step back, catching her arms with both hands and steadying her.

A half-smile teased his mouth, but Rachel noticed his breath came quickly. His eyes took her in, from the jaunty hat perched between her curls down to the dainty slippers that peeked out beneath the broad swell of her gray skirt. He nodded his head in approval as he released her.

"I can't truthfully say I'm sorry your clothes were lost. You make a fetching companion in that traveling suit. The color is very good for you. Did you know that you have gray flecks in your eyes?"

"No, I've never noticed." Rachel responded, a little breathlessly, a flush burning her face.

"You do. In fact, you're eyes are fascinating, in a moment they can change from hazel to fiery emerald."

Rachel raised an eyebrow and merely commented, "Really?" Then she turned from his disturbing eyes, not willing to acknowledge his compliment. Sweetwater awaited her and a long trip in between. Silently she told her clamoring heart that somewhere between here and there she would sort out her strange emotions. Meanwhile Daphne and the carriage waited to take them to the train and the last leg of her long journey home.

SIX

Rachel sat with her eyes riveted on the hills and valleys streaming by the smudged train window. The rhythmic sound of wheel striking rail seemed to whisper "Sweetwater" as each turn brought her nearer home.

Young, tender leaves gowned the forest outside her window in pale, green splendor. Here and there she caught glimpses of a late blooming dogwood, reluctant to surrender its April glory. The smaller trees nestled beneath splendid tulip poplars raising their yellow flower-tipped limbs heavenward with trunks straight and tall.

A swift moving stream ran beside the track briefly to fall out of sight somewhere in the low lying land beyond. Rachel could almost smell the delicate fragrance of swamp honeysuckle that she knew were opening their delicate pink blossom beside the streams and rivers. Suddenly her heart lurched as nostalgia gripped her with a longing for home.

Just then a forest of virgin pine timber came into view and memories of pine needles carpeting the timberland of Sweetwater intruded on the present. She could almost feel the pricks and sticky resin that clung to her bare feet as a child when she had searched for wildflowers beneath the majestic evergreens. They had left Macon and Savannah behind them and just ahead were Atlanta and home.

The 190 mile trip from Savannah to Macon had taken nine and a half hours. It would have proved tiring for Rachel if she hadn't been so excited. She even managed to rein in her usual impatience when she discovered on arriving in Savannah the train wouldn't depart until 1:30 p.m...

They spent the ensuing hours in Meredith's office and after a delicious lunch of fresh baked bread and seafood gumbo, they boarded the train and pulled out of the stately old depot.

The landscape had gradually changed as the train made its way out of Savannah for twelve miles to the Ogeechee River where it followed its northwesterly course across coastal plains for some eighty miles. Diverting its course to connect with Sandersville, it crossed the sandy soil of Washington County where it picked up the Oconee River westward until it entered the piedmont area of Georgia and reached the Ocmulgee River at Macon.

She smiled. Her father had once told her that this rail line and she shared a birthday. The building of the Central Railroad of Georgia had begun in December 1835, at a projected cost of $10,000 per mile. He had explained to her that the route was chosen because the more densely populated area would provide more goods and riders as well as slave labor after harvest season.

Financial problems plagued the project. When she was two there was a labor dispute with Irish immigrants because of the delinquent payment of their wages. When they walked off the job and marched into town, a militia armed with cannon met them. That incident became known as the War of '37. An Irish priest negotiated terms with the company and work resumed. Ultimately the line was completed to Macon by 1844 and Rachel had traveled these very same rails with her parents on a trip to Savannah.

They didn't arrive in Macon until a little past 11:00 p.m. They had to change to the Macon and Western Railway for the remaining trip to Atlanta and it wasn't scheduled to leave until 7:15 the next morning.

Meredith had friends on a plantation just outside of town so he rented a buggy and drove them to Maplewood, the home of John Dupre, friend and business associate of Andrew's.

Thoughts of the Dupres rekindled the strange emotions she had experienced while in their home. She relived the tense moments when they arrived.

Even though the hour was late, the Dupres' were up and welcomed Andrew warmly. Their gracious hospitality extended to Rachel, calming any apprehension she felt that they might be intruding at such a late hour.

John Dupre laughed at her discomfort explaining Andrew had wired them of his visit and assuring her his friend knew he and his wife, Annette, were night owls. Anytime day or night his house was open to Andrew Meredith.

Dupre remembered meeting Rachel's father in Charleston many years before and sympathy flared in his dark eyes as he gave her his condolences.

However, the warm welcome did not include Daphne. Annette Dupre gave her a cool acknowledgement. Nodding only slightly in Daphne's direction, she turned to Job, their butler, and asked him to show Daphne to the servant's quarters.

Rachel observed with interest Daphne's response. Up to this point she had been treated as Rachel's equal. Either because people took her to be Rachel's maid or because she traveled with the renowned Andrew Meredith, who had a substantial financial interest in the railroad, she rode in their car without objection.

But here in another's home, where Andrew's word was not law, she was relegated to a servant's role. Perhaps she was free but in Annette Dupre's home, she would receive no greater privilege than the ebony slaves waiting in the wings to fulfill their mistress's command.

Golden eyes sought Andrew's questioning. He nodded his head and smiled reassuringly. Daphne dropped her head and responded softly to her hostess, "Thank you." But not before Rachel saw the pain that touched her eyes.

And once again the mystery of Daphne rose to haunt Rachel. She puzzled over the strange relationship between the two. Andrew had freed this beautiful woman of color. He treated her with the care and respect of a family member, as if there were no difference in the color of their skins. Annette Dupre had made it abundantly clear what she thought of the relationship and her disapproval of Daphne. Rachel puzzled over the apparent lack of censure toward Andrew. It all seemed directed toward the young woman.

Despite Annette Dupre's reaction Rachel refused to believe that the Andrew Meredith she was coming to admire would flaunt an illicit relationship in the face of his friends. To do that would insult his friends and place Daphne, whom he treated with the greatest consideration, in a painful position. Yet that was exactly what had happened.

Rachel had glanced toward the butler and the parlor maid. Shocked, she noted the hostility of the mistress mirrored in both sets of eyes as they looked at the young woman.

Sarah the maid, stepped forward, her movements lithe and graceful as a panther's, "You come on with me, gal, and step lively, Marse Dupre' he wanna visit with his guest widout no interruption."

Daphne's head lifted as she raised her chin, and turned to follow, her eyes narrowed, glittering with anger.

All heard Sarah remark as she left the room, "Course I don know wha we gonna do wid you, but I reckon we'll find you a pallet somewheres. It may not be up to yo usual standards but it'll jest have to do."

An uneasy silence followed the exchange as Andrew turned to stare at the now empty passageway. An embarrassed laugh escaped John Dupre as he explained, "You know how it is, Drew. Just like with horses there's a pecking order to be observed."

Andrew looked at his friend hard before remarking, "But they're not horses, they are people. Same as we are, flesh and blood with emotions and needs. I guess that's why I'm here, John. I need to ask you some questions. To find out where you stand."

While late evening passed into the early morning hours, Andrew Meredith sought answers from his friend in the privacy of the library.

After Annette Dupre had retired, Rachel Gregory contemplated the events in the drawing room and for the first time considered what Daphne's life must be like. What had Andrew Meredith done to her? He had freed her from slavery. His kind treatment had lifted her from one world yet she was forbidden entrance into the other.

Thus Andrew Meredith had become her only world. The only place she belonged was in his life. Now Rachel understood Daphne's possessive attitude toward her benefactor. He gave her world existence.

Rachel shuddered as she saw the truth. Daphne remained in bondage as if she had never been set free. And as surely as she was captive still, so was Andrew Meredith her prisoner. A strange sense of loss and foreboding gripped Rachel as she closed her eyes to a sleep that had refused to come.

The steam engine belched a billowing column of smoke from the wood-fired boiler abruptly bringing Rachel back to the present. She noticed the locomotive was straining on steeper grades as it entered the red foothills encompassing Atlanta. Before arriving in Macon the hills had taken on the red tinge of clay and now the train struggled through gorges bordered by tall banks of dense, crimson soil.

The woods and hills looked more and more like home and she considered Sweetwater, comparing it with the Dupre's home, Maplewood.

After being a guest of Balmara and the Dupre's, she had to agree with her aunt. Most plantation homes of the middle and northern portion of the state were crude compared to the homes of coastal Carolina and Georgia.

Although Maplewood failed to equal the palatial surroundings of Balmara, the house bespoke of wealth and genteelness. The Dupres hailed from Charleston and they brought the coastal ambience of aristocracy inland with them.

She had to admit Sweetwater lacked that essence. What seemed expansive and luxurious when she was a child, in comparison with these two places, proved more utilitarian than elegant. But it was home and that was where her heart longed to be. Yet, as the train sped homeward thoughts of ways she could upgrade it filled her mind. The nesting instinct latent in every woman's soul suddenly awakened in Rachel Gregory.

⌐══════════════⌐

The locomotive slowed as it approached the hodge-podge buildings of Atlanta and pulled into the wooden structure that housed the trains of the Macon and Western Railway.

Now they would either have to change train stations and go by rail west to Fairburn or north to Marietta and then by carriage home or rent a carriage for the entire trip from Atlanta.

However one traveled, getting from Atlanta home was no easy task. The journey home consisted of rough terrain, bad roads and the Chattahoochee River to cross. The river had proven a perpetual problem in the shipment of goods from her father's mill. Ferry operators charged exorbitant prices until her father and Governor Charles McDonald, owner of Sweetwater Manufacturing also on Sweetwater Creek, threatened to build a bridge themselves. Realizing the potential threat to their business, the operators came to terms and the plan was abandoned.

Her father and the former governor had gone so far as to incorporate a railroad company but the plan had been abandoned as too expensive. Now how she wished it had become a reality. Home would be many hours nearer.

Andrew opted for Marietta. Mr. Wilkie had an office there and he had telegraphed him when they would be arriving. He expected the attorney to meet them at the station.

She and her father had always chosen Marietta, just north of Sweetwater when they returned from Savannah or even Charleston. Often they would visit Dunmeade's, a local store and warehouse that sold Sweetwater yarn from McDonald's mill and her father's.

Later on in the afternoon he would visit the warehouses where he stored cotton for his mill and then the two of them would return to the hotel for tea, where they would spend the night. Early the next morning they would start for home.

It was at the hotel that Rachel first encountered the differences between upcountry and coastal culture. Marietta was a resort area where many from the tidewater plantations came to escape the heat and fevers of summer.

Her Aunt Letty had implored her father to build a house in Marietta, for the sake of his daughter's refinement. Adam Gregory had turned a deaf ear to her pleas and Rachel had breathed a sigh of relief. A bitter smile turned the corner of her mouth downward as she remembered her contentment to stay a "country girl".

Perhaps if they had moved to Marietta, she could have avoided the years she spent away at school and then in Europe under Aunt Letty's tutelage. Maybe if she'd been here where she belonged when her father had needed her, she wouldn't be ill prepared to shoulder the responsibilities before her. Culture and refinement were not prerequisites to successfully raising cotton and manufacturing yarn and fabric.

A sigh escaped her and Andrew turned from the train window, lifting a questioning eyebrow.

Rachel's cheeks flushed, "Just wool gathering. Thinking about the `might have beens'."

Brown lights in his eyes warmed, his voice soft, encouraging, "Coming home after a long absence does that to one. But don't dwell on them, they only deplete your energy and you will need all that you have."

Apprehension flashed in Rachel's unguarded eyes as he touched her hidden fear. Their eyes held for a moment, hers seeking encouragement and strength from his. The train jolted to a halt, ending the brief encounter. But not before Daphne noticed and turned her face from them, pain again washed her tawny eyes. When she stood up, determination set her face as she reached for her reticule.

Rachel and Andrew followed her, gathering up their belongings and the trio exited the train. Outside carriages waited to load their luggage and transport them to the center of town to a large impressive brick and steel passenger depot where Rachel would commence the last leg of her long journey home.

Randall Wilkie waited patiently by the tracks as the passenger train pulled in beside the Marietta Depot. A long sigh expelled the air in his lungs but did nothing to ease the dread that lay inside him like cold steel.

Had he been a profane man, he'd have cursed the circumstances that brought him to this vigil. But he wasn't and instead sorrow burdened him down.

He caught sight of Andrew Meredith's familiar face through the train window. Beside him sat the source of Randall's sorrow. Auburn curls escaping beneath a small pillbox hat framed a face dominated by those striking eyes so dear to him.

Seven years ago he had gone with her father to see a vibrant young girl off to school and then on to Europe. Now she returned a woman. And he still loved her. Loved her with all the devotion a childless man can have for a daughter he wished were his own. He had loved her mother. From the moment he had seen Adam Gregory's new bride from Charleston, Randall Wilkie had loved her from afar. His adoration of her had kept him single; his integrity had kept her pure. He never once considered betraying his friend; never once revealed his heart to her. Instead with determination of a devoted friend, he had sought to make her life easier. To cheer her up when she missed the lowlands of Carolina, to assist Adam in business decisions, and to be the godfather to their child.

When she died, he too, had grieved. But his grief could not be assuaged by a child, or any evidence of a love shared. Instead, as his love had remained private so must his anguish. In the darkness of the midnight hours he bore his torment like the man he was. But his friend who had a daughter to live for had squandered her future in the name of grief and Randall Wilkie could not forgive him for that.

Now the emerald eyes of her mother looked out from the daughter's face and found his. When she saw him hope ignited them, the anticipation so poignant he had to drop his head. How could he find the words to tell her that the life she once knew no longer existed, that for all practical purposes, she had no future?

A growl of anguish rolled from the throat of this gentle, loving man and for a moment he hated his dead friend and the legacy he had left this exquisite creature. How could he tell her that there was no way? Her father had dissipated her future in self centered attempts to appease his pain.

He looked at Meredith and wondered just how much he might have told her. Then he looked back at Rachel and knew. The hope shining in those unsuspecting eyes told him. Randall Wilkie was the one left to shatter her dream.

"Oh, Anna," his heart cried out, "would to God I had an answer, but Adam destroyed all my options."

He sighed, straightened his shoulders and stepped toward the door, a feigned smile plastering his face.

As she bounded out of the train, the studied composure of the last several months dissolved the moment she reached him. Throwing herself into Wilkie's arms, she cried, "Uncle Randall, it's been so long . . .", then the tears came. The dammed up grief released as she clung to the last bastion of the world she once knew.

Wilkie held her tightly. Her pain dampened the shoulder of his black coat while he patted her back gently murmuring soft words of comfort. His face above her bowed head contorted with the misery of an aching heart which wants to make things right and can't. His sad eyes bore the knowledge of more pain to come.

Meredith turned from them, giving them the benefit of this moment. He intuitively knew that later Rachel would suffer embarrassment knowing her facade had slipped allowing him to witness the tendered soul behind her studied self-sufficiency.

SEVEN

Rachel pulled back and looked up into Randall Wilkie's face. An embarrassed half-smile tugged at her mouth amidst the salty stream of tears trailing down her cheeks.

Suddenly remembering her traveling companions, she turned to find them. They awaited her from a discreet distance. Andrew had turned his back to her, giving her the privacy of this painful moment. Understanding and appreciation toward her benefactor warmed Rachel's heart briefly.

Then her face flushed as her eyes encountered Daphne's who stood watching the tender scene. The young woman gave her no quarter. She stared, intrigued at the metamorphosis of this self-reliant, self- contained woman.

With her eyes still on Daphne, Rachel straightened her back and lifted her chin defiantly. Then turning to Wilkie, apologized.

"I'm sorry. I don't know what overcame me. It's so good to see you and to be back home."

Randall Wilkie's hands clasped her shoulders as he looked deeply into her eyes. Then he asked, his slight lisp magnified by the raw emotions tearing his own soul, "Tis time, my girl. You've carried too much grief too long without any outlet. And who would be the better one to share it with than your Uncle Randall who experienced it first hand, too? You know I loved your mother and your father as if they were my own family. You are the daughter I never had."

Rachel took the handkerchief Wilkie offered and dabbed at her eyes, wiping away the tears.

"But I didn't have to make such a public display. Anyway I'm all right now. Do we leave for Sweetwater right away?"

Pain flickered in Wilkie's eyes, "There are some legal matters you need to take care of at my office in order to settle your father's estate. I thought it would be better to attend to them before you go home. I've reserved two rooms in town for tonight."

"We're not going to Sweetwater today?" Rachel questioned softly.

"No, my dear, I felt it would be better for you to wait until tomorrow."

Rachel dropped her head for a moment and then, determination set her features as she replied, "Whatever you think best, Uncle Randall."

"That's my girl. I think you'll find the accommodations most enjoyable. You've never stayed at the Fletcher House."

Randall Wilkie pointed to an impressive brick building that hugged the tracks beside the old train depot.

Rachel looked about her for the first time, then in amazement turned to look toward town. A strange and unfamiliar vista met her eyes. New buildings abounded while old, familiar ones had disappeared. In the center of the town square was a fenced in park with horses hitched outside the fence here and there. Eastward and across the street from the park she recognized the courthouse constructed during the time she was away at school. She had watched its progress the few times she had returned by train. She remembered the impressive two story brick building with columns on every side had been completed in 1853. She noticed many familiar merchant stores as well as the Howard House, one of the hotels, where she and her parents had stayed, were missing. She exclaimed, "What's happened to Marietta?"

Randall Wilkie smiled, "A lot since you've been away. You remember the two fires we had in '54 and '55? They couldn't compare to the one that engulfed the town in April of 1857."

"Is that what happened to the Howard House?"

"Yes, completely destroyed it."

"How did it start?"

"The blaze started down in the in the cellar of Sabal and Tennent in Colonnade Place when a candle ignited some turpentine. When the whole place blew, the two men in the cellar barely escaped with their lives. In fact the whole square barely escaped it. The fire destroyed several doctors and lawyers' offices, jewelry stores, Denmead's warehouse and other retailers. The square was pandemonium with everyone trying to evacuate their merchandise. Plows and boots were all mixed in with volumes of law books, surgical tools and fine fabrics. A swift spring breeze spread the fire so rapidly that we were afraid it would carry on to the residences."

"It must have been a frightening experience."

"Yes it was. The whole town turned out to fight the fire. Some people pasted wet blankets on their roofs. That's what saved Will Root's drugstore."

"I remember Mr. Root's store. Didn't he have large iron shutters?" Rachel asked her heart pounding.

"That's right, he just closed those shutters and even though the flames came right up to his store, it was spared. I don't know what would have happened if the Atlanta fire department hadn't come to our rescue. People for miles around could see the flames lighting the night sky. When morning came, the Howard House, fourteen stores and the post office were gone. It was really a traumatic experience. But good came of it." Wilkie shook his head, a faraway look in his eyes.

"What good could possibly come of a tragedy like that?"

"The way the community pulled together to fight the fire and help one another. In fact that very month we finally organized a fire department."

"And about time I'd say." Rachel said her present pain pushed aside as she vicariously lived the horror of the past. Then as an afterthought she recalled Randall's office must have been in the path of the fire.

"Did you lose your office?"

"Yes, but I was able to save my books, files and some of my furnishings." He shrugged as if to dismiss his loss as insignificant.

But something in his countenance conveyed to Rachel a message of profound loss.

By this time Andrew and Daphne had joined them and heard the last exchange. Andrew put his hand on the attorney's shoulder in a strange comforting gesture as Randall turned to him. The attorney seized his hand in a hearty squeeze, greeting Meredith with enthusiasm. His welcoming smile included Daphne before he asked, "Are you about ready for some lunch?"

"Hungry as a bear, I'd say, what did you have in mind, the Fletcher House?" Meredith asked.

"As a matter of fact that is what I had in mind since they serve the best meals in town. However, I've opted to have them deliver lunch to my office where we can eat with more privacy."

Rachel knew Daphne was the reason they wouldn't be dining in the restaurant. Wilkie's thoughtful gesture to his business associate would avoid any chance of an unpleasant scene.

"I'm really not very hungry but I could use a cup of tea," Rachel replied.

"No sooner said than done. Lunch should be at my office in not more than ten minutes. Meanwhile, Andrew, I've arranged for my man to carry Daphne on out to my place after lunch. Trudy will see that she is looked after, but I thought perhaps it would be more convenient for you to stay in town since you have so much business to take care of."

"Of course. That was my plan."

When Rachel arrived in Randall's office, the nostalgic aroma from old books and aged leather forced memories of her father to catapult her into the difficulties of the present and the anxieties in the future. Illusions of a simple, pleasant journey had cocooned her and her traveling companions during the trip from Savannah. The fantasy came crashing down around her when she fell into Randall Wilkie's comforting embrace at the Marietta depot. Since then the realities of life had intruded and destroyed the warm intimacy the three had shared on the trip north. Lunch proved delicious and filling but conversation lagged as the atmosphere became strained.

Her traveling companions had seen her emotions stripped naked and she felt weak, ashamed. Grief had tracked her down and finally had its say.

Now vulnerable from it, the apprehensions that had plagued Rachel in the pre-dawn hours in Savannah rushed in. Suddenly she was more relieved than disappointed that she would not return home today. She was glad to delay it until the morrow. For the moment her heart seemed too tender to face an empty house with only the ghost of her Father's memory. Tomorrow would be soon enough.

Rachel barely toyed with her food. Finishing before the others, she sat in silence as Randall and Meredith discussed the depressed cotton market of the year before and the disastrous impact on local planters. She looked around her, unable to concentrate on the conversation.

With surprise and, not a little alarm, she noticed the sparseness of Wilkie's office. Missing were the hand rubbed cherry furnishings, which only left the two soft leather chairs she had relished as a child. Often her father would leave her there to devour a good book in the comfortable masculine surroundings while he finished his business. Randall or his associate would always provide her with fresh tea in the summertime and hot cocoa in the winter months.

Now the office was neither comfortable nor inviting. Rather it was austere in its meager utilitarian furnishings without the masterpiece paintings on the wall or even a rug to cover the rough, wooden floor.

Perhaps the fire had destroyed the furnishings, but why had he not replaced them? Even the office he occupied was in the shabbier part of town where the less than successful attorneys congregated. Something more than the fire two years ago had happened to Randall Wilkie. Somehow the wealthy Mr. Wilkie had fallen on hard times.

Andrew Meredith pushed his chair back, scraping it across the bare pine floor and jerking Rachel back from her musings. "I see your man has arrived to pick up Daphne."

A large black man entered the offices, his hat folded in his hand, his head slightly bowed. The rays of sun streaming through the western window danced across his broad shoulders and glistened on bulging muscular arms that proclaimed him a valued field hand. His simple homespun clothes were clean, but much mended. Outside a wagon waited and Rachel wondered where the fancy carriage and the uniformed footmen of years gone by were? Was it because of who Daphne was or did he retell the story of the austere office inhabited only by Wilkie?

Daphne looked from the man through the window toward the waiting wagon as Rachel caught the briefest look of distaste in her eyes before a facade of indifference masked her face.

When she left, Andrew picked up his jacket explaining," I know you two have a lot of business to attend to as do I. I want to look up Robert Goodman this afternoon. I have a few things I'd like to discuss with him."

Wilkie cocked an eyebrow toward Andrew, "Goodman? Some of the folks around here don't like the politics he's been spouting in his paper. You knew him before he came to Georgia, didn't you?"

"Yes, at Yale. He was an upper classman when I was a freshman."

Randall chuckled, "The locals say that's what ails him. He got foreign ideas while he was up there in Connecticut."

"I've recently been accused of that myself." Meredith added his face serious.

"Do you?" Randall asked pointedly, no amusement warming his eyes.

"Depends on what you mean by foreign ideas." Meredith retorted.

Randall Wilkie breathed in deeply, then let his breath out slowly, the sound slicing through the charged silence of the room, "I don't exactly know what I mean. The firebrands around here accuse Goodman because he feels that disunion is not an option."

"Well, Randall, I guess if that's your definition of foreign ideas, I plead guilty."

"Not mine, Drew, but many of the people in this area. I just want to warn you that it might harm your business prospects in this area if you get too close to Robert Goodman. He has strong beliefs and he doesn't hide them under a barrel."

"I made a decision this week. I've been too worried about my business to take a stand. Now I must at whatever the cost."

"You are fortunate my friend you have enough resources that you can afford to stand for your convictions. As you can see," Randall made a sweeping gesture around his office, "I can't afford that luxury."

"The time is coming when everyman will have to make a stand. Whether he can afford it or not. My time came this week. That's my real mission this trip. To see how many men stand with me and will work to keep us in the Union."

"Then you've picked the right place to begin. Robert Goodman is your man for he has his hand on the pulse of the public and is committed to the union. He can tell you where to begin."

"That's what I had hoped. It'll be good to see Robert again." Andrew Meredith replied as he went through the door, determination holding him ramrod straight.

A sigh escaped Rachel as she stared at the broad-shouldered Meredith as he walked out the door and away from her. Randall Wilkie looked at her, a curious light in his eyes.

"What do you think of Meredith, Rachel?"

"I don't know him well enough to form more than a cursory opinion of him. He has been more than considerate of my needs, courteous and hospitable," she answered evasively.

"I didn't ask you how he had treated you; I asked you what you think of him—as a man?"

"Uh, I really don't know. From my observation, he seems to know what he wants in life and gets it. I suppose he is an honorable man—."

"You just suppose?"

"Well I hardly know him. He is successful in business and apparently respected, at least his power is. Then there's the obvious consideration and affection he shows toward his aunt and niece. But then there's also—."

"Daphne." Randall finished what she was unwilling to say.

"Yes, there's Daphne." Rachel paused twisting an auburn tendril escaping and resting on her cheek. Then no longer able to contain her curiosity she went on, "Who or what is she? I've never witnessed anything like this. He treats her with the same respect he accords me. Why he treats her as if she were white."

Randall chuckled, "I don't know. All of Savannah whispers behind his back asking the same question and drawing their own conclusions. They accept his behavior because he is a power to be reckoned with in that port city, but here he will not fare so well. Although he is wealthy and has some holdings locally, his influence is not as great. People will not turn their head here and pretend she doesn't exist. That's why I sent her to Waverly. There's no need to arouse the people anymore than necessary. He'll be doing plenty of that with his politics."

Rachel pressed, "What do you think, Uncle Randall?"

"I think that Andrew Meredith is an honorable man with whom I do business and his personal relationships are none of my concern unless they interfere with commercial affairs."

"In other words, it's expedient for you to turn your head and pretend she doesn't exist, also."

Disappointment touched Wilkie's eyes before he answered quietly, "It could be that or maybe I just trust Andrew."

"That's the difference between a man and a woman. To me Daphne would have to be explained before I could completely trust him."

Wilkie looked up sharply, holding Rachel's eyes, "Are we talking about business affairs or an affair of the heart?"

A blush colored the lovely Rachel's face as her heart pounded an affirmative reply even as her lips denied it.

Andrew Meredith opened the half-glass door of the newspaper office and a brass bell jingled, barely audible amid the clop, clop and whoosh of the steam press where the printed sheets rolled off ready for market. The pungent odor of ink stung his nose as he paused just inside the door waiting for his eyes to adjust from the bright sunlight washing the street.

In the darkened interior, he failed to see his old friend. A gruff, gravelly voice spoke caustically from behind Drew. "Well if it isn't Andrew Meredith, the rich planter and broker from Savannah. What are you doing gracing us with your presence?"

Andrew whirled toward the voice amusement dancing in his eyes, "Goodman, You haven't changed a bit. It's a wonder you have any friends left, considering your gracious hospitality and your vociferous opinions."

Goodman wiped his ink stained hand on the apron he wore around his rotund body then extended one large, calloused paw toward Meredith as he growled, "Humph, can't say that I do. But at least the ones I do have are genuine, which is more'n I can say for most folks. I'd wager few people really know who their true friends are."

Meredith smiled genuine affection warming his eyes as he gripped his friend's hand, "You're probably right about that but wouldn't hurt you to warm up a bit. You scare 'em off before you give them a chance."

"I don't have the time or the stomach for buttering people up. I am what I am, take it or leave it." Goodman retorted.

Meredith chuckled as he released his hand, "What's a mystery to me, is how you ever managed to capture Martha Ann's heart?"

"Guess she appreciated a "man in whom there is no guile," the newspaper man quoted, an affected scowl not hiding the twinkle in his eyes.

"I dare say you showed her a side you hide from the rest of us."

"Perhaps. But 'tis important a person weds with their eyes wide open. I did nothing to convince her I had qualities I lacked. Martha knew just what she was getting—a man who worked hard and had little time for the amenities of life. Too many important issues in life to waste time with social frivolities."

"Sometimes one can get too bogged down in responsibilities to realize some of life's blessings," Meredith remarked more to himself than his friend.

"Perhaps, Andrew. That's where a good woman like Martha comes in. She's good with the social aspect, she softens out my rough edges, and then she keeps some balance in my life. But I can't be casual about life. I fully believe each of us has a mission to fulfill for which we are accountable. I learned responsibility from hardship at an early age. Changes your outlook on life," he explained matter of factly, without a trace of self pity.

Meredith knew he referred to his being orphaned at twelve and forced to earn his own way. Even at that early age Goodman had had a passion for newspapering and had already acquired type setting skills, but was forced to turn to marble cutting to earn his living. However, he never let the hard manual labor deter his love of learning and pursued it from Latin and philosophy to history and mathematics. Determined to return to his beloved newspapering someday, he realized that he needed at least a year in law school to supplement his education. On a marble-buying trip to New England, he visited Yale and decided to attend. Andrew, still in his teens and a brand new student at the school, met Goodman, by then almost a legend with his strong convictions and outspoken comments.

Suddenly Andrew's memory transported him back in time and he remembered the awe he had felt for the student who seemed to live surrounded by controversy, "You always did rile people up."

"Most people do who have strong convictions."

"To say you have strong convictions would be putting it mildly," Andrew quipped.

"How about you, Meredith?"

"Me, what?"

"I don't remember your convictions, I remember you as a mediator."

"Don't you think a mediator can have convictions?"

"I suppose so, but sometimes they have to compromise."

"That's bad?"

Goodman nodded his head, "When a principle is involved. That brings us back to why you're here. Why you wanted to see me."

"I want some advice."

"About what?"

"How to be a mediator without compromising a principle."

Robert Goodman threw back his head and laughter rolled from deep within him, clearing the scowl from his face and relaxing the stern wrinkle of his brow. Finally he reached out to his friend and grasp his shoulder with a giant gnarled hand, "Friend, I've never been a mediator. I've always stirred up, so why come to me?"

"Because I'm convinced we share the same principles . . ."

"About what specifically?"

"The horror that is about to be visited on our land."

"I'm surprised. I figured you for the typical plantation owner. Either a firebrand panting to show those Yankees a thing or two or else hiding your head in the sand thinking it will just go away and leave our life as it is," the publisher remarked dryly.

"I have tried to ignore it," Meredith admitted. "I've diversified my holdings with northern and foreign investments just in case there is a war which I know the South cannot win. My plan was to protect myself and my holdings as best I could and just ride it out."

"You've had a change of heart?"

"Yes."

"What?" Goodman probed, his eyes narrowed, riveted on Andrew's.

"It has something to do with what you said about a mission and responsibility."

"How's that?"

"A visit I had this week pricked my conscience and made me realize that "to whom much is given, much is required," Andrew shifted his gaze breaking eye contact, uncomfortable with being forced to reveal his innermost feelings.

"And?" Goodman asked, not dropping his eyes, giving Meredith no quarter, forcing him to the soul of his convictions.

"All things considered I can survive an economic disaster with minimum loss, but I've come to terms with myself—my responsibility goes beyond self-interest. I am duty bound to work for what I believe in."

"Which is? . . ."

"While there is still time, to do everything in my power to preserve the union," Andrew responded, a quiet conviction in his voice.

Robert Goodman nodded his head, a pleased understanding lighting his eyes. "Drew, our convictions are the same, our roles differ. My job is to stir the people and call those to action who believe as we do. Yours is to try to mediate and convince those who are vacillating between two opinions."

"That's where you come in. I need to know who those people are and I need to organize them."

"Some of them don't want to openly support the union because of reprisals by their neighbors. Social pressure is a powerful tool, that's why I have so little patience with society." Goodman said his voice tinged with disgust.

"Perhaps that's a role I can play. Society is a fact of life and condemning it won't change it. We're going to have to use it for our purposes . . . ."

Goodman interrupted impatiently, "Like I said, our roles are different. Like left hand and right we'll work together—I'll stir up and you persuade. But if we can't turn the tide in Georgia by the presidential election next year then we've lost."

"You think it hinges on the presidential election," Meredith queried.

"Absolutely. If by some miracle Lincoln is elected, there'll be no question, Georgia will secede."

"Lincoln elected? Impossible. He's a dark horse. I go up north often, none but the strident abolitionists support the man. I can't see him being elected."

"There is a danger of his getting it by default. If the south fails to consolidate behind one candidate and they split their support then he could be elected."

Fingers of apprehension danced down Andrew's spine as he thought of the possibility and the consequences. Suddenly his mission took on a new urgency as he turned to his friend and stated simply, "Let's get to work."

Robert Goodman nodded and moved toward the files he had been compiling, hoping for a moment like this and a man who could share his mission.

EIGHT

Rachel's chair crashed to the floor, the sound exploding against the ominous silence that punctuated Randall Wilkie's revelation. Unable to speak, she grasped the edge of the old scarred desk for support. The floor rushed to meet her and she weaved unsteadily. From beneath the lip of the desk an errant splinter of wood pierced her finger and a drop of crimson blood oozed out. But she didn't notice. The inner pain racking her soul momentarily obliterated the physical world. Her eyes, round and dark, seemed to fill her pale face. Finally her voice returned and she protested softly, the words halting, "The mill is not mine?" She shook her head, her heart rejecting what her ears had heard. "How could that be? I can't believe it."

Randall Wilkie looked at her from across the old familiar desk that separated them, his tortured soul burning in his eyes. Rachel, so preoccupied with her own horror, failed to recognize his pain.

"It's true. Would to God that I had better news for you." Then he reached out to her, his whole being pleading for her to understand, to survive this blow and what was yet to come.

"Uncle Randall what happened? Surely father would have told me. Why didn't I know?"

"He wanted to protect you," Randall hedged. The moment he had dreaded for months had arrived. He could no longer delay an explanation. Yet, he stood before her buffeted with indecision. Did he tell her the whole truth? He couldn't bring himself to tell her that her father had wasted her inheritance with drink and gambling.

He still had to tell her that she had lost far more than her mill. How could she understand that the father she had known and loved had died with Anna? Since Rachel had not been there to witness his deterioration, would she believe him?

Without telling her the truth how could he get her to accept Andrew Meredith's generous offer? It was her only hope of survival.

Why had Meredith left? How he wished he had the man here with him to tell her. But he had insisted the situation was too delicate for a stranger to intrude on. Of course he was right. Randall Wilkie was all that she had left except her self-serving aunt in Europe and she'd have to return to her soon enough.

Only Andrew Meredith's generous offer could prevent her from returning as a penniless relative, otherwise she would receive a cold welcome from her father's sister.

He'd observed Letty while she stayed with Adam. She cared only for prestige, position and wealth. A penniless niece would prove a hindrance to her. Inwardly Randall shuddered, thinking of the meager existence Rachel would have under those circumstances.

"Protect me? How can keeping the truth from someone protect them?" Her voice echoed down the chamber of his conscience pressing him for an answer, a decision.

Yet he remained unwilling to administer that final blow, to destroy the image she carried of her dead father. How could she bear the loss of everything dear to her and to then have the comfort of her memories torn from her in one devastating blow? Instead of answering, he moved around the desk and enveloped her rigid body in his embrace, in a vain attempt to comfort her.

She felt his hesitation and looked up, searching his face. She recognized that he concealed something, his eyes told her, and in that moment of shock, she misinterpreted his tender concern.

Rachel pulled away, pain and now doubt, making her resistant. Her tone turned softly accusing, "It was a small but thriving business when I left."

He heard her words, a simple declaration, but the hint of

suspicion tinged her voice, driving a dagger through his tormented heart.

Did she think he had contributed to her misfortune? If she only knew. The sparseness in his own office reflected the extent to which he had gone to save his friend. He had given until there was no more to give, and then when he had nothing left, he had borrowed. When he could borrow no more, he went to Andrew Meredith and asked for his help.

It was true, he did convince Adam to sell the mill, but his motives were pure. He did it, trying to avert disaster, trying to circumvent today. But he had failed, and now because of someone else's mistakes, he stood on the threshold of losing the only thing in this life that meant anything to him . . . Rachel.

He could see it in her eyes. She needed someone to blame and he was there and involved. His eyes held hers and he took a deep, ragged breath before answering, "The truth, Rachel, is that your father lost much more than the mill. Half of Sweetwater is gone, the rest is mortgaged. Most of the slaves are gone.

Rachel's full red lips parted, her mouth forming a small "o", her eyes uncomprehending. Then when she finally received what he said, she pressed the back of her hand to her mouth to stifle the scream of denial welling up inside her.

Wilkie reached out once more, trying to pull her rigid body into the shelter of his embrace. In that gesture, he sought to comfort her but more than that to re-assure himself. He needed to know she would still accept his devotion, but she stood unyielding, a hard light glittering in her eyes.

Finally when she could speak, Rachel stepped back, pushing him away, rejecting his comfort, "You still haven't told me how Father could have lost so much."

"The last year's financial panic caught many planters by surprise. When the price of cotton fell, they couldn't pay back money they had borrowed against their crops. All they had to loose was their property. None of us escaped."

"None?" Rachel's questioned, unbelieving.

A wan smile parted Randall's face as he gestured toward the sparsely furnished office,

"As you can see I didn't escape, either. Our community's prosperity was tied too closely to cotton. When the planters lost money, they didn't have any to spend on goods and services and the depression in the north cut demand for cotton goods. Lessened demand resulted in production cuts at the mill. Adam had borrowed heavily and couldn't pay it back so he sold all that he could and still survive,"

"Why had Father borrowed so much money?"

"That's just a customary practice, borrow for planting, pay back at harvest," Wilkie hedged with a half truth, unable to put more pain on her with a full revelation.

"Then why did you bring me back to—nothing? Did you have some sadistic notion to torment me with the what might have beens?" Rachel spat out cruelly, each word hurled like a dagger.

Wilkie looked at her and shook his head sadly, "Rachel, Rache—."

"You're here because I requested you be brought here," Andrew Meredith's clipped tones reverberated through the charged room. Neither Rachel nor Randall had heard him enter the office.

Wilkie looked toward his friend, his eyes pleading for help as Rachel whirled toward the door and Meredith, "And what is your concern in this matter?"

"I own the mill," Meredith stated matter of factly.

Rachel jerked her head back toward Wilkie, "Is that true?"

"Yes, Rachel."

"It seems that Mr. Meredith was spared the financial disaster that others encountered . . . ."

"That's true to some extent. My holdings are more diversified, and I—."

"You were able to take advantage of those who needed help . . . . There's a name for people who prey on other's misfortunes." Rachel's voice rose, hysteria bubbling close to the surface, "Is that how you amassed all your great wealth or just some of it?"

"Stop it, Rachel, before you say more you'll regret." Randall Wilkie commanded sharply, "Drew gave your father a liberal sum for his mill, more than it was worth, in fact, and now he has made a very generous offer for Sweetwater."

Rachel cringed inwardly as the fragile illusion of life as she thought it would be shattered into a million pieces. Her voice dripped with acid as she turned those green eyes, fired now with the gall of disillusionment, full force on the tall stranger with whom she had spent these past few days. "How noble of you Mr. Meredith, to fulfill your promise to a dying man."

"Nobility was not my aim, Miss Gregory, but I am a man of my word. I did make a promise."

"A promise? More a carefully orchestrated charade to take advantage of me like you obviously did my father."

Randall Wilkie blurted out, "Rachel, it isn't that way at all. Listen to his proposal. It is your only hope."

Rachel's pale face now flushed with anger as she faced her father's friend, "And how could you betray me like this, Uncle Randall? What did he promise you that was more important than my friendship? To restore your fortune if you delivered Sweetwater?"

Andrew Meredith's jaw tightened, his dark eyes cold, "It would pay you to listen to my proposal and stop your foolish accusations. I will give you enough for Sweetwater to clear the mortgage and you will have a nice dowry or nest egg until you marry. I will also pay for your passage back to your Aunt, since she is your only living relative. I understand that you do have a suitor in France?"

Embarrassment compounded her anger and she snapped, "That's none of your concern. I plan to stay at Sweetwater."

"Only until December, if that long, Miss Gregory." Andrew answered tersely, his voice controlled, "because that's when your note comes due and you don't have a crop planted or enough slaves to cultivate it and nothing to live on until then."

"If you're going to foreclose then why did you bother to offer to buy it? Is your conscience bothering you belatedly?"

"I don't hold the mortgage, but the man who does, did take advantage of your father."

"I'm looking at the men who took advantage of my father, but you won't take advantage of me!" Fury banished for a moment the anguish churning inside of Rachel. Suddenly she found in Andrew Meredith a focal point on which to vent all the conflicting emotions tearing her apart.

As the afternoon sun filtered through the leaded glass door bathing Rachel in a golden aura, a white-hot hate forged in her. It buried the guilt she had wrestled with since her father's death and masked her disappointment, fear and uncertainty. For that moment, Andrew Meredith became the sole object of the hatred energizing her. His broad shoulders bore the blame.

Randall Wilkie stepped up to Rachel, and grasping her arm, protested, "You're wrong about both of us. Believe what you will about me, Rachel, but listen to Andrew. He's your only hope of survival."

Rachel jerked her arm from Wilkie, "Listen to him? I've heard all that I care to hear from either of you." She turned on her heel. Walking toward the door, her taffeta skirts rustled as her shoes played a somber requiem on the bare wooden floor, breaking the heavy silence draping the room.

Andrew and Randall stared toward the now empty doorway, neither speaking. Then a deep sigh reverberated from the older man and Meredith turned toward him.

Wilkie's face paled to the color of death and perspiration beaded his forehead. Andrew shook his head, "Get hold of yourself, Randall. She'll come around as soon as she cools off. She had a big shock."

"She thinks I have defrauded her and her father. I've been like her family. How could she believe that of me?"

"She won't. Rachel just took her disappointment out on you. She's not ready to receive the truth yet."

"I didn't tell her the truth."

"You what?"

"Not the whole truth anyway."

"Why?"

"I couldn't bear to tell her how Adam lost his fortune."

"Someone will. And it is better coming from someone who cares for her."

"I just won't put that on her right now."

"Do you have any idea what is going to happen when Banks gets hold of this?"

"How can he do more harm than he has already?"

"If he manages to persuade her not to accept my offer, she'll loose what little she has left—the equity and the few remaining acres of Sweetwater."

"I won't tell her now."

"Well, I will." Andrew answered in clipped tones as he turned on his heel and walked out.

The late April sun peered out of a cloudless azure sky, shining straight into Meredith's eyes as he turned westward down the dusty street. His boots created small dust swirls, coating his fawn colored trousers as he made his way toward the Fletcher House. He noticed little about the perfect spring day except to voice curt greetings to familiar merchants sweeping out their shops. Occasionally he tipped his broad brimmed hat to a vaguely familiar lady he encountered mid-block.

His mind, filled with Rachel, failed to recognize those he met and his face set in such a stern countenance none dared detain him with conversation. So on down the street he strode, determined to capture his illusive prey and force her to listen to reason.

He entered the lobby of the grand hotel, but she was nowhere in sight. The clerk had not seen her. Bewildered he left the ornate building and retraced his steps back toward town, perusing the shops along the way. Amusement briefly lightened his face as he thought how like a woman to go shopping when she was upset. But amusement quickly turned to aggravation when he failed to find her. After he searched the small shops adjacent to the depot without success anxiety overtook irritation.

Unwillingly his heart began to pound and his breathing came

short as he entered the depot. The interior was dark and he had to wait for his eyes to adjust. Then eagerly he scanned the occupants, but no fiery emerald eyes blazed back at him. Only weary passengers waiting on slick, wooden seats turned curious glances his way.

A child's pitiful wail mingled with the clickety clack of the teletype sounding off behind the caged counter but no husky voice threaded with fury spoke his name. She had disappeared.

Andrew approached the agent, querying him brusquely. He had just come on duty and knew nothing. Andrew turned impatiently and walked away, interrupting the man mid-sentence and leaving him feeling somehow to blame.

When Meredith stepped out into the sunlight once again, shopkeepers were closing their doors and preparing for their journeys home. With the shops closed where else could she go?

With a shrug he made his way to the Fletcher House once more. Maybe she had returned. The clerk looked his direction and shook his head to the unasked query burning in Andrew's eyes.

Now apprehension full blown, bloomed in Meredith. How could she disappear? She knew that she had a room here for the night. She should be here. But where was her luggage? The clerk said it never came. Puzzled, he bent his head then chuckled with more relief than mirth. She went to another hotel. That made sense. She was so mad; she refused accommodations provided for her by him.

Why that little stubborn miss. He had his hands full with her. A smile forced his lips apart. He'd had his hands full ever since he laid eyes on her. His smile broadened as self-knowledge dawned. He had always relished a challenge. He pushed the leaded glass door open and stepped out into the late afternoon sunshine a new determination forged every step.

Thirty minutes later his smile had faded, instead impatience prompted by worry furrowed his brow. He had searched every hotel, every shop that remained open. Rachel had disappeared.

He whirled on his heel and headed for Randall's office, maybe she had returned. When she had a few minutes alone to think, she realized her mistake. She must be there now, apologizing to her friend. He was right all along. Hadn't he told Randall as much?

Relief eased the lines binding his face. His pace picked up, anticipation he dared not examine put a spring in his step.

Relief proved short lived when he found Randall Wilkie's office locked and empty. With a sinking heart he peered down the street, fighting the unreasonable panic bubbling within him.

NINE

The wind whipped Rachel's curls across her face stinging her cheeks and bringing tears to her eyes. With each lurch of the buggy, her bonnet danced wildly up and down her back as its ribbons clutched her neck. She removed a hand from the reins she held tightly to push away a thick tendril blinding one eye. When the vehicle careened wildly on the rough road, she stubbornly refused to slow her pace. Flicking the reins, she drove the horses even harder.

Jacob Emory sat on his front porch some 50 yards away and watched. His piercing black eyes narrowed in his weathered, lined face. He shook his head and muttered to his short, ample wife standing beside him, "Whoever that fool woman is, she'll never get where she's going in one piece,"

Bertha Emory's large, china blue eyes followed his, then widened in alarm. She handed her husband the slice of strawberry pie she held in her hand. Large juicy berries glistened under a cap of rich cream and nestled on a flaky crust.

"Mm" remarked Jacob breathing deeply as he savored the fresh baked aroma that permeated the air. Briefly distracted from his vigil, he looked up, a tender light in his eyes as they fastened on his wife of fifty years. Patting the swing beside him in a mute invitation, he turned his attention to the road once more. "Have you ever seen such goings on?" Jacob nodded toward the departing buggy, by this time only Rachel's back was to them.

Bertha sat down beside him, her gaze fixed on the careening

buggy, "No, can't say as I have. Wherever she's a going, she might not make it. Wonder what her hurry is? Say, Jake, don't she look kinda familiar to you?"

"No, can't say as she does. Anyhow she's going at such a lickety split, didn't have much time to notice. Why, mama, did you think so?"

"Seems like I've seen her before."

"Must be somebody who just got to town 'cause that's one of Lively's rigs from down at the livery stable."

"Well, how could that be? She didn't have no luggage with her." Bertha protested.

"Could be she's having it sent out later."

"Wonder where to?" Bertha mused, the mystery bringing a welcome excitement to their usual after supper ritual. "Hope it ain't far, cause it'll be dark soon. Don't seem fit for a young woman to be out like this in strange country and it coming on night."

"Well, she shore acts like she's headed for a fire."

Rachel was. The fire of remembrance beckoned her over the hills and through the valleys as her final destination neared. Two miles more and she would be on Sweetwater property. The rage that had driven her out of Randall's office and straight to the livery stable lay like burning embers somewhere inside of her. However, the urgency to see Sweetwater before the sun set, taking the last remnant of day with it, momentarily superseded her anger.

Rachel recognized the Emory place, a small farm nestled among other forty acre farms like it bordering Pine Ridge Plantation which adjoined Sweetwater. Her wild ride prevented her from seeing the couple who watched her in wide-eyed wonder. Had she slowed her journey and looked toward them, Bertha would have recognized the little girl, now turned woman, who had toddled after her children on those rare occasions when Anna Gregory would visit. But she didn't and Bertha Emory was left to fret about the vaguely familiar apparition that had briefly and wildly appeared on their horizon.

Jacob and Bertha Emory's eyes were not the only curious eyes that noted Rachel's arrival. As the racing horses left the neatly cultivated

Emory acres behind, the road entered a rolling forest of loblolly pines that marked the beginning of the Pine Ridge Plantation.

On a tall bluff overlooking the dusty road, Walter Banks perched firmly in the saddle of a magnificent roan stallion. Pleasure flushed his broad face bordered by long unruly, sideburns. Surveying his acreage, he relished his recent acquisitions as only a man can to whom possessions represent the substance of his manhood. This late afternoon ride was his daily ritual; this savoring of his accomplishments, the highlight of his day,

Rachel's buggy rounded a curve and came into view, capturing his attention. His short, squat body tensed in the saddle as a thin stream of tobacco trickled from the corner of his wide mouth and trailed down his chin. His fat cheek bulged from the ample plug he had wedged in it, giving comic relief to an otherwise repugnant countenance.

He sat enthroned like a statue while his close set, beady ocher eyes, staring from beneath craggy red brows, followed her until she drove out of sight. Then he spoke softly to his mount and they moved off as one, the needle strewn ground muffling the sounds of their movement. Horse and rider skirted the road; and with the woods shielding them from sight, followed Rachel from a discreet distance.

Rachel began a meandering descent and knew that soon Sweetwater Creek would come into view. Excitement pounded her heart in cadence with the horses' hooves so she remained oblivious to her audience.

The road divided at the creek and the right branch followed it to the small mill that had been her fathers and on beyond to the larger mill and settlement of New Manchester. Rachel took the left which led to Sweetwater and home. She heard the muffled roar of the shoals behind her filling her with an impatient nostalgia. She hurried the horses on, and Banks watched as she lifted from her seat to catch a glimpse of the foaming water as the last rays of afternoon sun danced on the creek turning it golden.

How many times had her father paused on a trip from town and let his little daughter shed socks and shoes and wade in the shallow edges of the rolling creek. Often times he would take her home with dripping skirts only to be scolded by Agatha who predicted dire consequences to her baby's health. None of which ever came to pass.

Warm memories eased the tension in Rachel's face for a moment. The furrow in her brow smoothed as she thought of Agatha and the comforting welcome awaiting her from the massive black woman. How surprised and pleased she would be to see Rachel. How relieved Rachel would be to have those black arms enfold her in the haven of her broad embrace.

A wisp of a smile touched Rachel's full red lips and Walter Banks had his first glimpse of her beautiful face. He had arrived at the fork before her and reined in his powerful steed. Hidden by the drooping branches of an ancient cedar tree, he watched her progress toward him. He stood immobilized, entranced by her wild and windblown beauty. But in the split second she turned her emerald eyes toward him, her beauty exploded a desire in him to conquer and possess her. Whether she proved married or single, he vowed to have her. This creature was what he had searched all his life for. He needed this woman.

Walter Banks was a self-made man. From a dirt floor hovel, this middle child of twelve grew up vowing to break loose the abject poverty that bound his childhood and caused him to endure the cruel taunts and laughter of other children. At fifteen he left his widowed mother to fend for herself and his younger siblings and struck out on his own.

By the time he was twenty-five he had clawed and connived his way into a better life, but his 200 acre cotton farm on a Mississippi bayou failed to satisfy his definition of success. Poverty had forged within him an insatiable need for power and prestige. He sold his farm and used the proceeds to stake himself on a Mississippi Paddle wheeler. With his innate ability to sense a person's weakness, he preyed on the weak and took their money.

Before many months, he had a boat and then a casino in New Orleans. However, his occupation barred him from the social acceptance he so craved. Once again he pulled up stakes, sold his assets and made his way to Georgia, far from the muddy Mississippi and the reputation he had earned. Here he found a plantation and a lifestyle he thought would bring him the power and prestige for which he yearned.

He had the land. The palatial house he built had no peers. Yet somehow the acceptance he sought eluded him. The community received him with a friendly facade, but they withheld invitations and genuine friendships. He remained an outsider wanting in. He acquired more possessions and seized more power, but nothing he attained vanquished the little barefoot and hungry urchin who clamored inside the man.

When his eyes found Rachel, his imagination and desire ran rampant. Here was the answer to his nightmares. With her on his arm, she would crown his grasping achievements and then doors would swing open to him, hearts would stand in awe. This exquisite creature would banish the childhood taunts that tormented his mind.

Mercifully Rachel's eyes failed to see the threat that awaited her just beyond the forest's edge. Her mind filled with home and Agatha. She sighed, recognizing for the first time that what she felt about her nurse transcended status and color. Agatha was home to her grieving heart. Agatha was the only family she had left.

In short she loved her. If she had been white and free, she would have loved her no more. Because she was a slave and black, she loved her no less. She needed her as a person, a companion, a confident. Somewhere within the heart of this Southern born and bred girl an ember stirred, unrecognized by Rachel, but the long journey to wisdom had begun.

She anticipated the scolding she would get about her disheveled appearance. No matter, Agatha was Sweetwater and Sweetwater was home. Both awaited her with a welcome balm so needed by her battered heart.

In the distance the lingering light dappled through the pale green of newly gowned maples. She was almost home. Involuntarily she slowed her pace and, for the first time since making the turn, she gazed out over Sweetwater property. Amazed she noticed that previously cultivated fields lay fallow, unattended. A crop of weeds and briers covered the ground. She smelled no freshly turned up earth, instead the pungent odors of creek and forest filled the air.

Anticipation gave way to misgivings, churning through her as the anguished words of Randall Wilkie teased her mind. Could it be true? She dismissed the painful memories and urged the horses forward. They responded with a final burst of energy, their bodies lathered from the fierce pace she had demanded.

The buggy whirled around the bend in the long drive and there before her like an apparition from the past stood her beloved Sweetwater, outlined by a pink and golden sunset.

She jerked the reins, stopping the tired horse abruptly. A low moan escaped Rachel as she took in the house. Chickens ran freely through the yard, paint peeled from the proud white boards and windows and doors hung in various states of disrepair. No scolding Agatha stood on the porch to welcome her; no faces black or white greeted the errant mistress, no candles burned within. Sweetwater appeared deserted. But it wasn't. Just beyond her vision Walter Banks watched and smiled triumphantly as he turned his steed toward home. His curiosity satisfied.

Rachel leaped from the buggy. A sob caught in her throat, as she shook her head, rejecting what she saw. Yet even as she ran up the steps and across the broad front porch the words of Andrew and Randall reclaimed her memory.

Pausing at the front door, she pushed it open. The hinges groaned as its sagging bottom scraped the heart pine floor. She called hesitantly, "Agatha?"

Only silence responded, and then a scurrying sound greeted her as a large rodent ran across the hall causing Rachel to jump back with a screech. Disbelief washed her face as she walked from the entrance hall into her father's library where she found only disarray and scattered pieces of furniture. His large oak roll top desk was gone. His two lounging chairs of supple oxblood leather as well as the library table where she studied were missing. Relieved she noted the shelves still held his favorite volumes.

She made her way through the first floor room by room. Each step she took made a footprint in the dust covering the fine heart pine floors. The rugs her father had purchased in Charleston were missing as was her mother's harpsichord but the rest of the furnishings in the parlor and the dining room seemed intact. Protective sheeting covered all the large pieces creating ghostlike images and lending an eerie ambience in the gathering darkness.

Rachel shuddered and looked for a lantern before attempting to investigate the second floor. Her heart raced as her mind tried to comprehend the meaning of what she encountered. In the kitchen pantry she found a lantern and matches in their usual place. Soon a reluctant flame burned on a wick that needed trimming, reflecting from a smoked glass chimney.

Holding the inadequate light high and in front of her she mounted the broad staircase, plain and austere compared to Andrew Meredith's Balmara. The steps creaked familiarly, provoking painful memories of the times they had betrayed her when she sneaked out of bed to steal a peek at Santa. Her father somehow always heard and with burly arms would scoop her up and carry her back to bed.

The first room at the top of the stairs was her parent's room, with a deep breath she held the lantern before her and entered. In this room everything appeared intact. Her eyes caressed each familiar piece of finely carved cherry furniture. The large room had windows, now dark in the gathering dusk, but facing east and the morning's dawn. Her mother, an early riser, would welcome the day perched on the window seat with a steaming cup of tea in her dainty hands.

Mosquito netting draped the carved four poster bed placed strategically to catch the breeze and the morning sun. The room remained as she remembered it and she turned from it reluctantly to continue her inspection down the hall.

She surveyed each guest room down the long hall, some had their furnishings and some were partially empty. Finally she arrived at the large room at the opposite end of the hall. It was her room with floor to ceiling windows on two sides and a door opening onto a balcony with commanding view of the meandering Chattahoochee in the distance.

A low moan of denial tore from Rachel's throat as she entered her room. It was completely empty. Her mind clamored with an unwanted memory fighting to surface. The image of another room facing a river with a bed so similar to hers, or was it identical? Fury suppressed broke through the bubbling in her throat and engulfed her.

She lifted the jib window and stepped out onto a small balcony that faced west toward the river and the last ribbon of light as it bade the day farewell. Suddenly all her composure dissolved. Sobs tore through her as the pain of disillusionment, disappointment and anger flooded her like a rampaging river that leaves its banks out of control, dislodging and uprooting everything in its pathway. It washed away all remnants of her self confidence leaving only a sense of loss and loneliness which reached to Rachel's inner most being.

The tears poured out in what seemed an unending stream. They came to mourn her father, to mourn her mother, to mourn for Agatha. But most of all they gushed forth washing away her precious dreams and aspirations. When they were gone, she had lost that last fragile thread that keeps life going—hope and in its place lodged bitterness.

Her throat was sore from crying, her eyes red and swelled, yet she had no power to stop the release of emotions pent up since her mother died. Destructive emotions she had pushed down and buried layer by layer now came pouring out. They were dislodged and uprooted from so deeply within her she had denied their existence. Now they made themselves known in one cataclysmic dam burst.

She turned back toward the window. Night settled in around her like a velvet mantel as she stepped back into her empty room. The lamp had long since sputtered and died, leaving it draped in a suffocating blackness. Her shoulders still jerked in uncontrollable spasms and she stumbled. Suddenly waiting arms, outstretched in the darkness, grasped her.

TEN

The scream caught in Rachel's throat as a hand closed over her mouth. Strong arms clutched her tightly in the oppressive darkness of the room, pressing her against a hard, muscular frame and the rough texture of a man's coat.

Too expended to resist, too defeated to care, she waited limply, with only her pounding heart raising an objection. Then Andrew Meredith's voice spoke quietly in her ear, his head bowed his cheek pressed to hers.

She had failed to hear the footsteps that had followed her into the room or the voice that called her name. But he had heard her sobbing and now his heart ached, "Rachel, don't be afraid. It's Drew. I'm here, now. Everything's going to be all right. I'll look after you."

She made no sound, then her body began trembling, first her shoulders, then spreading until every sinew, muscle and bone shook as a sapling caught in a cyclone. Meredith moved his hand from her mouth and a strange sound gurgled from her, and then intensified with each shudder of her body, until finally she pushed away from him and threw her head back. Gulping for air, gales of hysterical laughter filled the room.

The moon, pale and wan, peeked through the trees and filtered its light into the room, relieving the blackness. Andrew shook Rachel gently but still the maniacal laughter rolled. Then she wrenched in his hold, turning her face to the side and tears wet his hand. Consternation gripped Andrew Meredith's features as helplessness overcame this self-reliant man. He tried to draw her closer somehow to reach through her hysteria, but this time she pushed free of him and stepped back.

She stuttered, laughter subsiding some, "You're gonna ta—take care of me—?"

"That's what I said and I . . .."

"A-a ma-man of his w-word," Rachel continued, haltingly, still unable to control her trembling. With her eyes dark and wide in the dimness, she backed away from him until the corner of the room imprisoned her, halting her retreat.

"Yes," Drew replied remaining where he was while alarm added a gruffness to his voice and set his face like granite in the semi-darkness.

Then the gurgling began again and hysteria threatened to engulf Rachel once more, "You to-took care of me-me already,"

"I what?" Meredith puzzled.

Rachel lifted her arm and in a sweeping gesture screamed, "All of it, everything I had and loved" Tears streamed down her face and laughter turned to sobs, "You took it, you took it. Even my furniture, you took it. Now I have nothing and nowhere to go. You win. You're too powerful to fight."

In three long strides Andrew crossed the room to her and grabbed her by the shoulders as understanding penetrated his alarm. His tall frame towered above her, "Rachel, Rachel I've taken nothing!"

"The mill?" She insisted.

"Not taken, bought."

"The mill was my father's dream; he'd never give it up unless he was forced to."

"He was. But it was his own excesses that forced it."

"I don't believe that. You and Uncle Randall took advantage of him. I can see how you might do it, but how could Uncle Randall betray my father? He was his friend. How can greed do that to a person?"

"Greed is not the word for it. Grief and dissipation. Your father threw his wealth away with drink and gambling."

Rachel put her hands to her ears and screamed, "No, no, no. I will not allow you to malign my father and destroy his memory."

Andrew captured both Rachel's hands in his, pulling them from her ears and forced her chin upwards. Looking into her wide, sad eyes he crooned, "Oh, Rachel, how I wish I could do otherwise. But it's the truth and you must face it."

"You don't have the truth in you," Rachel hurled at him, as she jerked away from him, her hysteria changing to anger.

"You don't know me that well, but you do know Randall Wilkie."

"I only thought I did."

"You do. He's the most honorable and self-sacrificing man I know. Do you know why all his wealth is gone?"

"Disastrous cotton market, he said."

"That's only part of it. He couldn't survive the market fall because he had already sacrificed too much trying to save your father." Meredith's voice, now matter of fact, continued slowly and steadily, trying to re-assure her.

"Then why didn't he tell me?" Rachel demanded; her eyes narrowed.

"Because he didn't want to destroy your memories,"

"Obviously you don't mind," she snapped. Tears and hysteria receding.

"I do mind, Rachel, but when your memories threaten your future and distort the truth they become expendable. I refuse to keep the truth from you when it will destroy Randall Wilkie."

"How could my memories destroy him?" Rachel queried through tight lips.

"They've made you condemn an innocent man. The truth is he stripped what little assets he had, giving to your father." Andrew answered brusquely.

"Why?" she asked, still not convinced.

"Because, he was trying to save Sweetwater for you."

"I don't believe you. He connived with you—" Rachel hotly protested.

"A look at his office and at his home, if you would care to go there, will show you the fallacy of that statement. He is a broken man.

His fortune gone."

"But how do I know what you say is the truth? You own the mill. And Randall talked you into it," she accused resisting the persuasion in his voice, unwilling to let her guard down.

"It is true he talked me into buying the mill, but it was in a last ditch effort to save Sweetwater."

"But it didn't save Sweetwater?"

"That's because your father sent half of the money to Europe to your aunt."

Rachel winced. His words brought back the memory of Aunt Letty complaining that her father had sent a mere pittance to cover her expenses. She never saw any of the money personally because her aunt had said it barely covered her expenses up to then. An involuntary shudder escaped as she remembered the letter she had written to her father asking for more and the feeling of being an unwelcome burden.

Pushing back the wave of guilt that washed over her, she demanded, "What about the rest?"

"He gambled the other half and lost it instead of planting his cotton crop."

"My father was no gambler," Rachel denied.

"You're right. He was like a lamb led to the slaughter."

"How would you know? Were you there?"

"As a matter of fact I was."

"And the slaughterer no doubt."

Hardly. I've worked too hard for what I have to risk it on a game of chance. Especially one that's rigged."

"Then why didn't father object."

"He never knew."

"What do you mean by that?"

"He was too much in his cups and the man he was playing with is a shyster and card shark. Not only that, his major objective was to take your father's land and holdings. If I hadn't bought the mill, your father would have lost it to him."

"If you and Uncle Randall were such champions of my father,

then why didn't you do something to stop him?"

"Randall tried to. Your father was belligerent and the other man threatening. Since the man was our host he could do little. Now that I look back, I believe the whole dinner party was a set up for cheating your father out of his property. I didn't try to interfere. Felt like it wasn't any of my business."

"Made it easier for you to get your hands on Sweetwater."

"Rachel, if I had wanted Sweetwater that way, why would I offer you many times more than it is worth now?"

"There must be more to the story than you're telling me. Surely he saved enough for spring planting. I know my father would never have been as foolish as that," Rachel protested.

"Maybe the father you knew wouldn't have but ale has made a fool out of many a man. When planting time came last spring, he mortgaged the plantation but the crop failed because he didn't have enough labor to tend and harvest it."

"What about our slaves?"

"Sold off or leased out. He had only a skeleton staff left. Far too few even to keep up with ordinary plantation maintenance."

"What happened to the mortgage?"

"He traded part of the land and all of the slaves."

"But you said there was still a mortgage on it?"

"Right before your father died, he borrowed more money on the place."

"But how did Uncle Randall try to help him?"

"He gave him money to send to you, to plant his crops, to buy raw materials for the mill. Money your father never repaid. When he thought your father was going to lose the mill, and he had no more to loan, he mortgaged his own property. When cotton prices fell he had no profit to pay his mortgage so he sold his valuables and moved to a shabby office which hurt his business. You know how fickle society can be. They prefer attorneys with proper addresses."

"I'm sorry I just can't believe that. Why on earth would any man do that for someone else?"

"Because he was trying to preserve your heritage."

"My heritage? Why?" Rachel questioned, her brow furrowed.

"Because he loves you. Completely and unselfishly as he loved Anna."

"Mother? How dare you say such a thing! There was never anything between my mother and Randall Wilkie," Rachel protested, her voice raised, shock rounded her eyes.

"Of course there wasn't. Randall is an honorable man. He loved your mother purely and from afar but he loved her no less. That's why he never married. He grieved for her, too, but he understood what your father never did, your mother lives on in you."

"How do you know this?" Rachel probed, masking the curiosity that demanded answers.

"I guessed it when he came to beg me for help when his assets were gone. I couldn't understand his involvement and dedication to a man who seemed determined to self-destruct."

"He told you this?"

"Only the pain in his eyes confirmed my probing." Meredith admitted.

"Why did you bring me back?" Rachel fired, changing the subject abruptly as some subconscious warning flared.

"So Randall could see you once more."

"Once more?" Her heart pounded in ears suddenly afraid to hear.

"He's ill." Andrew answered quietly.

"How ill? Is he going to die?" Rachel insisted.

"Aren't we all?" he evaded.

"You know what I mean," she snapped, impatience and fear sharpening her voice.

"If you mean how long will he live? I don't know the answer to that. I just know he was afraid that he'd never see you again."

"So out of the goodness of your heart you . . .?"

"No, Rachel because of the goodness of his heart. It cost me little more than time."

"I thought it was because of a promise you made to my father."

"I did. But it was because of Randall Wilkie that I promised."

"You were not a friend of my father's?

"Only a business associate."

"Why not a friend?"

"The father you remember, I never knew."

"Then who did you know?" Rachel asked softly, reluctantly.

"I knew Adam Gregory, a man whose best friend was a bottle of ale, who used his friends and, selfishly, threw away what he had because he wouldn't let go of the past."

"How did he do that?"

"By focusing on what he had lost instead of being grateful for what he had left."

"What?"

"You and the legacy of Sweetwater that would live on. Nothing could bring your mother back, but as long as he had his daughter he had part of her. "

"Don't you think he knew that?"

"He didn't act like he did. He sent you away then threw away your future. Don't do the same thing, Rachel. The present and your survival are more important. See the truth."

"What truth?" she asked, afraid to hear the answer.

"Life as you knew it and hoped it would be has changed. Face it and determine to survive," Drew encouraged softly.

"But all I've ever wanted was Sweetwater," she declared softly, as she lifted her head and her eyes, large and dark in the shadows of her empty bedroom, held his.

In that moment all Andrew Meredith's stern resolution to send her back to her aunt melted and he knew that Sweetwater was all he wanted, too. Because Sweetwater meant Rachel. And Rachel had captured his heart.

Shaken to his very core, Andrew reached out a hesitant finger and traced the curve of her cheek down to her chin then lifted it so he could look into her eyes. Gently he murmured, "And little one, what do you want with Sweetwater?"

"Don't you understand? The very roots of who I am are buried in the soil of this place? I could never be happy in Europe. You asked me if I had a suitor over there. Yes, I did. But on the way home I realized no human love could take the place of my attachment to this land. It is my identity, my very life. Without Sweetwater, I'm only a shell. And now it's gone."

"Rachel, Rachel. You're more than a place on the map. You're a living being. This place is only sticks and stones, soil and rock. It has no life."

"Without it I have no life."

"Rachel, you can't mean what you're saying."

"Andrew, you don't understand. This place is all that I have left of who I was," Rachel explained her face pleading, forgetting for the moment her hostility and suspicion.

"But that's the past Rachel, who you are now is what matters."

"But who am I now? Without Sweetwater I belong nowhere. No family, nowhere to go."

"Your aunt, your suitor," he suggested as his heart lurched at the thought.

"I was a nuisance to my aunt because I didn't fit in with all that court foppery. When my father's support fell below what she expected, she let me know I was a burden. After father's death she begged me to stay because she thought I'd be wealthy. Yes she married nobility, but most of what they had was a title, not the funds to live the lifestyle she craved. She thought I was the key to that."

"And your suitor?" he asked afraid to hear the answer.

"No, he was wealthy and a fine man. He worked hard. But I don't think he would ever be happy here because his roots are someplace else, he has a responsibility to his family. I could never be happy anywhere but here. I didn't even tell him how to find me and he's too proud to ask my aunt."

"Did you love him?"

"Maybe, what's love?"

Andrew chuckled, a strange relief flooding him, "I think that if you really loved him, you'd not have to ask that question and Sweetwater wouldn't take precedence over him.

Rachel shook her head in objection, "you're wrong. No man will ever mean as much to me as this place."

Andrew shook his head sadly, "Then you're destined for a lonely, unfulfilled life."

"Aren't most women? Seems like they marry more for convenience and then something other than their marriages, whether it's their home or their children, becomes primary in their lives. With my aunt it was social position."

"Was that the way it was with your mother?"

Painful memories of her mother's shining face and sparkling eyes greeting her father washed over Rachel, and she dropped her eyes, "No, of course not. But look at the pain losing her caused my father."

"It didn't have to be that way. That's the tragedy. Your father was blessed with what few men ever have and he squandered the blessing. Now you have to suffer because of his bad choices."

"You seem determined to malign him. Why do you hate him?"

"Not him, Rachel. I have no patience with waste and I hate what he's done to you and to Randall Wilkie. Bad choices never just affect the guilty, the innocent always suffer the consequences. I don't want to destroy your father. In fact I want to forget the past except what we have to deal with to insure you a future."

"We're back to that. I have no future," she reminded.

"What were your plans?" he asked.

"To continue with the plantation and the mill."

"The mill is gone and only a fraction of the plantation is left." Andrew reminded gently.

"So you see I have no plans. There are few employment opportunities for women, you know."

"Beyond marriage, you mean."

Her laugh made a brittle sound in the room, "No prospects, I'm afraid."

He chuckled, "How about me?"

"Don't you think that's sacrificing a little too much for your friend?"

"Wha—?" he puzzled.

"Uncle Randall," she reminded.

"I wasn't even thinking of Wilkie."

"Then I can't accept your grand sacrifice." she retorted sharply, feeling angry and humiliated that he would make fun of her.

Andrew heard the anger in her voice and in her eyes misread her humiliation as distrust and blame. Not accustomed to a woman's rejection, he answered coldly, "I guess there must be another answer, but it will have to wait until morning. Come on it's time we got started back to town."

"I'm not going back to town. I'm staying right here, this is my home."

"Miss Gregory, you cannot possibly stay here tonight. It's much too dangerous. It was foolish enough of you coming out here in the daylight by yourself."

"Never the less, I'm staying. I didn't travel all the way from Europe to run away. I don't know how long I'll get to stay, but I'm going to live here while I can. I need to think."

"You're an exasperating woman. Don't you ever co-operate with anyone?"

"I don't know, I just know what I'm going to do tonight is stay here." Rachel insisted.

"All right I give up. Let's see if we can find some more lanterns and I hope you ate enough lunch to satisfy you until morning."

Before long Meredith had candles burning in Rachel's parents' bedroom and together they found linens for the bed. When he had helped her make the bed, he bade her good night and unknown to Rachel made his way to the abandoned caretaker's cottage where he kept an overnight vigil tossing and turning as the auburn haired beauty invaded his dreams.

ELEVEN

Walter Banks' stallion whinnied in the woods just beyond Sweetwater Manor. His early morning ride ranged several miles farther than usual. Curiosity had drawn him like a magnet.

From his hidden vista on the southern end of the house, he watched two horses grazing side by side, a saddle neatly stowed on the porch banisters and a carriage standing idle. All was calm and in order, that is except Walter Banks' pounding heart. Nothing in the past few months had played into the scheme of his plans as what he had observed last evening and now.

Rachel Gregory may have failed to hear Andrew Meredith's arrival the evening before, but Banks had not. He had just turned his mount toward home when he spied Meredith riding at break neck speed around the last bend in the road along the creek. Following him as he had followed Rachel earlier, the furtive planter had seen Andrew take the front steps two at a time. Banks lingered in the gathering darkness until he saw light flickering in an upper bedroom. Then he left for home, a smug satisfaction glowing in his beady eyes.

Now he was back, his imagination running rampant as his heart exulted over his unexpected good fortune. He knew he stood on the threshold of achieving his long held objectives. The final chapter was being written before his eyes, the tools to his success were housed within Sweetwater Manor, waiting to be utilized at the right moment.

The early morning sun streamed through the southeastern corner of the broad kitchen windows and silhouetted a tall, solitary figure standing in the middle of the room.

Rachel awoke; something startled her from a deep sleep. For a moment she felt disoriented in the strange surroundings. Memory crashed down on her and she leaped out of bed. She was home at Sweetwater and someone was in the house with her. Wafting beneath her closed door, the nostalgic aroma of sausage and coffee greeted her while sounds of activity below her confirmed she was not alone.

"Agatha?" could last night have been a bad dream? She looked around her; no familiar childhood furnishings greeted her eager eyes, only the tester bed and highboy gave mute evidence that this was her parent's room and last evening was a reality. But who was down below? Could she have been mistaken? Had Agatha come back?

Throwing her rumpled traveling suit over the undergarments she had slept in and leaving her hoop and crinoline collapsed on the floor where she had stepped out of them, Rachel dressed in seconds. Pausing only to run her fingers through her tangled locks, she rushed from her room and down the long staircase, her heart drumming.

When she rounded the corner to the kitchen, shock stopped her. Andrew Meredith stood in her kitchen, a towel draped around his waist and his shirt sleeves rolled up. He whistled a merry tune as he stirred something in a pot on the familiar cast iron stove. Coffee boiled on it and a small platter of golden sausage links graced the harvest table in the far corner of the kitchen.

Outside Banks waited patiently. His patience was rewarded as a second figure entered his line of vision. This time the sun's radiance outlined cascading curls and a full skirt which fell unrestricted by hoop or crinoline and clung to the soft curves beneath it. His heart pounded with anticipation, but his curiosity would know no more for the pair moved away from the windows and disappeared from his view.

Suddenly the aroma of frying sausage and coffee drifted through the air denting his consciousness. Hunger pains reminded Banks that his own breakfast had been delayed by his early morning eagerness. He waited a few minutes longer; then satisfied he could see no more, he turned toward home in anticipation of the bounteous sideboard of food awaiting him.

Amazement left Rachel speechless for a moment. The grimy kitchen she had explored in search of matches and candles the night before, now scrubbed clean, fairly gleamed. Two plates of willow blue China were set with coffee mugs beside them. Rachel's stomach growled a silent greeting before her tongue found utterance. Finally she exclaimed, "Mr. Meredith, what are you doing back here?"

Andrew turned sharply toward her, jolted from his reverie, "Oh, I never left."

"You what?"

He looked at her squarely before replying matter of factly, "How could I? You were too stubborn to return to town, and it was too dangerous to leave you here alone."

"But that's—", She protested.

"Improper?" he laughed, "Don't worry; your reputation is not compromised. I spent the night in the caretaker's cottage and who's around to carry tales anyway? "

"Where did you get the food?" she queried, her heart still racing. "And the kitchen, it's all cleaned up."

"Found some canned sausage, coffee and brown sugar in the root cellar. Couple of hens obliged us with some eggs. Sorry we don't have any bread or cream for your coffee, but after missing supper last evening I figured just about anything would taste palatable. And as for the kitchen, never could work in a dirty room." He explained as he turned back to the stove.

"Well you are a man of many talents, Mr. Meredith," she observed, amazed.

"Natural result of being thrown on your own at an early age. You learn to fend for yourself. Now sit down, Miss Gregory, enjoy your first meal at Sweetwater." Meredith commanded.

"Perhaps my last?" she asked softly as she sat down docilely.

Her pain reached his heart and caused him to speak curtly,

covering his own emotion, "Perhaps not if you're willing to do what it takes to survive."

"I've already told you finding a husband is out of the question and other than that, it would take a miracle," she retorted her voice reflecting his sharpness.

He turned toward her with a plate of pale golden eggs in his hands. His eyes held hers for a moment, as he too, sat down. Then he chuckled but his look held no mirth and replied evenly, "Since you turned down a perfectly good offer last night, I guess we need to find that miracle."

Her eyes narrowed for a moment as she saw something puzzling in his countenance, but it was gone before she could decipher it. So she shrugged, slightly embarrassed and feeling awkward that he would mention his inappropriate jesting of the night before. "Do you have a suggestion?"

"You could accept my offer to buy Sweetwater."

"Then you would have it instead of this mysterious mortgage holder. My situation would hardly change," she protested.

"I disagree. This way you'd have some money," he reasoned.

"Very little after I cleared the mortgage," Rachel observed dispassionately.

"That's right, but don't you think that little is better than none." Meredith asked pointedly.

"When it runs out I'll have no place to live and no way to make a living," she reminded him.

"By that time maybe your suitor will come back."

Emerald lights fired in her eyes, "I've told you that's over, he would never leave England. Anyway what a detestable thing to do. It would be no more than using him. "

He threw up both hands in a mock defense, "Just making a suggestion. Trying to find out what sounds best to you."

"Nothing sounds best to me but to stay here where I love and where I thought I belonged."

"Then do it."

"I believe that's what you've spent last evening and this morning telling me I cannot do." Rachel's voice raised, exasperation with him and her situation ready to boil over.

"I've been thinking. In fact didn't do much sleeping in that broken down cottage last night so I thought of a possible solution. I know it isn't what you ultimately want, but at least you would have a livelihood and a place to live," Meredith said, his voice persuasive.

"What's that?" curiosity filtered through her despondency.

"Sell me Sweetwater and you stay here and manage it. Many women with absentee husbands have been forced into that position and were successful."

"But Sweetwater would never be mine."

"You'll lose it either way, Rachel. This way you'll have the money and you won't have to leave. I'll even sign an agreement that if anything happens to me, ownership will revert back to you." Meredith interrupted.

"And you'll accomplish exactly what you set out to accomplish," Rachel accused quietly.

"What's that?"

"Take Sweetwater for your own."

"How many times do I have to tell you, I'm not the villain in your situation? What could I possibly need with Sweetwater enough to cause me to plot and scheme for it?" He demanded, frustration flushing his face.

"If I knew the answer to that, Mr. Meredith, then I'd understand why my life is in shambles."

"Very well, Miss Gregory," Andrew responded, his eyes suddenly hooded, his voice cold, "I see you must blame someone for your misfortune rather than face the truth. But the simple fact is, I'm your only way out."

"If what you're telling me is true, then why are you interested in Sweetwater at all?"

Andrew Meredith paused before answering. Her question pierced his soul stirring a truth he wanted to deny. When he spoke, he chose his words carefully lest he reveal more than he intended. He explained, "My interest is only minimal. It is more a matter of convenience. Since I have a factory here, it would be convenient to have a place to stay when I come as well as a supplier of raw material. It would be efficient for me to have a plantation that could supply the mill with cotton and other commodities."

She responded coldly, "Have you considered the impropriety of your staying here with me living here?"

His mouth turned up in a cynical half-smile, "Not exactly but something could be worked out."

"Then there is the problem of so little property. You said a large portion of the land had been sold off. North Georgia land is not as productive as the level coastal plains it requires more acreage."

Surprise raised his brows, "Why, Miss Rachel, you surprise me with your knowledge."

Ignoring his barb, she pressed, "Why would you consider a place with so little land? Surely there are more suitable places available around here?"

Andrew grew impatient as Rachel pressed him toward a truth he refused to admit. That he wanted Sweetwater because Sweetwater meant Rachel was merely some vague suspicion not yet fully formed in his own mind. His studied answer denied his inner turmoil, "It seemed appropriate that your father's estate would stay intact."

"But you took care of that when you took my father's mill."

"Take it, Rachel? Take it? I told you I bought the mill. Paid more than a fair price. I've never taken anything from anyone."

"Except Sweetwater!"

"I'm trying to buy Sweetwater, not take it." His voice rose as exasperation pushed him near anger. It had been many years since Andrew Meredith had allowed himself the luxury of anger. But this woman aroused raw emotions within him that he had never experienced.

"But since I have no other option, isn't that the same as taking it?"

"No, I'm offering you an opportunity. Taking it is what Walter

Banks is going to do if you don't accept my offer."

"Walter Banks?" she queried.

"The neighbor who has steadily bought up the land adjoining the north boundaries of Sweetwater, then finally more than half the acreage between the house and his plantation."

"I don't remember a Walter Banks."

"He's a newcomer who's hungry for power and social acceptance. He has the mistaken notion that property will buy that for him." He explained his lips tightened in disapproval at the thought of Banks.

"Is that what you're after, Mr. Meredith?"

"A man can't buy respectability. He is either honorable or he's not. Banks is not an honorable man."

"And you are?"

"Yes." His answer curt and without explanation.

"And just what is your definition of honorable?" Rachel hurled at him.

"Honesty, hard work and loyalty."

"I guess you feel that you meet that criteria but personally I'm not at all convinced. I can't see that there is much difference between what you're doing and what you say Mr. Banks is going to do. Both of you have destroyed my future."

"If you can't see the difference then you have willfully blinded yourself to the truth," Meredith responded through clinched jaws, dangerously near explosion.

"What truth?"

"That it was your father and not me who destroyed your options; that life as you once knew it is over; that you've got to have the courage to accept the past and face the future as it is, not as you wish it were."

"And your proposal will do that?" she demanded, unbelieving.

"It's your only hope," he persuaded.

"But Sweetwater will never be mine again—", she reminded, her voice breaking.

"Never is a long time, Rachel."

"But it's mine now," she protested.

"Come December and it won't be."

"Why December?"

"The note is due. Then it'll all be over. You will have no options left."

"Maybe not."

"You can't survive, because you have no other way to raise the money. You have no crops planted, no labor to work with and the house and outbuildings are in shambles."

"So what would be different if you bought it?"

"I have the financial means to supply an adequate labor force to get a late crop in the ground and to do the repairs necessary."

"There's a question of enough land." she reminded him.

"I have an option on the adjoining 2000 acres."

"You what?" she gasped.

"Part of the Tower Plantation that adjoins the backside of Sweetwater."

"So that's it! You've got to have Sweetwater to give that acquisition any value," she concluded, suspicion once again clouding her features.

"It is only an option."

"That would be no good without Sweetwater," she accused.

"In a way that's true. But look at it this way, Rachel, Sweetwater is no good without that option."

"Explain it anyway you wish, Mr. Meredith. The truth is evident. You want Sweetwater and now you have your chance. You might say my disadvantage became your advantage," She spat out.

Suddenly Andrew wearied of trying to persuade her and responded, his voice cold, "Believe what you choose to believe. I see my offer as a definite advantage for you but as far as I'm concerned, you can take it or leave it. I'm extending my trip further north and plan to return in three days. You will have until then to accept my offer; at that time it will be withdrawn."

TWELVE

Ablue bird swooped down from the branch of a dogwood tree and perched uncertainly on a partially collapsed fence post. Its brilliant blue coat and orange brown breast glowed, appearing almost iridescent in the bright morning sunlight. It quarreled at Rachel who sat quietly in the shade of an old, gnarled apple tree starring unseeingly at the outraged bird. Unable to bluff the intruder, he flew away not willing to enter the small hole in the cedar post that he called home.

The sun filtered through pale green leaves and caressed her face but the pleasant warmth went unnoticed. She sighed deeply as anxiety filled her being and a cold helplessness stole over her members paralyzing her for the moment of any productive actions.

Andrew Meredith had left. Angry and definite he had stated terms that she refused to accept. He said he'd return in three days, how could she survive three days?

Her total aloneness washed over her anew and for the first time since her father's death she really came to terms with what it meant to be without family or assistance. Her only thought had been to return to the haven of Sweetwater. But the home in her memory was one far removed from this disastrous reality.

Now she sat alone without hope devoid of any plan of action. Her only chance of survival resided in giving up the very thing that had brought her here. The question she had demanded of Meredith echoed through her mind. Why had she come?

Outside the fence, the livery stable horse foraged for grass. A mirthless chuckle caught in her throat. He had better prospects among the weeds than she had in all of Sweetwater.

She hardly had enough food left for two days. She had only a little money left, no servants, supplies, not even the horse was hers.

Her desperation turned to fury. How could Meredith leave her helpless like this? What kind of man would leave a woman unprotected and not provided for? A grimace darkened her lovely features as bitterness wooed her receptive heart whispering a lie to believe." A man determined to have his way," the poison murmured," what better way to bring her to terms than this?"

Reason struggled with her anger reminding her that it was she who ran away to Sweetwater. He had merely followed to offer assistance. Yet the lie within her persisted. Of course he offered help, but on terms she had to refuse.

A grim smile parted her face distorting her beauty, firing her eyes with an ugly light as she chose to believe the lie. Leave her destitute and helpless and she'd have to acquiesce. That was his game plan.

A shudder racked her body blocking out the warmth of the warm April sun. She needed help. Someone to talk to. Someone to tell her what to do.

Randall Wilkie's face swam before her and she reached out her hand as if to clutch a life line. She'd hitch up the buggy and ride over to Uncle Randall's. He'd tell her what to do. Then her hand dropped back to her lap as yesterday's memories reminded her that he was Meredith's friend. Who could she trust? Uncle Randall had betrayed her. Her mind insisted while her heart denied it.

Hoof beats on the long driveway startled Rachel from the war raging within. Hope quenching bitterness, she turned toward the noise. Her heart pounded with unexpected relief—maybe Meredith had returned.

But it was not Andrew Meredith's tall, erect figure that greeted her eyes. But rather the short, squat presence of Walter Banks seated high upon the back of his magnificent roan stallion.

For a moment the splendid steed distracted Rachel from her pain and her visitor. Her sojourn in Europe had left her an appreciation and love for fine horses.

Refusing to be ignored, the rider removed his wide brimmed straw hat and, lifting it in his pudgy hand, waved a friendly hello.

Rachel rose hastily, brushing the grass and debris from her crushed traveling skirt. She shielded her eyes with her hand and responded hesitantly, searching her memory for any remembrance of the broad face beneath the thinning red hair.

Satisfied he was a stranger, she stood poised waiting for horse and rider to come to her. She squared her shoulders, summoning all the dignity she could muster in her present circumstances.

"Can I help you?" she asked her voice bolder than her heart.

"No ma'am, it's I who have come to assist you, if I may." The stranger crooned as he approached the apple tree.

"And who are you, sir?" Rachel demanded, her heart pounding.

"I'm Walter Banks, your neighbor."

The name stirred embers inside Rachel. Strangely familiar and foreboding, a warning teased her memory; yet she could not bring it to her consciousness and so it was that need overrode caution igniting a spark of hope within her.

"How did you know I am your neighbor?" she asked, her voice softer more appealing.

"News travels fast in a small community, Miss Gregory."

Rachel's lips favored him with a cool smile remembering how it used to be. "You even know my name."

"You've been expected."

"The welcoming party didn't quite make it."

"Well, ma'am. Let me rectify that oversight." He drawled as he hefted himself out of the saddle, landing eye level with Rachel.

"That would be most kind, sir."

"What can I do for you?"

"I don't even know. It seems that my situation is rather hopeless. I had no idea I'd find my affairs in such disarray. Maybe you could start by telling me what has happened here since my father died."

"Ma'am you have my heartfelt regrets about your situation. But Walter Banks is here to see to it that you get what's coming to you. I made that promise to your poor sick papa."

"Mm. Seems a lot of people made promises to my father. Exactly what did you promise him?"

"To see after you ma'am," he assured, his tawny eyes stared into hers unblinking.

"How did he propose for you to do that?"

"Well he had his ideas, but we won't go into that now. I just want to assist you in any way that I can."

"How much do you know about my father's business?"

"We were intimate friends, your Pa and me. I moved into the community right after you went abroad. Your father and I took an immediate liking to one another. We had so much in common. I had just lost my wife and we shared grief together. Liked to socialize together."

Painful accusations that Andrew Meredith had made surfaced and she asked, "Drink and gamble?"

"Oh, now, Miz Gregory, you know your Pa. He was an upstanding citizen who didn't participate in no riotous living. If he had, we wouldn't have been friends, cause I'm not a mind to live a lifestyle like that. Now toward the end there when he was so sick and in pain, I won't deny, we'd occasionally lift a tankard of ale together. Sometime we would have a game of cards to take his mind off his troubles."

Rachel's eyes met Walter Banks, hope firing the emerald lights within hers, "Are you sure that was all there was too it?"

"Of course I am. Your father was one of the finest men I've ever known. Now you might hear some gossiping tongues, but believe me they're only tales. There were some people who hoped to take advantage of your father when he was so sick, and they spread rumors about him." Banks assured her.

"Then what explains this?" Rachel questioned, waving her hand to include the house and land.

"Your father spent his money trying to find a doctor to cure him.

After he lost his mill, he didn't have the income or the energy to save Sweetwater. I did what I could to help him, but I couldn't restore his health and he was too proud to let me take care of his business. I did what I could, but when he died the darkies ran off. I rounded up the good ones and looked after them at my place. You know they're just like children. If a white person doesn't provide for them, they can't survive."

"Our slaves are at your house?" Rachel asked.

"Some of them, Miss Gregory. I took care of them just like they were family."

The man's apparent benevolence encouraged Rachel to probe further, "What happened to our furnishings?"

"Some of them your father sold, others people looted. You know how it is when a house is left vacant."

"What happened to the house servants?"

"Your father sold most of them and some of them I leased, the rest ran off."

"How can I get them back?"

"Why I'll bring the ones back that I've been looking out after. But we need to take stock and see what you need. Besides aren't you afraid to stay out here all alone except with just the slaves?"

"I'm not afraid, but I am going to have to sell Sweetwater. You see I don't have the financial assets to stock the place or even to plant crops. I have no other alternative but to sell. I understand there is a mortgage on the place due in December."

"Miss Gregory, don't you worry your mind about that. I hold that mortgage and while I can't afford to just forgive the debt, I will be very understanding. I loaned that money to your father to keep him from selling it to Andrew Meredith."

"Meredith tried to buy Sweetwater?"

"Sure he did. I bet he's the one who wants you to sell to him. "

"Yes, he is," Rachel agreed.

"You can't trust the man." Banks spat out.

"I don't know about that. After all he did pay for my passage back from England and has been most considerate in seeing me home."

"Only so you would sell him Sweetwater. He knew otherwise that I had the mortgage and would never let him get his hands on my good friend's property. I didn't have any idea until this week you'd be returning home or I'd have seen to it that Sweetwater would have welcomed you back. Meredith knew what faced you. Didn't warn you did he? Did he bring you out here and just leave you?"

"He didn't actually bring me, you see I . . .," Rachel stammered.

"Well bring you or not, how could anyone who calls himself a man, bring a lovely lady like yourself all the way across the ocean and never tell her what she's facing?" Banks asked, then added logically, "except that he wanted to shock her into selling her property."

"I can't judge his motives, Mr. Banks, but I do know that I have no other choice but to sell."

"Well I would buy it before I'd let Meredith have it. That's how he's made millions. Taking advantage of people. Don't let him have it." Emotion raised his voice.

"I believe until December, I still retain the right to choose to whom I sell it," Rachel countered quietly.

"Of course you do." Banks agreed, bringing his emotions under control, "I meant nothing by that more than showing you that you do have an option—some bargaining leverage. The man wants your property. I don't want him to have it. But I have a better idea," Banks persuaded.

"Are you a miracle worker? I need a miracle."

"For Adam Gregory's daughter, I'd do my best."

Rachel chuckled, the heaviness pressing her down, lifted some, "And what do you propose?"

"I bring your hands back, loan you the money to get by and plant your cotton crop."

"On what collateral?" she pressed.

"On your cotton crop."

"What about the mortgage due this winter?"

"I told you we'll worry about that later." He dismissed the question with a wave of the hand. "Because your father was my friend,

I'd consider it a privilege to help his daughter."

"Thank you, Mr. Banks. Your generosity and commitment overwhelm me." Rachel murmured.

"Now to the practical help. It's obvious to me that you can't stay here in this house until it is refurbished. Suppose you stay in my home for the next couple of weeks until your place is livable?"

"Sir?" Rachel gasped.

Banks chuckled, "Perfectly proper. My maiden sister is mistress of my home and an adequate chaperon to even the most severe critic."

"Really, Mr. Banks, I appreciate your concerns, but I prefer to stay at Sweetwater, regardless of the inconveniences. I will accept the return of our labor force but I insist on staying here."

Disappointment flared in his eyes for a moment before he agreed softly, "I understand, it's been a long time since you've been home."

His apparent understanding touched Rachel's heart and threatened to dissolve her last bastion of reserve, "Thank you for your kindness. I will repay you."

"I have no doubt about that; however, your happiness would be ample repayment. I'll send supplies and manpower over this evening. I'll also try to find you an overseer, but that may take awhile.

"I'll look forward to getting to work." Rachel agreed, her emotions under control again. Then added, "Is Agatha at your place?"

For a moment Bank's muddy eyes flared with some unreadable emotion, then hooded, he responded, "Agatha? I don't believe I know anything about an Agatha."

Rachel saw and heard what he said, yet something within her couldn't accept that Agatha was lost to her. Somewhere somebody knew where she was. Rachel would find her, she had to— Sweetwater would never be Sweetwater without her!

THIRTEEN

Andrew Meredith pushed his mount harder as the mid-day sun beat down on both horse and rider. He rode toward Marietta as if escaping from an enemy army. And maybe he was.

He had expended his anger and frustration but now a hoard of unwelcome emotions pursued him as the memory of angry eyes and a shattered life refused to retreat.

His mind told him that he had done the right thing. Obviously temporarily abandoning her was the only solution. Give her time to think. Rachel was a stubborn woman and the only way to make her understand her need was to make her face it. Painful as it might be, she had to come to terms with her predicament. When she realized her future depended on accepting his help, they could begin to build her future. If she let go the past, then he could render the help his heart dictated.

But what if she didn't come to her senses? What if something happened to her way out there? He didn't want to consider that. Maybe he'd send supplies out with the livery when they delivered her luggage and picked up their horse and carriage. He would make sure she had a weapon and food, and then he knew she could survive.

The compromise pacified his heart and he slowed his pace, giving his mount some belated consideration. Slowing to a trot and settling his mind somewhat, freed him to consider the appointments he had waiting for him.

The day before, Goodman had mapped out a plan of action

after they looked through his files. Today Andrew was headed for the Sedgefield Plantation just northwest of Marietta and south of Cartersville. He understood the plantation was small and the proprietor, Mr. Williford, a man of modest means.

Goodman believed that the strongest union sentiment rested in the hearts of the yeoman farmers and smaller plantations in the piedmont and northern regions. That would prove a distinct disadvantage for Andrew since it would pull him farther from home base where his influence might be greatest.

However, Goodman had traveled around the state keeping his ear to the ground. He remained convinced that the hot bed of secessionist fever rested in the elite planters. The coastal aristocracy and the mid-state plantations with their vast holdings of land and slaves would fight hardest to hold on to their way of life.

Goodman readily agreed that Andrew lacked credibility with the middle class. Coming from Savannah with his obvious wealth could provoke both a regional and class resistance to his efforts. But it was a chance he resolved to take. Had his decision been made earlier, he'd have had the time to build a relationship with these strangers. But the editor believed that time was running out. They only had until the presidential election. The outcome would determine the destiny of the South.

Andrew admitted to himself that if he failed in his task, he would have to accept the blame. It was his own procrastination in coming to terms with his conscience that hampered the process. He had waited too long. Refusing to face his responsibility, he had hoped someone else would get the job done. Now maybe it was too late.

However, there were some wealthy transplants in northern Georgia and if they shared his convictions then they could be a valuable resource base. One man, Godfrey Barnsley, lived on a vast plantation, Woodsland, near Rome. His wife, Julia Scarborough, had been a wealthy Savannah socialite but died in mid 1840's.

Meredith didn't know Barnsley personally but had heard of the transplanted Englishman who had made and lost several fortunes in cotton. Goodman was less sure about where Barnsley stood but urged Andrew to search him out.

If he had time this trip, he would search him out, but now his primary goal was to see Thomas Williford. Goodman felt the planter's support would prove vital for any measure of success. He had unionist leanings and had respect and influence in the community and surrounding area. It was up to Andrew to persuade him to use that influence.

If only he could garner enough support for a strong coalition of union sympathizers, then maybe they could head off the fire-eaters. Goodman remained convinced that union sentiment in the state was strong but that the radicals were more vocal. Well he'd see. He understood apathy and he recognized it as their greatest enemy.

Andrew arrived in Marietta around noon and headed straight for the livery stable. He exchanged his horse for a new one, paid Rachel's bill and hurried to Denmead's to order her supplies. He found a used navy colt someone had exchanged for a saddle and he purchased it with a wry smile. He had the clerk load all six cylinders and apply the caps, being careful to place the hammer on the safety pin to guard against accidental discharge. Andrew was confident that would be sufficient for her protection. He returned to the livery stable with the purchases and the proprietor assured him they would deliver the items to Sweetwater before dark.

As an afterthought Andrew ask the puzzled attendant not to mention who had sent them. He hoped she would think it had been Randall; otherwise she might question the strength of his resolve. Then he headed for Wilkie's office.

Disappointment clouded his face as he encountered a locked and empty office. He had needed to alert the attorney to Rachel's predicament and ask him to check on her. More than that he needed the reassurance from another that his plan of action was the right one. The shop keeper next door informed Andrew that Randall had failed to come in, and according to him, that was an uncommon occurrence.

Meredith turned back toward the Fletcher House, weariness and an empty stomach suddenly overcoming him. He knew that a lonely meal would be the only fortification he could expect for the difficult task that awaited him. Resolved to put his personal turmoil aside for the next few days, he entered the dim interior of the familiar hotel.

Meredith swung into the saddle and headed south. His past three days had been hectic. Only time would tell if he had been successful politically, but personally his visit with the Williford family had left him pensive about his own life.

Nothing would satisfy Tom Williford and his wife, Varina, but that he stay with them. The simple bounty placed before him at each meal proved delicious and filling, but it was the genuine hospitality extended him that touched his heart. The whole family accepted and pulled him into their large family as if he were a part of them.

When he observed the warm and gentle repartee between family members and saw the pride lighting Tom's eyes, a longing took root in his heart. Missing in his own life was that feeling of place and the sense of continuance a man had when he looked into the eyes of sons and daughters and knew that his life continued on in theirs.

He realized for the first time what price his quest for material success had really cost him. All his elegance and riches could never equal what Tom Williford had seated at his long table. His strong, stalwart sons responded with respect, his gracious daughters smiled shyly with eyes of love as he teased them lightly and his wife of forty years still gazed at him with adoring eyes.

The first evening, Meredith spent observing Tom and his family. The next day he brought up the subject of politics.

Tom Williford had provided a sympathetic ear. His union sentiments were present but unfocused when Andrew first talked with him. Like Andrew, he had chosen to push his misgivings away, concentrating on providing a living for his large family.

Typical to most northern Georgia landholders he owned only a few slaves, no more than ten. He had three house servants who assisted his pleasant wife in the feeding and caring of his extended family. His family consisted of three daughters and ten sons, some of whom had families of their own. As patriarch of his large brood, he felt the responsibility of his role keenly.

He and his ten sons worked beside the field hands cultivating his small plantation. By hard work and thrifty living they eked out an adequate living but wealth would never be theirs.

Many of their fields were long and narrow, the shape dictated by deep ravines dissecting the land. Other fields were interrupted by large outcroppings of granite rock on hillsides which made planting impossible.

The best soil lay in the rich bottom land bordering the several creeks that crossed the land. It was here, as the Cherokee Indians had only a generation before them, they grew corn. By necessity a large part of it was set aside for their own consumption, but what surplus they had left, they sold or ground in a water-powered grist mill located on one of their fast moving creeks.

Their life was one of toil and at times leanness, but they garnered joy from the simple pleasures of life. Close family ties, all the family lived in the main house or somewhere nearby on the acreage, gave them a sense of community.

But it was their strong faith in God which sustained them. Their lives and activities were rooted in the white washed board church with gothic windows and steeple pointing heavenward. They had built the edifice with their own hands and worked long hours to pay for the bell whose sweet tones were forged in France. It was there they came to rejoice in God's blessings. Within the hallowed walls they pledged their life and love in marriage and it was there that they mourned their loved ones who had gone on before them.

Their plain and simple lifestyle, even the way they worshipped their God had little in common with their elite counterparts in the coastal low country and across the southern "black belt".

Yet they loved the South and cherished her traditions. Being a southerner was their identity but deep in his heart Williford admitted, he struggled with the issue of slavery. Somehow, he felt it was wrong to own another, yet even his own beloved church condoned slavery.

He admitted he could see little wrong with their stand. He treated his slaves like family. Surely they had a better standard of living with him than in some remote jungle in Africa.

And then there was their salvation. Because of slavery, they had given up their pagan gods and served the only true God. He remarked that all of his people worshiped in the same Baptist church he did. Even though they were restricted to the balcony, they were destined for the same heavenly home he was. Yet, his conscious whispered, it was only then that true freedom would be theirs.

Andrew listened intently as the man poured out his heart. Tom Williford unburdened himself to this stranger because he intuitively knew that his guest struggled with the same misgivings.

Finally when he had emptied his heart, his gray eyes looked straight into Andrew's and declared. "Am I a unionist? I believe the South's best course of action is to remain in the Union. Neither I nor my family would ever fight for the preservation of slavery. But if the South secedes and war comes, I know my boys will go. They won't be fighting for slavery but for the South's right to decide her own destiny. When my boys go, I'll do everything in my power to support their role and to preserve their future, but until that time, Mr. Meredith I'll do what I can to preserve the union. Cause when my boys go off to war some of them won't come back and those who do, life as they knew it will be over. Just tell me what you want me to do."

Informal meetings all over the county filled the next two days. Williford carried Andrew to homes and offices of farmers, merchants, clergymen and attorneys. The aging farmer omitted no one he thought might have a sympathetic ear. Some were receptive, some reluctant, only a few proved disinterested.

On the final afternoon, Tom carried Andrew to his small church. He had planned a meeting for the community at large and news of it had spread by word of mouth. Williford felt that if he held the meeting in the church, they would be less likely to encounter a hostile reception.

Surprised, Andrew encountered a large crowd already gathered at the church. Benches had been set up outside the sanctuary and long tables with picnic baskets on them waited beneath the towering tulip poplar trees.

Andrew cast an inquisitive eye toward Tom and the older man chuckled, "Entertainment around here is scarce so they use every opportunity to fellowship. I must warn you though since it is a community wide gathering, you're bound to have some opposition."

Meredith took a deep breath and let it out slowly, "I understand. I've expected it before now. I'll choose my words carefully."

"That's wise. We don't have many fire-eaters up here, but you are at a disadvantage—you're not a local."

Tom Williford mounted the church steps and immediately the buzz of conversation hushed. It was evident that Tom Williford's respect in his home extended to the community at large. Robert Goodman, the publisher, hadn't exaggerated when he said Williford was the key to the area's support.

"We've called this meeting tonight to introduce my new friend, Andrew Meredith from Savannah, to you. He's been visiting in my home for the past three days and I've come to respect him and his point of view. Although he hails from the lowlands of coastal Georgia he has the same concerns we do about what's happening in our nation and state. You'd do me a favor if you would give him a listening ear."

Andrew stepped up on the top step and looked out over his audience. Curiosity brightened most of the female eyes while the men looked wary, inviting him to convince them. He became acutely aware of his finely tailored garments as his eyes took in the bright calico dresses of the women and the homespun simplicity of the working men who sat before him.

His highly polished boots of the softest leather offered a rude contrast to the work brogans that most of the men were wearing. Class distinction prevailed as his audience surveyed him with a critical eye, noting his elegance. He knew in an instant his sole credibility rested on the reputation of Thomas Williford. But at least he had a starting point.

He chose his words with great caution while keeping a warm smile on his face. He complimented the beauty of the area and the work ethic of the people. He praised Tom Williford and thanked him for his hospitality. The women smiled and the men looked only a little less wary. With the sixth sense of a gifted orator Andrew knew that he had crossed his first hurdle successfully.

Then with proper humility, his voice low and persuasive, almost conversational, he explained to them he was only on a fact finding tour. Then with subdued passion, he told them of his fears and hopes for the South and the nation. He assured them that his only purpose was to find others who shared his concerns; he meant no condemnation for those who felt differently. When he had finished he turned to Tom who asked for questions.

The question and answer session went smoothly until finally the questions lagged and an uneasy silence indicated that it was time to adjourn. Just as Tom started to dismiss the crowd to the picnic table where supper waited, a tall man in the back of the crowd stood up. With cold black hair and eyes that matched, he said nothing for a moment, just stared at Andrew. Tom looked from one man to the other, then puzzled asked, "Yes, friend?" Andrew realized with a start that he was a stranger to Tom.

The grizzled bearded man rocked back on his heels, and, hooking his thumbs behind his suspenders, began to speak in a slow, mountain drawl, "I'm not from around here. I've come down to visit my cuzzins, the Gradys." Andrew saw Tom's jaw clinch even as the expression in his eyes never wavered.

The stranger continued. "They couldn't be here tonight. They wuz killin' a hog. That's why I'm here, I brung it to'em." A few in the crowd chuckled and he added, "I see some of you'uns knows what I'm talkin' bout and ye'd be right thanking it ain't the right time of year fo no hog killin', but when yo hungry and that be all ye got, well ye do what ye gotta do. I bet this fancy dressed fellar fillin' our ears with all this high falutin' talk wouldn't know a thang about hog killin' or being hungry, neither."

Tom interrupted, "Mr.?"

"Joe Grady's my name and I'm over to here from Alabama." He explained.

"Well, Mr. Grady, did you have a question? We're just about ready to break for supper and of course you are invited to break bread with us."

"No, sah. Ye ain't ready to eat, yet. Not tills I have my say."

"Very well, have your say. But be brief." Tom's gentle voice held a hint of cold steel.

"I want to know how come it is that this here fellow thinks he's got anythin' in common with the likes of us."

"I'm a man just like you are, Mr. Grady and—," Andrew began.

"Well, ye are dressed like one, but yo fancy words are smooth as snake oil. I want to know do ye raise corn and cotton like we do?"

"Yes."

"Do ye turn the soil and eat the dust behind the back end of a mule from sun up to sun down?"

"Not exactly . . . ,"

"No course ye don't, ye got plenty darkies to do that for ye. And ye don't have to worry ye can't feed yore family if'n it rains yo crop out, neither. My cuzzins woulda starved if'n I hadn't brung that hog to them cauz their winter store wuz gone and harvest time is months away. Ye can't understand that. All ye can think about is who's gonna be President. Whata I care who's president or if'n yore colored folks be free or slaves. That don't concern me none. All that people like me cares about is trying to keep food on the table for our family."

Here and there a few heads nodded in agreement while others watched Tom Williford closely. Andrew started to answer and Tom interrupted.

"You have a point, Joe. When our personal times get painful, we don't have any time or effort to look beyond our own need. I was guilty of that until Mr. Meredith came and he admitted to me that he, too, had been apathetic."

"Apa wha?" Joe asked, his bearded face contorted.

"Not caring, leaving it to someone else to take care of, thinking it won't affect me—you know," Tom's lips parted in a cool smile.

"Yea, and I don't care. Ain't nobody in this room but them what's got a lot to loose need to be bothered. Way I sees it, you and that rich fellow there just wants us pore folks to help you keep what ye got."

"You are wrong there, my friend." Tom persuaded gently only the taunt lines in his jaw revealed the control he was exerting.

"I ain't wrong." then turning to Andrew he demanded, "Tell me what dif'renc it makes to me if'n yore slaves are free or not, if we make our own way outside the Union er stay in it. I ain't got no slaves. I'll still have to work same as always; plowing pore rocky land; trying to make enough to feed me and my wife and chil'ren."

"You have sons?" Andrew asked.

"Shore do," he grinned proudly.

"How many?" Andrew probed quietly.

"Four of 'em if'n it's any of yore concern."

"How old are they, Mr. Grady?"

"They be fourteen, fifteen, sixteen, and eighteen." He added sheepishly looking at the crowd and garnering a growing support, "I woulda had one tween sixteen and eighteen but he up and died of the measles. I gotta passel of li'l gals, too. Pretty but not worth much when it comes to making a living."

"Joe, I don't have any children." Meredith continued, the tone of his voice conciliatory, "And you're right I do have houses and land, servants and slaves to do my bidding. I don't have to worry about providing for my family because in the first place, with the exception of an elderly aunt and a niece, I don't have one. In the second place, I've been blessed with wealth: but I don't have anything to loose compared to what you do if we secede."

"How's that?" Grady growled, his belligerence tempered now with curiosity.

"If the South secedes, we'll go to war," Andrew answered calmly, determined to win this first skirmish.

"Why?"

"Because the North will not allow us to leave."

"Ain't that our right?"

"Whether it's our right or not is not the issue we're dealing with here. You said it didn't affect you. I say it affects you much more than me. If we leave the Union, there will be a war and you'll lose your sons. My risk is small compared to yours. Wealth is replaceable, children aren't."

"Well if'n we went to war, don't mean my boys would have to go," Joe hedged.

"They would be forced to go by conscription. You would, too. Then who would plow your rocky acres? Your wife and girls would or go hungry. Not one soul sitting in this group can say that this issue is not vital to your lives." Andrew took in the whole congregation with his eyes.

Not willing to concede Joe almost shouted, "Ain't a yankee alive that can out shoot my boys."

"Only if they have guns and ammunition with which to fight. We don't have what it takes to arm a fighting force. The North is industrialized, our industry is agriculture. The South cannot win a war and if we leave the Union there will be war." Andrew replied.

Grady sneered, "What is yo real reason for scarin' us. I just bet you own some of them Yankee factories. Do you?"

A low murmur swept around the room before silence curtained it as the crowd moved forward in their seats to hear the answer. Even Tom Williford turned toward Andrew a question in his kind, gray eyes.

"As a matter of fact, I do. I have shipping and ship building company in Boston," Andrew began.

"I know'd ye wuz a Yankee lover. No wonder yore fer the union. Ye jez don wanna lose yo southern business." Grady accused, while the audience sat still and silent mesmerized by the exchange.

"Perhaps it does look like that to you and maybe others in this room."

"Shore do." He looked around the room a victorious smile plastered on his face encouraging others to agree with him. A few heads here and there nodded their agreement.

"Well it isn't true. My wealth will survive whether there is war or not. My heart and my convictions are at stake here. I am a Southerner; my desire is what is best for the South. I am convinced that if we leave the Union it will mean the destruction of all that we hold dear. Our families, our homes, our livelihoods and, for many of us, our lives.

"Well, mister, if yo heart bleeds fo the South so, then why don't ye jest sell yo Yankee holdin's. Then folks come a heap near believin' you."

"Perhaps your right, Mr. Grady. If my northern holdings damage my credibility then I will divest myself of them."

"You'll do what?"

"Get rid of them," Meredith explained.

"When?" Joe Grady pressed.

"As soon as I return home." Andrew replied his eyes holding Grady's.

Grady, like a young bully unwilling to acknowledge defeat, dropped his eyes and sat down with one parting shot, "I don' believe ye. Come back when ye do, Maybe then I'll take a listen."

Andrew smiled stiffly, "Like I said at the beginning, I came to listen and to share my observations."

Pausing he looked at the faces starring up into his. Some agreeing, more doubtful. The task he had before him seemed impossible and for a moment, he struggled with the temptation to give up, to let someone else try. The cost was going to be too high. But suddenly a great burden seemed to settle on his shoulders as he imagined what their future held.

As if compelled by an inner conviction he could no longer contain, he explained, "You're free to believe what you wish, but I am convinced that my role is to make people aware of what's ahead. Anything less and I would fail myself, my country and, most of all, my God."

A hush fell over the audience as no heart seemed immuned to the sincerity of his plea. Tom Williford's gray eyes fastened on him first in amazement, then with understanding and approval.

No one in the room was more surprised at Andrew's response than he. Andrew Meredith, like most men in the South, called himself a

Christian. But unlike some he had a clear cut understanding of a point in time when he had settled his eternal destiny.

At the age of sixteen, he received his salvation in the storm tossed hole of a ship. An Irish evangelist had led him to place his faith in Jesus Christ and that night was forever etched in his memory.

Because of that commitment, strong Christian ethics and good morals ruled his personal and, later, his business life. But until that moment he had been unaware that God had an intimate interest in his life beyond dictating his personal values system.

He had never considered that the God who forgave him might have a special purpose for his life. He had devoted his life to hard work and amassing a fortune.

Now all that he had accomplished and all that he possessed seemed inconsequential as he faced the sea of faces before him. They appeared as defenseless lambs waiting for slaughter, ignorant of what was to come. Suddenly a sense of responsibility toward them and others like them transcended anything that he had ever encountered and in that instant Andrew Meredith's life was unalterably changed. He knew that whatever the cost or sacrifice might be to him personally, he had been commissioned a watchman called to warn his people.

FOURTEEN

Robert Goodman, with a journalist's keen eye saw the new determination in Andrew Meredith's eyes, the firm set of his jaw and he knew this was not the same man who had ridden out of Marietta three days before.

After they talked, he understood the Meredith who had left his office earlier was a man on a mission, the one who returned had received a divine commission to which he had dedicated himself, whatever the cost.

The editor was jubilant. Imagine a man so committed, he vowed he'd give up part of his holdings for the sake of credibility. Now that was the true test of commitment—a man's willingness to sacrifice.

He had hoped for a long time someone would catch the vision, would understand the importance. Never in a thousand years would he have dreamed that the wealthy Mr. Andrew Meredith would be his crusader. But what better choice. The intelligent and articulate man had become the impassioned one. Along with wealth and influence what more could he ask for? Talk about miracles.

The rotund editor frowned midway through his jubilance. As great as his attributes were, he had some major hurdles. First of all his work in Savannah would prove frustrating. Too many of his cohorts wanted nothing if not secession and war. He'd be wasting his time talking to them. Crazy lunatics, the Lord himself couldn't talk sense into them. But then who would ever thought Andrew Meredith would . . .? Suddenly Goodman believed in miracles.

As to the problems facing Meredith, the biggest was that young colored woman. Andrew needed to ditch her. That girl surely was a mystery. Up here mystery wouldn't outweigh the outrage. That kind of thing didn't set well. People were straight laced. They didn't cotton to even the appearance of evil.

Couldn't say he blamed them. He tried to walk the straight and narrow himself. He'd found out the hard way, God's laws were for his protection, not restriction. Yep, he'd tried it both ways and the straight and narrow made life easier and a lot more fun. That wasn't to say Meredith didn't, but it just had the wrong look about it and people were too quick to make up their own minds when he never offered an explanation.

Goodman decided he'd have to tell him the situation but he dreaded it. He'd heard that was one subject Andrew Meredith could prove a might testy on.

Like it or not, he'd have to deal with it. Maybe on the coast those big plantation folk with lots of slaves winked at that kind of goings on, whatever it was, but not up here. Slaves were slaves and they knew their place; and if they ever won their freedom, they'd still know their place. It was a long way from the quarters to the big house and North Georgia planters didn't take that hike.

If any did, they were ostracized in society. No, his man had to be beyond reproach and that little gal would have to go. What Andrew needed was to get married to a nice North Georgia girl. Then folk would forget and forgive those Savannah rumors. The portly publisher smiled as a list of prospects danced in his head. Preferably one with land. Not too much, just enough to make him acceptable in the community.

Robert Goodman leaned back from his cluttered desk, pushed his visor up and patted his pot belly, grinning like a Cheshire cat. Finally he had a committed disciple.

Andrew exchanged his exhausted mount for another and told the livery man that he was shipping two horses to be stabled there. He expected them to arrive the following week. Expecting to make frequent trips to Marietta and the surrounding area, he wanted to make sure he had a decent mount. If Andrew Meredith enjoyed anything in life it was a fine horse. If he detested anything it was a poor one.

His experiences with the livery stable so far had left a great deal to be desired. From now on he'd see to it that he had his own. He would leave an extra in case Rachel should need one.

He thought of her at Balmara when he had come upon her unawares during an early morning ride. He had paused to watch her ride, marveling at her horsemanship. When he had caught up with her, her shining eyes told him that they shared an appreciation for fine horses. She told him that she had loved horses as a girl but it was only after she went to Europe that she came to appreciate fine horses.

When she came to her senses, he would ship some of Balmara's finest stock to Sweetwater. He had a hunch this climate would be more suitable than the coastal lowlands for a breeding farm.

Suddenly Rachel exploded in his mind. Andrew had little time to worry over her these last few days although fleeting thoughts of her teased his memory now and again but his journey to self-discovery had not included her. Now sure of his direction and calm in his determination, she returned to haunt him.

Worry and hope picked up his pace and he pressed his horse onward sharply. How had she managed in the interim he had been away? He chuckled. He had no worry as to her safety, once she had that weapon he had sent.

He had no doubt she could use it. She had told him her father had taught her to shoot. Suddenly the memory of her defiant magnificence on the Savannah Riverfront flooded his mind driving out everything else. He laughed aloud. Who in their right mind would approach her if she had a weapon? Rachel definitely was not a wilting violet. While he admired her courage and boldness, her independent spirit proved a thorn in his side. It seemed to delight in frustrating his plans, his plans for good and not for evil, as she so insisted.

His laughter turned to pensive consideration. He prayed she was safe, yet he hoped her three day experience had been unpleasant enough to make her reasonable. How could it have been anything else? She only had enough supplies to sustain her. Without manual labor, her living conditions would be barely tolerable. Sweetwater needed total refurbishing and major repairs. She had neither the money nor man power to do it. Even she would have to admit the job was beyond her without help. And help was exactly what Andrew Meredith had to offer. But on his terms, because they were the best for her.

His horse slowed some as it mounted the last steep grade before the road leveled off and joined the creek road. Andrew glanced at the moderate sized white clap-board house nestled among tall maples with a dirt yard swept neat and clean. The friendly middle-aged couple rocking on the broad front porch waved a friendly hello and Andrew made a mental note to ask Rachel about them. They might prove helpful to her in the days to come, especially if they had known her when she was a child.

Meredith had an uneasy feeling as the thought of her neighbors brought Walter Banks to mind. Knowing the man's determination for power and prestige, he wondered what kind of problems he would present to Rachel. If it hadn't been for Walter Banks Rachel might not be in the position she's in, he mused. Then shook his head. The blame lay solely at Adam Gregory's door; Walter Banks just took advantage of the situation. But that would not happen again. Now he'd have to deal with Andrew Meredith—that is, if Rachel had come to her senses.

The distant roar of the rapids announced Sweetwater Creek and despite his outward calm, Andrew's pulse accelerated. He turned the corner and rushed toward his destination. Finally the long maple lane came into view and his heart lurched in anticipation. How would he find her? Penitent and agreeable? Had she come to terms with the past so that she could believe and trust him? Surely three days of solitude would bring her to her senses, but then again there was always the chance that it hadn't. If she chose to cling to her past and refused to accept the truth then he knew she would heap the blame on him. Making him helpless to assist her.

The house loomed just ahead. The sun blinded him and he could only see the angled lines outlined in radiance. He rushed forward eager to see her. How would she receive him? Enemy or rescuer?

The drive shifted to the left revealing the front of the house. A handsome roan stallion foraged for grass beneath the hitching post where he was loosely tied. The debris that had littered the yard was missing and the old house looked cleaner, lived in.

Puzzled, Andrew looked about him and then peered behind the house where three black men were hammering on the loose boards that had been hanging on the side of the barn. He noted that repairs had been made to the house as well and apprehension darkened his eyes. Obviously Rachel was even more resourceful than he had given her credit. But she couldn't have managed alone, maybe Randall?

Just as he reached the hitching post and dismounted, the door opened and Rachel stepped out onto the front porch. Dressed in a simple calico covered with a muslin apron, without hoops or crinoline, she looked like any ordinary housewife. Her hair was pulled up in a severe topknot with wisp of it escaping here; the curls damp from perspiration caressed her neck and framed her face. Her rolled up sleeves and homespun apron verified that she had been hard at work. On closer inspection, he noticed that the long jib windows facing the porch were so clean he could see the parlor now set to rights.

"Miss Rachel seems that you've been hard at work. The place is looking better," he commented pleasantly while he grappled with the mystery.

"It's not what I remember, but all I need is a little time and it will," she answered through tight lips, her eyes like ice.

A dull ached grew somewhere in the middle of Andrew's chest as he saw the coldness in her eyes. He walked toward the porch, his heart like a lead weight.

His plan had failed. He didn't know why or how, but it had and now he fully understood the risk he had taken. All she needed was time! TIME? What about resources?

"It's going to take a little more than time, I'm thinking but we've already been through that I believe." He responded pleasantly as he paused below her at the bottom of the steps.

"And that's why you're back, I imagine."

"Yes, it's been three days." He placed one dusty boot on the bottom step.

"And you always keep your word—to a woman or a dying man," she snapped.

"I endeavor to," he replied evenly, but his eyes wary.

"Especially if it's in your best interest."

"Are we going to rehash that again?" he asked, this time irritation tinged his voice.

"The truth nettles."

"Not the truth, Miss Rachel. It's your refusal to face it that is our problem." He stood where he was, not daring to approach her, not wanting to.

"Oh, I've faced it and all my suspicions have been confirmed," Rachel replied, the icy aloofness melting into anger.

"Then you've gotten the wrong information from somewhere. I told you the truth!" He exclaimed, frustration raising his voice.

"About what?" She demanded

"Everything! Your father, the mill, Sweetwater plantation." He lifted his hands in exasperation. "But I'm not here to argue with you. I came for your answer. Believe what you will, I need to get home."

"My answer is no, no, no."

"And you my dear will suffer grievous consequences if you choose to be so foolish." He warned.

"Are you threatening me, Mr. Meredith?"

"Of course not, just a friendly warning. I don't want to have to pick up the pieces when your stubbornness tears your life apart."

"Don't even consider the possibility. As soon as you're out of my life, I can start putting it back together."

"How?" he puzzled, "Did you discover a buried treasure?"

"No, something more precious than that. I discovered a true friend to me and to my father before me. Someone who wants to help me keep what was mine, not take it from me."

"And who, may I ask, is this generous benefactor?"

"The very one you maligned!"

"I haven't —" he protested.

"Walter Banks, my neighbor."

"WALTER BANKS?" he all but shouted.

"Yes. He has loaned me the money and sent the manpower over here for me to reclaim Sweetwater."

He shook his head wearily, "Rachel, that man is your enemy. He will destroy you and take away everything that is dear to you."

"I think that is quite enough, Meredith," spoke a high pitched voice behind Rachel as the door opened and Walter Banks stepped out of the shadows.

Andrew ignored Banks and looked up into Rachel's eyes, his pleading, "Rachel, don't do this. You'll regret this decision the rest of your life. If my plan didn't suit you we'll find another. Just don't be deceived by this man. He took what was rightfully yours from your father and he's going to destroy you."

Banks slowly extended the arm he held down by his side, and Andrew Meredith looked squarely up the barrel of the navy colt revolver he had sent to Rachel. A metallic click parted the air as Walter Banks cocked it, and readied it to fire with the slightest touch of his index finger.

His voice cold and threatening, deepened, "Meredith, the lady said, 'no' and I'm telling you to leave. One touch of this trigger and your wearisome face won't be seen around these parts anymore. Ain't a jury in the county would convict me, protecting this little lady like I am."

Andrew's eyes slid up the barrel of the gun and fastened on the yellow, bilious ones challenging his.

Like a person detached from reality and observing from afar Rachel watched in horror the scene unraveling before her. In her heart she knew that Banks would kill Andrew Meredith, given the slightest provocation. Something in his expression told her that he would welcome the opportunity. She jerked her head toward Andrew and in that moment fingers of admiration pierced the hate and anger bounding her heart toward him as she looked into his eyes which showed only courage and a certain strange fearlessness.

"Shoot if you wish. My life is not in your hands, Banks, but in God's," he challenged then turned toward Rachel, boldness changed to sadness. "Believe me, Rachel, I never wanted anything but your good. Take care, my dear, you're in treacherous waters."

With those words he turned his back on the pair and walked unhurriedly to his waiting mount while tiny seeds of doubt peppered the deep recesses of Rachel's heart.

FIFTEEN

April skipped into May in a blur of activity for Rachel. True to his word Banks sent several slaves back to her and loaned her money. She wasn't sure how much and she had an uneasy feeling in the pit of her stomach. She wanted something definite but as yet he had forestalled any accounting.

Walter Bank's had lived up to her every expectation. He anticipated her every need in advance and met it. When she needed something he paid for it. When she protested he said they would settle up later, assuring her that her frugality had impressed him. And in all his help he remained the perfect gentleman.

Not knowing exactly what she had to work with or what liabilities she might be incurring kept her uneasy so she did without everything but what was essential. Her diet and that of her slaves was limited, to cornbread, pickled pork, dried fish, eggs and occasionally greens but she never complained.

Hard manual work along with her restricted diet caused her to lose weight. Her cheekbones became prominent and her green eyes appeared even larger in her thin face. But she never noticed. Her life was too busy surviving to worry about what she wore or how she looked. She discovered some homespun dresses that Agatha had worn and wore them to work in. They proved more comfortable without need of hoop or crinoline. And they were easier to laundry.

Andrew's niece's fine clothing hung in the tall walnut armoire along with Rachel's purchases shipped without comment from

Savannah. At first she would occasionally caress the fine fabric longingly as she opened the wardrobe to find her brogans, then finally they lost their enticement. Now untouched for weeks they hung as a monument to the new direction her life had taken.

Her world consisted of intense labor from sun up to sundown. Her primary objective remained fixed in her mind to rescue the only thing in her life that mattered, Sweetwater. At whatever the cost, no sacrifice seemed too much.

For the first crucial weeks, the only faces she saw were black except for a daily visit from Banks. And his meant no more than theirs. She ceased to think of him as a man, to her, he had become only an essential element in achieving her goal. So she gave little thought to her appearance or how she might impress him.

Always clean and neat, with her hair bound in a tight chignon and often covered with a broad straw hat, she received him in work clothes. And it was so that the realities of life dealt with any lingering superficial pride she might have had exchanging it for character and purpose. And in the exchange her beauty intensified.

Walter Banks' scheme proceeded on schedule, but the daily contact with her fire and beauty drove him to an impatience he could barely conceal.

His visits became a daily ritual. He came to inspect the outside work, have a word with the slaves, then join Rachel on the porch for a cup of tea. He'd have preferred something stronger in a more intimate environment, but he had a role to play and he dedicated himself to it. He relished the time when he could put pretense aside and Rachel would be his possession, but for the meanwhile the charade continued with Rachel the dupe, willingly blinded by her fixation with Sweetwater.

The work force he had provided at first was far smaller than she needed, but she did as most North Georgia planters who lacked the large labor forces of further south, she made do with what she had. Most were Sweetwater slaves and before long she felt at ease with them. The first two weeks they repaired the house and essential outbuildings. She left the ramshackle overseer's cottage for later and did little cosmetic improvements to Sweetwater Manor because she felt the need to conserve her resources.

Getting the house clean and livable brought a superficial joy to Rachel as it restored the sense of belonging she had lost. Her heart rejoiced in being home while her hectic physical pace forestalled the nagging doubts that plagued her since Andrew Meredith walked out of her life.

She could ill afford to waste her energy in grappling with the thoughts that teased her mind the day he left. Acknowledging she might be wrong would mean he really had her best interests at heart. That could open a Pandora's Box of implications concerning the intentions of the man who had come to her rescue. And she had penned her hopes on him.

Since her peace of mind demanded that she believe her assessment of Andrew Meredith had been correct, she cocooned her doubts and inner warnings in layers of denial until finally the whisper of her conscience fell silent.

Just before May exited, Banks hired an overseer and brought a wagon load of his own field hands to prepare her fields for their precious seeds. Planting was about a month late, but he assured her cotton needed warm earth to grow, and the warmer weather would give them a boost. Perhaps if they received sufficient rain and the weather stayed hot, there might be a chance for her crop to make it. The timing couldn't have been better as far as available labor force was concerned. His cotton had been in the ground three weeks so he had laborers to spare.

As to what they would do when harvest time came nearly 200 hundred days later when she had so few laborers of her own and his would be busy in his own fields she shuddered considering it. Then she told herself that everything had worked out so far and she refused to borrow trouble.

The afternoon Banks brought the new overseer over and the events that soon followed were forever etched in her mind. Each time the memory returned, apprehension plagued Rachel.

That afternoon a tall, massive man rode into her yard on a fine looking paint next to Banks. His narrow face and sallow complexion looked strange atop his muscular bulk as it swaggered in the fine tooled leather saddle. His wide-brimmed straw hat, curled up on one side revealing yellow, straw colored hair, sat low on his forehead and shaded piercing eyes set too close together. They gave one the feeling they observed everything, cataloguing it for future reference. A beak-like nose curled over thin lips that looked as if they'd never smiled.

Banks introduced Sam Pritchett to Rachel and when his probing eyes took her in from head to toe a chill she couldn't deny ran down her spine and she shivered in the warm summer sun. Pritchett gave her a knowing look, his face almost cracked in a sly smile, but not quite. Banks had engaged him as her overseer explaining that planting time had come and almost gone so time was of greatest essence.

Rachel agreed despite her misgivings, knowing that it was past time to get those precious seeds in the ground. For when those seeds bore fruit, its harvest would set her free! All of Sweetwater would be hers at last and she would have to depend on the generosity of no one.

The next morning, Pritchett arrived just at daybreak and a wagon full of slaves followed with several teams of mules bringing up the rear. Banks had loaned some of his best hands to do the plowing. Before the week was out, the smell of fresh turned earth greeted Rachel as she stepped to the back door and surveyed the activities going on behind and on each side of her house.

Gone were the tangled vines and briers that dominated the fields when she arrived. Instead neat furrows of manicured crimson soil cradled the hope of her tomorrows.

Down toward the small creek rushing to meet Sweetwater, her workman cleared several acres of new ground to be planted. She recognized the risk in using flood plain for planting, but she took it knowing that bottom land was the most fertile, able to produce the greatest yields.

One evening she awoke to gentle rain pattering on the roof and smiled knowing each rain drop gently nourished a thirsty seed.

She walked the fields, searching for the first tiny plant to burst forth. The morning after the first shower, she found tiny stems peeping timidly through the earth. Everywhere she looked rows of green met her eyes and she rejoiced.

Walter Banks found her, kneeling in the dirt beside a row, hands and dress stained. "Miss Rachel, what in the world are you doing out here? You are ruining yourself in that dirt. You shouldn't be walking in this plowed field this way,"

Rachel laughed, "You sound like, Agatha."

A shadow passed over his face, "What?"

"Agatha, my servant. She always rebuked me for my unlady like ways."

"I never meant you were unladylike. What I meant was you shouldn't be walking around in this plowed field. Those workers might get the wrong idea."

"This is my land, this is the only way I can see it. And I will oversee what is going on here," Rachel snapped.

Banks crooned, "Of course you will. I just hate to see you wearing yourself out like this. I only wish you would allow me to do more to assist you."

"You can! I want you to set up an accounting. I need some idea of what my liability is going to be. Thus far I have no idea how much you've spent."

"Now, Miss Rachel, Mr. Pritchett and I are going to take care of that. You don't need to worry your pretty head over at all."

"Nevertheless, I want you to go over the accounts with me."

"Well I have with Sam."

"Sam doesn't have to pay you back."

"Of course, you're quite right, my dear. I don't want you unduly concerned about your debts to me," he laughed, "I won't charge you much interest."

"Tomorrow then?" Rachel insisted.

"If you insist." He conceded.

The next afternoon Banks arrived, leading a beautiful golden palomino mare with ivory points and flecks of gold glistening in her burnished coat. A snow-white mane rippled in the gentle breeze as she raised her head and flared her nostrils, reflecting her proud Arabian ancestry. As if sensing Rachel's admiration, she arched her neck and her tail, prancing around on coal black hooves.

"To whom are you delivering that exquisite creature?" She asked, an ill-concealed longing in her eyes.

"To the exquisite lady standing before me," Banks declared a sly grin parting his face. For the first time his tone held a hint of familiarity, but Rachel, too entranced with what her eyes beheld, failed to notice. However, Banks noticed that he had gone unrebuked and took heart.

"For me? You know I can't afford a horse like this. I was thinking to ask you if you had any grade horses I might buy, but this one—." She sighed her face sheathed in the first genuine smile he had ever seen and she dazzled him.

"It's a gift." He said softly.

"You know I could never accept a gift like that from you," Rachel said, a frown erasing the smile as reality crashed in.

"And why not?" Banks insisted.

"Because it wouldn't be proper." Rachel argued.

"Who would know?"

"You and I."

"I figured you'd say that, so I'll make a deal with you. Suppose you just pay me for her when your crop comes in," Banks persuaded.

"I wouldn't be able to afford her then either." Rachel protested half-heartedly.

"Sure you would. Since she is a palomino I won't be breeding her so that greatly decreases her value. Anyway, I'd be willing to carry part of the debt another year."

His reminder jarred Rachel back to reality, "Mr. Banks, what I've been working for is to be free of all entanglements. As beautiful as that mare is, she isn't worth staying in debt for. Thanks, but no thanks." Rachel tried to turn before he could observe the unabashed yearning in her eyes.

But he had seen and pressed his advantage as he tied the mare to the hitching post, "I understand, Miss Rachel, believe it or not I've been there before myself. Tell you what. Suppose I just loan her to you. She needs exercising everyday and you need a horse to ride your fields so I'll loan her to you. When your crops come in, if you can afford her I'll sell her to you for a fair price."

Rachel walked around the hitching post and placed a hand on the horse's muscular flank. "What's this lovely lady's name?"

"Sundance."

"Yes—what else would it be!" Rachel smiled as the sunlight caught the golden flecks in her coat, turning her iridescent. Brushed and groomed, Sundance felt like velvet to her fingertips as she ran them along the mare's back. Rachel looped both arms around her neck and Sundance whinnied, turning her small well- shaped head toward her new friend. When the palomino reached down and nuzzled her, the last bastion of Rachel's studied resistance melted.

"I guess I could do that. She does need exercising and I do need a horse."

"Sure you could."

"Sounds too good to be true. I've really wanted something to ride." Rachel agreed, her will power crumbling.

"You've really needed something. Pardon me for saying it Miss Rachel, but it don't look seemly you walking around the fields like you do."

"Why? What do you mean by that?" Rachel puzzled.

"You're the mistress of this place and you need to look at your slaves from the advantage of a saddle."

Rachel's brow wrinkled. He rushed on to explain. "If you deal with your people when you're down on their level it causes them to forget their place."

"Why that's the most ridiculous thing I've ever heard," she protested.

"No ma'am. I've been in this business a long time, and if there's anything I know about it's how to get the most out of my people. You just gotta keep 'em in their place, that's all there is to it. That's why some folks worry all the time about insurrections. They got slack about discipline and their place. Some of them even let their people learn to read. Taught them right in the classroom with their own chil'ren, didn't matter to them it was against the law. Sure enough they get high falutin ideas and the next thing you know they were trying to take over. I say just keep them in their place and they'll be happier and so will we."

Rachel stared at Banks intrigued, "So that's how it's done, huh?"

"Yes ma'm, that's how it's done." Banks nodded his head.

"Well, Papa never mentioned anything like that. He just taught us to treat them well and they would reward us with loyalty and hard work."

"Miss Rachel, your Pa was the finest man I knew. And kindhearted, too, but the workers I got from him didn't want to work. Took me a few weeks to get them in the groove,"

"And how did you do that?" Rachel probed, her curiosity peaked.

Walter Banks smiled benevolently, "Just had to remind them where their place was and what was expected from them. That's what I want you to do. We don't want them to regress, now do we?"

"I don't remember ever having any problems on our place when I was growing up," Rachel disagreed.

"You probably were too young to remember," Banks countered.

"There has been none that I know of since I returned home," Rachel reminded.

"That's cause of Sam. He's a good man."

"I suppose so. But I had no problems before he came," Rachel objected.

"They knew I'd be coming everyday," Banks said, expanding his chest and rocking back on his heels.

Rachel abruptly changed the subject as a strange uneasiness stirred her, "Did you bring your records so that we can see what I'm going to owe you?"

"As a matter of fact I did." Banks confirmed as he reached into his saddle bag. "

Walter Banks left a stunned young woman when he had ridden away from Sweetwater in the gathering twilight. His figures for repairs and planting appeared astronomical to Rachel. When he factored in what she would need until harvest along with the mortgage already due in December, she knew that she needed a miracle.

That night sleep refused to come and when it did, she dreamed of Andrew Meredith. His eyes filled with sadness stared into hers as his voice spoke words of warning. She awakened and punched her pillow with clinched fists. Finally when day broke, she came to terms with her anxiety. She would work and not worry. Sweetwater would be hers one way or another.

June rushed into July and fortune smiled on Rachel. The proper mix of sunshine and rain nurtured the cotton and corn. As they raised their stems heavenward, it looked as if Sweetwater would have a bumper crop. Maybe a miracle stood between the neatly plowed rows of cotton and corn. Her spirits soared.

Each morning just after dawn, she was in Sundance's saddle checking her fields. It was almost as if she could measure overnight growth. The conversation with Banks about her position among the field hands gave her food for thought. His obvious success with his own labor force gave credence to his argument and she refused to be closed minded toward any productive suggestion. So she observed the workers.

Some of them were Sweetwater people and some came from Pine Ridge. The first thing she noticed was the silence that cloaked her fields like a heavy mantel. Not even the normal friendly give and take of conversation reached her ears.

On similar early morning rides with her father she remembered broad white smiles parting black faces as they greeted them and joked among each other. Then someone would begin a spiritual and as others joined in, it reverberated across the field like a rising tide. But no singing lightened her laborers' load; they bent their backs to toil in fields as quiet as a tomb.

When Sam Pritchett rode his paint row by row, with a riding crop perched in front of him, all hands kept eyes averted, acknowledging neither Pritchett nor Rachel as they rode by.

One morning in mid July, the air lay heavy, the stifling heat more like August. A sudden flash of lightning parted the sky and the ground shook with rolling thunder. Black eyes rolled in terror as some dropped their hoes and ran toward their quarters. Pritchett whirled his mount and intercepted them as another flash of light pierced the sky. His horse reared as did Rachel's but both kept their seats and Pritchett shouted at the workers to return to their work.

All but one returned even while looking fearfully toward the heavens. A young girl not more than fifteen and slender as a willow reed, dropped to her knees where she stood and put her head in the dirt covering her ears with her hands and wailing loudly.

The overseer was out of his saddle and standing over her before Rachel could reach him. The riding crop made a whistling noise as it cut the air and bit into the thin garment covering the young girl's shoulders. He raised his small whip even higher for the second lash when Rachel arrived just in time to grab his hand. The force of it jerked her off her horse but deflected the second blow from reaching the young slave.

Pritchett looked at Rachel; a cold loathing chilled his eyes. Fury engulfed Rachel almost blinding her as she jerked the crop from his calloused hand. "You come to the house," she commanded her voice low and threaded with steel.

"Directly, Ma'am." He challenged, his voice oily and confident. "When I've finished here, Miss Rachel."

"You're finished now, Mr. Pritchett. Get your belongings and leave."

"You're mistaken Ma'am. I take my orders from Mr. Banks and he told me to look after you." An arrogant smile turned one corner of his mouth up as his eyes slid over her and he added, "And that's what I aim to do."

Rachel shivered in the morning heat. "You work for me. You'll do as I say,"

Pritchett chuckled as one who knows he has the upper hand,

"Not as I see it. It's Mr. Banks' money that's paying me, it's Mr. Banks' money that's buying the seed and feeding these darkies. It's even Mr. Banks' money that pays for your food and the soap that washes that pretty skin. Far as I'm concerned he owns you just like he does these workers 'cause come December this land you call yours will be Walter Banks, too and so will you."

"I will?" She repeated shaken.

He threw back his head, an evil, shrieking laughter rolled from this throat, "That's right cause ain't no way this little crop gonna get you out of debt. Mr. Banks is depending on that."

"Walter Banks told you that?" Rachel shouted, her face ashen.

Pritchett's smile broadened in victory as he leaned over putting his face close to Rachel and whispered, "Why'd you think he hired me? To see to it that come December you ain't got no other choice unless you wanna become one of those fancy women down in Atlanta."

The crop whistled through the air as Rachel lashed him across his face, leaving an ugly red cut across his cheek.

Black rage exploded in Pritchett and unleashed his boiling hatred of women. Choosing to forget the eyes that watched and disregarding the carefully orchestrated plans of Walter Banks, he reached for the woman who stood before him.

His long muscular arms grabbed Rachel by the shoulders and shook her until her head bobbed like a torn rag doll, then his hands moved around her throat picking her up by her head, his thumbs wedged beneath her chin. The chain that held her mother's locket dug into her neck as he twisted it with his fingers. Then he moved her up until her wide staring eyes looked straight into his beady ones. He whispered through clinched teeth, that no woman could do to him what she had and live to tell about it.

His fingers closed around her windpipe and Rachel's life passed before her eyes. With blinding clarity she realized that he could kill her and survive. The innocent eyes that watched in horror would take the blame. The law would execute them for the crime Sam Pritchett committed. Just as her eyes closed and he squeezed the last ounce of breath from her, his grimy hands suddenly released their hold, dropping her. She fell limp and gasping for breath in the soft earth as Sam Pritchett pitched forward, his massive body penning her to the tender plants beneath her.

She pushed against the dead weight that pressed down on her, finally struggling out from under her burden. A crimson, sticky substance soiled her hands where she had pushed against his limp form. The blood oozed from a deep gash in the overseer's parted skull and dripped on her dress, staining it. She shuddered and wiped her hands in the dirt and looked up into the frightened eyes of the young girl, a hoe in her hand, "I didn't kilt 'im did I Ma'am?"

Rachel reached out hesitantly and touched Pritchett's neck, then gingerly searched for a pulse that wasn't there. Terror seized Rachel, as she turned back to the frail servant and slowly nodded.

SIXTEEN

A sea of dark faces crowded around Rachel and only the whistling wind broke the silence. Then a forlorn whimper burst from the young girl and pandemonium broke out.

The low mournful wail penetrated Rachel's stupor as she commanded the young woman, "Hush, it was only an accident. You didn't mean to do it. You saved my life, he would have killed me. We'll tell the authorities and that will be the end of it."

A young man stepped forward, his ebony form tall and sinewy, and drew the young slave into his powerful embrace. She clung to him, the moans turning to silent sobs that racked her body. Rachel recognized the young man as one of Sweetwater people but his little friend belonged to Banks. His intelligent face and strong body marked him as a man of great value."

"Ma'm you can' tell no 'ffcials wha happent here. "

"Well, I have to, but it'll be a simple case of self-defense."

"Ma'am", he dropped his head in a respectful gesture, a pleading in his eyes, "If'n you kilt him, twould be, but not wid Lizzie killin' him."

"I can see little difference, she defended me . . . ."

"Heap big dif'rence ma'm. Lizzie be colored."

"What's that got to do with it? They'll have my word."

"First place if one of us touches a white person, theys lynched wid out no trial. That Marse Banks and Pritchett, they be head of the slave squad and all the peoples on it bees their friends. My Lizzie ain't got a chance." His arm gripped the young girl tighter and Rachel saw he loved her.

"Well what other choice do I have? We have a dead man here. He stays at Mr. Banks plantation and I'm sure they converse every night. It isn't as if he won't be missed. And besides you expect me to cover up a crime?"

"Well, Miz Rachel, if'n Lizzie hadn't done what she done, ya wudn' have to be a makin' no decision lak that, now wuds ya?"

Truth erased any tinge of insolence from his statement and Rachel's heart pounded, panic bubbling inside of her

"Well what do you suggest?" Mistress asked slave, white asked black, the educated sought wisdom from the uneducated and in that moment of need, a bond formed.

"Ya let me handle it, Miz Rachel. Jest don' say nothin' to the authorities and gives us a little time. Why don' ch'a go visitin' today? You ain't been off'n this place since you come. We'll takes care of everythin' and when theys ask you where is Mr. Pritchett, ya can answer truth ya don't know. Now ya go on up to the house."

"What are you going to do?"

"Gonna perteck Lizzie, but ya don' be needin' to know hows we gonna do dat."

"If you run away, you'll be caught and brought back, and then you'll both be hung for sure." Rachel protested.

"Is yo gonna send after us, Miz Rachel?" his eyes holding hers.

"Of course not, you mentioned the slave patrols yourself," Rachel snapped, her nerves on edge.

A sly smile parted his face, relieving for a moment the stern heaviness that bound it. "Don't ch'a worry about that none, Miz Rachel. I knows how to care fo my sweet Lizzie. Now I ken marry her."

Rachel puzzled, "Why haven't you married her before now?"

"I didn't want none of my chilrin' belongin' to Marse Banks so I wudn't marry Lizzie at all. He's a wicked man."

Icy fingers of fear clutched Rachel's heart. The young worker's words reminded her that she too, was in bondage to Walter Banks, placed there by her own willfulness and pride. Suddenly she wanted to give these young people a chance she didn't have, a chance to be free. "All right, what's your name?" she asked.

"Samuel ma'am. Like the young prophet. My mammy gave me to de Lord like his ma did. She tol' me to listen out fo His voice maybe He mought speak to me lik'n He done to the Bible Samuel. He do speaks to my heart some."

Rachel smiled despite her misery, "And did He tell you what we're to do now?"

Samuel big dark eyes stared solemnly into hers as he answered, "I don't rightly be a knowin' if'n it be de Lawd or my heart, but me and Lizzie we got to run fo it."

Rachel responded, "What do you propose to do?"

"If'n you goes a visitin' then nobody will be comin' round to ast bout that Pritchett and dat'll give us some time. We gonna takes one ob de mules and Pritchett's horse so's it won't run back to Marse Banks place. That'll give us time to git away. Since we staying over heah now, Marse Banks won' miss us'n til dey find Pritchett's body. By dat time we'll be safe."

"Safe— Where?"

"Miz Rachel, we's cain't ev'n tell ya dat. Den we mought not be safe."

"What about the patrol and their dogs?"

He smiled, "Jest trust me. All ya's have to do is let nature take its course. When dey's find de body, then dey'll see who's missin', after dat dey'll start looking fo me and Lizzie."

"Will you come back, Samuel?"

"No'm I cain't, if'n I jest take Lizzie to a safe place and leaves her, den come back, den all our peoples be punished. Nobody believe dis little one could a kilt dat big monster. This' a'way, they'll thank I kilt him."

Rachel sighed, and stole a look at the grotesque figure sprawled in the field, "Whatever you think best. As soon as you get ready to leave, come to the house I'll have something for you."

Samuel replied, "I druther not come back to de house, Miz Rachel, case Marse Banks comes around."

Rachel nodded her head, "I'll come to the quarters as soon as I clean up."

Samuel added, "And Miz Rachel. Yo best brung dat dirty dress yo be wearing. We need to burn it."

Rachel looked down at the large brown stains and shuddered, "Of course," and vowed to end her practice of wearing Agatha's homespun. She'd never be able to look at one of them again without seeing the dark spots.

Mid morning had arrived before Rachel let herself out the back door and made her way toward the slave quarters, a paper in her hand. No longer dressed in homespun, an exquisite riding habit of cinnamon velvet graced her figure and her hair lay in soft coils beneath her hat.

She had taken great pains with her bath and toilet. The simple farm woman who had entered the dilapidated house emerged from it as a moth from a cocoon, beautifully groomed and ready to rejoin society. Such was her mission for the day.

Her horse stood saddled and readied for her mid-morning jaunt to where she had yet to decide. In her hand were manumission papers setting Samuel free and permission papers for the couple to travel in case someone stopped them.

Samuel took the papers from her and looked at them, "What these be fur, Miz Rachel?"

Rachel pointed to one, "This paper is a manumission paper Samuel, that sets you free. The others are travel papers signed by me in the event someone stops you."

Samuel asked, his voice choked, "Free, Miz Rachel? You be settin' me free?"

"I know it will mean little to you in these parts as long as you're a fugitive, but if you go beyond the influence of Walter Banks, these papers will mean something to you. I only wish I had the power to set Lizzie free because your children won't be until she is." Rachel explained.

"Yassum, dat's why I'd heap ruther see my Lizzie free than me since then our babies would be. But you cain't hep that none and I'll always thank ye fer what you tried to do fer me." Samuel replied.

"I will do what I can on this end." Rachel promised.

Samuel handed both papers back to Rachel, "Miz Rachel if'n we get caught wid dese papers on us, yo'll be in heap o trouble."

"But this is your freedom, Samuel," she urged.

"Yes'm and sum day I'll git 'em. Right now ya jest keep 'em fer me. It'll hep my heart just a knowin' I'm really free. If'n all dis dies down den I'll be sending fer 'em, don't ch'a worry none."

"I wish you godspeed and safety. Now we'd better both get busy." Rachel turned toward the house and her waiting horse, her heart in her throat.

She cantered down the shaded, maple lane leaving Sweetwater behind. As she turned onto the road, she put Sundance into a full run. It was the first time since receiving the horse that she dared let her have her head, now she fled, leaving the terrors of Sweetwater behind if only for a few hours.

Today her only mission was to flee and for the moment she wanted to put as many miles as possible between her and Sweetwater. The memory of Sam Pritchett's grotesque form haunted her mind and the guilt that she had let his death go unreported burdened her soul.

Her need to confide in someone was desperate. For the first time since the morning Andrew Meredith had walked out of her life, her aloneness closed in on her, almost suffocating her.

Her breath came in short gasps as her throat threatened to close up. She needed to talk to someone. Someone, strong and honorable and wise, who could tell her what to do. Suddenly a desperate need brought the face of Andrew Meredith to her mind and in that moment her conscience broke free. From beneath the layers of denial where she had buried it, the truth confronted Rachel on that rain spattered road, vindicating Meredith while demanding a response from her. Tears of remorse steamed down her face. But she knew they came too late.

More than anything else she needed and wanted the haven that Andrew Meredith had offered her. But Andrew was gone, lost to her because of her own stubborn will. Now there was nowhere else to turn. No one who cared.

Then whispering through her sorrow, echoed another she had wronged. At the crossroads Rachel wheeled her horse toward town.

Three hours later, the familiar landmarks of Marietta flashed by. She had ridden it in nearly record time even for a man. Only the stamina of the Arabian blood coursing through the flashy Palomino she rode and the adrenalin pumping through her own veins made it possible.

On the outskirts of town she paused at a small creek, slid off the saddle and let Sundance drink from the cool water. Then she took a handkerchief and dampened it in the cool brook and freshened her own face. After putting her hat and hair to rights, she bent over a still pool in the stream, and saw that she was once more presentable. From a large fallen log, she climbed back into the saddle and soon horse and rider were headed down the last leg of her journey toward reconciliation.

Bitter disappointment washed Rachel's features as she found Randall Wilkie's office empty and locked. She inquired in the shop next door only to learn that he had not been in for several days. The proprietor told her that his office hours had been quite erratic during the spring and that Randall's health had not been good. The shop keeper added that he had heard Mr. Wilkie was looking for someone to buy his practice.

Apprehension plagued Rachel as Andrew Meredith's words played through her mind. Meredith had brought her home for one reason, Randall was ill. She had been too wrapped in her own miseries and had dismissed Andrew's warning, now it came back to torment her. She thought of the precious hours and days spent blaming an innocent man and bringing pain when she could have been relieving it.

Practically flinging herself into the saddle again, she hurried down the street and back the way she had come, rushing toward Randall's house and a reunion she hoped would not come too late. No longer did Rachel seek comfort, but eagerly flew to give it. And in the change of purpose, her own problems retreated.

Randall Wilkie's face failed to greet Rachel when she arrived flushed and breathless at his front door. Instead, peering through the oval glass insert, the china blue eyes of Bertha Emory fastened on the young woman.

For a few seconds, recognition eluded both women, then the older woman's widened in surprise and curiosity twinkled in them as she opened the door for Rachel, "Well, Miss Rachel, it's been a long while since I've seen you. You're all grown up but I'd have recognized you anywhere, you've got your mother's eyes, God rest her soul. Finest woman I ever knew."

Meanwhile Rachel searched her brain for recall. The ample woman's sweet face proved familiar, but apprehension and fear pushed her name somewhere deep into her consciousness. Eluding her recollection, it played a game of hide and seek.

Bertha Emory's very nature was to put people at ease and added, "I'm Bertha Emory. I live about half-way between you and Mr. Wilkie. Your mother used to buy eggs and butter from me when Sweetwater supply ran low. You'd come and play with my children."

Suddenly recognition dawned on Rachel and a sense of peacefulness soothed her soul for a moment. Pleasant memories of a large, happy brood of children and happy laughter transported her for a brief moment to a time when her world seemed secure.

Rachel stepped through the double-cased doorway and into the broad, dog-trot hall running from front to back porch. Its only interruption was a simple staircase leading to the bedrooms above. Three doors on each side opened into the rooms beyond.

A hoarse voice jolted Rachel's reverie as Randall Wilkie called out from his study at the end of the hall. Bertha Emory's answered pleasantly, "You've got a caller, Mr. Wilkie and a mighty pretty one at that." Then turned to Rachel, "Why don't you take your hat off, my dear, so he can feast his eyes on that beautiful hair of yours,"

Rachel heard Randall chuckle, "That's the only kind I'm at home to."

Bertha put her hands on her broad hips and sashayed into his study, teasing, "Well, I guess I'll have to be gittin' then."

Randall Wilkie's voice mellowed as Rachel heard him answer just beyond the door and her view, "I forgot to include beautiful, Bertha. That means you."

"Shaw, Mr. Wilkie, you best put on your specs, Jacob's the only one who thinks I'm beautiful" Bertha protested.

"Most people are blinded to real beauty. Bertha, the beauty of your soul lights your eyes. Believe your Jacob. He knows what he's talking about. In fact you're both beautiful and I couldn't have managed without you."

"Well thank you, Mr. Wilkie, Jacob and me are proud we could help out, you've always been there for us and now it's our time to repay you. But now then, just look what I've got in store for you—." She began as Rachel entered the room. A lump caught in the throat of the kind housekeeper when she observed the unvarnished adoration and hope light the attorney's eyes.

Rachel paused just inside the door and handed Bertha her bonnet. Then her eyes widened with astonishment, as she turned toward a rice-carved bed facing the window. Sudden fear raced her heart as her eyes encountered her friend. Propped up by several pillows, Randall Wilkie reached out a fragile hand toward her. His dressing gown hung from his emaciated form and his dark eyes looked enormous in an ashen face. But for a brief moment delight rose above pain and restored their familiar twinkle.

Rachel raced to his bed and kneeling on the floor beside him took the hand he offered as tears of sorrow streamed down her flushed cheeks. Wilkie took the corner of the sheet and wiped her tears away and gently inquired, "What's this, my love? Why do you cry? Tis a time of rejoicing, not sorrow."

"Oh, Uncle Randall, I've been so wrong—" Rachel began and Bertha Emory quietly slipped from the room closing the door behind her.

"Rachel, there's no need for this." Randall protested.

"I've wronged you. When you tried to help, I accused you of terrible things. Can you ever forgive me?" Rachel pleaded, the flow of tears once again threatening.

"Forgive you? There's nothing to forgive. I only wish I could have protected you . . ."

"You did all that you could and more," Rachel began.

Sadness overtook the lingering joy in Wilkie eyes as he shook his head, "It wasn't enough."

"More, much more than you should have done. And I was so blind. Blind to everything," Rachel continued, "Andrew Meredith told me what you did. How can I ever forgive myself? I have made a mess of everything."

Randall caressed the hands holding his, "You mustn't say that, little one. God forgives freely and when He does it behooves us to accept it and forgive ourselves. I learned to do that."

"Whatever for, Uncle Randall?"

"For loving another man's wife."

"My mother?" she asked.

"So Andrew told you everything," he observed sadly, "Yes, it was your mother. At first I coveted her, and was jealous of my friend. Then when God showed me the sin hidden in my heart, I repented of the covetousness, but I could as soon quit breathing as stop loving her, so I made a commitment to myself and my God."

Intrigued Rachel asked, "What commitment?"

"I vowed never to defile her or sin against Him by making my feelings known to her, and that I would spend my life protecting her and working to strengthen her marriage."

"How could you do that?" Rachel asked, her mind in turmoil.

"It wasn't easy at first, but after awhile, I found my fulfillment came in her happiness."

"And you were never tempted to break your vow?"

"Never." His weak, hoarse voice answered with renewed strength.

"How, why?"

"Because sin destroys and I loved your mother too much to destroy her."

"Oh, Uncle Randall, you were cheated out of life." Rachel cried out, tears freely streaming down her face.

"Don't cry for me, Rachel. I got an unexpected bonus."

"What?" she asked, disbelief furrowing her brow.

Randall winced through his smile, as pain darkened his eyes, "You. When you were born it was as if God had given me a channel where I could let my love flow unrestricted, and then in the end I've failed you."

"No, no, no, I won't accept that." Rachel protested, "You did everything you could and more than you should have."

"Andrew told you I've lost most of my worldly possessions and the rest are mortgaged?"

"Yes," she admitted dropping her head in remembrance and shame.

"Don't you worry about that, my dear. My remaining time appears short and success or failure in this life is not measured in the material things one possesses, but rather whether or not we've been found faithful. That's my concern now, my dear. I couldn't remain faithful to my vow. I'm going to leave you unprotected and destitute."

"Of course you're not, Uncle Randall. I'm making out fine," she lied.

Wilkie placed a finger beneath Rachel's chin and forced her to look into his eyes, "As long as you are in league with Walter Banks you are not doing fine, you are in grave danger."

"What do you know about Walter Banks?"

"Word travels fast in these parts. Especially when it's a braggart like Banks. You talk about forgiveness, how can I face my Maker knowing I've left you at his mercy?"

"Don't even talk like that, Uncle Randall." Rachel commanded, "You're going to get well, I'm going to see to it."

"My dear, it's not in your hands or mine, but in God's and if he calls me home soon, I'm helpless to assist you. I've failed you."

"How can I lose you when I've just found you again? Why does God take everyone that I love?" Sorrow and guilt gripped Rachel and the sobs began again, as she laid her head on his chest,

Heartache for her superseded the pain racking Randall's body as he caressed the soft curls of her head bowed before him, "We aren't given to understand all God's plans or purposes, my dear. But this I know, He will provide for all our needs,"

Rachel grasped his words, and jerked her head up. Looking up into his eyes, she attempted to comfort him with them, "Then, see, you ought have no worry for me. God will provide for my needs."

"Yes, sweetheart, if we're obedient and don't willfully step outside his Divine protection. But sometimes when we do, he allows us to suffer the consequences of our actions."

The words like daggers pierced Rachel's soul as the morning's events flooded her memory. She dropped her head, not willing for Randall to see the burden of truth visible in her eyes.

Once again his hand raised her chin forcing her eyes to meet his. He stared into hers for a long moment before inquiring, "Little one, have you compromised His direction?"

"You already know the answer to that," she confessed.

"What are you going to do about it?"

"There's nothing I can do about it except pray for a good crop and hope that will rescue me."

"What will you do until then?" He pressed.

"Go on like I have been taking every precaution to be frugal."

"Banks is financing you totally?"

She nodded, "I had no alternative."

Wilkie smiled sadly, "You did have one other."

"But it no longer exists."

"Are you sure?"

"Oh I'm sure," Rachel said the pain of regret firing her emerald eyes, "I hurt and humiliated him. His decision was final."

"Maybe not."

"It was. I've not heard nor seen him since."

"It's up to you, Rachel. You did the humiliating; you spurned him, now you have to make amends."

"I know, and I will, but if I do that now it will only look as if I'm using him. I just couldn't ask him for assistance. Like Agatha used to say, 'I've made my bed, now I'll have to lie in it.'"

"To what extend will you go in order not to ask Meredith for help?"

"Whatever it takes, I guess."

"Oh, my dear, you have no idea what you might be letting yourself in for." Randall pleaded, "Put your pride aside, before you allow it to destroy your life."

"It wouldn't do any good, Uncle Randall. I saw it in his eyes. He told me the decision was up to me. I chose and I'm going to have to live with the consequences. . . ."

"Even if it means as Walter Banks wife?"

"Why—why do you say that?" Rachel's face blanched. The thought had never crossed her mind.

"Because that will be the only solution left to you if you're not able to pay him off in December." Wilkie observed.

"He told me not to worry, that he'd work with me, if I couldn't." Rachel parried, not willing to face the possibility

"Do you have his promise in writing?"

"No." She admitted, her heart pounding.

"Ask him for something in writing. Then prepare for that probability if he refuses. Tell him you want me to draw up an agreement and if he won't I beg you, go to Andrew Meredith. He's still your only hope."

Rachel smiled a stiff smile, attempting to assure Wilkie, "You forgot my crops. They look as if we are going to have a bountiful harvest."

"Then more's the reason you should go to Andrew now while you still have something to offer him." Randall pleaded, "If the crops fail, and it's a long time between now and December anything could happen, you will be at the mercy of Walter Banks. Don't burn your last bridge, Rachel. I have nothing left with which to help you."

"I don't want you to worry about me. I'm young and I'll think of something. I want to cheer you up. What can I do to make you easier?"

"Contact Andrew Meredith." He said weakly, his eyes fluttering shut as a wave of pain engulfed him.

Rachel cringed, feeling helpless before the throes of his racking pain. She grasped his hand and he gripped it tightly until his anguish had subsided some. Then looking at her he smiled, "Promise me?"

"I promise to do everything I can to protect myself."

He nodded his head. "I guess you wouldn't be Rachel if you set that fiery pride aside, but don't let it destroy you."

"I won't." She consoled all the while knowing she could never bear to throw herself on Andrew's mercy. Suddenly despair engulfed her as she considered what her future held because of the grotesque image of Sam Pritchett's body, buried somewhere beneath the clay of Sweetwater, invaded her senses. . . .

SEVENTEEN

The sun had dropped off the horizon like a fiery orb leaving in its wake, fingers of pink and gold, gilding the clouds in iridescent colors.

"Jacob, would you look at that sunset?" Bertha exclaimed. "God's handiwork overshadows anything man can do."

He pulled the wagon off the road onto a bluff. Cleared off and readied for a late planting, it offered a better view. He waited patiently for her to get her fill, chuckling, "I know, Mama. You don't want to miss it. You never know how many more you got left."

"Oh Jacob, you quit joshing me. I know the Lord's got somethin' a lot more beautiful than this waiting for us. But if you don't enjoy all the little things life has to offer you, the heartaches will fair overwhelm you." She sighed.

Rachel looked at the woman who sat beside her in the jostling wagon. What a simplistic view of life, she thought. Yet, maybe that was the secret to Bertha's twinkling eyes and serene presence.

The younger woman gazed toward the western sky and in the awesome beauty before her realized that she had rarely paused to consider, much less savor the simple beauties in life. Rather she had pushed ahead toward her immediate goals while her single focus trampled over or passed by anything or anyone that might distract. Until now, that is, and in Bertha Emory's homespun philosophy Rachel Gregory glimpsed tragedy in her existence. Torn and shattered dreams strewed the pathway of her young life and the only true joy she could remember were the times in the distant past when her Mother and Father had paused with her for moments such as these.

Rachel looked westward toward the glorious light and for a moment all her problems seemed insignificant next to the grandeur and majesty before her while quietly her heart reminded her, that the same God who painted the sunset cared about her. No solutions for her problems flooded her mind, neither did her difficulties dissipate, but somehow, somewhere deep inside her a fragile kernel of hope sprouted. The hope encouraged her the rest of the way home.

Rachel's emotionally charged visit had exhausted her and when she started to leave, Bertha Emory insisted that she wait for Jacob who would be coming with the wagon to pick her up. Then they would tie her horse behind and take her home.

Rachel hesitated but when she thought of the long ride home alone with only her fearful thoughts as companions, she acquiesced. And a good thing she had because twilight approached as they turned into the shadows of the long drive leading to Sweetwater. Rachel breathed a sigh of relief, at least she had missed Banks' daily visit and it would be tomorrow before she faced his inquisition. Maybe by then she would have thought of some answers.

When morning came, Walter Banks arrived on Rachel's doorstep several hours earlier than his usual afternoon visits. Thundering up the lane on his stallion, he left a cloud of dust in his wake. He bypassed the house and headed straight for the fields.

An hour later he tossed the reins of his horse to a young slave boy brushing Sundance and took the porch steps two at a time. Rachel observed it all from an upstairs window. She had waited in the shadows, brushing her hair and dreading the encounter that awaited her.

By now Banks knew that Pritchett was gone, it only remained for him to question her before he began his search in earnest. She stretched out a hand before her and noted that it trembled. Nora, her lone house servant who doubled as cook also, knocked on her door and informed her that Marse Banks had arrived and was in the parlor awaiting her.

Rachel peered in the mirror and a wry smile parted her tense face. By design she had brushed her hair until it shone. She tied a ribbon through it allowing the thick tresses to cascade freely down her back. Her hair along with the white muslin dress trimmed in blue ribbons and sash made her look young and innocent. She had chosen her attire with care. But her face appeared pale above the tall collar that encircled her neck so she pinched her cheeks, bringing color to them in an attempt to conceal her troubled heart.

Walter Banks paced the parlor, his riding crop drumming an impatient requiem on his dusty britches. His boots were caked in fine clay dust from the field and a ring of perspiration beaded his head where his hat had been. A noise behind him caused him to wheel impatiently on his heel only to freeze as his eyes beheld the vision of white loveliness that had entered the room behind him.

For a moment Walter Banks forgot Sam Pritchett, his grand scheme for Sweetwater even his cold and calculated plans for Rachel's future evaporated along with his customary calm facade. Her beauty drove all else from his mind. It left him speechless and aware of nothing but that his heart and his mind cried in unison, she would be his, whatever the cost.

If Rachel had hoped to throw him off balance, she succeeded beyond her wildest expectations. In their day to day contact throughout the last weeks and months, Walter Banks had grown accustomed to her beauty and magnetism. His objective had not changed nor had his determination lessened, only his motivation had been buried somewhere in the process of achievement.

This morning when his mind railed against the unexplained, and impatience chaffed against the unexpected, she floated into the room and reminded him that this woman was his ultimate goal and possessing her motivated all his schemes. In that moment he vowed to himself that nothing this side of heaven or hell would stand in his way.

When finally his voice returned, Walter Banks asked softly, "Why Miss Rachel, don't we look nice this morning? Are you expecting visitors?"

"Not really. But you can never tell, now can you?" Rachel responded, a forced smile on her lips.

"You go a visitin' yesterday? I missed our regular cup of tea."

"As a matter of fact I did. Thanks to you and Sundance, I had a way to go."

"Maybe bringing you that horse wasn't such a good idea after all, if you're gonna be running off like that without telling me first." He gently reprimanded.

"I didn't know I needed to ask your permission, Mr. Banks," Rachel's smile remained fixed, while her eyes turned to green ice.

"Not my permission, dear." Banks slipped into a familiarity that sent cold chills of revulsion up and down Rachel's spine. "It's just that I was worried since I feel responsible for you."

"Well, sir, set your mind at ease. You are not responsible for me beyond honesty and fairness in our business venture."

Banks moved closer to Rachel and picked up her hand, raising it to his lips, "Surely you must know my concerns reach much further than our business association."

Unable to contain it, Rachel shuddered at his touch, a response Banks observed and his smile faded, his face hardened.

"No, I'm afraid I didn't," Rachel responded, fear replacing revulsion as she read a threat in Banks tawny eyes,

"Surely you know, Miss Rachel, that the terms I have offered you are way beyond anything I would offer just in the line of business."

"I realize and appreciate your generosity but I fully intend to repay you for everything you have provided."

"There are some things that money can't repay, my dear," Banks replied, his voice smooth.

"Is that a threat, Mr. Banks?"

"Of course not. Merely a suggestion that my assistance has been more one of the heart than the head. Usually I am a more astute business man than I've proven with you."

"Perhaps you did it because of your friendship with my father." Rachel suggested, her heart pounding with the direction the conversation was taking.

"Perhaps at first, but mere friendship would never allow me to take the risks I have for you." His eyes held hers.

"I'm new and naive in the field of business. I would have never knowingly taken advantage of you, Mr. Banks. Please accept my deepest apologies," Rachel hedged.

"It's not your apology that I want, Rachel" Banks replied, all pretense dropped.

"I'm afraid I don't understand," Rachel stammered.

"I want you." He said plainly.

"Me? How?"

"I want you on my arm, to sit at my table, to preside over my drawing room. I want your beauty, your grace to be exclusively mine. In short I want you to be Mrs. Walter Banks."

"This is so sudden, Mr. Banks," She murmured weakly, her knees trembling.

"I think we can dispense with the formality, call me Walter." He commanded.

"Err, Walter." the name stuck in her throat, "I've been so concerned about Sweetwater I've given no thought toward personal relationships at all."

"Then you'd better start now. Especially since you have no other choices."

"You don't know that. I have a suitor in England. A Duke as a matter of fact." Rachel argued, pulling at straws.

Walter Banks threw back his head and laughed. The harsh sound echoed through the room. "If you had any other options you wouldn't be standing in this room, all dressed up for me."

Rachel's morning scheme crashed down around her and she knew her carefully orchestrated charade had been a mistake. She should have gone about her business as usual. Then she thought of the field and Sam Pritchett's hideous body lying lifeless between the rows of tender cotton.

"I'm so overwhelmed, Walter. I had no idea you felt this way, I just need a little time. You understand, don't you?" She smiled as warmly as her frozen heart would allow.

"Of course, Rachel. I understand." Banks replied and he did. A smug smile parted his face telling Rachel they both knew she was a conquered captive. "Now to the business at hand. Have you seen Sam Pritchett?"

Rachel's eyes widened in her pale face and she answered honestly, "Not since yesterday morning."

"Where did you last see him?"

"In the field next to the creek. You know the new ground that they cleared for cotton? Why?"

"He didn't come home last night and he's not in the field this morning. You sure you haven't seen him since?"

"Of course. As you already pointed out I was gone yesterday."

"And where did you go?" Banks barked, all pretense gone.

"To see Randall Wilkie," Rachel answered.

"I'd advise you to stay away from him."

"I'm sorry but I can't do that, Walter."

"You'll do as I say, my dear." Banks answered, his voice cold and hard.

"Randall Wilkie is an old and dear friend," Rachel protested.

"Then why wasn't he here to help you instead of me?" Banks mocked.

"You know why. He hasn't anything left to help me with,"

Banks curled his lip and sneered, "That's what happens when a person is too weak to fight for what he has."

Rachel defended softly, "He's dying, Walter."

Banks cocked his head to one side, a triumphant light flared briefly in his eyes before he checked it, "Oh, really? Sorry about that. I don't know him very well, but he seems to disapprove of me for some reason."

"I really need to spend some time with him."

"Well, maybe, but you have too many duties here to be out running around the county. But I must say I do approve of your new style. It becomes you. By the way, the Dunbars are having a ball Friday of next week. I will pick you up mid afternoon in my carriage." He stated, re-enforcing his new status and leaving Rachel no quarter to doubt that from now on, his forum ruled.

Rachel merely nodded her head, accepting the role she had to play until harvest time set her free.

Shortly after noon the storm that had threatened the day before came crashing down. Wind and rain pelted the countryside for hours. Water ran in rivulets across the yard and fields as creeks and river rushed to their brims but held without spilling over. But the deluge of water served a dual purpose.

Young thirsty plants drank deeply while telltale human scents floated away hampering tracking dogs and delaying search parties.

After the storm cleared and for the remainder of the week, Walter Banks searched Sweetwater and all the surrounding area for Sam Pritchett without results. When he discovered that the two slaves were also missing, he sent patrols out looking for them but the dogs had nothing to track.

He posted wanted posters for the slaves, offering a reward, but no one came forward with any leads. It was as if the earth or maybe the river had swallowed them all, both black and white. The slave patrol figured the Chattahoochee held the answer. It wouldn't be the first time the treacherous Chattahoochee imprisoned victims by pinning them beneath the rocks and rapids that riddled her shallows and channel.

But Banks couldn't believe Sam Pritchett was in the river. Maybe the slaves but not his henchmen, he was too smart for that. He concluded that some trouble from his past had driven him away. Yet, unexplained, his belongings still resided in Walter's bunkhouse as if waiting for the man's eminent return. Uneasiness teased his soul that Rachel knew more than she pretended. He smiled suddenly realizing that Sam's disappearance might prove more beneficial in the long run than his overseeing had.

Content with those observations, Walter Banks called off the search and rode back to Pine Ridge to prepare for the festivities of the evening.

Relishing what this evening should accomplish and the many more to come, a smug smile lighted his face and he hummed a tune.

In his mind's eye he could see his ornate carriage with his pair of matched grays pulling up to the broad front steps of the Dunbar's Greek revival mansion. He decided that they would arrive late so that most of the guest would already be present. He wanted everyone to note his entrance with Rachel.

He planned to set tongues wagging and men envying. With Rachel on his arm he knew he could break down society's final barricade to him. She was the key that would open the door he craved more than anything else. The elusive goal that all his wealth and power had been unable to attain for him, respectability and genuine social acceptance.

Besides her beauty and grace, Rachel was one of them. Who would dare deny her acceptance into her rightful place in society? And with her acceptance, her husband's place. As a daughter of a respected community leader her place was secure, as her husband, he would step in to fill the place her father had held before her mother died.

Yes sir, this would be the last party that would include him on their guest list because they needed his business.

―――――――――――――

A hush fell on the crowd, starting at the ornate double entrance doors of the Dunbar mansion and sweeping around the room, as Walter Banks entered the door and walked into the hall with Rachel Gregory on his arm.

Those who had their backs to him, heard the hush and turned to look and all fastened their eyes on the exquisite woman dressed in a ball gown of pale green silk trimmed with point lace, a wide velvet sash accenting her tiny waist. From her thick auburn locks swept up and held in place by her mother's mother of pearl combs, to the tips of her satin slippers peeping from beneath ivory lace ruffles cascading down the front of her dress, they fixed their gaze on her. Some gawked with ill conceived admiration, some with envy, but all with curiosity.

When she passed, whispers began behind her as a low hum of conversation began again. At first the beauty with Banks seemed only vaguely familiar, and then the hum of conversation grew like a rising tide as someone put the puzzle together and whispered her name. They had heard Rachel was back but none had seen her. Most had dismissed it as rumor, considering the shape Sweetwater was in. But here she was. The boyish girl-child who had left their community had returned a ravishing beauty.

The few young men left who were her age and had not taken a bride, rustled restlessly in the crowd. Each wondered what she was doing on the arm of the despicable Banks and plotted how they could whisk her away.

The music began and as the Dunbars stepped out to begin the dancing, Walter Banks took Rachel's hand and, bowing over it, led her onto the pink marble floor.

His technique proved flawless with each step timed to the beat of the music, but he moved like a wooden soldier, precise but devoid of grace and suppleness.

Since he was no more than an inch taller than she, they stood practically eye to eye. His stared into hers like golden serpent ones rarely blinking. When his arm curved around her she grew rigid, pulling as far away from him as possible, even as his hand pressed demanding and hard against her waist. He noted her resistance and his eyes narrowed, a warning flashed.

Rachel's back ached before the first waltz finished and panic bubbled inside her as she wondered how she could endure the rest of the evening. But curiosity and intrigue rescued her. As soon as the last strands of the waltz died, and with only perfunctory permission, a young blade whisked her away from her captive. She looked up, relief flooding her body, into the twinkling hazel eyes of Will Brown, with whom she had climbed trees and picked berries as a child.

As his dark head bent to hers he whispered, "Oh, Miss Rachel, how you have changed."

Rachel smiled gratefully, "Why, Will, I can't imagine what you mean."

As the night wore on and, despite the possessive tawny eyes that followed her every move, Rachel went from one partner to another renewing old acquaintances. Finally the merry tempo of the music invaded her senses and for a while she escaped the realities that pressed her and gave herself to the music.

When she paused to catch her breath, three young men rushed to bring her punch. Their neglected sweethearts glared from the fringes of the crowd while mamas of unmarried daughters looked on in alarm, all but forgetting about the man who had brought her.

The dance was winding down when a tall man, elegant in his evening clothes, pushed his way through the crowd. Ignoring the line of young men waiting for another dance with her, he tapped her on the shoulder.

"I believe you promised me this dance, Miss Gregory?" He softly commanded more than requested. A cool smile parted his lips.

His eyes had fastened on her the moment she entered the room. He watched her dance with Walter Banks and his pulse raced. Then he noted something akin to fear subduing the fire in the large green eyes, dominating her face. He saw how thin she was and sudden worry besieged him. He had stayed in the shadows for hours, just observing, not wishing to be noticed before his eyes could drink their fill of her.

Now he had come to claim her. For mere observation from afar had proved woefully inadequate. He needed, if only for a moment, to touch her hand, to hold her in the curve of his arms and to hear her voice speak his name.

She looked up into his eyes and he saw an avalanche of emotion flood her being as the emerald fires ignited and she whispered breathlessly, "Andrew."

EIGHTEEN

The sun was bright and hot on the dusty road to Powder Springs as Andrew Meredith cantered toward Randall Wilkie's house. He had finished his conference with Goodman who had given him the only encouraging news he'd had since he left Marietta three months ago. He learned Tom Williford was working hard and having some success in his organization efforts northwest of town. The editor had lined up several more meetings this trip, west and south of Marietta, but first he had to see Randall.

He dreaded the visit, hated to see his friend suffer. Like most men of robust strength and good health, Meredith felt inadequate in the presence of pain and misery because he had no way to ease it. As a man of action he equated true comfort with solutions, he had yet to learn that real consolation came from genuine caring.

He found it hard to accept Randall was dying; even harder to imagine his visits to the Marietta area without basking in the gentle man's wisdom and kindness.

Thoughts of Randall once again brought the specter of wide green eyes back to haunt him. He tried to banish them back to the area of his mind where he had imprisoned them in April. When he had walked away from her, he had willed to put her out of his mind.

Since his newly found purpose had all but obsessed him, his efforts to put her out of his mind had been somewhat successful. He had worked day and late into each night in pursuit of his commitment. His days were too filled with activities, his nights with meetings to have time to think of her during his waking hours and when he slept it was the dreamless sleep of exhaustion.

His commercial enterprises continued to prosper and he had a prospective buyer for his northern industrial holdings. A British nobleman would be in Savannah when he returned.

The new course his life had taken proved challenging. Goodman was right. Most of the coastal planters had closed minds concerning secession. They felt the slavery problem was not the only vital issue in the South's survival. The question of tariffs proved a real threat and had been a source of controversy for years between the two sections.

Reluctantly he could see their point. It would seem if the South wanted to remain an economic power, she needed free trade. Since she exported three fourths of her raw goods while importing all her manufactured goods, a tax on imports would result in higher prices. Then they would be forced to seek their goods from the North or pay exorbitant prices for imported goods. The North wanted the lucrative business that was going abroad while Southern planters felt the North wanted to dictate where they made their purchases. They felt the industrial states would ultimately drain off their wealth either through taxes or their own high prices. The lack of industry was the Achilles heel of the South, but Drew's arguments reminded them the same problem existed if they seceded and went to war.

To them secession meant possible economic wealth and freedom, because they felt Southern free trade ports like Savannah and Charleston would capture trade from busy northern ports where tariffs were in force. To Andrew secession meant a war they could not win, the message he faithfully proclaimed to an increasingly hostile audience. He remained a watchman whose warning was rejected. Now he had returned to Marietta to visit with his friends in search of encouragement.

Instead of the encouragement he sought, Rachel came crashing into his life again. Rather than a steady mind and clear thoughts all he could think of was the way his heart leapt when she had spoken his name last night. Her face swam before him and he saw her eyes filled with sadness and something akin to fear.

His encounter with her had been the briefest of moments. He had whirled her only halfway across the room, and exchanged only pleasantries when Walter Banks tapped him on the shoulder and possessively captured her away. The memory of her countenance as she stared back at him over Banks' shoulder invaded his sanity, tormenting him.

But what could he do? She had made her decision and obviously her destiny belonged to Banks. His heart fought what his mind concluded that for good or evil she had chosen Walter Banks. The memory of her expression haunted him until he dismounted at Randall Wilkie's front door.

Bertha Emory answered his knock and ushered him in to see Wilkie. She had turned his study into a bedroom, she explained as they walked down the hall together. The stairs had become too difficult, so she and Jacob moved his bed in among the books and things he loved so much. Felt they'd be a comfort to him if anything could.

Meredith inquired about the few remaining slaves that Randall had and she told him, they had to be sold except for one house servant and one field servant. She hoped Mr. Wilkie could hold on to them because she only looked after him during daylight hours. She laughed, "When dark comes my Jacob wants me home. Course you know we'd do anything in the world for Mr. Randall and if he needs us then we're here."

Andrew patted the kind woman on her shoulder as he turned toward the study door, "I know you will, Mrs. Emory. But I want Randall to have all the help he needs and you and Jacob can't do everything. Please let me know if there is anything I can do."

Bertha looked at him for a long minute as if she wanted to tell him something, but thought better of it.

Meredith noticed and pressed, "How is he today? Anything else I should know?"

"I've been wrestling with this every since you knocked on that front door. Mr. Wilkie's took a turn for the worse. It happened the afternoon that pretty Rachel Gregory came to see him. When she walked in, his eyes lit up so's I thought she was just the medicine he needed, but all it has done is drag him down. I think he is worried about that miss."

Andrew's eyes narrowed as he asked, "Did he tell you what she said that might have upset him."

"He won't talk to me, maybe he will to you. Anyway you might be able to help if it's a problem she has. He's not in any shape to help anybody and I think he's grieving over that very thing. Keeps railing against his helplessness. Now you know, Mr. Meredith, that can do nothing but harm."

"What does the doctor say?"

"He says he's done all he can and wants Mr. Randall to go up north to see a specialist. But he won't hear of it." Bertha explained exasperation written in every line of her face.

"Why won't he go?"

"He hasn't told me, says it won't do any good. But between me and you I believe it's the money. He just hasn't the resources. You know what a proud man he is. He's resigned to the worst."

Meredith nodded as he opened the door and went in. Randall's eyes were closed and Andrew was glad he had the time to regain his composure. His friend's deterioration during the past three months overwhelmed him. Always lithe and slender, his friend was scarcely more than flesh and bone. His hair had thinned and now was totally silver; his breathing, labored. Emotion misted Andrew's eyes and he vowed to ease whatever burden he could from the man he had grown to love as a friend and almost a father.

Randall's eyelids fluttered opened and a genuine smile parted his face, easing away the lines of pain and fatigue, "My friend, I'm so glad to see you," he said as he held out his hand, the fingers long and bony.

Andrew grasped his hand gently, fearing he would crush it, and sat down beside the bed, "Randall, why didn't you send for me?"

"I didn't want to disturb your work."

Meredith forced a chuckle, "Work will always wait, people are what count,"

Randall laughed, bringing on a spasm of coughing, and then said weakly, "Am I hearing these words from the lips of the busy entrepreneur Andrew Meredith?"

"Guess I'm getting older. Priorities do change you know."

Randall looked at him hard, then remarked, "It's more than your priorities that have changed. Something has happened to you, Andrew."

A flush colored Meredith's face as he admitted, "I guess you could say that. But it does affect priorities."

"Why don't you tell me about it?" Wilkie encouraged.

"There's not a lot to tell, Randall. My life has taken on a new direction of sorts."

"Some reason for that?"

"I'm a little embarrassed to talk about it, but I guess there's no other way to explain it, but there is a new spiritual dimension to my life."

Randall nodded, knowingly, "When you're in my position, you realize that's the only really important aspect of your life. I only wish I had realized it earlier then other areas of my life would have been affected. Am I right in assuming that is what has happened to you?"

Relieved and surprised his friend understood, Andrew continued with freedom, "One day I realized that God had an overall purpose for my life beyond amassing a fortune. Actually my wealth doesn't impress God much and you know what? It isn't as important to me anymore either."

"When did this revelation happen?"

"On my trip to Cartersville. I don't know if you could actually call it a Divine revelation," Meredith laughed, embarrassed.

Randall queried, suppressing a smile, "Why?"

"I didn't see an angel or hear trumpets," Meredith explained, shrugging.

"Well what did happen?" a twinkle returning to Wilkie's weak eyes.

"It was just an overwhelming conviction in my heart that God had a work for me to do."

"What work?" Randall urged, his eyes now turned serious.

"Immediately it is to warn the people and work to avoid the bloodbath that's going to be poured out on our nation."

"Blessed are the peacemakers," Randall murmured under his breath.

"What?"

"Oh, nothing. You said 'immediately' was there more to your conviction?"

"I suddenly realized that all my life belongs to God and what I do with it is of great concern to Him. In short, He has a plan for it and I'd do well to consider Him before I make my own plans."

"I'll say you did get a new direction," Randall exclaimed.

"It has changed my proprieties."

"Have you been happier?"

Andrew laughed and shook his head, "I can't say that I have. Mostly I've been frustrated, but in the midst of the frustration, I have discovered a strange peace and contentment. I'm finding out that when God gives you a task, it doesn't mean it'll be easy or even that you'll be successful."

"You gonna give up?"

"If it were my project . . .yeah. But since it's God's, I better not."

"Wise decision. Sometimes He uses what we term failures to test our faithfulness. It doesn't take faith or much dedication to continue when we're successful, but it does when we can't see results. God go with you, my friend."

"Enough about me, I came to see about you. How are you doing?"

"That's a foolish question," Randall chuckled,

"Is there nothing that can be done?" Andrew asked.

"I don't know of anything. The doctor is mystified. I've been failing as you know since that bout of influenza in '57 and it's really accelerated in the last four months. I just get weaker and weaker and now this cough plagues me. I'm resigned to the inevitable."

"What about other doctors?" asked Andrew, man of action.

"I know there are some good ones in the Northeast, but I doubt

I could endure the trip," Randall said.

"Well, man, wouldn't it be worth a try?" Andrew urged.

Randall shook his head, "There is something else you can do for me though."

Andrew eager to assist, "What? You just name it."

"Rachel Gregory."

"Oh, Randall, give me a task I can accomplish. You talk about frustration. I've done everything I can for that girl. It's like fighting cobwebs to help her. Not only does she just refuse my help, but blames me for everything wrong in her life."

Wilkie held up a hand, "Andrew, I don't think she blames you anymore."

"Then she needs to come to me and ask for help."

"Her pride won't let her."

"There, you see . . . we're right back where we started. I can't help her until she wants me to."

"Please, Andrew." Randall begged.

Conscience buffeted Meredith as he saw the pleading in his sick friend's eyes, "Forgive me, Randall. I let my frustration overrule my compassion for a moment."

"It's easy when your heart's been trampled on," Wilkie observed.

Andrew's pulse raced even as his lips denied, "My heart has nothing to do with this, and I've tried every way I can to help her. She has chosen Walter Banks' help and that's the way it'll have to be. Maybe things will turn out all right. She's probably just what he needs. I know he wants what she has, her land and her family position in the community. She wants Sweetwater so an alliance between the two might be just the answer."

"She doesn't want Walter Banks."

"Well she arrived on his arm at the Dunbar's last evening."

Randall suppressed a smile, "You saw her there?"

Andrew nodded, "Just passed pleasantries with her for a moment."

Randall pressed, "You didn't talk?"

"What's there left to say? She made it abundantly clear before I returned to Savannah what she thinks of me and my help."

"Things have changed."

"What things?"

"She didn't tell me much. She did say she was sorry for the things she said."

"To me or you?"

"I guess she meant both."

"For you I am glad that your relationship is restored. She loves you. She doesn't love me, Randall; in fact she thinks I'm the reason for all her problems. I think if Miss Gregory needs anything, she'll have to ask for it. I get tired of getting my hand bitten every time I try to give her a bone so to speak."

"I'm afraid for her, Andrew. Something is going on that she's not telling me. She's in trouble. Won't you at least ask around?"

Andrew looked at his emaciated friend and nodded his head "I'll make a pact with you, Randall. If I can find some medical help for you in Boston will you consider making the trip if I see what I can find out about your Rachel?"

Randall responded, "Drew, more than anything I wish I could, but you know I don't have the financial resources to pursue that."

Andrew sighed, relief softened his features, "But we know someone who does, don't we?"

"I won't take charity."

"It's not charity. I need you and I have more money than I can spend in a lifetime, don't you think that the God who enabled me to make that money cares enough for you to direct me to use it for your good? "

"What about Rachel's good?"

"Only if you'll agree to let me help you."

"For Rachel, I'd even take charity. Find out what you can, Andrew, then do what you can to save us. But hurry. Time is running out for both of us."

The first order of business for Andrew Meredith when he arrived back in Marietta was the telegraph office. He wired his Boston manager to make an appointment with the best lung specialist in the city as soon as possible. Then he wired his Savannah office to inform his prospective buyer he would be late arriving in Savannah but would join him when the steamer, the Anna Maria, left for Boston. Meanwhile he would be welcome to wait at Balmara while awaiting his return. Lastly he wired the Central Georgia Railway office to send him a private car for his use, one equipped with a comfortable bed.

A wry smile parted Andrew Meredith's face as he stepped out into the sun kissed summer afternoon. He felt better. He had to admit, he enjoyed being in control. Feeling that he could actually do something to help his friend buoyed his spirits. Then his smiled broadened. Now came the tricky part. Maybe he could dictate to industry and they catered to his demands, but Jacob Emory was another matter all together. How was he to persuade him that he could do without Bertha for a few days?

He knew he'd never agree for her to go to Boston, but there would be no need. He would have Daphne's willing assistance once he got to Savannah.

His trip to the Emory household that evening proved as successful as his telegraphs. Jacob cooperated and even offered to accompany Bertha when he found she would be returning by herself in a private car. The two would spend a couple of nights in Savannah at Andrew's expense and return home quickly and in style. Since neither Bertha nor Jacob had ever visited the port city, both seemed thrilled at the prospect.

While Andrew visited with the congenial couple he brought up the return of their neighbor, making discreet inquiries about Rachel. They had very little information to contribute about her welfare, but when he mentioned Walter Banks, Bertha's round pleasant blue eyes sparked uncharacteristically. "Now that's one for you," she sputtered.

Jacob patted her ample shoulder, "Now Mama you don't know

anything for sure, just rumors."

"Well, it's not rumors when I see all kinds of strange people coming and going down this road in the early evenings and returning during the wee hours, setting old 'Blue' to barking and disturbing our sleep. Now is it, Jacob?" she demanded.

He sighed and nodded his head in agreement, then cautioned, "But it is rumors as to what is going on while they are down there."

"This is a Christian community, and we didn't have the likes of anything like this until that gambling man brought his New Orleans' ways to Georgia."

"There's nothing we can do about it."

Meredith sat quietly, taking in the conversation but not willing to betray his real interest. Finally when it became apparent that they could offer no further information, he said his goodbyes and left. He felt the Emorys would offer a safe haven for Rachel if she had an emergency. That is if she would contact them.

From the Emory's, Meredith back tracked to town, hoping Robert Goodman was still at work. He knew that if anybody could help him the knowledgeable editor could. Goodman didn't disappoint him. After the editor pressed Andrew about his interest in the strangers, he nodded in agreement with Randall's assessment of Rachel's peril and elaborated on the veiled insinuations Bertha had made. After an hour's visit Andrew left with pertinent names, addresses, and occupations for all the out of town visitors Walter Banks had entertained. Amazed, Andrew asked the editor how and why he had gotten this information. Robert smiled his Cheshire grin in response and reminded him that he was talking to a newspaper man.

Meredith left the newspaper office relieved that the names at least offered him a starting point. He could give Randall some hope.

He realized his task would prove difficult; maybe even require a trip to New Orleans. Goodman warned him that he would have to work subtly lest Banks get wind of what was afoot and force his will on Rachel. Meredith knew that all the medical help in the world wouldn't be able to save Randall if that happened. Randall's welfare was his only motivation for getting involved, he kept telling himself.

―――――――――――

The morning clouds hung low and threatening in the southwest. The air was heavy and the heat clung like a wet blanket, suffocating. Rachel stood on the back porch and watched the boiling gray sky.

Bolts of lightning parted the heavens and rolls of thunder crashed around her. When the wind whipped up, the rain started. It came down in horizontal sheets, so thick she could barely make out the outline of the barn. She heard her mare whinny and she knew she was pacing the stall with flared nostrils and arched neck.

Somehow Rachel wished she were in the barn with her. The weather unnerved her this morning and a sense of loneliness overwhelmed her. Nora was in her quarters and the big house creaked and groaned as the wind swirled around it. No human voice to respond if she called. And this morning Rachel longed to hear a voice.

But not just any voice. His voice. The voice she had heard briefly two nights ago, the one that was music to her ears. The one Walter Banks had forbidden her to hear again. But even his veiled threat could not prevent her mind from playing the sound of it over and over again. The special timbre of it when he had told her she looked lovely even yet raced her heart. The memory lingered of the one who had told her the truth, who promised her a future if she released the past. The one she had rejected in favor of another. She shuddered.

Now from the shelter of the porch she watched her future bow and nod its head row by row in the acres of green before her. A grim smile curled her mouth and she knew the source of her anxiety. The weather had never frightened her. Until now that is, but her hope of breaking free rested on the mercy of nature.

She heard the roaring before it arrived. Then a warning ping hit the roof before the very air turned white. Frozen egg-sized missiles fired against the barn, the house and hurled on the porch where she stood horrified. When the storm expended itself, the yard and fields lay covered in two inches of hail and an eerie mist rose up from the ice swirling around the house wrapping it in a gray shroud. Only here and there a leafless green steam pushed up between the layers of ice. And Rachel knew Sweetwater was gone and with it her freedom.

NINETEEN

Walter Banks found Rachel, her dress caked in mud, kneeling beside a fallen, stripped stalk of cotton. With her back to him, she failed to see the brief gleam of satisfaction that touched his eyes as he took in the destruction surrounding her. But the momentary pleasure he experienced at her misfortune was short lived before reality settled in on him once more.

The winds and destruction of nature had visited Walter Banks, too. The storm had skirted his property, only hitting part of his fields but the damage occurred in the ones planted in cotton and corn, his money crops which he could ill afford to lose.

However, the losses that the violent storm claimed today were insignificant in comparison to what his greed had cost him at gaming tables set up in his own parlor the night before.

Short of cash, he overextended his credit and now Abram LaRoche of Baton Rouge and New Orleans held the mortgage on Pine Ridge. With most of his crops destroyed, he could hardly afford to pay LaRoche in December when the note came due, and the Louisianan was anything but a patient man. If Banks failed to pay him, all that he had worked to accomplish would fall into the gambler's hands.

Gambling with LaRoche was nothing like fleecing these inexperienced Georgia lambs. LaRoche was a professional and Banks knew better. But the stakes were high and gambling was in his blood. Somehow when gold coins gleamed in the candle light, he seemed helpless to the lure, even when he knew the risk was too great.

It wouldn't have been so bad but that game was the final one of a season of losses to other Louisiana visitors. He had wagered and lost most of his liquid assets.

When LaRoche dangled the high stakes before him, he saw the chance of gaining everything he had lost plus some. But when LaRoche had refused to accept his marker without collateral, Pine Ridge was the only substantial asset he had left. In the heat of passion, he had not hesitated to comply. The pile of gold coins centering the table blinded his judgment and he wagered his future, much as he had induced Adam Gregory to do the same thing last year.

Other participants in the game had dropped out and, as if by design, it came down to LaRoche and Banks. With the flick of a card, history repeated itself, but this time it was Walter Banks not Adam Gregory who had lost. He had mortgaged everything with only a little capital left to continue on.

Now he was on a mission to save himself. The earth beneath him strewn with the remnants of Rachel's hope offered the salvation he needed and the woman who kneeled before him would give it to him. He no longer had the time to wait and play her game.

Rachel owed him money. Lots of it. Too bad he'd have to sacrifice Sweetwater to get Pine Ridge back, but hard choices had to be made sometimes and this was one of them.

The rash of emotions buffeting Banks wiped the brief flicker of satisfaction from his face, just as Rachel turned toward him. She lifted her large green eyes to his. They dominated her face as usual but disappointment glazed them putting out their fire, but no tears trailed down her cheeks, instead a peculiar resignation set her countenance.

A mask of concern slammed down on Banks' face as he leaped from his saddle and crooned, "Oh, my dear, you've lost everything." His hands reached out to touch her shoulders and she stiffened.

"It would seem so, Mr. Banks." She nodded dully.

"I'm afraid it's much too late to get another crop in the ground." He shook his head as he looked toward the rows of bare cotton stalks a few standing rigid while most bowed, bent and broken.

"Did your place escape?" Rachel asked, through tight lips, her look disinterested.

Banks observed her closely before answering, and then shook his head. "The storm spared the piney woods but visited my fields. Most of them resemble yours. We have a serious problem, Miss Rachel."

"At least we know that I have, Mr. Banks," she responded, her voice brittle.

"No ma'am, we both have. I have overextended myself helping you," Banks lied, "and now neither of us has a crop left to cover our expenses. I can't wait until December, Miss Rachel. I'm going to have to call my loan."

"You know I can't pay you." Rachel replied evenly, her eyes boring into his.

"I know you can't but you have Sweetwater." He replied in sugary tones.

"What will taking Sweetwater do?" She asked her tone even, emotionless.

"I have an option of selling or mortgaging it until I get out of the difficulties I'm in at the moment," His voice hardened.

"I thought I had until December." She parried as one small fist clinched hidden in the folds of her muddy skirt.

"Circumstances have changed and you have no hope of satisfying the mortgage in December." A glimmer of triumph lighting his eyes.

"But I have until then to try." She reminded.

"Perhaps the original mortgage, but what about the money I've advanced you?" Banks countered.

"The agreement I signed? You said it wasn't due until after harvest time," Rachel protested half heartedly.

"You didn't read the agreement carefully, my dear. A clause stated that if the crop met with an unexpected disaster, the note would automatically come due and I could collect at my discretion." Banks explained, his voice articulating each word as if his tongue savored it.

"Without prior notice?"

"No, you have a three day grace period," He chuckled, a mirthless sound, "What can you possibly do in three days that you haven't been able to accomplish in several months?

"Sell Sweetwater to Andrew Meredith," she bluffed, her eyes sparked suddenly unwilling to give up without a fight.

The leering grin faded from Walter Banks face as his reptilian eyes narrowed to mere slits and he stepped close to her. Banks grabbed Rachel's arm and she winced as his fingers dug into her flesh, "I wouldn't try that, my dear." His voice threatened in syrupy sweet tones. "If you want to save that monument to your past, you'll deal with me."

"How can dealing with you save Sweetwater? I believe you've already broken that promise, Mr. Banks."

Banks' fingers tightened on her arm cutting off the circulation, "I told you to call me Walter." He demanded.

"Well, Walter, didn't you?" She jerked her arm free.

"No, merely a minor change in expediting them. The plan is still the same." Banks explained his eyes evasive.

"And that—?" She questioned

"For you to retain Sweetwater."

"In light of what you've just demanded, how can that be possible?" Rachel demanded

"Marry me." He urged, a triumphant half-smile cracked his face.

"How will that change anything?" Rachel questioned, her heart hammering her chest.

"When you marry me, as your husband I can mortgage Sweetwater until I have recaptured my losses. You would still possess the title and be mistress of all the land between here and Jacob Emory, some ten thousand acres, the original estate your father owned. Otherwise I take possession of it and then it's mine to sell or mortgage and you're left with nothing, not even a roof over your head and no money to provide one. It seems to me, sweetheart, you have no choice."

"In other words, sell myself to you in exchange for Sweetwater?" Rachel replied, her voice steady.

"If you want to put it that way. But what choice do you have? I thought Sweetwater was all that mattered to you. No price too much to pay." He taunted and the words she had spoken to Andrew Meredith came back to haunt Rachel.

She stepped back and her green eyes raked him from his thinning red hair to his mud caked boots, then answered, "I was mistaken."

Walter Banks moved toward her, rage fired his tawny eyes erasing the smile from his face. He leaned close to her face, "Careful, don't offend me, I have a long memory. If you think Andrew Meredith is a more palatable choice, let me remind you, he walked out of your life, I was there. And if you think one of those young whelps that rushed you at the ball the other night will come to your rescue, think again. Most of them are spoken for already. But beyond that, Miss High and Mighty how would your society friends feel if they knew Meredith spent the night with you? "

Rachel's face blanched, "He never spent the night. . . .."

A triumphant, evil laugh erupted from Banks reverberating across the fields and swallowed up in the green shadows of the forest beyond, "I was there watching in the woods. Two horses, one light in the upstairs bedroom. I was back the next morning, observing that cozy breakfast for two. Even your exalted social position couldn't withstand behavior like that. In fact you've been gone so long you have to reclaim it anyhow and you'll never do it conducting yourself in such a wanton manner. If it is made known, your former friends wouldn't want you anymore."

"Then why would you want me, Mr. Banks?" Rachel questioned softly as the musty odor of damp earth filled her nostrils suffocating her.

"What happened that night between you and Meredith makes no difference to me as long as no one else knows, because possessing you will give me what I want in this community." he explained.

"How?" Rachel asked.

"By opening doors in society that have been closed or only reluctantly opened to me thus far. I'll always be an outsider to these people something my wealth can't overcome but as your husband, that will be remedied." A cold smile touched his lips as his eyes slid over her, he added, "And then there's the bonus I will get marrying you, a beautiful wife who will be the envy of every man not to mention the pleasure of having you totally under my control."

Rachel shuddered involuntarily, "Suppose Sweetwater and social position don't mean that much to me anymore?"

He laughed, "I know better and if you're thinking Andrew Meredith is your solution, forget it."

Rachel protested, "He offered me a business opportunity and it is much preferable than belonging to you."

A malevolent smile parted his lips but never touched his eyes, the pupils shrunk to black pinpoints staring, mesmerizing her. His voice husky, he murmured, "You think it's Sweetwater he wants? He wants the same thing I do—you. But for different reasons. He wants to rescue the fair maiden, but he'll change his mind when I get through with him. I'll tell him how many times that I called on you and the favors you swapped me for Sweetwater. Your chances will be ruined when I'm finished. Andrew Meredith's honor wouldn't let him accept tarnished goods."

Banks grabbed her arm as it whistled through the air, an open palm aimed at his cheek and sneered, "That won't help, Rachel. You know he'd believe me, because he knows what this place means to you."

Rachel quivered in defeat; the past rushed in to greet her as Agatha's warning from long ago echoed through her mind, "OK, Missy. Whatever you sow, you're gonna reap."

"Oh, Agatha, why must harvest time be so wretched?" Her heart responded.

<hr>

The late afternoon sun warmed Andrew Meredith's back as he cantered toward Holman's Livery. The journey had been long and hot and the thought of a cool glass of water, a clean room and a cool bath at the Fletcher House spurred him on.

He'd been gone a week and the trip had proved more frustrating than successful. He felt burdened down with the despair a watchman feels when his warnings of imminent danger go unheeded.

The small farmers he met had been congenial and even shared his political persuasions, but apathy and concern with their immediate lives left them unresponsive to Andrew's warnings. Sporadically some of them had suffered severe damage during the weather that had moved through while he was there so understandably their present losses took precedence over any future risks.

Not one person gave him a commitment to assist in organizing for the coming elections. When he compared the passiveness he had encountered here with the passion of the coastal fire eaters, he despaired, his task appearing impossible. He shrugged admitting to himself that he had done his best. What more could any man do? Still Andrew Meredith didn't like failure.

Putting his trip behind him, he planned the remaining few days before he would return with Randall to Savannah and on to Boston. His agent in Massachusetts had found a doctor who had made a career of researching lung diseases. His stellar reputation and eagerness to take the case eased Andrew's mind, giving him hope that Randall might find help. At least maybe he had a partial solution for one of his problems. The trip wasn't an entire waste of time.

Andrew climbed the grand staircase that led to the second floor of the Fletcher House and the more elaborate guest suites. The aroma of freshly baking bread wafted upward from the kitchen and his stomach growled reminding him that he had missed lunch. They would serve dinner in about an hour and he looked forward to a bath and fresh clothing while he waited. Suddenly weariness engulfed him and his steps slowed as he executed the last few stairs.

The past week proved so emotionally and physically grueling that he looked forward to boarding the train back to Savannah. That part of the stress had come from being near Rachel he refused to admit even to himself. Rather he blamed his new found commitment and the heartache of seeing Randall Wilkie in the dire physical and emotional state he was in.

Somehow all the energy he expended during his 12 -18 hour work days in the port city never exhausted him like the last two trips to North Georgia had. He smiled. He wanted to retreat back home where he could find some peace and solitude. Daphne ran a well ordered household where he could find quiet sanctuary. Quite a contrast to his life before she became a part of it.

A strange misgiving touched his heart and a frown furrowed his brow. Gnawing doubts about Daphne that he refused to acknowledge plagued him. Had he benefited or crippled her by his preferential treatment? He knew that she refused to associate with her own people. Her treatment in Macon by the Dupres pointed out the rejection she would encounter in the white world. She remained devoted to him and clung fiercely to her position in his life.

Despite the fact she was a gifted artist, he had to admit, taking care of his affairs was her only priority. He had discovered her talent quite by accident. He had arrived home from a trip a day earlier than expected and had discovered her sitting in the windowed alcove behind his desk. She had her paints and easels set up and capturing the bright afternoon light, she brought the lawn and gardens bordering the black waters of the river to life on her canvas.

He startled her and she jumped to her feet scattering paint and easel in every direction. That was one of the few times he had seen Daphne's cool demeanor pierced. He recognized that it was not that she was in his study; he had given her full access to the room to use in his absence. No, it was rather as if he had discovered some dark secret about her. He smiled remembering her confusion and the resulting conversation.

She explained that she only painted now and then to relieve boredom when her work lagged. Andrew chuckled to himself. He knew that was a fabrication, Daphne's job was endless and she was tireless in the pursuit of excellence in it. It still remained a mystery to him why she denied how gifted she was or admitted that her art was important to her. But he knew better, no one could be that gifted and it mean so little to them.

He had encouraged her to finish the landscape and pursue her art but she refused except for now and then she would paint for pleasure. Now the finished landscape hung beside the window whose view she had captured, but her life remained dedicated to Andrew Meredith, managing his household while finding her identity in her importance to him.

He admitted this young woman of beauty and talent was sacrificing her life for him. It suddenly occurred to him that, although he had set her free, she still remained in bondage to him as surely as any slave he had. Maybe more so because the slaves had personal relationships, Daphne had none. Vicariously she lived life through him.

The furrow deepened in his brow as self-examination forced him to admit he had not been too insistent that she pursue her interests. The truth was she made his life easier. She ran his household faultlessly and her dedication provided him a comfort zone that he cherished. He never considered before what would happen to her if he married. A wife would rightly assume the role of mistress of his household, the role Daphne fulfilled in every area save two.

But he had no immediate plans to take a wife and there was very little he could do about Daphne from here. But the disturbing thoughts continued to plague him curtailing his anticipation of the sanctuary that awaited him at Balmara.

The tepid water of his bath served to refresh him somewhat and lift his spirits. He deliberately pushed aside any further considerations about Daphne and turned his mind to even more perplexing thoughts—how he was going to help Rachel Gregory and free Randall's mind.

He had the names and information Goodman had provided, but what to do with them was another matter. New Orleans was a long distance and the chance the men would come while he was in Marietta seemed unlikely. Well, if it took a trip to New Orleans then so be it. With that commitment made, he dressed and went down to greet the tempting aroma wafting up the stairs from the kitchen.

TWENTY

The British nobleman lounged carelessly in the carriage, his long legs stretched out in front of him, his hands cupped behind his head. Daphne sat beside him while heavily draped windows and doors kept curious eyes out and the stifling heat inside.

As the two waited for the train towing the special car from Marietta, he studied the beautiful young woman through half-closed eyes. She presented an enigma to him. Exquisite and gifted, her life seemed inalterably bound to the host he was yet to meet. He could only speculate what forged such implacable bonds.

By her own admission she was free. He had reason to believe she could earn a reasonable living pursuing painting. He had discovered her work as he explored the upstairs gallery at Balmara one rainy afternoon. When he had, he knew he had found unusual talent, one that he could and would market for her in England. He had sought out Miss Matilda asking who the mysterious artist and subject was. He was not surprised to learn the subject was Meredith's absent niece, but surprised to discover the D.D. was none other than the beautiful woman who served so efficiently as household manager.

When he had confronted her with his discoveries and ventured his ideas, she rejected them out of hand. In fact, for the first time the reserved exterior she presented cracked and allowed him to see something of the emotions that seethed behind the composed facade and efficiency that bound her.

At first she denied the potential, making light of her talent. She told him it was only a frivolous past time that she pursued on long winter evenings. But he knew better. The portrait of a young girl was done with such detail it almost looked like a mirror's image. But it was in the girl's very essence captured on canvas that Daphne revealed herself as true artist rather than simply skilled technician. The young woman's eyes sparkled with mischief yet touched with a longing of some sort.

He had returned to the painting time after time the following days, captured by the young girl, feeling that if she walked through the door they would already be intimate friends.

With a little promotion he knew that people would line up at Daphne's doorway for portraits of such quality. She had laughed at that reminding him this was the South. He didn't quite understand what she meant by that but, he pressed, if she was free why did she need stay here? When he had suggested that she make her way north where there would be a ready, rich market, she responded, her eyes blazing, that Balmara was her home; her job was to care for Mr. Andrew.

So he sat in the shadows and wondered what manner of man could hold a woman captive in such a way? Who was this man that he was about to meet as the long overdue train pulled into the steamy Savannah station.

Andrew stepped out onto the platform and scanned the small waiting crowd. Then he caught sight of Daphne as she waited beside the tracks. Just in front of her stood a tall, broad shouldered youthful giant with golden hair. His refined features of slender nose slightly flared at the tip and high cheek bones as well as his confident bearing marked his nobility but his generous mouth which turned up at the corners and laughing azure eyes displayed none of the characteristic arrogance. With his blond good looks resplendent in the bright sunlight, he looked like every boy's dream of manhood. Daphne leaned toward him and said something then pointed toward Meredith. He looked up, his bright blue eyes locking on Andrew's deep brown ones where curiosity collided with reserve.

He moved toward Andrew and thrust out his hand. His lips parted in a friendly smile revealing even white teeth while his eyes, wide and guileless, looked straight into Andrew's, "Hello, Meredith, I'm Philip Duval, from England."

Suddenly Andrew Meredith felt very old.

The trip from Savannah to Boston had taken more than two weeks with the ship pulling in at ports of call at Charleston, Wilmington and New York. Although Andrew chaffed at the leisurely journey it proved time enough for the nobleman's effervescence and vitality to disarm Andrew Meredith's usual reticence toward strangers.

Philip's genuine warmth captured hearts like a friendly puppy, putting people at ease. Andrew Meredith proved no exception. Before the trip was over, Andrew felt that he had acquired a new friend as well as a business associate.

Randall Wilkie visibly perked up from the hours Philip spent talking to him as he sat wrapped up on deck in the gentle salty breeze. The weather had been splendid and Andrew noticed Randall's coughing had diminished with the sun and breeze putting some color in his wan cheeks. However, it was the spark of hope igniting his eyes where earlier only resignation had reigned that encouraged Meredith most. Andrew wondered how much of it was due to his own promises that he would try to help Rachel and how much was due to seeing a new physician. If he knew Randall, it was his assurances about Rachel. But Andrew doubted the proud, emerald eyed beauty would seek him out, but he kept his apprehensions to himself. Sighing deeply, he pushed the nagging worries to the back of his mind; there was little he could do from the rocking deck of a ship.

The days in Boston flew by in whirlwind succession. The first order of business was to get Randall settled in Dr. Larson's small, but well equipped, hospital. After a thorough examination, he remained hesitant of giving Andrew any hope that Wilkie would survive. Andrew had to live with his promise to expend every effort to diagnose the problem and then, he hoped, to treat it successfully.

Both doctor and patient realized his recovery chances rested in proper diagnosis and Randall committed himself to assisting in every way he could. The most important ingredient, hope, had already been set in motion. Andrew left Randall encouraged with his impression of the good doctor and the knowledge that he had done all that was humanly possible for his friend, now his survival rested in the hands of God. He prayed that the doctor would be a successful instrument in His hands.

The remaining days in Boston, Andrew spent at his shipping and ship building factory on the Boston waterfront. Philip Duval spent long hours with him, observing the operations, talking with employees and going over the accounts.

Philip surprised Andrew with his knowledge of shipping and manufacturing. When the young Briton understood the accounts with only a cursory explanation, he surprised his older friend even more. Philip's carefree demeanor and good looks belied the business acumen that rested beneath his easy going deportment.

He finished his perusal of the business mid way through the second day and made Andrew an attractive offer for both his townhouse and businesses. Since Andrew had not planned to sell the comfortable brownstone house where he, Aunt Maltilda and Laura had lived, he asked time to consider the offer.

Philip shrugged nonchalantly and informed him he would be out the remainder of the afternoon. So he picked up a flat package wrapped in brown paper that he had brought with him from Savannah and disappeared, leaving Andrew to uninterrupted consideration.

That evening an impatient Andrew waited dinner for a tardy Philip. When he finally arrived, the same package tucked beneath his arm, his eyes danced with excitement. He waved a hand toward Andrew and entered the hall calling for Daphne.

She answered from deep within the house and Philip rushed toward the sound of her voice, ignoring the elegant table set for two in the dining room. Puzzled, Andrew heard the soft murmuring of voices then heard Daphne's raised voice, "No. I told you, Mr. Philip I was not interested. This is none of your concern. Please let me be."

Daphne's tone shocked Andrew. He had never heard her raise her voice to anyone before. With his heart pounding, he walked swiftly down the hall in search of what made her angry.

Andrew found Philip in the hall outside the kitchen grasping an unframed portrait of Aunt Maltilda. Daphne stood in front of him, her hands on her hips the brilliant golden lights in her eyes blazing.

Andrew took one look at the portrait and demanded, "From where did this come?"

Philip, his hand lightly balancing the portrait, "From your house."

"I've never seen it." Meredith exclaimed, unbelieving.

"I thought not. And I'll wager no one else would have either if I hadn't found it hidden away in the alcove behind my room at Balmara."

"Did you do this, Daphne?" Andrew asked.

"Yes, and I would thank you both to leave it alone," she replied, her whole body trembling.

"Why do you have it?" Andrew demanded of Duval

"I borrowed it to test a theory I had." He answered with a slight shrug of his shoulders.

"You stole it, you mean." Daphne accused.

"If I had stolen it, would I have brought it back?" Philip asked calmly.

"That's beside the point. You took something that was mine without my permission, Or do you think because I'm a woman of color I don't own anything or have any rights?"

The smile slowly faded from Philip's face, the excitement wiped away by pain, "Daphne, you must know better than that. I was only trying to help you."

"You're meddling, Mr. Philip. Your kind of help will ruin my life." Daphne cried, her eyes bright with threatening tears.

"Philip, what's the meaning of this? Daphne calm yourself, I'm sure he meant no harm." Andrew commanded.

"I went to an art gallery because I wanted an expert opinion. I thought she was good but wanted someone else's judgment. The proprietor was excited and demanded to know who this mystery DD was. I asked him if he might have a market for an artist such as this and he said yes. In fact wanted to buy Aunt Maltilda's portrait at a very respectable price. With that encouragement I went to three more galleries, and received the same reception except each one offered me more than the one before," Duval explained excitement firing his eyes once more.

"You wanted to sell Daphne's painting? Why?" puzzled Andrew.

"Why, man?" Philip almost shouted, "She's great. A talent too good to be hidden away. She can earn a living with her talent."

"She doesn't need to earn a living. I provide for her more than adequately." Andrew retorted, his tones clipped. The muscles in his jaws twitched.

"That's what I told him, Mr. Andrew. I have a job, all the job I want or need." Daphne whimpered, a tear trickled down her cheek, the controlled, efficient young woman dissolving before their eyes into vulnerable girl.

Andrew watched the two of them, looking from one to the other, mystified at the exchange and mesmerized at the transformation of Daphne. Before him stood a Daphne he'd never seen, one he didn't know existed. In all the years he had known her since she left her mother, he had never seen her cry nor had he glanced behind her calm exterior.

Philip's eyes softened as he took in her discomfort and he crooned softly, "Oh, Daphne, I would do nothing to hurt you. I only wanted to prove to you, your worth."

Daphne, wide eyed and sorrowful, gazed at the handsome young lord and pled, "Why can't you understand. My worth is what I can do for Mr. Andrew. This art is only for my own amusement."

Her words pierced Andrew's conscience like a fiery poker resurrecting the memory of his earlier misgivings.

"No I can't understand, Daphne. I don't understand a woman who could deny her God-given gift or a man who would require her to." Philip said softly.

"You don't understand the circumstances. He didn't require it,

I gave it freely. That's all I want out of life," she protested and dropped her head in humiliation.

"Circumstances? I can see you must love him very much," Philip pressed, forgetting Andrew's presence in the room.

Daphne's head shot up, wounded pride lighting her eyes, "Not the way you mean, Mr. Philip. I have an obligation to Mr. Andrew."

"No valid obligation would result in sacrificing this." Philip insisted as he pointed to the painting. Then he shook his head and added, "It has to be something more."

She nodded, "Respect and admiration."

"That's not enough, Daphne. Life is more than obligation, respect, and admiration. It's fulfilling our potential with our God-given talents and beyond that loving, family relationships blessed with a spouse and children. That's my aspiration; really what life is all about to me."

"When you're white, Mr. Philip. In my world life is survival. In Mr. Andrew's world I can survive." Daphne explained fighting to gain control of her emotions.

"There's a great deal of difference between living life and merely surviving," Philip charged, his voice breathless.

"That's more than enough for me. Now if you please, sir, I'll take my painting and I'll hear no more of this." She took the portrait from him and, turning, walked quickly out the door. Once again under control, she escaped, her back ramrod straight, the old facade settling around her features.

Philip stared at her retreating back until she was out of sight, then turned to Andrew, his eyes bright with frustration, "Andrew Meredith, how could you do that to her?"

"Do what?" Andrew hedged.

"Enslave her. You didn't set her free. She's in bondage more to you than any slave you have. And in doing that you are cheating the world out of her glorious gift and Daphne out of fulfillment. How could you require so high a price for mere physical pleasure?"

The warmth of Andrew Meredith's dark brown eyes frosted turning them cold black as he remarked through clenched teeth, "What you don't know, you should not form an opinion on, Duval."

Philip stared back into the frigid depths of his new friend, before remarking, "I'm sorry. Perhaps I've come to the wrong conclusion, Andrew. I had heard about some of the strange customs in the South and while in Savannah—well I could only assume that the bonds that held Daphne were stronger than housekeeping duties and gratitude. Perhaps I was wrong."

"You are wrong. The reason Daphne is with me is to protect her from that very practice you're alluding to. I know what all Savannah whispers behind my back. And I've allowed them to, because as long as they think that about her she is safe from any lechers who might prey upon her."

"But I don't understand her allegiance to you."

"Perhaps she understands she's safer."

"No, it's more than that Andrew. Your very protection has destroyed any life she might have. Has she any hope of husband or family?" Philip questioned, his blue eyes darkened with pleading.

"If she wants one." Andrew answered brusquely, his eyes not quite meeting Duval's.

"That's it. Does she want one?" Philip took a step closer to Meredith, pressing his point.

"I haven't asked." The older man answered evasively

"Are there any prospects around?" Philip responded, not willing to let go.

"None that I know of." Andrew admitted, forcing his eyes to meet Philip's.

"What about from her own race?" Philip asked softly, less militant now that he could see the struggle in Andrew's eyes.

Andrew shrugged, the memory of Daphne in Macon at the Dupre's home surfacing, "She doesn't make friends easily with her own people."

"That's what I mean. You've elevated her from her own world causing them to reject her; yet, your world refuses to accept her. She has no world but yours."

227

Andrew protested, "Don't you think that's sufficient?"

"What about when you take a wife?"

"I'll come to that decision if it ever arrives."

"Meanwhile Daphne only lives vicariously through you and if you marry and your need for her is gone, her life will be over."

"There are many things you don't understand, Philip." Andrew replied coolly as Philip's words and observations echoed the very misgivings he had encountered in Marietta only two weeks before.

"I'm sure that's true, friend. There is much about Southern culture I don't understand, but I do know human nature and I understand the importance of a person using their God-given gifts. We're only stewards of the life and talents we're given. It's a terrible tragedy when we waste them."

"I appreciate your concern for my business, Philip, but really don't you think I'm the one who can best make those judgment calls?" Andrew asked between tight lips.

"Not necessarily. Sometimes we're too close to a situation to evaluate it properly. That's the only reason I spoke. I have enough confidence in your integrity that I know you would rectify a problem if you knew it existed. I guess I took on the momentary role of a watchman, if my warning offended you please accept my apologies." Philip said as he placed a comforting hand on Andrew Meredith's resistant shoulder.

But Duval's gesture failed to comfort Andrew because all he could hear ringing in his ears and reverberating into every crevice of his conscience, "If a watchman warns the city and the city heeds not . . . ." The same call to action that had motivated him over the past weeks and months now came back to haunt him, only this time he was the recipient of the warning. The question was what would his response be? How could he? A chill played up and down his spine as he responded abruptly, "Let's eat, Duval. Our meal is getting cold," closing the conversation and daring Philip to reopen it.

TWENTY-ONE

The train slowed its progress as it made its way across the Chattahoochee and began its ascent through the bare branched forest toward Marietta. It was late November and months since Andrew Meredith's last trip to north Georgia.

He had not intended that he would delay the trip so long, but August and September passed quickly. Frequent trips to Boston to check on Randall and to assist in the transition of his businesses from his hands to the capable ones of Philip Duval, had filled the months and no time seemed convenient to return.

When October brought the calamity of Harpers Ferry, he told himself he needed to remain in Savannah to bring moderation in the midst of fiery tempers. John Brown did more to aggravate Meredith's mission than anything thus far. The fanatic madman became a symbol no amount of common sense could convince away. In the north he became a martyr and in martyrdom, a hero. To the South he embodied all that they dreaded and feared, causing them to broaden their suspicion to embrace and equate anyone who was a unionist as an abolitionist. The rift widened and Meredith's task became more difficult each day and in some cases downright dangerous or so his friends had warned him.

With his frenzied political activity, he suddenly felt a need to divest himself of some of the responsibilities that bound him. Realizing he would no longer have any need for a residence in Boston, he agreed to sell his Brownstone to Philip. Yet it saddened him that a chapter of his life was closing.

Sometimes Philip would accompany him on his trips. Other times he would be away in Charleston, sometimes New Orleans and even as far north as Washington and New York. Duval's first visit to America was proving an informative one. He left no stone unturned which aroused his curiosity.

Andrew occasionally suspected his friend of simultaneously lining up markets for Daphne's art work as he visited around the country. Neither had mentioned their conversation concerning Daphne again, but it lay between them a wedge that had, for a while, dampened their budding friendship. Yet he dared not let himself dwell on that subject, yet unresolved and festering in his soul.

So Andrew hurled himself into harder work and a frenzied life, fighting the two specters that haunted him, one with eyes of topaz the other with eyes of emerald, neither settled. Resolutely he had pushed both to the back of his mind, hoping somehow they would resolve themselves and knowing better. But each time he entered Balmara, Daphne's presence and efficiency remained a silent, painful reminder. The lovely plantation had ceased to be his haven of serenity.

His reluctance to deal with Rachel's problems came to an abrupt halt when he received a note from Robert Goodman. The note informed him that LaRoche had returned to Marietta along with it the editor had included an announcement from his newspaper announcing the engagement of Anna Rachel Gregory to Walter Banks. It stated simply that on the Friday evening following Thanksgiving she would become the planter's bride in a simple ceremony at Sweetwater Plantation.

Now he had to make an effort to confront the problem, because Randall waited expectantly, slightly improved in health and asking about Rachel. Up to this point he had stalled. He could no longer. Yet he remained at a loss as to a plan of action. She had refused to ask for help. He could only surmise that Randall had been wrong about her distress. Perhaps she had sorrowed over his illness and the attorney mistook it for remorse over her predicament. Whatever it was, Meredith had to learn the truth. If she needed help, he would be there, but he refused to disrupt another man's wedding without cause, even if he was a swindler like Walter Banks.

Pain that he had buried and denied for the past months suddenly engulfed him with memories of her dark beauty encased in Banks arms as she danced away from him. The thought of her belonging to the wily planter for a lifetime crashed in and his stomach gave a sickening roll. In that moment of truth it was hard to deny that his search for a solution had not wholly been fueled by Randall's need, but by his own as well. He realized he had delayed action because he hoped time would raise her frustration enough to sacrifice her pride. Obviously it hadn't and now he had to consider if Walter Banks might not be what she really wanted.

Philip Duval sat on the seat next to the window and took in the scenery, the excitement of discovery lighting his face.

"Now how far did you say it was on up to Barnsley's place?" he asked Andrew. He planned to visit Godfrey Barnsley and his sons in Adairsville. Godfrey, an Englishman, had been a companion of his father when they were boys and Philip wanted to pay his respects as well as satisfy his curiosity about his large plantation. For some strange reason he wanted to see for himself how well an Englishman fit into Southern culture.

Despite his heavy heart Meredith smiled at his friend's vibrant enthusiasm, "Maybe about thirty miles or so I'd say."

"I hope I can get a decent mount at the livery in town. You know Englishmen, they like a proper horse." Philip announced, his brow slightly furrowed beneath his thatch of unruly blond hair.

"I can assure you that you will have a mount worthy of you at your disposal," Andrew chuckled

"Oh?" he questioned his eyes bright, expectant.

Andrew knew that a compassionate heart as well as the mind of a shrewd business man hid beneath his light hearted behavior. Neither seemed to dampen his boundless energy or his inexhaustible curiosity about the country he visited, especially the South.

"It might surprise you to know that Americans, especially Southerners share your English love of good horse flesh." Meredith replayed dryly.

"Didn't mean to imply otherwise, old chap. You have some fine horses at Balmara." Philip hastened to assure. "Remember I tried everything in your stable? I even tried your own black Thunderbolt. Now there was a ride. They told me that only you could ride him. Before I got off him, I believed them. Whew! It was the ride of my life."

"It just so happens that I have two of my personal horses stabled in Marietta. One is Thunderbolt's son, Stormy, a grey thoroughbred, the other a flashy Arabian mare, Fantasy. Both are excellent stock. I needed to have one that would take the rigors of these side trips I have been taking," Meredith explained.

"Two horses? Why two? Surely you can ride only one at a time." Philip rejoined, his inquisitive nature fired again.

"I thought someone else would be using the other. It didn't turn out that way, though."

"Someone else? You have a lady love up here, Meredith?" Philip inquired teasing, "No, it couldn't be that. If that were the reason you wouldn't be offering it to me. Anyway I can't imagine any lady turning down Andrew Meredith's attention."

"You might be surprised." Andrew chuckled again, covering a vague discomfort at the path the discussion veered.

Philip's deep blue eyes met and held Meredith's for a moment. Something akin to understanding washed away the levity in his eyes as he remarked, "Sorry, Drew, I shouldn't have teased about that. I know how you feel."

"I don't think so. It isn't what you think." Andrew protested.

"I recognize regret in your eyes, for I've seen it in my own." He explained matter of factly.

"Regret?" Andrew asked, curious despite himself.

"Yes, didn't realize I was in love until I had lost her. Fact is she was an American girl, Southern. Met her in France where she was visiting an aunt. Guess that's why I'm so interested in Georgia and cotton plantations. She had grown up on a cotton plantation and talked of nothing else but returning to it."

"What happened?"

"I let her get away." He explained simply.

"Why?" Andrew probed.

"Because of my own foolishness. I couldn't stand her aunt. She was interested in nothing but her own upward social climb. She decided that her niece was the ticket for her advancement if she could snare a duke. She selected me as the candidate, not that she didn't have her eyes searching for alternates in case I failed to come through.

She fairly pushed the girl on me. Every social engagement I attended she would pounce on me, telling me about her niece who was arriving from America. I managed to refuse her every invitation and resisted any occasion that might bring me in contact with the woman. Finally in exasperation, I returned to England and avoided that part of France for three years. I thought by that time she would have managed to marry her off and it would be safe to return.

The first day I arrived, I went riding and came upon a young woman sitting in a meadow and watching the river meander down below while her horse grazed nearby. When she looked up at me, her beauty and the vitality in her eyes captivated me so I stopped and spoke. Afterwards we met often in the afternoons. Some days we would ride like the wind over the meadows, other days we would sit, watching the river and just talk. This went on for several weeks during which time I found myself attracted not only to her but her South. That's why I want to see what she loved."

"What happened?" Andrew encouraged

"Guess who the girl was."

"The woman's niece."

"None other. I found out about three months later. She had told me her name, but since it was different from her aunt's I didn't press her for any details or about where she was staying. She always refused to let me see her home and the touch of mystery all added to the spell, you know." Philip explained with a shrug.

"That seems a little odd, Duval from a young man who was smitten." Meredith observed with a wry smile. "Didn't you meet her at any social functions?"

"Avoided anywhere I knew the woman would be, because I had heard her niece was still unmarried." Philip answered with a grin.

"Still seems a little odd that you never discussed her personal life." Andrew insisted

"In retrospect, I believe she didn't want me to know who she was. Her aunt's maneuvers must have proved humiliating to her." Philip explained a thoughtful light in his blue eyes.

"You're probably right. But why didn't you press her, if you were falling in love?" Andrew questioned, not willing to accept his answers, his heart torn for this unknown American girl.

"Meredith, you have to understand British nobility. At first I mistook her for an American relative of a local farm family who had elegance and class above her station. My family would have highly disapproved of a match like that. I wouldn't have considered marrying neither a French farm maiden nor their American kin."

"Oh, I see." Andrew observed a cool surprise widened his eyes slightly.

Philip sensed Andrew's censure and rushed on to explain, "That was then, not now, Andrew. If I had my time to go over it would have a different outcome. But you must remember, I didn't have any idea how smitten I was until I left her. Can you understand that? You don't realize how much something or someone means until you've lost them?"

Pain touched Andrew's warm brown eyes turning them dark as he ignored the question and countered, "Did the aunt find out about your visits?"

Disgust tinged the younger man's face wiping the sparkle from his eyes, "Oh, yes. She sent me a threatening note claiming I had ruined her niece's good name, demanding that I marry her. That's when I found out who the girl really was. I refused to give in to extortion and left for Cornwall, feeling the girl had duped me. I refused to risk association with a family like that."

"So that was the end of it?" Andrew encouraged.

"Only partly. When I went home, I endeavored to put the whole thing from my mind, but it proved impossible. Those eyes and wistful voice haunted every crevice of my being. Finally when I regained some sanity, I concluded the girl was an innocent party in her aunt's scheme. So I decided to return and marry her, then take her far away from her aunt."

"What about your family's wishes?"

"By that time I was so besotted by her memory, I was willing to take her as my bride if she'd been the milk maid. But actually since her aunt had married nobility and she was an American, it didn't present an insurmountable social obstacle as long as I remained in England. Americans, especially wealthy Americans, are viewed differently. They rather have a class of their own."

"What happened?" Andrew urged, his curiosity fired.

"When I went back to France to confront the aunt and rescue fair maiden I learned she had returned to America." Philip answered with a sad half-smile.

"Well, man why didn't you follow?"

"The proprietor of the local inn said she had returned to marry. I felt I had no right to disturb her wedding since I had abandoned her as I did."

"Didn't you at least ask the aunt for her address?" Meredith asked, his voice rose in disbelief.

"I couldn't abide the thought of encountering the woman. I felt like ringing her neck not to mention my heart's own torment. I spent only the one night and returned home the next day." Philip shook his head and dropped his eyes and continued his voice husky, "She still haunts my every memory and the regret is still bitter as gall. I am interested in American business ventures, but more than that, the trip has been a catharsis. I want to lay the specter of her to rest. I thought maybe I could if I came here and dispelled the mystery of this land she loved so. If I could think about her, in her own surroundings, happy with someone suited to her, and then maybe I could get on with my life. So you see that's the secret of Sir Philip Duval IV, only son and sole heir of Sir Philip Duval III."

Andrew clasped his friend's shoulder, and replied, his own voice hoarse, "I'm sorry, Philip. I wish there was something I could do."

Philip caught Andrew Meredith's warm, brown eyes, a compelling look in his vivid blue ones, "You can, Drew. If you find love, don't let it get away. Overturn every obstacle; pursue every avenue until you secure it. Nothing is quite as painful as living with regret."

A band clasped around Andrew's heavy heart as he wondered if Philip's admonition to him had come too late. Meredith turned from his friend and gazed out the train window where Marietta's red brick station nestled beside the tracks. He had arrived at his destination, but had he waited too late?

TWENTY-TWO

The pungent odor of printers' ink greeted Andrew as he let himself into the newspaper office. Robert Goodman lounged at his cluttered desk, his back to the door. With his feet propped up on a pile of strewn papers and his familiar green visor pulled down low on his forehead, he appeared mesmerized by what he held in his hand. The tinkling brass bell that announced his friend's arrival failed to disturb the editor's concentration.

Andrew grabbed the old oak chair that he sat in and spun it around on its creaking swivel. Goodman's feet scattered papers over floor and desk. The older man jerked trying to regain his balance to the chuckles of his younger visitor and rasped, "Andrew Meredith, I might have known it was you. Why the ink has hardly dried on the note I sent you, and here you are. So it's just Randall Wilkie's welfare you're interested in eh, my boy? "

"That's what I told you and I'll stick to my story, you old reprobate." Andrew chuckled. For the first time in days the heaviness that had constrained him lifted some.

"You'll have a hard time convincing me, Meredith," Goodman growled.

"Wouldn't even try. Tell me, is LaRoche still in town?" Meredith asked.

"He was yesterday and I hope he hasn't left yet." Robert answered.

"Have you been able to learn anything else that might be of some help to me?" Andrew's eyes brightened with expectation.

"Maybe. My man, Tim, befriended one of LaRoche's young henchmen and was able to garner a little information from him. Seems LaRoche came calling 'cause he's in something of a cash flow crisis. I knew he'd tried to get up a game of chance locally without much success. The local folks have learned their lesson about these New Orleans visitors."

"And not a bit too early according to my observations," agreed Andrew.

"Well, err, right. Anyway seems he journeyed on out to Banks' place who, according to local gossip, usually welcomes him with open arms and invites a few men from south of here participate in a game of chance."

"Guess LaRoche was successful in getting up a game."

"Actually, he wasn't," Goodman reported.

Andrew raised an inquisitive brow at his friend, "Banks reforming?"

Goodman chuckled mirthlessly, "Not a change of heart, rather a change in fortune. That's what I thought you might find interesting and helpful."

"How's that?" Andrew questioned.

"According to Tim's source, Banks has been steadily losing to LaRoche as well as some other New Orleans visitors since last spring. The stakes were so high that he gave LaRoche the mortgage on Pine ridge to cover his wager. Guess what happened?'

"Don't tell me—he lost?" Meredith asked, his voice raised.

"That's right." Goodman confirmed, nodding his head.

"History repeats itself. His just deserts I'd say since that's what he did to Adam Gregory." Andrew observed.

"Rather looks like it. You think it's just retribution, do you?"

"I'd be lying if I said I didn't get some pleasure from his predicament." Andrew confessed.

"Nothing but human, Drew. But you can't absolve Gregory's guilt by blaming Banks entirely. In the final analysis a man is accountable for his own choices."

"Grief can do strange things to a man. None of us know how we would react," Andrew defended.

"Perhaps you have a point, and if Adam Gregory had been the only one to suffer for his bad decisions then I'd agree. But his was a selfish act in not considering that his daughter would be the ultimate one to pay. This is exactly what's happening now. Did you get my clipping?"

"Yes." Andrew answered tersely.

"I feel Walter Banks' predicament is behind this wedding."

"How do you figure that?" Andrew questioned.

"If Banks can get his hands on Sweetwater, then he can lift the mortgage off Pine Ridge."

"If he waits until December, it'll be his anyway." Andrew reminded.

"According to LaRoche's friend, his note on Pine ridge comes due before December. If he marries Rachel, then Sweetwater will be available immediately."

"Could be she wants Walter Banks." Andrew insisted sharply, his tone revealing far more than his words.

His friend peered at him for a long moment over round, gold rimmed glasses pushed down on his nose before he replied, "That's not logical, my friend. Why would she want the man who is responsible for her problems?"

"She blames me, not Banks for her problems."

"Why? Don't you think it's time to tell me the whole story?" Goodman encouraged.

The crusty old editor listened attentively while the evening shadows lengthened as Andrew Meredith poured out the problems with which he had grappled since Rachel Gregory had invaded his life withholding from his friend only the tumult raging in his heart because his mind and tongue even yet denied it. But his wise and concerned friend knew because he saw it in his eyes.

When Andrew finished his story, his burden felt lighter from the telling of it for he had carried it alone far too long.

Robert Goodman sighed, "The poor lass."

"Obviously you weren't listening, Robert." snapped Meredith, "She has refused help; therefore, she must not need any. I am only trying because of Randall."

"Maybe so, but, whatever your reasons, you need to consider this, where could she turn, Andrew?" Goodman reasoned. "You walked out of her life, by your own admission. She thought your help withdrawn and you took Randall to Boston. She has had little contact in the community since she returned so there is no one here she dare approach. Without marrying Banks, she will have no home, no money, no way to earn any and no alternative to return to her aunt. What other choice does she have?"

A strange struggle warred in Andrew's soul as a glimmer of hope ignited and he asked, "What should I do then?"

"Your first course of action, as I see it is to find LaRoche. Are you staying at the Fletcher House? That's where Tim said LaRoche was staying."

"Right, Philip Duval and I are sharing a three room suite there.

"Philip Duval?" Goodman narrowed his eyes, his mind churning for a memory.

Andrew laughed, knowing the editor was trying to remember. He took great pride in never forgetting a name or a face. "You don't know him. He is the British nobleman who bought my Boston holdings. He's gone up to the Woodsland to visit Godfrey Barnsley. Won't be back for a couple of days."

"Oh, I see. Well back to LaRoche, if he's as short of cash as he seems to be, you might be able to buy Banks' mortgage from him because I don't think he's interested in acquiring a Georgia plantation. If you can deal with him then you'll have the leverage you need with Banks." Goodman advised with a nod of his head as he thoughtfully patted his protruding paunch considering the possibilities.

"Suppose I do persuade him to part with that mortgage, then what? I don't know how I'll help Rachel without her asking for it." Andrew mused more to himself than to Goodman as he stood up to leave.

The plump editor followed the younger man to the door and paused beside it. Reaching out one gnarled, ink stained hand, he grasped his shoulder. He stood an arm's length away and looked into Andrew Meredith's eyes, "Andrew, my boy, I found that the good Lord has a way of giving us wisdom and opening doors to us when we're trying to walk in the path He's leading us. Sometimes He doesn't open the door until the last minute, that way we learn to trust Him. You just do what you know to do and I have no doubt the next step He'll provide. You deal with LaRoche, and then trust God to provide you with the next step."

Andrew sighed and a half-smile played at his lips, "That's difficult for a "take charge" kind of man to do, my friend."

"Then maybe that's why God has you in this situation. Do what you know to do, then leave the next step to Him. You won't fail."

"Thank you, Goodman, I needed that reminder, but I'll say you're the most unlikely preacher I've ever met."

"Why do you say that? God uses messengers in all shapes and forms, even a crusty old newspaper man. Now you go on over to the hotel and rest a bit."

<hr/>

As it turned out, Andrew had plenty of time to rest. Two days later, an impatient Andrew Meredith entered the Fletcher House dining room for an early dinner. He had cooled his heels waiting for an elusive LaRoche. The desk clerk assured him several times that Mr. LaRoche was still registered at the hotel and had not returned to New Orleans so Andrew Meredith was left to wait and worry, neither of which suited him. His mind dragged up a thousand reasons he needed to be somewhere else, not the least of which his young niece was returning to Savannah. Her visit to Virginia had lasted eight months and he had missed her.

However in the months of separation Aunt 'Tilda had convinced him it was time to send her away to school. His heart shuddered at the thought, but finally he had agreed. Perhaps in the spring. It would take them that long to get her ready, his heart insisted.

———————————————

Candles on tables dressed in Irish linen cloths bounced light softly from two mirrored walls in the dining room, bathing it in a translucent golden aura. A cold November wind whistled around the brick building, cocooning the patrons inside where a warm fire crackled in the large fireplace while the fragrance of cinnamon from baking apples permeated the air.

Only a few customers occupied tables as the dinner hour had not yet arrived, but Andrew, hungry and out of sorts from his waiting, found a table near the door and sat where he had a broad vista of the customers who entered.

The nearly empty hotel seemed strange. During the summer it operated at capacity, usually filled with people who traveled from coastal and southern Georgia, to enjoy the cooler summer temperatures and bathe in the therapeutic springs that abounded in the area. But when the cold winds of winter blew, only the hale and hearty left warmer climate to venture north. Most of the guests were there on business, not pleasure.

Local couples drifted in as he waited for his dinner. Some of them he recognized, others were strangers. Not wanting to invite small talk, he merely nodded to them with an occasional wave of his hand. His forbidding countenance hardly invited them to linger so he enjoyed his meal in solitude.

He was having an after dinner coffee when three strangers entered the room. They chose the table just in front of his and he had time to scrutinize them carefully without their noticing.

The two younger men were short and stocky, while the older was tall and spindly with long thin black hair peppered with streaks of grey. A finely tailored coat and britches did nothing to disguise his coarse features or give him the aristocratic impression his attire sought to convey. On the contrary his clothes only emphasized the incongruence, making him almost a caricature.

But it was the dark eyes sunk deep in his thin, swarthy face which caught and held Meredith's attention. Cold, but alert, they darted to and fro throughout the room as if accessing the clientele while he listened to his companions.

His long slender fingers drummed uneasily on the table and Andrew noticed they appeared delicate and out of place on him. A man of few words, he answered his companions in grunts and monosyllables. Beneath his waist coat, the telltale bulge of a derringer heightened Andrew's suspicion that the man was a gambler.

The waiter drifted across the room and spoke to the trio as he handed each a menu, "Welcome, Messrs, we are so glad to have you visit with us again. I suppose our north Georgia weather is a welcome change from the weather in New Orleans."

The short, blond man looked up an affected arrogance in his eyes, "Welcome change? Maybe during the summer, but not this time of the year. However, it's been awhile since we've been in New Orleans, you see, we've just returned from Macon. It was plenty cold down there . . . ," his response cut short by a silent reprimand from the cold eyes across from him.

The gregarious young man abruptly turned his attention to the elegant menu, whose golden curls and flourishes presented the evening's fare. Andrew's attention now riveted on the trio, his heart pounding. Could this be? A too talkative younger man and a swarthy man with wily countenance?

"Of course, Mr. LaRoche, we will cook it to your specifications." The waiter replied to a question from the older man and Andrew Meredith thanked God for his bountiful blessings and perfect timing.

Andrew left the dining room and made his way to the desk where the clerk confirmed that indeed LaRoche was the Ingus LaRoche he sought.

So it was that Andrew Meredith, impatience and despondency forgotten, spent the midnight hour huddled in a back room of the Fletcher House with a stranger named Ingus LaRoche. As the night marched steadily toward day, astute business man battled gambler in negotiations. Andrew's only hope of a solution for Rachel's problem rested in the hands of this unscrupulous gambler. Yet Andrew never revealed the urgency his heart felt. With quiet determination he held his ground and when the eastern sky streaked with pink and gold both men had won.

Andrew rose from the bargaining table, stiff and tired, but he possessed papers that cost him a small fortune. Compared to the ultimate victory they represented, he counted the price negligible.

His success had far outdistanced his anticipation for not only did he hold the mortgage on Pine Ridge, but Rachel's note on Sweetwater as well. Banks' addiction had not ended with his August losses, but in September had driven him to part with his only hope of satisfying LaRoche, Sweetwater. The only leverage Banks had over Rachel now remained the living and planting expenses she had incurred since her return and what Andrew held in his hand far outweighed that sum. He smiled the taste of victory sweet.

For the few hours remaining before morning fully arrived, Andrew slept the sweet sleep of relief knowing that finally he could encourage Randall. Still the unanswered question remained would she ask for his assistance and if she didn't how could he help her? He clung to his decision not to barge in without some invitation.

The choice of survival was ultimately up to her.

After Andrew filled in a jubilant Goodman about his success, he could hardly refuse to attend to the political visits south of Marietta, toward Sweetwater that the editor had arranged for him.

This trip he met with open hostility. The results of John Brown's actions in a small town in Virginia had spread like ripples on a pond, raising fear and prejudice where there had been moderation. Not only did Andrew encounter simple backlash from the demented man's deeds, but someone had fanned fearful hearts with lies about him.

The crowd that stood before the little white Methodist church just north of Fairburn bristled with belligerence toward Andrew. Word had spread before him that he was a Southerner turned abolitionist, tainted by his northern industrial holdings. For the first time in north Georgia, the seat of moderation, Andrew Meredith's message received outright rejection.

The earlier sweet taste of victory he experienced in his negotiations with LaRoche, turned to bitter dregs as he rode back to Marietta, a cold November wind stinging his face. His political endeavors had been futile and as far as he knew, Rachel Gregory's marriage remained imminent. Hunched in the saddle, he concentrated on the warm bath he would order as soon as he arrived in town and refused to think of the fast approaching Friday when Rachel Gregory would pledge her life and loyalty to Walter Banks. Because he had no idea how to stop it.

TWENTY-THREE

Arriving at the door of his suite, Meredith paused, puzzled. The door stood slightly ajar. He stepped into the parlor of the three-room suite and looked around cautiously. The heavily curtained windows darkened the room, diminishing his ability to see. Suddenly the unbidden fragrance of lilacs teased his nostrils and unwanted memories crashed into his mind. He vehemently threw his mud spattered overcoat onto the chair and turned toward the bedroom when a movement behind the door caught his peripheral vision. Whirling with outstretched hand, he grabbed crisp taffeta and soft flesh.

"Hello, Andrew." Her voice was low and hesitant, arms trembling beneath his grasp. A heavy veil draped from a jaunty hat covered the face she turned toward him. He could hardly make out her features.

"Rachel! What in the world are you doing here?"

"I'm here to see you," she answered and he heard her voice tremble.

Checking his emotions, his voice gruff, "Have you any idea what you've done now?"

"I suppose so. I was really on my way to Savannah."

"Why Savannah?" He asked his heart unwilling to hope.

"To see you." She answered simply.

"How, why?" He asked, mystified.

"The train. Bertha and Jacob Emory dropped me off at the station. I had missed the train so I came here and got a room for the night, that's when I discovered you were here. I—I saw your name on the register."

She dropped her head, not willing to meet his eyes.

"How did you get in? Who saw you?" He demanded, his voice low but intense, as he bent to light a lamp.

He saw her determined chin raise ever so slightly and he could imagine the defiant look firing those emerald eyes hidden beneath her dense veil.

Soft, apologetic words denied the countenance he envisioned but could not see, "Only the maid saw me and even she couldn't see my face. I paid her to let me in your room. "

Andrew released his grip on her arms and said, "I'm quite flattered, but don't you think this is a little unorthodox even for you."

"Not when you're desperate." She replied breathlessly.

He took her arm again, but this time gently and led her toward the camel back settee, "Have a seat and tell me about why you've come."

"I want to accept your offer of employment, if it's still available."

"I withdrew it when I left." He hedged. His heart hammered his chest as he struggled to remain aloof.

"Do you have an alternate?" She asked, all the usual spirit missing from her voice.

"Why are you interested now?" He asked, as he sat down opposite her and stretched his long legs out in front of him. He looked at her closely hating the veil that hid her glorious eyes and hair from his view.

She breathed in a ragged breath, "It's either that or marry Walter Banks."

"And you think I'm the lesser of the two evils." He observed dryly.

A flush mounted Rachel's face, hidden from his view, "You didn't require marriage,"

Her words stung Andrew, piercing through the armor shielding his heart from her, "I believe I did offer that option, but you turned me down handily, as I remembered."

"You were jesting, what he is demanding is no joking matter. He is an evil man," Rachel replied.

"I could say I told you so, but I guess there wouldn't be any point in that." He responded choosing to ignore her response to his proposal.

"No, none whatever." she snapped, reflecting some of her old spirit.

"Exactly what do you want me to do?" He asked.

"Forgive me, Andrew." She pled softly, her voice breaking.

"For what?" He questioned, emotion sharpening his.

"For everything I accused you of that wasn't true," she answered.

"Well, that's rather a broad apology since you accused me of every bad deed and plot conceivable, along with blaming me for all your problems." He observed.

"I was wrong. I see now, you were trying to help, not hurt. And I desperately needed—need your help." Her voice sounded on the verge of tears, his heart melted.

"What's happened?" He asked, more gently now.

"A hail storm destroyed my crops last summer and Banks demanded immediate satisfaction. He gave me a choice, foreclosure or marriage. I managed to forestall the marriage by telling him I was in mourning, but now he has insisted I go through with it. I tried to but I can't. "

"You have until December." Meredith reminded.

"No, the agreement I signed when he advanced me money for repairs and planting allowed for immediate foreclosure." Rachel explained, now her voice dull, the threat of tears waning.

"What a foolish thing to sign." He observed evenly while checking the black rage toward Banks bubbling inside him, threatening his tightly reined composure.

"What choice did I have?" She asked.

"If you remember I gave you a generous one." He reminded, straightening up from his lounging position, only a clinched fist giving evidence to the wraith of emotions tearing him.

"I know but Sweetwater would have no longer been mine." She explained twisting the lace handkerchief she held in her hand.

"It still won't be. It's just a question of whether you'd rather Walter Banks own it or me. Isn't that what it's down to?" He asked through tight lips.

"No, he said if I'd marry him I would retain ownership."

"Then maybe that's what you should do since Sweetwater is the only thing that means anything to you." Andrew answered sharply.

Rachel shuddered, "Andrew, I told you I was wrong. A thousand Sweetwaters wouldn't be worth marrying Walter Banks."

He stared at her trying to see behind the veil. Trying to see what she really meant, what she felt. But her soul remained hidden from view and he resisted yielding. Unconsciously he had encased his heart in amour now he clung to that fragile protection. Surely she knew, as he did, that a promise from Walter Banks meant nothing. She might marry him and still loose the only thing in life she wanted. His effort at self-preservation made him appear cool and unyielding.

Rachel squirmed under his direct gaze and dropped her head. He leaned toward her and lifted her chin. "Rachel, if you've come to me sincerely then take that confounded hat off so I can see your face. I never did like to make a deal with a man if I couldn't see his eyes."

"I'm not a man," She answered sweetly as she reached up and pulled her hat from her head. Long tresses escaped with the hat pins and fell around her shoulders, as the fragrance of lilac encased them in the soft shadows of the room.

A half-smile raised one corner of his broad mouth as he struggled with rampant emotions, "You'd do well to remember that when you try to do business."

"Why?" She pressed.

"Because creation and society have made you vulnerable. If you were a man—well never mind. Back to your problem."

"Yes?" She encouraged, her full lips parted expectantly, her eyes bright with threatening tears and his heart wavered. He would have been safer with her hat on.

"It seems that you're deeper in debt than you were when I made my original offer. You now owe Banks for the repairs and the cotton crop that is lost by the way."

"That's true but you'd be out no more than you would have in the beginning. You would have had to repair the place and you would have had to pay for planting the crop and would have lost it so see, you'll really be no worse off," Her woman's logic pleaded.

"How much do you owe him?" He snapped, not wanting to remember she had obligated herself to Banks.

"I'm not sure," she hedged.

"Not sure?" he thundered and she flinched.

"I trusted him," she defended weakly

"We kept a weekly accounting, but I had no idea that I had agreed on foreclosure if there was a crop disaster," she admitted weakly.

"How do you think I can help you?"

"I don't know."

"What are you willing to do to help yourself?"

"Swallow my pride and come to you, tell Walter Banks I won't marry him, and then do whatever you want me to do that is ethical, legal and moral."

"Anything?"

"Anything—be a house servant, field hand, whatever it takes to earn my keep. Like I said whatever you want."

"Oh, Rachel," his heart cried out silent, secret confession, "If you only knew. I want you, to hold you, to protect you, to care for you, to love you. How I would have given you Sweetwater, the world if you had only wanted me, but even now—it's only survival you need."

He didn't answer for several long minutes. He stared at her as his emotions fought with self-revelation. She saw the strange light in his eyes and hers widened in fright.

She mistook it for disgust and rejection, and her heart sank as moment by moment the silence hung heavier between them, each immersed in their own private agony and neither understanding the other.

Finally he spoke, the strange light masked now, and she wondered if she had really seen it.

"Rachel, the first thing you need to do is ask Banks for a signed document stating every penny that you owe him, when he gives it to you then you tell him you are not going to marry him, but will pay him back in full." His words, crisp unemotional.

"What if he won't agree to that?" she asked.

"Then you let me handle it." he answered quietly.

"I don't see how you can persuade him anymore than I can," she objected, apprehension mingled with fear in her widened eyes.

"Are you afraid to confront him?" He asked, ignoring her objection.

She lifted her chin defiantly and looked at him a fierce brilliance firing her eyes, "Yes, but I will do what you require."

He chuckled, relieving the charged atmosphere in the room. "Rachel, you will not be alone. I will be in the next room and frankly I would welcome the opportunity to confront Mr. Banks and persuade him to cooperate. Don't worry I will get his cooperation. Then you and I can decide what role your future holds."

Rachel shuddered, "There's something else you need to know."

"You haven't told me everything?" He asked, his eyes alert, serious.

"He's threatened me."

"Yes, I know. Something I don't know?" He asked.

"To spread tales about you and me throughout the community. He said he knew you spent the night—He watched in the woods."

Andrew lunged to his feet, the rage that threatened boiled over, "That weasel—,"

"There's more. He said he would tell you that I had . . . ," Rachel stopped, dropped her head and flushed.

"Go on—", Andrew urged, cold steel threading his voice.

"I can't," she objected.

"If you want me to help you, you will," he demanded, taking a step toward her.

She winced and his heart melted. Her voice threatened tears and her words stumbled out, "He said that he would tell you I had traded him immoral favors for Sweetwater and that you would believe him."

Andrew clamped his jaws together and demanded through tight lips, "Did you?"

"No, no, no. Never! If I couldn't marry him, surely I couldn't do that." She dropped her head and sobs racked her body. Andrew turned his eyes from her pain, ashamed that he had questioned her.

"OK, Rachel stop crying, I had to know the truth." His voice sounded harsh and unfeeling disguising the ache in his heart.

"Do you believe me?" She asked, her eyes pleading as tears trickled down her cheek.

He knew how much Sweetwater meant to her, he didn't know just how far she would go to preserve it. He remembered her defiant claim that she would keep Sweetwater whatever the cost and hesitated a moment before answering, curtly, "Yes, I believe you."

Rachel noticed his hesitation and her battered heart interrupted it as doubt. Slowly she raised her chin; a cold determination curtained the soft vulnerability that had just illumined her eyes. "I hope so, but I can hardly offer you proof of my innocence, now can I?"

He ignored her question and lost the opportunity to assure her of his confidence, to set things right between them. Instead he probed, his own heart churning for an answer to give it hope."Why was it important that I believe you?"

"Because I need your help and I was afraid if you believed Walter you wouldn't help me," She answered, her voice cold, her eyes daring.

His heart plummeted, her answer was not what it sought, so he replied a forced smile on his face, "I see. I applaud your candor, Miss Gregory," his voice laced with sarcasm, he added. "And I do believe you to be a woman of good character, but one who often makes foolish choices."

And so it was that each, wrapped in their own concerns, failed to recognize the other's need. Both missed the truth begging to burst forth in a restoring stream able to heal two hearts.

Rachel's full lips parted in a bitter smile, "Perhaps,"

Meredith's dark brows drew together in a fierce scowl, "Only perhaps?"

Rachel's eyes held his unflinchingly, "Very well, I have made some foolish choices. Will your revenge leave me no pride?"

"I'm not after revenge and pride is not what you need right now, Rachel."

"Then, Mr. Meredith, what is it that I need?" Rachel asked, her lip curled.

"We need complete honesty between us." Andrew demanded, even as his own lips refused to acknowledge the truth clamoring for release in his own heart.

"Which requires the complete sacrifice of my pride? Surely there's some modicum of retribution involved."

"I can't help you if you won't cooperate." He responded, then asked, his dark eyes boring into hers, demanding submission, "Are there any other tidbits of information I need to know but your pride is reluctant to reveal?"

They stood with their eyes locked in silent combat. Finally Rachel dropped hers and turned away as the image of Sam Pritchett's bloody corpse resting somewhere beneath Sweetwater soil invaded her mind. Involuntarily she shuddered.

"Nothing pertinent," she lied.

A loud pounding on her door awakened Rachel from the fitful sleep that had finally claimed her in the early morning hours. Bright morning light streamed into the room from the draperies, only partly pulled and bounced over the coverlet blinding her for a moment.

She sat up slowly in bed, disoriented for a moment. Her head throbbed. Gradually her surroundings took on a familiarity and she remembered where she was.

Hope struggled with an elusive sorrow within her as she threw back the covers and slowly got out of bed. One foot touched the cold pine floor gingerly, and then jerked back against the coverlet seeking a warmer landing. She shivered in her ivory flannel gown with cuffs and collar of heavy crochet lace.

She stretched toward the foot of her bed and her hand touched the soft velvet of her dressing gown just as the pounding on her door began again.

She climbed out of bed, placing her feet in the slippers just beneath the bed and shuffled over to the door. Standing next to it, she inquired in a slurred voice of disturbed sleep, "Yes? Who is it?"

Her heart caught in her throat as the demanding, shrill tones of Walter Banks invaded her room, "It's Walter, Rachel, open this door immediately."

"Walter, I'm not dressed. Come back later." She objected.

"I will not come back later. If you don't open this door immediately, I'll get the desk clerk to." He all but shouted.

"Don't make a scene Walter. What will people think?" She reasoned.

"I don't care what anyone thinks and the only way to avoid a scene is to let me in this minute." Emotion raised his voice to an even higher pitch.

Fear gripped Rachel and she pressed her back against the door, "Now, Walter, calm down. I'll open the door as soon as I'm dressed. Wait downstairs and I'll join you for breakfast," she pled.

"I have no desire to wait until you're dressed. Either you will open it now or I will have it opened."

Rachel cracked the door and peered around it. Her eyes encountered an angry gleam in Walter Banks' ocher, blood shot ones as his nose pressed in the opening. He smelled of stale tobacco and his suit appeared rumpled. "What are you making such a fuss about Walter?" Rachel crooned, her voice trembling as it tried to cover her fear.

Banks' pushed his foot into the narrow opening and shoved the door open. Rachel jumped back further inside the room. The morning's radiance outlined her with the softness of interrupted slumber enveloping her features. Wrapped in a deep blue velvet wrapper with her hair tumbling down her back in wild abandon, she stared at him, her green eyes wide and dark in her frightened face. She backed away from him and he followed her, leaving the door ajar.

Fury glittered in his snake-like eyes, but she faced him without flinching, "What's the meaning of this, Walter? We will talk, but only after I am dressed."

Bank's hand shot out and grabbed her arm, his short pudgy fingers digging into the flesh beneath her nightgown and wrapper. She jerked her arm, but he held her firmly.

"I'll call for the manager if you don't get out of here, Walter Banks," she threatened weakly.

"The manager is downstairs," he growled. Then reached behind him with the toe of his muddy boot and partially closed the door on curious eyes that were gathering in the hall as guests on their way to breakfast stopped to stare at the spectacle played out before them.

"Then I'll scream for help," She threatened as she backed across the room from him.

One quick step and he cornered her against the wall. Clamping one hand over her mouth, with the other he pinned her two hands behind her back. He leaned into her face, his breath reeking with rum, and threatened, "You can't afford to take that risk, my dear. You are at my mercy as you have been since you returned to Sweetwater. It would be to your advantage to understand that truth and to cooperate willingly. Now what are you planning holed up in this hotel?"

He released two fingers from her mouth so she could respond while keeping her pressed tight against the wall with his stocky frame.

Rachel shuddered and invented, "I—I came to town in order to get a few things for our wedding,"

"Is that why you bought a ticket to Savannah?" He snarled.

Her eyes widened in surprise. "Savannah?"

Banks laughed, his brows pulled together in a diabolical scowl. "I have my sources all over this town. If you think you can get away from me and return to your aunt, forget that nonsense."

"I don't know from whom you got your information, Walter, but I had no intentions of returning to Europe. You know quite well I can't afford a ticket even to Savannah."

Walter pulled her away from the wall holding her hard against him and propelled them both toward the tall bureau and Rachel's hand bag.

Dropping his hand briefly from her mouth, he rummaged inside the bag until he pulled out her train ticket. Pain shot up both arms as he twisted her wrists and rasped, "Didn't have the money, Rachel? You made a grave mistake, my dear, and you'll pay for it dearly."

Rachel twisted violently in his grasp trying to free herself as panic engulfed her. "Let me go. I'll go where I please and when I please. You don't own me, Walter Banks and you never will."

He tightened his grip on her and placed his thumb and forefinger like a vise on her chin, and forced it up. His face was so near hers she could feel his hot breath on her cheek. She struggled to turn her head from it as revulsion bubbled in her throat, threatening to erupt.

A triumphant cackle rolled from Banks, permeating the room with evil. His fingers moved from her chin to grasp her cheeks, indenting the dewy flesh on each side of her mouth, "You do as I command, my dear. I own you as surely as I own the black men and women that till my soil. Only owning you will give me a lot more pleasure. I've waited all my life to put your class to shame. Now through you I can. As my wife you'll make up for every slight I suffered from your aristocratic friends."

"I'm not going to be your wife," Rachel stammered through puckered mouth. "I won't marry you, now or ever, Walter Banks,"

He laughed his maniacal laugh again, sending cold shivers up and down Rachel's spine, "You have no choice, my dear. As a matter of fact, you'll be marrying me in a few minutes. Judge Argo is on his way up here to do the honors.

"Judge who?" she asked weakly.

"My friend from south of here," he bragged

"I won't marry you," Rachel objected again her voice gaining strength.

Walter pushed her roughly up against the bureau, its round wooden knobs jabbed her ribs, "You'll marry me, Rachel Gregory and you'll be a dutiful wi—."

"You heard the lady, Banks. She has no intention of marrying you. Now let her go and pick on someone who can defend themselves," a deep resonate voice contradicted from the partially opened door.

Banks whirled around and looked up into the cold black eyes of Andrew Meredith starring at him. Rachel fell limply against the bureau, her heart and head pounding as Walter released his vise like hold on her.

"Meredith!" Banks spat out the name, demanding, "You get out of here. This is my private affair."

"Then you shouldn't make your confrontations so public," Andrew drawled as he softly closed the door behind him and casually made his way toward Rachel.

Banks thrust his short stocky body blocking Andrew's way and reached his right hand inside his jacket pocket. Before he could retrieve the small derringer he had hidden there, Andrew Meredith had grasped the short stocky man's arm and, twisting it, twirled him around face first into the wall. Meredith held him there now a squirming and harmless threat. "Why, Mr. Banks, what an unfriendly way to treat a business partner."

Banks squeaked, "Turn me loose, Meredith."

"Not until you drop your derringer on the floor and promise to be good," Andrew spoke calmly, the light in his eyes clearly revealed he was enjoying the situation.

A loud metallic thud announced Banks compliance.

"Now kick it away from you." Meredith commanded.

Once again Banks obeyed and Rachel rushed forward to retrieve it without instruction, her heart hammering with relief and a strange excitement.

"Now turn me loose, Meredith." Banks muffled voice stammered between clinched teeth.

"Do you think you can be good, Walter, so we can transact our business?" Andrew crooned laughter in his voice.

"I have no business with you, nor will I ever." Banks shouted as Meredith released his hold.

"Now, now, Walter."

"Get out of here, Meredith, or you'll wish you had." Banks threatened.

"Contrary to that, Banks, if I leave, you will be in most dire straits."

"This only concerns Rachel and me. She is betrothed to me and you are interfering with our wedding," Banks exclaimed as he turned toward Meredith anger flashing in his eyes.

"Miss Gregory broke her betrothal; I was a witness to that. She is not going to marry you."

"She has no choice," Banks sneered.

"Oh but she does. It is my understanding that the only reason she was marrying you was one of finance. Extortion is against the law, Banks. What you tried to do to Rachel is against man's law and God's."

"Not extortion, Meredith, business. Rachel wants Sweetwater and I want her."

"How can you give her something you don't have?" Andrew asked softly.

For the first time fear sparked in Banks' pale, lashless eyes as they narrowed, held by the cold dark ones before him. Rachel's widened in surprise, confusion wrinkled her brow.

"If he doesn't have the mortgage on Sweetwater, then who does?" she asked, her voice breathless.

"Why don't you tell her, Mr. Banks? And while you're at it, tell her what happened to her father's fortune? Why don't you tell her all about the swindler and thief you really are?"

"I don't have to answer to you, Meredith. This is Rachel's business and mine. Believe me you'll pay for this interference."

"Rachel, am I interfering?" Andrew asked, never taking his eyes from Banks.

"No. I have no plans to marry Walter Banks whether or not he has Sweetwater."

"See I told you. Now I suggest we, you and I, Banks, amble on down to my room and give Miss Rachel some privacy. I'll talk to you later." Andrew smiled as he turned to look at Rachel for the first time since he entered the room.

The brilliance of the smile Rachel turned on Andrew rivaled the morning sun and Meredith's eyes revealed his heart's response. For that moment Walter Banks ceased to exist for them, only Andrew and Rachel inhabited a world locked in the radiance of her smile. But Walter Banks did exist, and his evil eyes took in the exchange and hope stirred where a moment before there had been only the promise of defeat.

TWENTY-FOUR

A demanding knock sliced through the heavy silence that draped the room. Rachel tensed, gripping the smooth, translucent cup, which held the last remnants of her tea, now grown cold. When Andrew Meredith softly called her name, she relaxed and relinquished the delicate china cup, placing it on a walnut teacart beside her chair. A half smile teased her lips before anxiety once again claimed her, narrowing her eyes. She stood and smoothed the imaginary wrinkles from her outfit with one hand while the other nervously touched her hair, now captured in a tight chignon at the nape of her neck.

Rachel sighed and opened the door to him, her heart in her throat. She knew that shortly Walter Banks would ruin her reputation in the community and by now the hotel guests who had witnessed their encounter would be hashing and rehashing it, but, strangely, the only concern knotting her stomach was Andrew Meredith's opinion of her.

She couldn't tell from his somber dark eyes taking in her fragile loveliness from head to toe. She had dressed demurely in a wool traveling suit of deep russet which highlighted the chestnut lights in her hair. Her pale face flushed under his scrutiny igniting the green embers glowing in her eyes. She opened the door wider and stepped back, issuing an unspoken invitation.

He shook his head, "Let's go downstairs to breakfast. It wouldn't be a good idea for me to enter your room again."

A bitter smile curled her lip," I can hardly do anything else that could make my reputation worse, could I?"

He smiled, "I can't say that you don't have a problem. I have threatened Banks, perhaps he will be quiet for awhile, but eventually he'll have his revenge. As for the people who had gathered in the hall, I wouldn't worry about them. Most were guests, curious strangers who seemed willing to assist you if I hadn't walked up. Whatever the outcome, you have to face it. Are you ready to go down stairs? We have a lot to discuss."

She searched his face, trying to read his thoughts, to see if he believed her innocence or the accusations she knew Walter Banks had hurled against her. His face remained closed, but courteous. She noted the fatigue lines around his eyes had eased from last night; maybe that was a good sign. Whatever the outcome, she knew that her future rested in Andrew Meredith's hands. She shuddered, from one bondage to another, would she never be free?

Andrew saw her shudder, "Are you all right?"

A brave smile parted her lips, "What do you think?"

"I think you're going to be better than you have ever been." He assured a curious expression on his face.

She lifted an inquisitive brow toward his, but he said no more. Offering her his arm, they went down the stairs to breakfast.

The hum of conversation paused as they entered the ornate dining room, and then increased in crescendo. Both Rachel and Andrew noticed, but neither commented. Andrew cast a furtive eye toward Rachel and smiled inwardly as she tilted her nose and chin ever so slightly and squared her shoulders. But when he saw the frozen smile that plastered her pale face, his heart broke.

He wanted to shield her from the pain of what was coming, but he couldn't. She would have to suffer the consequences for her foolish choices. People reveled in gossip and Rachel had fed their grist mill. All the power and wealth he possessed could not protect her now from society's ostracism; he only hoped he could help her endure it. He would if she would let him, but even that choice was hers.

They found a table and ordered breakfast, he insisting that she eat something. Then they talked.

Rachel's first question, the one that had tormented her while she waited for him to return, "If Walter Banks doesn't hold the mortgage on Sweetwater, who does?"

When Andrew told her he held the mortgage on Sweetwater, relief mixed with disbelief washed the anxiety from Rachel's eyes. She forgot the pain and humiliation surrounding her, as she exclaimed, "How did you get it, Andrew?"

"I had some help." He admitted.

"Who—how? It's incredible."

"Divine Providence mostly using people and circumstances."

"I—I don't believe I understand," she said, hesitantly a guarded look in her eyes.

"Do you believe in God, Rachel?" Andrew asked.

"Frankly I haven't given God much thought since He took my mother." she responded sharply.

"You sort of gave up on Him, then?"

"You could say that. It seems His only involvement in my life has been to take away everything that is dear to me." Rachel snapped.

"I'm sorry you feel that way, Rachel."

A tremulous smile played around her lips as her tone changed to a more conciliatory one, "I am vitally interested in hearing your story, but I'd just as soon you left God out of it,"

A frown wrinkled Andrew's brow as sadness touched his dark brown eyes, but he conveyed the bare events of his story, from Randall Wilkie's request to Robert Goodman's involvement, concluding with his encounter with LaRoche.

Rachel's eyes were round and bright when she finished, "You hold the mortgage on Pine Ridge, too?"

Andrew chuckled, "Unbelievable isn't it? How that just all "came about." Yes, I hold the mortgage and will until we get Banks' full cooperation. I hate to use coercion on any man, even a rascal like Banks, but force is the only thing he understands."

The sparkle in Rachel's eyes dimmed as a frown wrinkled her brow. Impulsively she reached out and grasped Andrew's arm resting on the table, "Andrew, you're in danger. I wouldn't put anything past Walter Banks. He may try to kill you."

Andrew's mahogany eyes fired with a strange glow as he stared searchingly into hers, "I know."

"But what are you going to do?" she exclaimed.

"Try to watch my back and not worry about it." He explained.

"How can you *not worry* about it?" Rachel demanded, her lips pursed.

"Because my life is not in his hands," Andrew answered quietly and Rachel remembered another time when Andrew Meredith had looked fearlessly down the barrel of a revolver held in the hand of Walter Banks. He had made the same statement and now, as then, wonder and longing filled her soul.

"Now we have Banks situated, what are we going to do about Rachel Gregory?" he asked, a long overdue smile crinkling the corners of his eyes.

"That's up to you, now isn't it?" She responded, no smile lighting her eyes.

"What do you want to do?" he queried.

"What I want to do is not an option." Rachel reminded.

"All the same, tell me."

"I thought it was to be mistress of Sweetwater, now I don't know. Survive with honor, I guess." She said quietly, then with a bitter chuckle she looked at the people sitting around her and added. "Perhaps I'll have to be satisfied with survival."

"You could have had that with Banks," Meredith snapped.

Rachel's head jerked up, startled at his tone. A mask slammed down extinguishing the warm lights in his eyes, but not before she saw the pain in them. And it puzzled her.

"No, Mr. Meredith, there would have been no survival and certainly no honor with Walter Banks," she said with a shudder. "So whatever your plans for me, I'll accept."

"Even if it means losing Sweetwater?" He asked, a strange intensity threatening his masked emotions.

"Even if it means losing Sweetwater," she sighed, her eyes downcast, her fingers toying with her fork.

"Rachel, my plans for you include Sweetwater," he began.

"How?" she gasped, looking up into his eyes, tiny emerald sparks exploding in hers.

"First thing we need to settle is how we're best going to ride this storm of social controversy you've stirred up with your overnight visit here. By the time Walter Banks finishes with you, you will have outraged this community with your actions. They won't forgive a single lady such indiscretion. They will ostracize you, refusing to invite you to any social activities. The church will discipline you if you choose to attend and you've killed all hope of marrying a local young man."

"I don't care about any of those things."

"But you will. You can't live in isolation. I tried it once, Rachel. Without others in our lives, we wither and die inside."

"I don't need anybody. Give me a place to live and a job to do and I'll get along fine." She contradicted, her head held high and rigid, while her chin trembled suspiciously.

"Rachel, don't lie to yourself again. You won't even have Randall here; he is away and may never be able to return."

"I know," she whispered.

"If you need no one why did you go to Randall?" He insisted.

"I . . .I had my reasons," she faltered as her eyes dropped, not willing to meet his.

"What reasons?" He demanded.

"I'd rather not go into that right now. Anyway it's nothing which need concern you. It's all in the past," She argued, trying to convince herself as the image of Sam Pritchett hung in her mind.

"I hope so, my dear. Because if you're holding anything back from me I can't help you, now can I?" He asked his voice persuasive as if trying to convince a small child.

"How can you help me?" she asked, looking at him finally, her countenance somber.

"Rachel, society forgives a married woman much more easily

than an unmarried one,"

"Now what can I do about that?"

"Marry me." He quietly suggested.

Astonishment flushed her cheeks and she drew in a quick breath, "Ma—marry you?" she stammered.

"Would that be such a distasteful consideration?" He asked, his eyes cold, hard.

"No, no of course not. I just don't understand the suggestion. Why would you want to marry me?" She explained.

"Gossip will link your name to mine. If you marry me then the gossip will die down much more quickly." He explained, in a matter of fact way, refusing to reveal his heart.

"But that would be unfair to you, too big a sacrifice to require."

"What?" He asked, perplexed.

"To marry without love,"

"Love is a commitment, Rachel. I'm willing to commit my life, loyalty and support to you. To protect you and provide for you—,"

"And what do *you* get from all this grand sacrifice?" she asked sarcasm lacing her words.

"I need a wife, children," he answered with a half-truth.

"But why me?" Rachel insisted.

"You need a husband."

"But that's a poor basis to begin a marriage. What would you expect from me?" She asked, her heart pounding at the idea.

"Whatever you could give me in return, which I hope would be commitment, in time affection and—children."

"That's it? . . .commitment, affection, and children?"

"Can any man or woman ask more than that from a relationship?"

"What about emotional involvement?

"I believe in time, emotions will follow commitment. Frankly I distrust decisions made in the heat of emotional passion. Most often they prove disastrous. If two people have complimentary characteristics with common goals and values, and commit themselves to each other, I see no reason why marriage between them wouldn't work." He observed attempting a logic that would explain away the truth, a reality he stubbornly refused to expose but that had set his heart pumping wildly.

"You think we are compatible?" She asked, looking incredulous.

He chuckled dryly, "So far compatibility hasn't exactly been our experience, but I think if we were dedicated to a mutual goal it might be."

"An—and, you think," Rachel stuttered in disbelief, "you'd be satisfied with compatibility and commitment?"

"You forgot children."

"Oh yes, children. And are they to be the visible assets of this investment we make on the grounds of compatibility and commitment?" She responded, her face flushed.

Her mind fought to accept his solution, to receive his logic. Andrew Meredith, wealthy, honorable and handsome was offering her the refuge of his name and Sweetwater. She should feel relieved, even thankful, yet she felt angry. Why couldn't she leap into the haven he offered without a backward look? But pain not relief gripped her heart, rejecting his logic. Instead a sense of deprivation overwhelmed her that threatened to take her breath away. She fanned her flushed face with the small handkerchief she held in her hand.

"Of course not. Every man wants a child to love, and to continue on after him. To pick up the mantle of his life and carry it on. I'm no different." He admitted, for the first time he spoke from his heart, and the truth softened his eyes.

Too absorbed in his unorthodox proposal to notice his moment of vulnerability, she sputtered," You make marriage sound so—so business like."

"Well, isn't it?" he reasoned and the moment moved on beyond recovery as cold logic shielded his heart from her, "Marriage like business, is an agreement between two parties based on certain stipulated criteria. From that union, if it is successful, will come affection, respect and children."

She shuddered and looked him in the face, shaking her head,

"I'm sorry, Andrew, but that can't possibly be an acceptable solution for my problem. I told you from the beginning I wouldn't marry for convenience. I tried it with Walter Banks and couldn't go through with it."

Stung, he recoiled, "Are you putting me in the same class with Walter Banks?"

"Of course not. You know better than that. You are an honorable man. As the wife of Andrew Meredith, I realize you would protect me, care for me and the community would esteem me because of who you are. I deeply appreciate what you have offered, but I simply cannot marry without love. It wouldn't be fair to either of us, especially you." She dropped her head, not able to meet his eyes, afraid he could read a truth in hers that even she didn't understand.

A cold chuckle broke the strained silence between them and he countered, "So be it. I have offered to marry you twice, Rachel. A man's ego is a curious thing, it doesn't receive rejection easily. The next time you'll have to do the asking."

"Only when my heart requires no more than a business partnership, Andrew." Rachel stated.

And as a man's heart too often processes words only as factual information, Andrew failed to perceive the subtle message which lurked behind Rachel's words. He only heard what was spoken. He missed the glimpse she offered into her very soul. Had he looked beyond the surface of her words and espied her real need and desire, he could have met her there where his own heart would have found hope. Instead they retreated from one another once again, each heart barricaded behind a wall of misunderstanding.

Andrew finished his breakfast of ham and eggs in silence while Rachel toyed with her blueberry scones and tea. Finally with the last bite, he pushed his plate back and looked at her with eyes devoid of emotion. Beginning in a dull monotone, he told her that he planned to make all the improvements Sweetwater needed and proposed she manage it in return for a place to live and a stipend based on a percentage of plantation earnings.

Rachel's green eyes widened in amazement at his generosity. He explained her percentage should be large enough to enable her to save for her future therefore freeing her at some point in time to choose her own destiny. He assured her a home at Sweetwater for as many years as she wished and he would will the place to her at his death."

Rachel's eyes grew wary at his overwhelming generosity and asked what he expected in return for his kindness.

He replied tersely, "Only a job well done. It's simply a matter of good business. I need you here if Sweetwater will be the success I intend it to be. I have found when one has a vested interest in a project, they are more apt to put their whole heart into it. You not only have a vested interested, but an emotional attachment, which will prove a winning combination, I should think."

"Then it's not charity?" She asked, a tremulous smile playing around her lips, her eyes serious.

"Of course not. I have ambitious plans for Sweetwater. I want to make it a showplace among north Georgia plantations. I want to encourage other planters as to what can be accomplished with efficient use of land and people."

"How do you propose to do that?" Interest fired her imagination despite the emotional turmoil tearing inside her.

"The first thing I'm going to do is to reclaim the acreage we need, then upgrade all servant quarters and build infirmary, barns and clear additional land." He explained.

Rachel caught the glitter of excitement in his eyes and wondered at it, asking "Why are you doing this? You already have Balmara."

A shadow crossed his face as he responded, "Let's just say I like a challenge. Balmara runs so smoothly with Agan in charge, it offers no further challenge."

"Agan?" she questioned.

"You met him. The young black with a West Indian accent. He came to Balmara from Jamaica when he was just a boy."

"Slave?"

"No, free. I recognized his intelligence soon after he arrived, so I freed him and hired a tutor to educate him. When Daphne arrived, they studied together."

"Tall with light skin?" she asked.

"That's the one."

"He met the carriage when I arrived. Seemed to be some kind of friction between him and Daphne, I recall."

Andrew chuckled, "I don't quite know what the problem is. They got along fine when they were growing up; it's just been the last few years that I've sensed some tension between them. But as long as their personal conflicts don't interfere with the operation of business I just leave it between them."

"He's in love with her."

"What?" Andrew snapped his head jerking up.

"The emotional kind," Rachel's lip curved in a humorless smile. "The kind that will interfere with your smooth operations sooner or later."

"Why do you say that?" Andrew demanded, his dark brows drawn together in a scowl.

"Oh don't worry, she doesn't return his affection," Rachel said quietly as she leaned toward him, a hard glitter in her eyes.

"Are you sure?"

"Quite sure. Does the young man do a good job for you?"

"No one could do better. I trained him personally from a young age."

"Don't be too confident of him. Love, the emotional kind, can do strange things to people. It can make enemies out of friends if they love the same person."

"What do you mean by that?" Andrew demanded.

"Nothing, except I read something frightening in his eyes. If he blames you for Daphne's rejection, then he might not be as dependable as you think."

"You're sure Daphne's rejected him?"

"Very sure and he hasn't taken it lightly."

"You must be mistaken. I would have noticed." Andrew objected.

"Not necessarily. It's the difference between emotion and logic. It was not what the young man did; it was the look I saw in his eyes when Daphne responded. He blames someone and whoever it is, will ultimately pay." Rachel shivered, remembering the night of her arrival at Balmara.

"I still feel that you may have read more into their conflict than exists, but at any rate I can do little until I return to Savannah. Meanwhile your first priority at Sweetwater is to find a capable overseer. Anyone Banks hired will have to go. Do you have one now?"

"Not now." Rachel admitted, her eyes downcast, not inviting more questions.

"We'll have to remedy that right away. We need a hard working man with good management skills, whose reputation is beyond reproach. That is not an easy task, but you've got to have one, the sooner the better."

"Whatever you think, I'd have no idea where to begin to look," Rachel responded mildly while her insides churned with the memory of straw colored hair and evil eyes, now closed forever.

"I'll ask around. Robert Goodman might prove helpful. In fact I'm sure he would."

They talked on for another hour, making plans and Andrew outlining his expectations of the role Rachel would assume. Her duties at Sweetwater would be almost identical to Daphne's at Balmara's, with one notable exception—she would serve as his hostess when entertaining out of town guests and business associates.

Finally as their discussion of plans and expectations drew to a close, Rachel asked the question that had plagued her, but she had been reluctant to address, "Mr. Meredith?"

Andrew frowned, "My close friends call me Drew."

She smiled a half-smile, "That's rather informal for a proper employer-employee relationship."

He chuckled, "Well, we certainly want to be proper, Miss Gregory. However, Mr. Meredith seems too formal for all that we've been through together, don't you think?"

She nodded, acquiescing, "What about Andrew?"

Andrew inclined his head, "Very well. Until you feel more comfortable with Drew. What was it you wanted to ask me?"

For the first time in months, she laughed. Then as suddenly as the sun looses itself behind a thick gray cloud taking its brightness with it, she sobered, "Andrew, this is a difficult question, and I know I've put myself into this situation. But how are we going to handle my being a single woman living in your home? Surely you plan to stay at Sweetwater during your visits to north Georgia?"

"I have every intention of doing so. If you'd accepted my proposal, then we wouldn't have a problem, but since you didn't I have an alternate plan. I want to move Aunt Maltilda and Laura to Sweetwater."

Rachel's eyes widened with pleasure. Matilda Burnes had been a delight the few days she had visited at the Savannah Plantation and everything she'd heard about Laura had sparked her curiosity. "Here?"

"The coastal climate can be deadly during hot summer months and Aunt Maltilda doesn't weather them well. Laura will be leaving for school in the spring and despite their bickering, Aunt Tilde is lonely when she is away. You and she could be company to one another while she would provide an ideal chaperon to keep the gossips satisfied."

"And I wouldn't wither away from lack of social interaction?" she teased.

"That's true," his eyes were somber, "Aunt Matilda and Laura rescued me and I didn't even know I needed it."

"Do you think she would be happy leaving Balmara?"

"She'll adjust as long as she has someone to talk to anyway I've decided to sell Balmara." Andrew announced. The response sprung from him, an unconscious decision made and announced.

Rachel eyes widened in surprise, then she paled as the specter of Daphne's beautiful face with hostile amber eyes haunted her memory, "What about Daphne?"

"Daphne will be staying in Savannah." He replied tersely without further explanation.

"Oh yes, you have a town house." She remembered a vague

discomfort and confusion darkening her eyes.

He rose from the table, closing the conversation, not offering an additional explanation.

As they made their way across the dining room, a sudden commotion in the lobby beyond captured their attention, easing the awkward moment.

A voice with a distinctive British accent drifted through the broad cased opening to the dining room and a broad smile of recognition parted Andrew's face, "I want you to meet a business associate and friend of mine from England. I think you'll like him."

"Perhaps he knows my friend—." she suggested, then stopped abruptly, and Andrew moved a step beyond her. His broad shoulder shielded her pale face as Philip Duval, barreled through the doorway, his blond hair tousled, and his cheeks rosy from a sharp November wind. His very zest for life filled the room encompassing those around him, leaving them wistful.

"Drew, you old renegade. I might have known you'd be—." Duval shouted, then stopped midway, his mouth gaping.

"Rachel Gregory, I'd like you to meet Sir Philip Duval-" Andrew began.

"Rachel!!!" interrupted Philip, in a reverent whisper, "Is it really you?"

Andrew Meredith twisted his head and shoulder to look at Rachel immobilized a half-step behind him. The delight in his eyes turned to surprise and then to dismay, his smile frozen on his face.

"Philip! Wha—How?" Rachel gasped.

The young nobleman covered the distance between them in two long strides, his arms outstretched. Grasping both Rachel's hands, he brought them to his lips in an act of homage. Adoration illumined his wide, blue eyes as he exclaimed in hushed tones, "Oh, my dear, it really is you."

"Yes, Philip. It is I." A tear trickled down Rachel's cheek as joy reached inside her soul, colliding with the pain and heartbreak of the past months.

"Don't cry, my love. I dreamed of this moment, but despaired it would never come." He exclaimed as he pulled her close with only the hands he held tightly separating them.

An astonished Andrew Meredith stood, his jaws slack, his lips slightly parted as he took in the scene playing out before him.

"But how, how did you find me?" she asked, her voice trembling.

"I didn't know I would. I've been trying to forget you, lest I ruin your marriage—?"

"My what?"

"You're—," he stopped and looked down at the hands he held in his, "not married?"

She laughed, her eyes bright with unshed tears, "No, whatever gave you that idea?"

"I returned for you and they told me in the village, you had left for America to be married." He exclaimed and tucked her hand in the crook of his arm leading her toward a crimson velvet couch beside a roaring fire, Andrew Meredith forgotten by both.

"No, my father died. So I returned to settle the estate. Oh, Philip, how wonderful to see you." She turned her face up to him, her eyes glowing with affection.

Belatedly Philip remembered Andrew and turned back to the shocked Meredith, "My friend, this is the girl I told you about. You have brought her to me. You have given me back my heart, Andrew. I can hardly take it in. Isn't it the most amazing thing you've ever seen, Drew?"

Andrew sadly nodded his head, his heart in his eyes, "Truly I've never seen anything like it."

Twenty-Five

Philip implored, "But, my darling, why can't you marry me and go back to England with me?" as he and Rachel rode across the winter browned meadows together, their cheeks and noses pink from the stinging December wind.

Rachel shook her head, a frown creasing her brow, "Can't you understand? I have no dowry. I refuse to come to you like some penniless waif."

"Why?" he demanded, "My family has more property and money than we can use in ten lifetimes."

"I know you don't need it, I need it."

"I don't understand." His face wrinkled, his eyes confused, "I'll give you anything you need."

"That's bondage. I need to feel I can bring something to a marriage."

"Oh, my darling, you would. You would bring my happiness. Without you my life is miserable. Isn't my happiness enough?"

Rachel laughed, "You, miserable? You have more zest for living than anyone I've ever known."

"That's only because I've found you. If I lost you again, I don't know how I'd bear it, truly. Forget all these excuses, Rachel. Give your heart and your hand to me."

"Perhaps I could if my aunt hadn't behaved so shamelessly, trying to pawn me off like she did." Rachel shuddered at the thought.

"I'm sorry I told you about what she did—, but I think any

relationship needs complete honesty."

"You didn't have to tell me, I already knew how she was. Why do you think I avoided telling you where I was staying or the name of my aunt? She determined to marry me off one way or another. I felt somehow she might have been behind your abrupt departure; however, I had no idea she would stoop so low to accomplish her goal. It was too humiliating for me to even consider coming to you then. I destroyed the only letter I wrote to you. But it would be even worse now without having a dowry." She looked at him with a half-smile and shrugged, "I'll be too old before I earn enough from Andrew Meredith for one."

Exasperation tensed Philip Duval's face, driving the usual good natured vitality from it. He and Rachel had been through this same argument several times over the last two weeks as they renewed their friendship.

During the days following Andrew Meredith's return to Savannah, they recaptured the joy they had formally shared in each other's company. And Philip found that the reality of Rachel equaled and surpassed his memories of her. He studied her in her surroundings, learning all that he could about her. And the more he learned the more besotted he became.

When a surprise early snow dusted the pine needles with white, they explored the forest. She had shown him Sweetwater and her eyes had glowed as she related the plans Andrew Meredith had for the place. And while Philip's heart rejoiced in her excitement, an indefinable dread dampened his.

Little by little she related to him the whole story of what had happened since her return. Leaving out only Sam Pritchett and his untimely demise, she explained her destitution, her betrayal by Walter Banks, and finally her indebtedness to Andrew Meredith.

When Philip heard about the exploits of Walter Banks and the gossip he caused, something akin to hate tugged at his gentle heart and he wanted to avenge her. Protecting her from any further harm almost obsessed him. When he returned to the hotel in the evenings, he worried that she might be in danger. The next morning at the earliest possible moment he would rush back to Sweetwater to reassure himself that she was safe.

Nothing, rumors, gossip, her poverty, dissuaded Philip's pursuit of her. If anything, it only incited him more. He had found what he had lost and this time he determined not to lose her again.

Each morning when he arrived from his long trip from the Fletcher House to Sweetwater Manor, Rachel welcomed him warmly. Her lonely heart found solace in his friendship, but she continued to find reasons why she could not marry him.

Once again she objected because of her dowry and he exclaimed, impatience raising his voice, "I told you a dowry makes no difference to me, and if not to me it shouldn't to you."

"Philip, what about my pride?" She pled, as she placed a restraining gloved hand on his sleeve. They rested their horses side by side, in a quiet evergreen forest surrounding them. Her eyes glittered like rare jewels beneath the green velvet hood that covered her auburn locks, keeping out the early December wind.

"What does that have to do with anything? Only our love matters. Love is more important than pride. You do love me, Rachel?" He asked, imploring her to say yes. But her heart resisted.

"You know how I feel about you, but I'm afraid. Love isn't always enough. Our backgrounds are so different. I would come to your world an alien. The fact I came empty handed would destroy my sense of confidence and self-esteem. And then what do I know about assuming the role of a future Duchess? How could I make you happy?" She argued her heart heavy within her. Affection for this man overwhelmed her, yet strangely she remained unable to accept his generous offer.

"I won't go back to England. I'll make my life here where you'd be happy." He urged.

"No, you must return, you have a responsibility to your heritage there and I wouldn't fit in," She insisted.

"Don't you understand, Rachel? After losing you once, I realize nothing in the world means as much to me as you. If I have to choose between my inheritance and you, there will be no choice."

"Perhaps you feel that way now, but when your children follow on behind you, your heritage will take on new meaning."

"I'll make a new heritage. Carve out a new life here." His eyes bright, willing to do anything to persuade her, "I'll buy Sweetwater from Andrew. That's it—I'll give you back your heritage and together we'll have a new one."

"No, Philip, you can't mean what you're saying. How could I ever let you make a sacrifice like that? What about your father? He'll disown you. He's probably chafing now because you're not with him, learning to assume your future role as his heir."

The truth of her statement pricked Philip's conscious, but he rushed on, "He misses my company, but I've been adequately trained to assume that role. Until my father's death, he is Duke and I am free to pursue my own interests. Why right now my title is purely complimentary and I'm little more than a commoner. But even my future is worth nothing without you. If I had a kingdom, I'd give it up if need be. Don't you understand? I lost you once because of my social responsibilities; I won't let that happen again."

"Philip, don't push me just now. I've been through so much—. I want what is best for the both of us, not only for now but in the years to come." She begged, confusion riddling her heart and tears welling up in her eyes. "I can't afford another mistake."

Catching her gloved hands between his, raised them to his lips and whispered, "Forgive me, my pet. I have only been thinking of myself. Of course you have much to consider, but above it all remember that I, Philip Duval, love you and want you for my own. No obstacle is too great, no sacrifice too demanding on me to win you. Marry me, Rachel, and I'll adore you all the years that God chooses to give me on this earth and throughout eternity as well."

The tears that threatened now ran over and spilled down her cheeks as she looked up into his eyes, cobalt with deep emotion. "Oh, Philip, you are so dear to me. Believe me, I am as concerned with your happiness as my own."

"Then marry me, Darling." He said, his voice husky. Philip leaned across the narrow space that separated their horses, and cupping her face between his hands, placed a long tender kiss on the full lips turned up to his.

———————————

Andrew returned from Savannah on the following week and checked back into the Fletcher House, once again sharing a suite with Philip. As promised, he had shipped enough supplies and labor to fulfill his pledge to Rachel concerning the complete renovation of Sweetwater. He had skilled carpenters and craftsman from Balmara in tow who could rework the interior and construct additional rooms to the house. He realized they would need more space since he planned to move Laura and Aunt Matilda to Sweetwater.

He had yet to relate his plans to his aunt and niece. Not that he anticipated any resistance, his Aunt Matilda would welcome the change; but he knew that once he did, his plans for Daphne would also have to be revealed, and he was still reluctant to address her situation.

He told himself that he needed more time to settle her future. Actually he was still at a loss as to what he could do for her. Rachel's warning about Agan increased his awareness of the young man and he observed him closely when they conferred on Balmara's accounts. Perhaps her warning had provoked needless suspicions in his mind, but he had observed a certain coldness he had failed to notice before. But since Agan's problem seemed linked to Daphne's he put it aside to deal with at a later date. Balmara's books were faultless, the plantation had turned a tidy profit and the staff ran like an efficient machine. What harm could happen in delaying by a few weeks the opening of that Pandora's Box? Anyway he could scarcely confront it until he had an answer, which he didn't.

The only personal problem he had addressed was Laura's schooling. As he expected she howled when he informed her she would be returning to Virginia to a boarding school in the spring. But her howls proved impotent, he had determined her course. When he met her at the train, his startled eyes finally saw the young woman she had become and he realized that Aunt Matilda was right. Her beauty and vitality needed channeling into a direction his love and permissiveness had failed to give.

Had he been willing to delve deeper into his own heart, Andrew would have found a comparison there between Rachel and Laura motivating his actions. He saw in Laura some of the same characteristics Rachel possessed. Beauty and strong personalities graced both women, only life and school had forged Rachel's into strength and character while Laura's, wild and free, had yet to be harnessed. He acknowledged his niece needed the discipline and training that school would begin and life would finish. He told her and ordered her wardrobe. When her howls ceased, her respect grew for an uncle who loved her enough to stand firm.

His brief two weeks at home had passed in a whirlwind of activity trying to assemble everything needed at Sweetwater while his own shipping business demanded much of his attention as well. Had he paused for introspection, he would have realized his frenzied schedule brought a welcome relief from the specter of Rachel and Philip together that rose to haunt him each time a brief lull in his work left any time for thought.

Despite his determination, his heart quickened a beat as he turned into the long lane leading to Sweetwater. Following him was an entourage of wagons filled with people and supplies. He had leased three boxcars to haul wagons, lumber, stock and workman. A thrill of anticipation ran through him at the thought of Rachel's eyes illumined with excitement when he had shared his plans with her. Now he could only imagine her response when actual construction began.

Along with construction supplies, he brought food from the well stocked larder at Balmara. Under Daphne's supervision, the slaves of Balmara had canned and dried the summer's bountiful produce. Fruits, vegetables and sausages filled the wagon that followed his carriage of burgundy and black pulled by a flashy grey, shipped especially for Rachel's use. He intended that she would have good food and decent transportation.

Providing for her physical needs comforted him, but the problem of her safety with an incensed Banks in the picture nagged him. The only answer was the right overseer who could provide the day and night protection she needed. The big problem was finding the right one. He had to be honorable, strong, wise and a hard worker who loved the land. So far all his efforts at locating such a man proved fruitless.

Philip Duval's decision to stay on in Marietta for a while had provided a temporary solution to his problem, but the news brought him mixed feelings of relief and alarm. He felt relief that Philip's constant presence at Sweetwater would offer Rachel temporary safety, but what about when Philip left? That is if Philip decided to leave without Rachel. Anxiety regarding the possibility of a Sweetwater without Rachel ate away at Andrew's insides, no matter how often he tried to deny it to himself.

However, Sweetwater needed a supervisor whatever Rachel's decision and Andrew determined, as the house came into view, his next project would be finding one.

For a week Andrew Meredith supervised the organization of the work crews that would turn Sweetwater into a show place. He planned to add a large wing on each side of the house. The upstairs addition would house bedrooms having bath alcoves like Balmara's while downstairs one wing would house new double parlors, the other a banquet size dining room. Each wing opened through oversized double doors into the present parlor where a wall would be torn away to make way for a grand staircase which would sweep down from the floors above. The large connecting rooms with tall ceilings, broad openings, and jib windows opening to the wrap around veranda would be airy and spacious while accommodating large crowds.

The plans called for a new kitchen to be added behind the house with a root cellar and storage bins beneath it. The wall separating the present kitchen and the old dining room would be removed and both rooms completely renovated into a library for Andrew.

When Rachel saw the plans, her eyes held all the joy he had

anticipated. Her full lips formed a silent "O" as she perused the plans. After her initial shock at the magnitude of his plans, she exclaimed as each room proved a new delight. She questioned how they would accomplish such a feat and still be able to live in the house. Andrew explained to her that the new wings and the kitchen would be completely constructed before renovations began in the old part of the house. When the workers moved into the old part, she could move into the completed part. While the construction would pose an inconvenience, it would not prove impossible to live there during it and she would have the additional advantage of being on site to supervise.

With Rachel by his side, he considered her wishes in every major decision. He set up a work schedule and organized work teams. Philip's presence shadowed their every conference, but he said little, his usual exuberance held at bay.

A frown often creased his forehead when he watched Rachel and Andrew bending over a set of plans side by side. Andrew would say something and Rachel would look up into his face with laughing eyes, her full lips parted in a delighted smile. Her happiness proved obvious to even a casual observer; however Philip's observation was anything but casual. As the days marched toward Christmas and Rachel's joy blossomed into full flower he could only be left to wonder, from whence came the source? Sweetwater or Andrew Meredith? When her days grew even busier leaving her with less time to spend with the handsome nobleman, he became a morose observer contemplating from the sidelines his chances of tearing her from a home that she so obviously loved or the man who provided it for her. Sadly he faced the possibility that if he wanted Rachel, he'd have to have Sweetwater. Would his friend be willing to part with it?

One morning when the December weather moderated and a sun warmed the cold winter air, Andrew and Philip arrived from Marietta in an exuberant mood.

At the front door Philip shouted for Rachel and she bounded down the stairs in her dress of copper merino wool setting off corresponding lights in her lustrous hair. Thick tresses looped in abundant coils on top of her head tiara style caught the morning sun as it streamed through the beveled glass, dividing the light into a rainbow of colors, and washed her in a shimmering aura. Both men stopped simultaneously, their mouths agape at the vision of loveliness she presented.

Seeing the expressions of the two men, she paused, "Now what's going on here? What do you two have up your sleeves?'

Philip recovering first, spoke. "Rachel, my sweet, Drew and I have decided that all work and no play make you a dull girl. Perish the thought, we can't risk a tragedy like that; therefore, your good friend and guardian of your good has decreed!"

"Guardian of my what? And just who might that be?" Rachel interrupted, her eyes wide, her lips trembled with laughter.

"Who else, but me? Andrew Meredith is your business partner." Philip emphasized, "I guard your heart." His teasing eyes growing serious as he staked his claim.

"And this guardian has decreed—?" Rachel encouraged, refusing to acknowledge his challenge.

"That you have a holiday. Andrew has agreed that we all go to town, dine in style at the Fletcher House and then make some Christmas purchases,"

Rachel's green eyes widened, her smile faded as she protested, "I can't go to town, face those people again!"

"That's exactly what you need to do, Rachel," Andrew commanded quietly. "The longer you wait the harder it'll be. Philip's right. You need a holiday and we need to make some purchases, so we'll have to bow to Master Decree's decree."

Rachel's hand flew to her throat, "I'm not dressed."

"You look lovely. Put on a warm cloak and I'll have Noah hitch up the carriage."

"Do you have any idea what people will say when I come to town with two men?" Rachel reminded.

"Something you're going to have to face or else leave this area. You might as well decide now if you can take it." Andrew declared, in a no excuse tone.

Rachel recognized there would be no escape, so she donned her heaviest cloak and soon found herself seated next to Philip in her new carriage. Since Andrew chose to ride Stormy and go on ahead, the two were left to capture some of the magic they had enjoyed before Andrew's arrival and Rachel's busy schedule had interfered.

With rosy cheeks and sparkling eyes, they alighted from their carriage at the Fletcher House where Andrew waited. A hush fell over the busy luncheon crowd as Philip and Rachel entered the dining room. Even Andrew's heart lurched when he observed the beautiful match they made as Philip's golden head leaned down toward Rachel's dark beauty, framed by the doorway of the gracious dining room.

The meal and the day proved perfect. They finished their purchases about mid afternoon and were leaving the final shop when they noticed a large crowd gathering in the small park across from the courthouse. Some leaned over the fence, some were inside the enclosure with their backs to the road, while others just sat on their horses but all appeared engrossed with source and message of a voice blaring from the center of the group.

Andrew took Rachel's elbow and moved her toward the livery when he paused midstep and, dropping his head, turned his ear toward the speaker, and listened intently, for they could not see the man from their vantage point. Then he muttered, a strange mixture of hope and disbelief on his face, "It can't possibly be but it is. There's not another voice like that—or another message."

"What did you say, Andrew?" Rachel asked a puzzled frown marring her smooth brow.

"Do you mind, Rachel?" He nodded toward the crowd.

She hesitated, an uneasy look in her eyes, "Do you think it is a good idea?"

"Don't see why not, I'll protect you," he grinned as he steered her across the street.

"You're part of the talk, remember?" She asked pointedly as she searched up and down the street hoping to find Philip to rescue her. Giving up, she looked toward the crowd where she spied Philip pressed in the midst of it, his body stretched tall so he could see, his eyes fastened on the unseen man with a booming voice laced with an Irish brogue.

Periodically some of the crowd would punctuate a particular point with a groan while others responded with a hearty "amen". The crowd consisted of mostly men with only a few wives sprinkled here and there, some with babies in their arms, but none present, man or woman, remained aloof from the influence of the dynamics of the moment.

Standing at the edge of the crowd, Rachel felt uneasy; her fear of gossip overwhelmed her. Soon her fear receded as the speaker mesmerized her as he had the rest of the crowd. Before long Rachel stood on tiptoe to get a better look at the muscular, balding Irish evangelist with saucer, green eyes and thundering message.

Spellbound, she listened, his quaint Irish accent charming her. However, gradually fascination changed to discomfort as his message pierced superficial curiosity and tugged at her heart.

When he talked about a personal relationship with a God who cared, who wanted to be a Father to the fatherless, an indescribable longing flooded her being but as he went on to explain that sin intervened in the relationship God desired with man, a strange sensation burned inside of Rachel. When the evangelist dared to proclaim every man, woman, and child had a sin problem which needed addressing, an angry denial flushed her face and, unwilling to hear more, she pulled at Andrew's sleeve demanding, "Let's go, Andrew, I'm cold."

Andrew shook off her request, "Wait just a few minutes, he'll be finished. I want to talk to him."

Rachel asked, her voice raised, "Talk to him? Whatever for?"

By this time the evangelist's message concerning the harshness of sin's consequences had agitated her so that she determined to escape from the man's disturbing message. Dropping Andrew's arm, she backed away, then turned, and fled to the safe haven of the livery while both Philip and Andrew stood captivated and unaware of her departure.

Rachel paced the floor in the small livery office. The nostalgic odor of aged leather and horses, mingled with hickory smoke drifted in from the barn and blacksmith's shop permeating the air around her, but she didn't notice. With her face flushed and heart still pounding, the man's message rang in her ears, *"All have sinned and come short of the glory of God; the wages of sin is death. But the gift of God is eternal life through Jesus Christ."* KJV

Rachel silently reproved herself for reacting so silly to the message of an obviously uneducated preacher. Why should his message disturb her? What could he know that she didn't? She asked herself.

Her parents required her to attend church regularly yet she never had heard anything like his message. They raised her as a good Christian, and as far as she knew she was still a good Christian. Rachel silently argued. And as far as her sin and God caring, what right did He have to expect perfection and service from her when He had taken away everything she had loved? Would a God who cared do that to someone He loved?

She shuddered as internally self-justification battled conviction for the destiny of her soul. Finally when she could stand it no longer, compromise won out over sweet solution and she promised herself that she would once again attend the church she had rejected since her Mother's death. Having promised, she could scarcely understand why the peace she sought remained elusive.

With determination she pushed aside the doubts that nagged substituting them with thoughts of Sweetwater, trying to focus on her joy in its transformation. A momentary respite had eased her inner ache when she heard Philip's pleasant lilting English answer Andrew's deep tones just outside the stable. Rachel hurried toward the familiar voices at the door; relief flooding through her only to collide green eyes to green with the source of all her anguish.

"No! No! No! Andrew. I will not have that man at Sweetwater. I know he is your dear friend and you have relished this reunion with him but he must not stay. I have observed him these past two days and he is definitely not what we need."

Andrew stared at Rachel in wide-eyed amazement. Shaking his head uncomprehendingly he exclaimed, "Why Rachel? He's exactly what I've been looking for—."

"I don't need him and I don't want him." Rachel shouted and stamped her foot.

Andrew's warm brown eyes frosted as he replied, "That's not your decision, my dear. I've decided to hire him."

"I don't need an overseer. He'll just rile the slaves, take your money and leer at me." She insisted, her voice lowered but her brows drawn together in a fierce frown.

"Roger? That's the most ridiculous thing I've ever heard. You're being totally unreasonable."

"What do you really know about him? Other than you met him when you were fifteen and he led you through some religious experience?" She fired back.

"That "religious experience" as you call it, is the most important thing that ever happened to me."

"I didn't mean to make light of something that is obviously very important to you, Andrew," she said, in a more conciliatory tone, alarmed at the sudden determination setting his jaw. "I just don't understand how you can make important decisions based on judgments you made when you were fifteen. We're talking about serious matters here."

Meredith clamped his jaws together, exasperation threatening to cloud his logic. He took a deep breath, then defended, answering slowly, "For many years he was a guest in my home when I lived in Boston, both in my foster parents home and then in my own home. When I moved to Savannah, he went out west and we lost touch with one another. You can't know what it means to me to find him again."

She answered softly, her tone persuasive as she took a step toward him, a hand thrown out in appeal "You see what I mean, your emotions are influencing your business decision. I can understand how you feel, but we must find a person with the proper qualifications, if you insist on an overseer."

Meredith barked, "My first criterion is integrity. I would trust Roger with whoever and whatever is dearest to me."

"Perhaps I was too hasty in impugning Mr. O'Callahan's honor," Rachel explained, her eyes wide and pleading. Then she lifted both hands and shrugged, adding, "But you know me, I speak before I think sometimes. This time I overreacted because you seem determined to go against my wishes."

"Rachel, I will consider your wishes, but I will make the final decisions, it's my duty and responsibility. Now give me a logical reason, rather than hysterical as to why I shouldn't hire Roger."

"He's a preacher, not a planter."

"He's a tent maker preacher."

"A what?" She asked, curious in spite of herself.

"He earns his own way so that he can preach the gospel free of charge." Andrew explained, expelling his breath in a long sigh.

"You mean he can't find a church that will pay him." Rachel snapped, in spite of herself. His reference to preaching and gospel resurrected a vague discomfort somewhere deep within her.

"No, that's not what I mean. He is an itinerant evangelist who wanted to preach the gospel to the entire country. He worked at various jobs to enable him to do that." Andrew responded, impatience sharpening his voice.

"There's a world of difference between being a handy man and running a plantation."

"He's not just a handy man, although he can do most anything he sets his mind to do and do it well. He has every qualification to do a good job here. He's hard working, he knows the land and he can motivate men to do their best." Andrew answered through tightened lips.

"How would you know that now, Mr. Meredith?" Rachel crooned, further annoyed at the turn in the conversation.

"Because in large part, he is the reason I have what I have today. He motivated a lonely, frightened fifteen year old boy to give his all and do his best in whatever work he found to do. I've endeavored to follow his challenge."

"There is a difference between a fifteen year old boy and seasoned slaves." She objected, her heart pumping wildly at Andrew's implacability.

"The ability to inspire is effective regardless of age or color, social position or lack of it."

"He doesn't inspire me."

"That's evident. I'm very curious as to why you're so resistant, Rachel. There's not possibly any way Roger could have harmed you." Andrew observed thoughtfully as he held Rachel's eyes, his own impatience waning.

"I don't trust him." She said, her lips pursed.

"You don't trust Roger?" He asked, his eyebrows raised.

"Not in the way you think. It's it's— the slaves." Rachel stammered.

"And what about them?"

"It's his attitude toward them. I don't think he believes in slavery." She whispered, glancing around as if someone might hear her.

"We haven't discussed that issue, so what could you possibly know about him to cause you to believe he's an agitator."

"He has strong convictions on everything and I'm afraid he might cause an uprising or—."

"Or what?" Andrew almost shouted.

"Influence you."

"Influence me, how?"

"To be an abolitionist."

"You think Roger O'Callahan can turn me into an abolitionist?"

"You seem to hold him in the highest esteem."

"My convictions are my own, not dictated by others, even someone I respect." A small nerve twitched in the side of his face, his jaw clinched.

"I'm not willing to risk it," She insisted.

"Risk what?"

"His influencing you and ruining all our plans for Sweetwater."

"Rachel, don't be ridiculous. This is just a smoke screen now tell me the real reason you object to Roger!" Andrew demanded, his patience at an end.

"Call it a personality conflict," she replied,

"Thank you for finally telling me the truth." He answered; a humorless smile curled one corner of his mouth.

Rachel's head jerked up and she sighed, relief relaxing her full lips into a petulant smile. "Then you won't hire him?"

"No, I will hire him. He is exactly the man I need. If it's just a personality problem then you'll just have to work through it." Andrew declared.

"You're going to, even over my objections?" She asked her voice rose in disbelief, her eyes round.

"Your need overshadows your objections, Rachel. When God presents me with a perfect answer to my problem, I'm not going to resist it. I've made up my mind, Roger O'Callahan stays, how you adjust to it—is up to you."

And Rachel saw in the set of his jaw, she'd lost.

And so Andrew hired O'Callahan and Rachel pouted. She remained cool to him throughout the remaining week, only discussing business concerns with him. Her ill humor crossed over into her relationship with Philip. At times she even responded to him with brusqueness when he would invite her for a ride or encourage her to pause from her work for a brief walk and cup of tea.

Meredith left the following week, amused more than worried with Rachel's petulance because he felt confident that given time Roger O'Callahan would charm her once she got to know him. And in any event whether Roger won her over or not, Andrew knew that he had made the right decision. He left assured that Rachel would be safe and that the work would get done. His only misgivings lay in another area. Philip Duval had insisted on staying at Sweetwater on through the holidays. He told himself Duval would be a hindrance to the progress by distracting Rachel. Andrew left Sweetwater with a divided mind, the peace that should have been his on the trip back to Savannah proved elusive, marred by the continuing presence of his friend, Duval.

Andrew refused to examine the unbounded relief he felt when in mid January a crisis at the Boston ship yards required Philip's attention and he had to leave Sweetwater to journey north. The crisis kept the young Briton tied up for several weeks, meanwhile Andrew's life seemed to float in an unexpected lull. He had yet to address Daphne's problem, or broach the move to Aunt Matilda and Laura.

With the holidays, politics seemed to drift in the doldrums and he devoted some extra time to his niece. He took her to the theater and escorted her around town on shopping sprees. The time with her seemed fruitful and he noticed she acquired a new interest in style and fashion. She seemed actually pleased when he hired a new dressmaker from Paris to design and make her new school wardrobe. Not once did he arrive home to find her sitting in the massive live oak, with long legs dangling from a large low limb. Now she greeted him at the front door, her hair and her attire in perfect order.

TWENTY-SIX

The weeks that followed Philip's departure, Rachel threw herself into the work at Sweetwater with no hindrances. She had yet to keep her promise to return to church, neither did she venture into town for supplies. Except for an occasional ride over to Jacob and Bertha's for fresh butter and milk, and if she were truthful the desire for fellowship, she stayed home. In staying home the only people she encountered were slaves and Roger O'Callahan. And she observed Roger O'Callahan, the muscular evangelist who looked more blacksmith than preacher, transformed almost overnight into efficient overseer.

Though she critically examined every action he took or decision he made, Rachel had to admit to herself that she had never witnessed a smoother operation than Sweetwater under O'Callahan's guiding hand. His administrative abilities were only equaled by his natural creative genius. His ability to visualize how each detail of the plans would look at completion and then bring that vision into reality was nothing short of miraculous. Under his supervision the dark walnut wood set aside for the grand stair case came alive with intricate carvings of nuts, fruits and vines, long before the staircase was in place. On rainy afternoons, she would see him take a knife himself and carve on the lustrous wood talking to the slaves as they worked.

He had no aversion to taking up a hammer and working alongside the slaves he supervised. At first Rachel was horrified then gradually noticed the respect his workers had for him. As Andrew predicted, the more Roger worked, the harder the slaves toiled and thanks to his expertise and Andrew's provision of a large work force, restoration of Sweetwater moved on weeks ahead of schedule.

At O'Callahan's insistence, he camped out in the dilapidated overseer's cottage, cooking over an open fire and sleeping on a straw mattress on the floor. Several weeks after his arrival, Rachel rode out to check the progress on the servant housing and infirmary and happened by the old cottage. She could scarcely believe her eyes. Where there had been debris strewn yard, now there was a neat yard with a low brick wall surrounding it.

Curiosity drew her like a magnet so she dismounted and wandered around the building, on impulse she opened the kitchen door and called out for O'Callahan. When no one answered, she entered and walked through the house, her mouth dropped in amazement. Every room had been repaired. In the long narrow parlor across the front of the house, additional shelves for books lined the walls from floor to ceiling on each side of the fireplace. The stone floor of the kitchen gave way to rich patina of heart pine floors, all clean and lustrous from buffing.

The sparse furnishings of the cottage consisted of only two beds, a table and three chairs but Rachel could tell the same loving hands had crafted them as well as the repairs on the cottage. Rachel wondered when he had found the time to accomplish all this, but more than that it was the warm ambience of peace permeating the room and issuing an inaudible welcome that mystified her. That strange indescribable longing which occasionally tugged at her returned to haunt her.

The relationship between Rachel and Roger gradually mellowed as she discovered the evangelist had no plans to force his beliefs on her. In fact their only contact concerned Sweetwater, their only discussions proved impersonal and business related.

As Rachel gradually relaxed her guard, her grudging respect for the evangelist grew. By the time Andrew returned in February, with an impatient Philip in tow, a truce of sorts existed between the two; however, to Andrew, she offered only a cool air of disapproval.

Work on the two new wings was well on the way and the new kitchen completed. Andrew and Philip's arrival prompted a celebration. Rachel reigned over her father's long banquet table in the old familiar dining room where soft candles flickered down the table and from sconces on the wall. Andrew had brought two more house servants from Balmara and they served the first meal cooked in Sweetwater's new kitchen.

Philip Duval, seated on her left could scarcely contain the excitement at being back with her. Andrew and Roger O'Callahan on her right were more subdued but their hearty appetites evidenced their appreciation and enjoyment of the first official meal in the old dining room since Rachel had returned. In a couple of months, the long table would move to the new dining room, but tonight a belated homecoming celebration took place, for it was the first time that Rachel had been able to bring herself to sit in her father's place. Before tonight, she had taken her meals in her room or at the kitchen table where she and Andrew had shared that first breakfast.

Now sitting here with the memories, she was glad that soon the table would be moving to a new room and Sweetwater would take on an entirely new look. For the first time she understood what Andrew had meant when he had urged her months ago to turn loose her yesterdays so she could go on to tomorrow, to replace sorrow with hope, memories with dreams. Maybe she could.

A momentary surge of gratefulness touched the coolness she held toward Andrew because of O'Callahan and she glanced up to find him studying her. Seeing something akin to pain mingled with despair in his dark eyes, her smile that had begun, aborted in confusion, and along with it, that first, hesitant step toward reconciliation.

Philip boldly reclaimed his ground, insisting Rachel take time out from her duties for him. She really had no excuses, no reason not to since O'Callahan had everything running smoothly. Any consultation Andrew did, it seemed not to matter to him whether she was present or not. Gone was the warm comradeship they had enjoyed pre-O'Callahan, so she ended up feeling left out and resentful toward Roger. It was easier blaming him than admitting her own mistake.

She had the highest respect for his abilities, but personally she still felt uneasy in his presence as if he might pounce on her forcing her to accept his disturbing theology. Try as she might, even the joy of watching the transformation of Sweetwater failed to completely wipe away the unsettling thoughts and feelings his words had provoked in her.

Like a melody without end, they played in the background of her mind. Like unwelcome guests, his admonition of the certain consequences of sin unresolved would crash into her mind and catapult the nagging doubt into full fledged agony. Yet she confided in no one. Who was there to ask? And always a still small thought would ask the inevitable—why not Roger? And she always rejected. Sometimes it would happen when they were together making construction decisions; sometimes it would happen when they discussed other plantation business. Sometimes it happened when she was in her bedroom all alone in the dark of night and couldn't sleep, but it happened and as long as the battle raged within her, she could hardly rejoice over his presence. Nor could she tell Andrew that Roger O'Callahan was welcome at Sweetwater.

This time Andrew and Philip stayed with Roger in his cottage, rather than the Fletcher House. The accommodations were a far cry from the luxury both had been accustomed, but neither guest seemed to mind. The cottage was much more convenient and Andrew relished the additional hours he spent with O'Callahan while Philip was ecstatic that he had more time to spend with Rachel. Rachel on the meanwhile wondered how she would ever get her domestic chores done.

In the ensuing months somehow O'Callahan had managed to construct one more bed so the three men each had a bed and bedroom of their own. Although the straw mattress he slept on would hardly be suitable for a British nobleman and a wealthy business man, he somehow managed to find feather mattresses to cover and pad the beds. Rachel later learned that he had obtained mattress, bedding and quilts from Bertha Emory who along with her husband Jacob had become close friends with the preacher.

Rachel insisted that the three men take their meals in the main house, and following the first celebration dinner, they moved back to the old harvest table from the kitchen. She retrieved it and placed it in the vacated old kitchen. With a warm fire licking the logs and crackling merrily in the stone fireplace and the long row of windows that let in the sunlight during the daytime, it turned into a delightful gathering room. More and more Rachel moved her accounts to the table, so she could work there taking advantage of the waning winter light and the warm fire.

One day O'Callahan came in with two slaves behind him, carrying a large drop front mahogany desk, "I just thought you might be enjoying this, ma'am. Since you be a doin' your ciphering in this pleasant room."

Touched by his thoughtfulness, she stood aside, speechless, as they gently placed the large piece of furniture. Instinctively she knew that it had been handcrafted by Roger himself. She was at a loss for words, but inside her heart thawed a little.

One afternoon in late February, when the sun's brilliance announced spring's imminence and the warmth of it stirred the seeds sleeping in their shallow graves, Rachel and Philip rode off to play while Andrew and Roger stayed behind.

Sipping a steaming cup of spiced tea, the two men watched as Philip gently assisted Rachel into Sundance's saddle, then hoisted himself on Prince Kafia, a new Arabian stallion, Andrew had brought to Sweetwater. They rode out with horses' necks arched and tails flying high in the crisp and crackling air. The bright sunlight caught and held the burnished copper tones in Rachel's hair and Andrew's heart rose to his eyes.

O'Callahan turned from the window just in time to witness his friend's moment of vulnerability, "Andrew, my boy, if you love her that much then why do you not marry her? She's a bonnie lass, needs reigning in a bit I grant you, but she's got the making of a gentle woman with the strength of steel. And who' but you could do it the better?" Although Roger had been in America for nearly 20 years, at times of deep feeling, he slipped back into the thick Irish brogue.

Andrew shook his head, "Marry her? She won't have me."

Roger's saucer eyes widened in disbelief, "Not be a having you man? I'm hard to be believin' that. You're a fine specimen of a man and any lass woulda be lucky to have ye."

"Nevertheless, she won't have me."

"Ye have been a askin' her, then I take it?"

"Twice, as a matter of fact."

"Me word! I'm not believin' such a travesty. What's the problem? Is it that young nobleman?"

"Perhaps." Andrew admitted.

"Shaw!!!" Roger exploded. "He's a fine young whelp, but he's not the man ye are. Surely she'll be seeing that by and by."

"Why? She's young too. Really too young for me . . . ."

"Now that's nothing but foolishness, that is, because Rachel, she'll be needin' the firm hand of an older man. I got my doubts that lil laddie'll ever be able to handle her, though he is a good and handsome boy. But tis a man I'm convinced she'll be needin'. Ya, a man like ye. Now what was her response to your proposal, did she reject your love right out now, did she?" Roger turned his eyes, as green as Ireland, unblinkingly on Andrew.

"I didn't exactly tell her I loved her, I offered to marry her. We did discuss love, but there was a disagreement about exactly what it was and she said no," Andrew finished running his words together, uncomfortable with Roger's probing.

Roger's wide eyes bulged, "Ye offered to marry her? Oh, my. And exactly what did you say about love that she couldn't live with?"

"I said love was a commitment two people made who were compatible.

"Oh mercy, mercy, my poor wee lassie, Drew Meredith! You made it sound as if love is a business agreement—!" O'Callahan exploded.

A flush tinged Andrew's face as heat began at the base of his neck and traveled upward, "Well, to me that's what love is. I find a woman to whom I want to commit my life to, which means I love her."

"What do ye feel toward her, son?" Roger probed, refusing to give him quarter.

"I don't want to explain to you how I feel, Roger. It's too personal." Andrew exploded.

"And I guess it's being too personal as ye say, to tell the girl ye love, how ye feel?" Roger insisted.

"That's different." Andrew responded, his hand drumming a rhythm-less beat on the old scarred table.

"And what's so different? Ye didn't tell her, now did ye?" Roger prodded, like a little green-eyed bull dog.

"No, no, and leave it be." Andrew demanded.

"I'll not be leaving it be, my boy. You're making the mistake of yer life." The evangelist fairly shouted throwing his hands in the air.

"How? If she wanted me, then she would have accepted my proposal." Andrew declared trying to close the argument.

"Not on your life, unless she was desperate."

"She was desperate but still wouldn't have me," Andrew commented, his soul opening some.

"Andrew, a woman has to be courted—,"

"I've taken excellent care of her—you know the whole story," Meredith's snapped.

"But tis obvious to me, you don't. These eyes can see both sides of the tale. What ye can't see is that ye both have a burr in your soul." Roger answered calmly never taking his compelling gaze from Andrew.

"A burr in our soul?" Andrew puzzled softly.

"I don't know what hers is, but I recognize yours, for sure." O'Callahan cocked his head to one side, his voice gentling some.

"What is it?" Andrew responded, interest and hope touching his eye

"Yar mom died when ye were a wee boy and ye grew up without love and affection. To say ye love someone was to risk ridicule, so ye put up a wall of protection around yar heart."

Andrew dropped his head, his heart pounded as his friend probed a painful truth, "Perhaps that's just part of my personality."

"Andrew, that wall is a'going to lose ye Rachel, if ye don't be admitin' it and doin' something 'bout it. I know that commitment, protection and faithfulness mean love to a man."

"And what's wrong with that? Love's not even love without commitment. "

"Tis true, but a woman is made out of delicate fabric, my boy. Her emotions are fragile. She's got to be told she's loved. Tis the Good Lord's way of keeping a man in touch with his own emotions." Roger explained.

Andrew looked up into his friend's eyes, confessing, "Sometimes emotions are painful, and sometimes people use them against you if they know about them. So maybe it's better to ignore them, wall them away as you say."

"No t' isn't. Neither for ye nor for yer lady love. If ye be keepin' your feelin's hidden, ye'll grow cold with 'em buried so deep. Then she'll feel like she's only a burden because ye have to take care of her. She doesn't understand the need a man has to look after the woman he loves."

"A burden? That's ridiculous."

"Yes, tis the way she'll be a feeling, and what's more she needs to be told she's lovely to look at. Have ye ever told Rachel how beautiful she is?"

"No," Andrew answered curtly to his friend's meddling.

"Well do you think she's beautiful? If'n ye don', ye're blind."

"What do you think? Of course she's beautiful. I've never seen a woman who could equal her beauty, but that's self-evident, isn't it?"

"Not with a woman, lad. If her loved one doesn't praise her beauty, she feels unattractive no matter how beautiful she is. The good Lord made her that way so a mysterious bonding can take place between a man and his wife."

"That's not reasonable or logical, Roger." Andrew sputtered.

"No tis nothing logical about it, in man's mind. But God worked out His own plan. Take me Becky fer instance. Now there was not a prettier lassie that ever walked the green grass of Ireland. When I would be a coming home, she'd get herself all pretty for me. If I was out of sorts and didn't comment on it, she'd go cry because a woman has to see her beauty reflected through the eyes of her beloved. The looking glass don't count, neither does the rest of the world, only what her love thinks. That's why the plainest of women can be beautiful when a man loves and appreciates her."

"A woman needs that, huh?" Andrew asked his face flushed as his conversation with Rachel played through his mind.

"Yes, along with being told she's worth something to the man who loves her lest she feel worthless. And a lot more. I was still learning when I lost me Becky." Roger added, his voice suddenly husky.

"I wondered how you knew so much about women and you not married." Andrew observed, trying to turn the conversation in a less disturbing direction.

"I was though. God blessed me with fifteen years of heaven on earth. I left Ireland right after me Becky's death."

"If you support love and marriage so, then why didn't you marry again?"

"Twas the Lord's will. When ye have had the best, ye won't settle for second best. God almighty ordained that I have me Becky and when He took her, I knew from then on, I'd make it alone with only Him to lean on. He's never failed me and from my single state, I've been able to devote me time to His work. I've traveled unencumbered when I needed to. With a wife I'd have to consider her needs. A man don't have the same ones."

"So you've just been telling me," Andrew chuckled.

"The question is have you been a listening?"

"Yes,"

"The next question is what are you going to do about it?" Roger demanded.

"I don't know, Roger, I just don't know—."

"Is there any moral or ethical reason that I don't know about that keeps you from pursuing that lovely lass?"

"Like what?" Andrew asked, his eyes narrowed.

"Like Daphne—"

"Not you, too, Roger." Andrew protested, indignation flaring in his dark eyes.

"I just want you to answer me question. What is your relationship with Daphne?" Roger insisted.

"I can't answer that—."

"If she's your mistress then you be breaking the law of God." Roger declared.

Anger flushed Andrew's face, "She's not, never has been, never will be and I don't know why you couldn't just trust me."

"Because she's another burr in your soul. You've got to get it out. If it's not your physically involved with her then what is the attachment?"

"I feel a commitment to protect her," he began.

"That be the same thing you've said about Rachel. Can ye tell me the difference?" Roger insisted.

"I made a commitment to look after Daphne, a vow I cannot break. Rachel is a fire in my bones; she fills my whole being with a longing I never knew existed. When I look at her, I want a home, a wife and children, her children. When she smiles, the sun dims in comparison, when she speaks my name, an angel choir sings. I long to put the world at her feet; to protect her from all pain, to wipe away every tear and to have her by my side for the rest of my days. In fact, I can hardly think of life without her."

"Oh my son, can ya not tell her that? The lass would fall in your arms."

"I don't know if I can or not. And anyway it may be Philip she wants."

"She ne'r wants Philip, but he may get her by default if ya don't fight for her."

"You're really convinced of that aren't you?"

"As sure as the bonnie sun rises in the east and sets in the west. But when she agrees to marry you, boy, what are you going to do with Daphne?"

"I have a responsibility and, yes, a deep affection for her

because— well I'm not at liberty to go into that."

"'Cause she's your sister, Andrew?" Roger's words echoed through the silent kitchen bouncing off the wooden walls as Andrew held his breath.

Then he slowly released it in one long shuddering sigh, "I was sworn to secrecy by her mother. After my foster parents died. You know the story—."

"Yes, after you ran away from home you joined the crew on the ship I sailed on," Roger assured him, his saucer eyes fixed on Drew.

"It was on the return voyage when I met you. The owner of the ship was on board and for some reason he took an interest in me," Drew continued.

"Aye I remember you made several other voyages for him. After the last one, he and his wife took ya to their home in Boston, educating and training ya in the shipping business as their own son," the evangelist said, nodding his bald head.

"That's right and since they were childless I became their sole heir at their deaths."

"Yea, and twas a fine couple they were, I know you missed them when they were gone. Such a terrible accident, their carriage overturning like that."

"I still miss them. They were fine people. But you know all the time I was in Boston, the terrible scene that drove me from home never left my memory," Andrew confessed.

"T'would be expected to haunt your memories," Roger agreed.

"It did and as a result, I had a real burden to find Rosa and try to make amends for my father's actions. After my foster parent's death I returned to the Charleston area where I visited my old home place and found that it had been auctioned off at my father's death. I learned that my brother had disappeared leaving behind an infant daughter with my aunt who lived in town barely supporting herself and my niece by dressmaking. I found them and began providing for them with yearly allowances. Aunt Matilda told me Rosa had been sold to a West Indies planter a few months after I left."

"So that explains Daphne's accent. Did you find her mother?"

"Yes, after many inquiries I found her and a beautiful young daughter. Rosa was very ill, dying in fact, but I'll never forget the joy on her face when I found her. She said she had been praying that Daphne would somehow be saved from the certain fate that awaited her. Beautiful young slaves were saved for trading to the flesh pots in New Orleans; up to that point she had kept Daphne's budding beauty out of sight, but since she was ill she couldn't continue to protect her."

"What did you do?"

"I went to the planter and offered to buy Rosa at a very generous fee, explaining that I knew someone in the states who wanted her, but she refused to leave without her daughter. Needless to say he was glad to get the money for a sick slave and a skinny youngster."

"Then what happened?" Roger moved up to the edge of his chair.

"She died before we could leave, but made me promise I would care for Daphne and never reveal her real identity. She had some twisted notion that the girl was in mortal danger if anyone found out her true identity. I could do nothing but promise. Rosa was in such a state of agitation, that I didn't see any problems with granting her wish so I did. Little did I know!"

"So you ended up in Savannah?"

"Ultimately. First I returned to Boston with Daphne. That's when I decided to bring Aunt 'Tilde and Laura to live with me."

"I remember that. You moved them during one of my visits to Boston. It seemed to work out."

"It all worked out fine. If they have ever suspected anything they've never let on. We lived there until the winters became too rough on Aunt Matilda, then I found a plantation in Savannah and moved my operations there. That's when my trouble began. By that time Daphne was a young woman, beautiful and educated, and she attracted curious speculation which I chose to ignore."

"But you can't any longer, Andrew," Roger reminded.

"I know. Talking to you has made my mind up finally. I'm going to sell Balmara, and set Daphne up in an art studio in Savannah. She is quite gifted. Thanks to Philip Duval who forced me to see that she needs to exercise it." Andrew admitted, his face drawn.

"How will she take it?" Roger asked.

"Badly, I'm afraid. Her entire security is in me. Too late I see the error in that, but I can't undo what I've done, just try to do the best I can now." Andrew turned his eyes from his friend and gazed outside toward the lengthening winter shadows.

Roger placed a comforting hand on Andrew's shoulder, "I know that with God's help you will do the right thing, my boy."

Andrew's breath came out in a long ragged sigh, "Being responsible for people's welfare is an awesome responsibility."

"Aye it is, but the Good Lord laid it on a broad set of shoulders. However, remember this, you take care of your responsibility to the best of your ability, but the choice of happiness lies within the individual. Comfort yourself with that."

Andrew nodded his head, "I know, but sometimes when you get so involved in people's lives, you forget that."

"Tis true, then you shoulder problems, the Lord ne'r intended you should. Keep it straight in your mind as you look after this bevy of women, you are to do what's best for them whether or not they approve. If ye'r guided by that, you won't get lost in the emotional fog of trying always to please them. What's best for Daphne, may not be what pleases her but ye have to do it anyhow for your sake and hers. Now what are you going to do about Rachel?"

"I don't know."

"You gonna move over without a whimper and let her go to that young Philip? That's not what's best for her."

"She needs to decide what's best, don't you think?"

"Then give her a choice, man! While you've been offering her a cold business proposition, Philip has been courting her like a woman needs courting. It's a wonder she's not already accepted him."

Andrew chuckled, "He doesn't have Sweetwater."

Roger nodded his head his hand stroking his chin, "Yes, and I'm surprised he hasn't tried to buy it from you."

"He has, but I'm not interested. As you can see I have important plans for Sweetwater. Actually having this plantation is a hindrance between Rachel and me."

"How?"

"I know how much Rachel wants Sweetwater, I'll find it hard to let down this so called "wall of protection around my heart" until I know it's me she wants with or without this place. The question is, how will I know?"

"When you love someone, Andrew, you have to risk being hurt. Until you are willing to be vulnerable you both will remain isolated from each other by your own fears."

"Then it seems we've reached an impasse."

"You haven't given her a chance." Roger pled.

"Perhaps, but I don't know if I'm ready to take that risk yet. You see she needs to decide about Philip. He loves her deeply and has loved her for a long time, and I don't want to do anything to hurt him."

"You're not thinking straight. Can you not think of what's right for Rachel. At least give the lass a choice."

"I'll consider it, Roger. That's all I can promise you." Andrew replied, a strange mixture of hope and anxiety racing his heart, as hoof beats sounded in the lane heralding Rachel and Philip's return.

TWENTY-SEVEN

The weather did an about face and the days that followed ushered in a new onslaught of winter weather. The cold wind's icy fingers slapped against the house and howled around the corners wiping away the memory of the brief promise of spring.

Housebound, waiting to attend a meeting set up by Goodman later in the week, an impatient Andrew failed to manage a moment alone with Rachel. Everywhere she went, Philip followed close on her heels. So with a full heart that ached to be emptied, Andrew carefully observed the two together.

She smiled sweetly at the Englishman, and they laughed together. While she treated him as a treasured friend, did she have that 'special glow' of a woman in love? As for Philip, was his vitality somewhat diminished or was it the pesky cough and cold he had contracted? As the week wore on, Andrew grew edgy with the forced inactivity so his need to confront Rachel grew day by day; yet he remained unwilling to try.

A small break in the weather prompted Rachel to request some fresh dairy products from the Emory's. Andrew volunteered to go, welcoming the opportunity to escape from his self-imposed prison. Surprise widened his eyes when Rachel suggested she might go with him since the cold rain had stopped.

Delighted, he had the carriage brought around hitched to two American Saddle bred horses he had imported from New York especially for Sweetwater. The biting weather fired their spirits and they were prancing and arching their necks, eager for the trip.

For a moment Rachel and Andrew admired the horses, a new breed recently developed in New York and Kentucky exclusively for road driving and harness racing. Andrew had been more than satisfied with their performances, and now he felt a new sense of pride as he gently handed Rachel into the carriage, knowing her appreciation for fine horseflesh.

A smile of satisfaction lighted his eyes and curved his lips upward as he tucked layers of warm lap blankets over her to ward off the chill. She nestled into the lush down coverlet covering the cold leather seat, and he tenderly pulled her mother's ermine lined cloak up around her ears, his hands lingering a moment when they touched her shining tresses.

She looked up at him, her green eyes questioning his. When her lips curled upward in a warm smile, Andrew knew her silent battle with him over O'Callahan had ended. He breathed a sigh of relief. One more obstacle laid to rest, but then another always seemed to take its place, he cautioned himself.

The drive to the Emory's ended too quickly. At first they laughed and talked of nonsensical things. Then they discussed the improvements at Sweetwater, his plans for establishing a horse breeding farm on part of the property, and finally the excellent work that Roger O'Callahan was doing.

Their visit with the Emory's was brief as the clouds darkened ominously and against the advice of Bertha and Jacob, the two headed back for the plantation before the cold, incessant rain began again.

On the way back their conversation turned serious as Andrew told her of his coming meeting and attempted to explain to her what his purpose was.

She told him the rumors Walter Banks had spread about his being an abolitionist, then asked without animosity, "Are you an abolitionist, Andrew? You sound like one, and of course there's Roger and his influence."

He chuckled dryly, "You won't give up on Roger, will you?"

"Oh I know when I've lost. I have accepted the fact Roger is a fixture around Sweetwater. Personally I'm not comfortable around him, but I will admit, he has done an outstanding job."

"Why aren't you personally comfortable around him? I can't believe he's been anything but a gentleman."

"It's not his actions, it's more his philosophy that disturbs me," Rachel hedged.

Andrew turned his head toward her, raising one brow, "His philosophy?"

"You know we've been through that before. You know his abolitionist leanings, etc." She responded, unwilling to admit the real source of her anguish. "But I didn't ask about Roger. I asked about Andrew Meredith."

"I'm a southerner who recognizes the South's vulnerability. Our whole economy is based on a faulty system."

"A real Southerner loves the South and our way of life." Rachel argued.

"Rachel, our way of life is ending. Whether we secede or whether we reach a compromise, our whole Southern way will have to change."

"Why do we need change? I can't think of anything finer than the way we live," Rachel insisted.

"Our lives are rooted in the institution of slavery. It will end but until it goes, the south is as enslaved by it as much as the very people we enslave."

"Perhaps Walter Banks was right about your abolitionist's leanings," she accused, her voice quiet but her eyes blazed.

"I've not allowed myself to consider the sins of slavery as much as the problems the institution presents to our future." Andrew confessed, as he gripped the cold reins tightly in his hands.

"It's not slavery that's the problem. It's northern industrialists trying to interfere in our business all because they want to shove tariffs down our throats and force us to trade with them," she argued.

"There's just enough truth in your statement to push this nation into war. The problem is not northern industrialists' self-interests but what our dependence on slavery has done to us as a section."

"The South is the finest, most genteel place to live on the face of the earth and slavery is a necessary part of that life," She objected.

"What you describe is mostly an illusion, Rachel. Only a relatively few people live like that and it's only temporary at best for them. Change is inevitable and the South has to be ready for that change. Slavery has kept us focused on an agrarian economy and away from progress which can only come with industrialization. That's why we're so vulnerable to tariffs and that's why we'll lose the war when it comes."

"You still think there will be a war?" She asked, staring into his eyes and biting her bottom lip.

"If we secede, yes, there will be one. One we cannot win. At this point, I'm not fighting slavery, I'm fighting to preserve the nation and save the South."

"How successful have you been?" She encouraged him to continue.

"Moderately so at first. There was much unionist sentiment in the northern part of Georgia, but I've seen it grow progressively weaker each trip I make. First I encountered interest, then indifference, lately open hostility." He finished with a slight shrug of his shoulder.

"Yet you keep on, why?" She asked, sincere interest firing her eyes.

"I have an obligation to warn the people, to let them know what's coming if they secede. When you know the truth you're responsible for sharing it."

"I don't understand why you feel this need if you know your efforts will fail." Rachel protested.

"I hope they won't, but even so I have to do what I have to do otherwise I couldn't live with myself. An awful bloodbath is coming, if I don't do what I can to stop it, the blood will be on my hands." He shifted his attention from the road to her, his dark brown eyes probing hers, as if willing her to understand.

Rachel shivered and drew her cloak up around her, "I don't like to hear that."

"That's the problem. No one wants to hear it. Change is coming. A new South will emerge but only the ones who are prepared for it will survive." He turned back to the road, his shoulders sagging with discouragement.

"You may be in danger, Andrew." Rachel remarked quietly.

"I know tempers flare at times," he agreed.

"I don't mean that. It's Walter Banks. I don't know a lot, but he has cohorts all over the county."

A bitter smile parted his face, "Don't you find your sentiments more in tune with his than mine?"

An embarrassed half smile curved her mouth and she stammered, "It's true, I do disagree with you about slavery. I believe it is necessary to Sweetwater's survival, but I admire the strength of your convictions."

"Thank you for that, maybe someday you'll share them."

"Whether or not that happens, I don't approve of Bank's tactics. His associates make up the slave patrol, but they go far beyond those duties. From bits and pieces I have heard, they act as a kind of vigilante group to police political thought they oppose. I wouldn't be surprised if that's not the source of the hostility you encountered at your meetings."

He turned his attention from the road to look at her, his eyes thoughtful, "You may be right, Rachel. I've seen some of the same hecklers in different parts of the county."

"I'm sure that I am. He has a lot to gain if he discredits you—,"

"Or kills me?" Andrew softly added.

Rachel jerked her head toward him, alarm widening her eyes, as she nodded slowly, "Or kills you."

They had not traveled far from the Emory's when Andrew rounded a curve, leaving the protective tall banks on each side of the deep road cut. A strong gust of icy wind blasted the carriage and both Rachel and Andrew gasped as small, darts of sleet hurdled into the protected carriage, stinging their faces. He pulled the carriage to the side of the road and stopped the horses whose ears laid back as they pranced nervously in their tracks

"I think we may run into some bad weather before we can get

back. Are you all right?"

"I'm fine," Rachel said through chattering teeth.

"We'll make a run for it and hope we can beat the weather home. I just hope that cloud is not between here and Sweetwater."

Andrew snapped the reins and the eager horses bolted forward. Neither he nor Rachel spoke as the carriage lurched over the bumps and reeled around curves. Meanwhile the sleet changed to an icy rain and before long an icy film formed on the trees and road providing a sparkling winter wonderland, while forcing Andrew to slow to a snail's pace as the carriage slipped in the sharp curves.

Finally the rain turned to snow. At first large lazy flakes floated from the heavens, coating road, trees and shrubs with an eerie white shroud, but before long flakes were coming fast and furious covering even the tracks left by the carriage. Their breath mingled inside the carriage leaving crystals in the cold air, as Andrew strained to see through the blinding snow in the darkening afternoon. The horses walked with heads down against the brutal wind and snow, feeling their way along.

They started up a narrow, steep grade that turned sharply to the right. With a high bank on one side and a deep ravine on the other, Andrew held his breath as the carriage shifted sharply and skidded sideways, the left rear wheel sliding off the side of the road and dangling over the steep side. The force of the skid threw Rachel against Andrew and his right arm reached out and drew her into his protective embrace.

She made no sound, just buried her head in his shoulder as he flicked the reins urging the horses to pull on. It proved futile. The road was too slick for them to maintain their footing and haul the impounded vehicle. The horses slipped and the carriage tottered precariously.

"Rachel, Can you climb out that door?" Andrew asked, nodding his head toward the right hand side.

"I think so, but what about you?"

"I'll keep tension on the reins while you climb out, else this carriage will end up with us both down there in that stream."

Fear darkened her eyes, "Wha—What about you?"

"I'll be right by your side, first you then me. It's just a matter of time until the horses fail and slide back into the buggy. And when that happens—" He explained evenly as he pushed her gently toward the door, sliding with her.

The carriage shifted toward the road as the weight of their bodies moved toward the right and escape. Andrew's arm, still enfolding Rachel reached out and groped for the handle finding it, he pushed. The door refused to budge. He muttered under his breath, "Frozen?"

"What now, Andrew?" Rachel asked.

Once again a strong gust of wind burst against the carriage rocking it and he felt the tension in the reins ease as the horses slid backward. With one swift motion Andrew released the reins and threw his shoulder against the carriage door, pushing Rachel to his front. The door flew open and Andrew leaped into the rocky road pulling Rachel and lap blankets out on top of him, just as carriage slipped off the road and down the embankment, dragging the helpless horses backwards, their eyes bulging with fear.

Andrew and Rachel sat immobilized in the wet snow and watched, horrified, from the road as the horses lost their footing. Just then the carriage reached a steeper edge of the ravine and toppled over the side. With a loud pop the wooden tongue snapped, breaking the bond that held the terrorized animals, setting them free to run up the road toward Sweetwater. Nothing now to impede its fall the stately vehicle rolled over and over, bouncing against sharp boulders that lined the steep banks until it stopped in a splintered heap upside down in a small stream that twisted through the base of the narrow canyon.

Andrew sat up straight and turned to Rachel encircled by his arms and lodged against his chest. His hands trembled as he pushed back her thick tresses that had come loose in her fall. He ran a caressing finger along the contours of her face as if to reassure himself that she was safe and in his arms. Gently he lifted her face to his.

Fear and relief burned in his eyes as he tenderly traced her brow, her eyelids, her nose, her chin and finally her lips. Seeing no injury he exclaimed, "Rachel, Rachel, I could have lost you. What a fool I've been."

He tightened his arms about her, gathering her into a fierce embrace, and bent his lips to hers.

Startled, Rachel pushed against him until the urgency of his kiss melted the last bastion of her resistance and she yielded her lips soft and pliable beneath his.

The smell of evergreen mingled with a faint odor of wood smoke enveloped them as the swirling snow coated them in white. Rachel's hands, caught against his chest, felt his heart thundering beneath the rough texture of his coat. Slowly she slipped them upward to his shoulders until one touched the back of his head bent to hers. Surrendering to his embrace, her heart reached its own crescendo in a thundering duet with his as Rachel experienced the haven of his embrace.

Finally when the snow had powdered her uncovered head and clung to her dark lashes, he lifted his head, still clutching her in a tight embrace. His eyes were large and dark with emotions, hers glowed like fiery emeralds. Neither could speak for a long moment.

Then with a shudder, Andrew confessed, "I love you, Rachel. From the moment I encountered you on that Savannah dock, you captured my heart. Wherever I go, those eyes of yours go with me. They haunt my dreams at night; the sound of your voice fills my mind. I want—."

Rachel touched her finger to his lips, "You love me, Andrew?"

"I love you, Rachel," Andrew repeated.

"Not obligation, but emotions?"

He chuckled and placed her hand over his heart, it still thundered like a herd of runaway horses. "Obligation alone can't do that, only a deep felt emotional response."

She smiled up at him, its brightness dazzling him in the darkness of the stormy afternoon,

"Oh, Andrew, you've felt like this and never told me, why?"

"I wanted to be sure you cared for me. But today when I realized how close I came to loosing you nothing mattered except how much I loved you. I wanted you to know whatever your response might be." He answered.

She dropped her head, nestling it in the curve of his shoulder, and confessed, "If you only had told me earlier, how much easier my life would have been."

He tightened his grip on her and, placing a finger beneath her chin raised her head to meet his kiss once again. This time his lips staked their claim and hers accepted. When he released her, both were short of breath, "I'm going back on my word to you, because this is the third time, but will you marry me, Rachel?"

Green lights mixed with warm flecks of amber danced in her eyes as she asked mischievously, "Why, Andrew?"

"Because I love you and I want to look after you, to care for you, to cherish you all the days of my life."

"How could I refuse an offer like that?" Mischief parted her lips in a smile, and then slowly faded as she encountered the earnestness of his gaze. Breathless she whispered, "Yes, Andrew, I'll marry you."

"What about Philip? I thought you loved Philip."

"At one time I thought I did, too, when you left for Savannah and Philip stayed behind, I realized what I felt for Philip was the deep affection for a friend."

"Philip will be very hurt, and I hate that. He's a fine man and a good friend."

She laughed, "Are you trying to talk me into marrying Philip?"

He pulled her closer to him, this time her ear to his pounding heart, "Never. I can no longer imagine life without you by my side. Up to now I had not dared hope, now hope has exploded into a reality, and I'll never let you go."

"I have already told Philip that I won't marry him." She said into his chest, her head buried away from the cold wind and snow.

"Have you told him why?" Andrew asked into her hair.

"Not exactly. I told him that my love for him was like a friend or a brother, but I didn't tell him I loved you." She murmured, not looking up.

"Neither have you told me." He said forcing her head up, so he could see her face.

"Wha . . .?" She stammered, confusion clouding her eyes

"That you love me." Andrew insisted, his eyes fixed on hers.

"Oh, yes, Andrew. I love you." She exclaimed.

"Even without Sweetwater?" He probed, a frown creasing his brow.

"But,— but, I don't have to make that choice, do I? All our plans—, " She paused, her eyes questioning, a battle within.

"I need the answer to that question, Rachel."

"I just told you that I love you," Rachel insisted, shaking her head and scattering snowflakes from her hair.

"Even if I told you Philip wants to buy Sweetwater?"

"What has that got to do with anything? With or without Sweetwater it's not Philip I love, but surely after all your investment you don't intend to abandon Sweetwater."

"No, I don't intend to sell to Philip. I was only testing you." Andrew confessed.

"That's not fair, Andrew." She protested.

"Perhaps you're right, my darling, but the needs of a heart aren't always fair. Maybe someday you'll be ready to give me your whole heart, with or without Sweetwater."

"Oh, Andrew don't," she begged, unshed tears glistening in her eyes.

"It's all right, my dear. You'll not always be in this bondage. When you're set free and your love is unencumbered perhaps then you'll even call me Drew." He gently told her and wiped away two lonely teardrops trickling down her cheeks.

She grasped his hand, bowing her wet cheeks against his knuckles, and longed for the moment she could give Andrew her heart unencumbered when she would be free of the mysterious shackles that bound her.

TWENTY-EIGHT

Daphne protested, "Mr. Andrew, you can't mean that!" Her eyes wide, questioning. The morning sun streamed in the windows of the alcove in his study and bounced off the cherry walls, washing her in a soft radiance. She stood ramrod straight, her small, square shoulders tense, only her trembling hands gave mute evidence that Daphne's world was falling apart.

"It's true, my dear." Meredith confirmed, rising from his desk. His own hands, unsteady also, gripped the smooth, satiny wood as he searched for some magic word that would ease her hurt. But he found none and only the agony of her heartbreak remained the moment's reality. A gentle breeze lifted the gossamer curtain and swirled about, encapsulating them in a gentle coolness, before it dropped to mingle its evergreen breath with the hint of lemon oil and leather permeating the room.

"You're moving and I won't be going with you and Miz Tilde? You're leaving me behind?" She questioned.

"That's correct. You'll stay here in Savannah, and I'll be moving to Sweetwater, along with Aunt Matilda and Laura."

"But what about Balmara?"

"Philip Duval is buying Balmara. And you will move to Savannah where I have purchased you a townhouse."

"But why?" Daphne cried, her composure threatened.

"For your sake and mine, Daphne." Andrew responded, slowly exhaling, while his broad shoulders, usually square and confident, drooped, the strain beginning to take its toll.

"I—I don't understand, have I displeased you in some way? Are you not satisfied with my work?"

Andrew Meredith's eyes darkened with pain as he saw her eyes brighten with unshed tears. He shook his head sadly, praying that he could convey to her the truth, that somehow her heart would receive it, "Of course not, Daphne. You please and have always pleased me in everything that you do."

"Then why are you discarding me?" Daphne asked; her hands rose in a helpless gesture.

Pain exploded in Andrew, his heart seemed ready to burst, "I—I'm not discarding you! I'm setting you free, truly free to be the person God intended you to be."

"I am free, Mr. Drew, You freed me, remember?" unconsciously Daphne addressed him by the name she only called him in private and to herself. In the emotion-charged air between them, neither noticed.

"No you're not, Daphne. You may have your manumission papers, but you have given up your life and your talents for my benefit. That's not fair to you. Philip Duval made me see that." Andrew explained, his voice husky.

"Mr. Duval should attend to his own business and stay out of other's affairs. He's caused nothing but trouble since he arrived." Daphne spat out, her eyes, now fiery, amber coals, her studied composure cracking.

"Don't blame Philip, Daphne. The blame lies at my door. He pointed out a truth that I knew but refused to acknowledge."

"What truth?" she snapped.

"That you are a gifted young woman who has sacrificed your talents to make my life comfortable." Andrew admitted, his voice tired. "Philip is right and I've decided to do what I can to rectify my mistakes."

"And ruin my life in the process?"

"Only if you allow it to. A life built on anything but truth is no life at all, Daphne. It's mere existence, waiting for tragedy to happen. I'm glad I faced it while there is still time to give you a chance for a new life."

"I don't want a new life. I want life to stay the same." Daphne responded through tight lips, her words clipped.

Andrew shook his head, "Life never stays the same, Daphne. It changes and we have to face the challenges. You have an opportunity to have a new and better one."

"Suppose I don't want this 'opportunity'."

"I can only assure that you have it, what you do with it is up to you. Only you can take advantage of it."

"How am I to take advantage of it? Without you?" Daphne asked her chin quivering.

"I've purchased you a studio that can be used as a gallery near the river. I trust you can sell paintings locally, but Philip is busy establishing you a network of galleries in the northeast where he is sure he can find a ready market."

"Mr. Philip oversteps his authority—" Daphne protested.

"Philip Duval is acting at my request. He has agreed to act as your sponsor."

"Why?"

"You will need someone to provide personal protection and business guidance until it is established and profitable."

"Why can't you do that instead of him?"

"I won't be here."

"You will be coming back to check on your shipping interests, I'm sure." Daphne protested.

"That's correct, but I won't be here to offer personal assistance if a need suddenly arises. I feel more comfortable leaving you in Philip's care."

"Why are you leaving? You could have done this and remained in Savannah," her voice rose, panic bubbling under the surface.

"I'm getting married, Daphne." Andrew said quietly, watching her reaction, his own heart beating furiously.

She flinched, then the angry fire that had sparked her eyes moments before disappeared as her emotions slipped behind an He nodded, "I love her very much."

Daphne shrugged, "I see. Then she is why I have to stay here."

Andrew's mouth curled in a humorless half-smile, "Not exactly. I'm doing what I think is best for you. I made the decision before Rachel agreed to marry me, but you're right, it wouldn't have worked. Rachel will want to be in charge of her own home, a house can only have one mistress."

"I hope you will be happy, Mr. Andrew. Miss Rachel is a very beautiful woman, but I don't think you'll have an easy life with her, she rather has a mind of her own." Daphne observed her voice even, emotionless.

"No, my life hasn't been easy since the day we rescued her from those ruffians, but I'm risking ease, safety for love. I believe it's worth the sacrifice. That's what I want for you, Daphne, love, a home of your own and the pursuit of your God-given gift. This change is for your benefit—"

"And yours—?" She asked a strange light in her eyes.

"And mine," he admitted.

In response Daphne smiled with her lips, her eyes still cool and distant, "Then I'll try, Mr. Andrew. I committed myself to labor for your happiness when you brought me to your home. If Miss Rachel is what it takes to make you happy, then I'll step aside."

"No, Daphne, not step aside, but step ahead where life awaits you. Not my life, but yours. Not one where you have to live vicariously, submerged in someone else's, but one where your own interests and gifts captivate you," He moved around his desk to where she stood and stared down at her, his eyes imploring her to accept his explanation.

"All I can do is try." She said and turning from him, asked, "May I go now? Ellie needs some assistance in the kitchen and you have guests for lunch."

Impulsively Andrew reached out to his half- sister and placed his hand on her shoulder, turning her toward him, "Promise me, you'll really try? Your happiness is very important to me."

For a moment their eyes locked, and then she lifted one brow, questioningly before she spun around and walked away.

Andrew turned back to his desk to face the tall windows and looked across the rolling lawn to the river's slow-moving black waters. He sighed, the river contrasted greatly with the rollicking Chattahoochee, but no greater contrast than his life would experience when he exchanged all of this for Sweetwater and Rachel. He had ambitious plans for his and Rachel's life together. To restore everything that had been her family's holdings was just the beginning. Thanks to Roger, attaining the first part of his goal was in view, but he had much more in mind.

Since his acquisition of the mill, he had little time or interest in it so he had opted to lease it out to the manager for only a monthly rental. However, when he and Rachel married that would change. He planned to take over management of the mill and to upgrade machinery and buildings. He wanted to expand it and give McDonald's mills at New Manchester some real competition. A thorough inspection on his last trip to Sweetwater had shown him it was in desperate need of some money and attention.

The current manager's treatment of his workers and the physical condition of the mill revealed gross mismanagement. He had given the man notice that his days were numbered at the mill. He had plans to bring in the finest equipment and build a village of comfortable and attractive houses for the workers, hoping that he could attain the same feeling of community there that New Manchester enjoyed. Yes, his life was facing some great changes, but as always a business opportunity challenged him.

He approached the change with mixed emotions. He rejoiced that his future with Rachel was finally settled. Soon after he had declared his love for her in the wind driven snow, Philip and Roger had tramped through the darkening afternoon with horses and blankets, rescuing them from possible harm.

Intermingled in his joy was apprehension and sadness. Rachel was to be gloriously, wondrously his. Yet he sensed that she still withheld a part of her heart from him. Roger had called it a "burr" in her soul, but Andrew comforted himself that it was misplaced security and only a temporary condition. Even when his friend had warned him, he countered that given time it would go away. His love closed his ears to the warning, but now in the dimness of Daphne's agony, he wondered.

Rachel had set their wedding date for the fall. And he knew that it would take him that long to transfer the operations of his Savannah businesses to his manager's capable hands. Both of them wanted the renovations at Sweetwater complete so he could settle Aunt Matilda and Laura in before their marriage.

His common sense told him they needed that much time, his impatient heart pushed to make Rachel his immediately. Forget social propriety; let Roger marry them at once. An uncanny fear tortured his heart that something might happen to steal his hope and new found joy. Love had come late to him and now he cherished it as a perishing man does an oasis in the hot desert sands.

But she had insisted and he knew that for her sake and his, time for a proper wedding would help quiet the wagging tongues. And he was willing to wait if it meant protecting Rachel, yet he chafed under the delay.

And then there was Philip. Andrew's heart lurched. It felt partitioned within him. One part of his heart reveled in what had taken place between Rachel and him, another ached for the loss his friend had experienced.

How could he forget the look of relief mixed with jubilation and unvarnished love on his friend's face when he and Roger discovered them unharmed in the snow. It was the morning after when Rachel told Philip about their plans. Like the gentleman he was, he had offered Andrew his congratulations with a smile, but in moments when he let his guard down, a sadness dulled the usual effervescence in his eyes. Until he had heard from Rachel's lips she loved Andrew, his heart had still dared to hope, but now whatever glimmer of hope he had was gone. His only solace was the prospect of her happiness and his respect for his friend. Andrew hurt for him, and tried to conceal the joyous anticipation that bubbled in his own soul.

Philip had returned to Savannah with him and was residing at Balmara. It was he who solved his dilemma with Daphne. As Philip pointed out, Rachel would refuse to marry Andrew unless Daphne was out of his life. His frown deepened as he longed to tell Rachel the truth about Daphne, but dared not. He only hoped that his wife would never question his integrity nor interfere with his commitment to the former slave girl, his half sister.

Thanks to Philip, maybe his wife need never be bothered about their strange relationship. Without him, Andrew knew that he would be at a loss for a suitable scheme for Daphne. She had to have a local sponsor and a protector. Philip had volunteered for the job, by offering to buy Balmara. Andrew agreed and asked Agan if he would stay on with Duval to manage the estate, telling him that by necessity Philip would be in England for long periods of time.

Thoughts of Agan intruded and some illusive warning left a vague uneasiness in his mind, and he wondered why the young man appeared reluctant to accept the position with Philip. He even thought that he had sensed a subdued resentment in him. Meredith shrugged, dismissing the thought. What possible resentment could he harbor? Hadn't he given him every opportunity available?

Daphne blinked back the tears that blinded her as she hurried down the narrow, dark underground passageway leading to the kitchen wing. She flinched as an unseen hand reached out from the shadows and grasped her arm, stopping her flight mid-step.

Her head shot up and her eyes widened as Agan Chero' stepped from between the massive timbers supporting the house and, grabbing her other arm, pulled her back into the shadows and so close to him she could see the veins in his neck throbbing.

She tried to wrench away from him, but his hands tightened,

compressing her shoulders and digging into her flesh. He stared down into her eyes; the dim light over her shoulders caught a mixture of desire and mastery burning in his. Daphne dropped her head, afraid of what she read in his eyes, unwilling to let him see her fear. But he had seen and now he chuckled, his deep melodious voice crooning in her ear, "What's the matter my sweet? You're not afraid of Agan. Are you? You and I are friends. But more than that we're allies."

"Friends?" Daphne questioned, her voice like ice, still refusing to look at him. "I think not."

His large eyes, ebony in the dimness, hardened, "Think again, because you need a friend. You need me."

"I don't need you—or want you," Daphne hurled at him, her heart pounding.

"What's that, my pet? Don't want me when we grew up together? Remember we ate together at the white man's table, we learned his manners and his methods together. We are alike, you and me." He whispered in her ear as he dropped his head over her bowed one.

"Maybe we grew up together, but we're not alike and we're not friends." Daphne declared through clenched teeth, her body rigid.

"Why, my love? Could it be because you have forgotten who you really are?" He asked in honeyed tones as his hands, caressing moved down her arms until they captured her wrists.

"It has nothing to do with my identity. What you wanted wasn't friendship," Daphne replied with a shuddered.

"I wanted your love," Agan's eyes glittered dangerously as he took in her response.

"Love at the price of betrayal is not love," She moaned as a tear trickled down one cheek.

He chuckled triumphantly, "Now look who is betrayed. You would have done well to have listened to me. You gave him your life and now he has dumped you for that green-eyed vixen."

"That's not true—," Daphne protested, raising her fore arms and twisting her wrists in his vice like grip.

"I heard it all. I listened inside the secret passage," He whispered, refusing to relinquish his hold.

"How like you, Agan. Mr. Andrew trusts you with all that he has. "

"But I still have to call him `Mr.'" He observed, his voice brittle with bitterness.

"He's been kind and generous with you yet you repay him with schemes and plots, spying and lies." Daphne defended.

"He did me no favors. I've repaid him well. His business is profitable, isn't it? "

"Yes, but I daresay a big portion has gone into your personal coffer."

Agan tightened his grip and pulled her closer, a strange light in his eyes, "Not my coffers, everything I do is for the cause,"

"Cause—you mean your own cause!" She accused, as she ceased struggling against him.

"Yes, one that you would have joined long ago if you hadn't forgotten your heritage."

"What kind of cause?"

"One that will save that beautiful hide of yours." He laughed, a malevolent sound in the shadows.

"I don't need saving. I have a future."

"In the white man's world? You'll never be accepted—," Agan taunted.

"I already have a market for my paintings—."

"In the South?" He probed.

"Not yet, but Mr. Philip has several prospects in Boston and other cities,"

He gripped her wrist, hurting her, "You needn't depend on that fancy dressed white boy to take up where Meredith left off. It's Agan's turn."

She shuddered, forcing herself to meet his eyes, "I don't know what you're talking about, but this one thing I do know, it will never be your turn, whatever that means."

"You'll change your mind soon and when war comes, you'll have no other choice." Agan disputed.

"War?"

"Yes, it's coming and it's our salvation."

"How much more could you want? You're free, you have a good life." Daphne asked, perplexed, her fear in abeyance.

"Free? I'll never be really free until I'm in control of my own destiny."

"You're free to leave anytime you wish."

"And be known as Andrew Meredith's "boy"? Agan spat out, his face contorted.

"Leave Savannah."

"And have to register my presence wherever I go? No, thank you."

"Then go up North where you don't have to register."

"But I choose to stay in the South, and when I get through not only will I be able to stay, the likes of Andrew Meredith will be answering to me."

"Agan, what are you planning?"

His face parted in a venomous sneer, "Nothing for you to worry your pretty head about. My plans are in order and before long you'll be anxious to participate."

"You're mad, Agan. Where is your conscience?"

"Unlike you, my sweet, I haven't forgotten who I am. I plan to help those who don't enjoy the so called privileges that I do, at least those who have the courage to join me."

"You don't want to help anyone, what you want is revenge. And revenge for what? Andrew Meredith has given you advantages far beyond anything you could have hoped to have and only shown you kindness in the meanwhile."

"Is it kindness to give a man an appetite for the things he can never have and then to deny him the one thing he wanted more than all others?"

"What has he denied you, Agan?"

"You, Daphne." Agan growled and she saw the unvarnished pain in his eyes.

"How?" Daphne whispered, her brows raised, her eyes round as fear and pity warred in them.

He saw the pity and bitterness curled his lip, "By chaining your devotion to himself and using you for his own purposes. I've hated him for that,"

"But you don't understand—It's not like you think, He's never used me." Daphne protested her voice low, pleading.

"I do understand. Because of him, you wouldn't give me a second glance."

"No, Agan. Because of your own bitterness. Your bitterness toward a man who has only done you good. You wanted my love. Perhaps I could have given it to you, but that wasn't enough, you required betrayal."

"The truth is you thought you were too good for me and you gave him your love when it should have been mine."

"Not love in the way you mean, Agan. Believe me, its deep affection and loyalty nothing more."

"Believe you? Believe you're not bound to the man by unspeakable passions?"

"I'm not. How many times must I tell you, it's only respect and appreciation that binds me to him?"

"No one would devote themselves to another for mere respect and appreciation. Tell the truth, admit it, admit there is more," Agan snarled at her shaking her by her wrist pulled up between them.

"I'm not at liberty to tell you more. Believe me, he has never laid a hand on me. He has only protected and cared for me."

"In turn for what?"

"My housekeeping services."

"He has a hundred slaves and an aunt who could do as much, why, you, except that you're beautiful and desirable?"

"Stop it, Agan. I've told you the truth, more I cannot tell you." She cried, tears now trickling down her cheeks from the pain in her arms and the pain in her heart.

"Don't lie to me to save Andrew Meredith, all Savannah knows and laughs at you. But Meredith will pay and all your defending won't save him."

"What are you going to do?" Alarm raised her voice.

"And wouldn't you like to know so you can run to him with your misplaced loyalty, but that won't last. When you really see him for what he is you'll come running to me. You're not ready yet. But you will be."

"I'll never take part in what you're doing."

"The wagging tongues of Savannah have been waiting for a chance to get at you. They won't buy your paintings and Philip Duval can't protect you. When Andrew Meredith dumps you for that fiery Rachel Gregory and leaves Savannah for good, you'll find out what it means to be black in a white society. You'll finally see what he's done to you. And when you do, you'll hate him as I do and then you'll come to me." Agan said, as he stepped out of the shadows into the center of the passageway, his mammoth body filling the corridor. Suddenly he released her wrists, a triumphant gleam in his eyes and added, "Meanwhile I can wait. I'm a patient man."

Icy fingers of terror raced down Daphne's spine as she shrank from him rubbing her wrists. She pressed herself against the wall, as she slid past him careful to avoid any contact with his body.

She heard laughter growl in his throat as she passed and it chased her down the dim corridor, embedding in her mind, waiting to haunt her future nights.

TWENTY-NINE

The heavens dissolved over Sweetwater and the surrounding area. For days the rain fell with only brief lulls. Small creeks overflowed and rushed over the land, washing away precious topsoil. Torrents cut gullies in fresh plowed fields and Sweetwater Creek gouged caves and tunnels along its tall clay banks, undermining the forest that rested atop and beneath disturbing bones long buried, but not forgotten. Finally with a mighty crash a towering oak whose broad spread of shallow roots succumbed to the inevitable erosion fell headfirst into the stream. It split the soft, faulty earth behind it and laid bare the unconfessed secret that stalked Rachel's dreams.

And so it was that Walter Banks during a brief lull between storms rode his mighty stallion to the very spot, trespassing deep inside the sanctuary of Sweetwater land. Dismounting for a closer look at the newly opened grave, he picked his way gingerly as his fine leather boots sank ankle deep into the gray miry ground, making a loud sucking noise as he lifted each stained foot and leaving a trail of water filled holes.

He reached out to the shroud-covered form, giving the cotton sheet a quick jerk. The contents rolled free, a garish vision of twisted, unclothed torso and yellow hair now the color of old brass. A triumphant sneer divided Bank's face, his short pointed teeth clasped together in vicious glee.

Although the worms and warm summer climate had done their work well and the skeleton had lost skin and tissue, leaving only sockets for eyes, and a face without form, he recognized what he had found, and rejoiced. For the long, bony fingers clasped a locket and a long, single strand of auburn hair.

Rachel paced to and fro in the former kitchen now transformed into an inviting study and grimaced toward the deluge that poured from the sky and cascaded from the roof like a thundering waterfall. Seeds waited to be planted in the waterlogged fields, but without a break in the weather planters would face another disastrous season. A crop disaster would make little difference to her personal future, but her pride and obsession with Sweetwater pressed her to succeed. The incessant rain continued to fall and once again her high hopes and plans appeared dashed by circumstances beyond her control.

Roger O'Callahan leaned back against the wall in a sturdy oak chair except for glancing at her from time to time, his attention was focused on the stick of wood and knife he held in his hand. He propped his feet on the fender of the new wood burning stove Andrew had sent from Savannah and whistled a tuneless melody as dark, life-like images emerged from the satiny smooth walnut he carved. "Miss Rachel, you might as well simmer down. Wearing a path in the floor will do no good."

"Will this rain never stop? We've got to get our crops in the ground." She snapped, as a bolt of lightning ripped the sky bouncing thunder across the roof until the whole house shuddered.

Roger chuckled, answering without lifting his eyes from the work he held in his hands, "Now don't you think the Good Lord knows enough about our needs to stop the rain when He sees fit?"

Rachel's heart constricted, his words resurrecting the misgivings that haunted her day and night, "It seems God delights in playing havoc with my plans."

"Maybe that's the problem, Miss Rachel, tis your plans, rather than God's."

"Whose plan was it that took my mother, my father and my future?" She demanded and Roger saw the burr in her soul glowing in her eyes.

"T'was God's, I reckon, Miss Rachel." Roger answered compassion softening his brogue.

"What kind of God would do a person like that?"

"I don't presume to know the answer to all the whys of what God allows, but I do know that He is a loving God, whatever He chooses to do."

"A loving God?" she asked, disdain raising her voice.

"Yes, one who loves you."

"If He loves me then why has He taken away everything that is dear to me?" Bitterness tinged her voice.

"Maybe he had to before He could reach you."

"That's not love, that's cruelty."

"Perhaps in yere own mind, Lassie, but you see the Good Lord knows us better'n we know ourselves. Tis true, He knows what stands in the way betwixt us and Him. If He can't get through to us, then He'll be removing the obstacles."

"You mean my parents were obstacles—."

"Now we'll not be a knowing that, but fer sure, they were your security. With them alive and looking after you so good, would you be a needing God?" Roger posed, his head down intent on his carving, giving Rachel her privacy.

"They took me to church," she protested.

"We're not be talking bout the same thing, Rachel." This time he looked at her capturing her eyes. "Some people substitute a good life and attending church for a genuine relationship with God."

His words approached the subject that had plagued Rachel the past months and her heart raced, yet her eyes glowed with defiance, "What more could He possibly want from us than that?"

"Oh He'll be a wanting good works and supporting His church, but that's afterwards."

"After what?" She demanded, her shoulders tense, her back

against the window.

"After He has you." Roger's quiet pronouncement exploded in the room, ripping open Rachel's defenses.

"And what does that mean?"

"A personal relationship with you."

Suddenly Rachel knew that the time had come to settle the doubts and agonies that had plagued her, taking her joy in Sweetwater's metamorphosis and tainting her love for Andrew. Intuitively she knew that all she need do was ask how. Yet still she resisted, reluctant to abase herself, unwilling to suffer the humiliation.

"Well everything's gone, but He still hasn't reached me." She observed calmly while inside her heart pumped wildly.

"Could it be that He's there but you aren't responding?"

Rachel's face flushed as Roger's words touched a truth lurking in her own soul, clamoring for release.

"Perhaps I'll respond when He finds a better way to show me He cares," Rachel snapped, denying the pulling in her soul.

"Oh, me poor, sweet Lassie. He could show ye no better way than by sending His own Son." Roger moaned, his large eyes sad, "Ye've got a river of bitterness and fear running through ye, Rachel. Ye're blaming God and afraid to love, what a tragedy. It'll be'a destroying your life and Drew's too, if ye don't confront it and come to the sweet Savior where there's healing. Ye'll never be able to give yourself to Drew or receive his love until ye face yeself."

A loud banging on the front door interrupted before Rachel could answer and she peered out the window, thankful for the interruption. She could see nothing so she excused herself and crossed the study into the new dining room. The insistent pounding began again and she heard a masculine voice call out, "Miss Gregory? Are you in there? I need to speak with you."

Rachel hurried to the door and opened it. Rachel's wide-eyed gaze encountered the kindly blue eyes of Sheriff Abram Holt and Walter Bank's beady gaze alight with some mysterious victory.

Rivulets of rainwater poured from their sagging broad brimmed hats and streamed down their backs leaving puddles of muddy water on the porch. Reluctantly, she opened the door wider in unspoken invitation but Sheriff Holt shook his head, "We won't come in, Miss Gregory. But I do have a few questions to ask you."

"Whatever about, Sheriff?" Rachel smiled up at him, ignoring Banks.

Holt reached into his pocket and pulled out an object concealed in the palm of his hand, "Miss Gregory, have you ever seen this?"

"What do you mean asking her that? I told you it was hers. I know it was I've seen her wear it too many times."

Rachel's face turned ashen as her mother's locket caught the gray afternoon light, she whispered. "It was my mother's. Why?"

"When was the last time you saw it?"

"I don't remember."

"Did you ever wear it?"

"I told you she wore it all the time. What are you trying to do, Sheriff? Whitewash this affair?" Banks growled.

Sheriff Holt's kind blue eyes turned to steel gray, "Banks this is my investigation and I will handle it as I see fit and you'll keep your mouth shut. Excuse me, Miss Gregory. Did you ever wear your mother's locket?"

"Why, yes. I lost it several months ago."

"You lost it?"

"Yes."

"Now you're sure you lost it, not someone took it?"

"What do you mean asking her questions like that, Holt? Do you want to give her an alibi?" Banks shouted, impatience pushing him.

"Walter, I hate to have you sit on that flashy horse of yours in the pouring down rain among lightning bolts, but if you don't hush and let me ask the questions that's exactly what I'll do. I'm the sheriff here. You have no official business in this affair."

"I most certainly do. Didn't I find that locket?"

"Sheriff Holt, what is going on here? Mr. Banks is not welcome in my home. If you have any questions to ask me, then you'll have to come again without Walter Banks. Another time would be more convenient for the both of us," Rachel said, a forced smile frozen on her face, and stepped back into the house, slamming the door behind her. Through the heavy wood she heard the two argue, then Sheriff Holt turned pulling Banks by the arm and she saw them mount their horses and ride away.

Rachel stood in the darkened entrance hall, her back pressed against the large front door. Fear paralyzed her for a moment, then a shudder started deep within her rumbling up and shaking her until her teeth chattered. She held on to the door with one hand to keep from falling while stuffing the other, balled into a fist, into her mouth to stem the moans that formed in her throat. Her eyes took in the exquisite grand staircase, the eloquent crystal gasoliers that hung suspended from the tall ceiling, and, finally, confronted the massive mirror with golden gilded frame shipped all the way from Paris. And in it she saw the contorted face of a woman who has faced the end of all her dreams.

***

Several hundred miles to the southeast of Sweetwater in Charleston, South Carolina another battle raged, one that would ultimately determine the course of the South and the nation.

The Democratic convention of April 1860, was underway and the fight to choose what voice would lead the people through the treacherous waters surrounding the slavery issue.

Charleston, the center of the hot bed of secessionist proved a poor choice for the convention and any hope of prevailing reason. Loudest and most eloquent of the fiery voices were the radicals such as the silver tongued orator, William Yancey. On the fifth day of the convention in an impassioned address he insisted the platform include a slave code for the federal protection of slavery in the territories.

The convention dominated by a Northern majority preferred the Douglas solution of self-government of the territories. When they refused Yancey's demands, he and his Alabama delegation bolted the convention, taking delegates from Mississippi, Texas, Florida and the majority from several other Southern states.

Three days before the convention Georgia and Arkansas met with five other Gulf States and agreed to walk out if Stephen Douglas were nominated. The Douglas nomination failed to materialize during the ten day battle in Charleston, for he was unable to garner the two thirds vote necessary to nominate him. Neither the voice of reason nor the persuasion of moderates like Andrew Meredith prevailed. At the end of ten days the convention adjourned without a nominee. Instead it ended with a schism so deep that it destroyed the only party with a nationwide constituency and with the destruction went all hope for the union.

———————————

Andrew Meredith arrived at Balmara from Charleston late in the evening, wet and discouraged. They had scheduled a second convention for June in Baltimore, but he recognized the futility of it. The radicals had their say, their determination to split the Union had prevailed. Six weeks would not change their minds; rather it would only give them more time to inflame the people with their impassioned rhetoric.

He shivered through his water logged clothing. A torrential downpour had greeted him as he stepped from the steamer on to the familiar Savannah dock. He could have spent the night in town, but a strange urgency had pressed him on to the plantation, now he stood puddling water in his entrance hall and longing for a bath and a dry change of clothes.

The house was dark; the servants were in bed since they hadn't expected him until morning. He shrugged. Maybe he'd have to forgo the hot bath he muttered to himself as he made his way to his study and the spiral stairs that led to his private quarters.

The candle on his desk still flickered, casting tall shadows on the wall. He fired the lamp beside the stairs and went to his desk to snuff the light when he spied a bright yellow envelop, unmistakably bearing a telegraph. Noting it was from Roger, he ripped it open. Fear and disappointment in national politics suddenly abandoned his thoughts as the terse message reached his heart, threatening his world.

<hr/>

Andrew Meredith drove his mount merciless through the wet bog. He knew the risk he took, one false step and his horse could fall, breaking a leg and he would be abandoned, lost somewhere in this moonless night. The darkness was like a suffocating blanket, he had already lost his way several times. His face bled from the scratches torn by errant tree branches flying back to hit him in the face, yet he pressed on, giving neither his horse nor himself any quarter.

This was his greatest challenge. Rachel waited at Sweetwater in danger of being arrested at any moment. Up to this point Sheriff Holt had been kind and considerate, searching every lead in order to corroborate Rachel's story. But all he encountered was an impenetrable wall of silence.

Circumstantial evidence was hard against her. Pritchett's body showed a powerful blow to the back of the head which ruled out self-defense and the fact he held Rachel's locket and a strand of her hair in his hand proved that she was present during the crime. Then there was the question of why she didn't report it if he had attacked her as she claimed. Her story of a slave rescuing her sounded thin given the punishment they risked even touching a white man. But how could she have buried him? Sheriff Holt delayed charging her on those grounds.

Rachel claimed the slaves that assisted her ran away and Banks searched for them. Banks claimed the slaves' bodies were found in the river washed ashore some ten miles downriver and the members of the patrol backed up his story. It was Rachel's word against theirs.

Andrew grimaced in the darkness, if only Rachel had confided in him, by not telling him the truth she had inadvertently assisted Walter Banks and Banks had done his job well. Spurred on by hatred of Andrew and lust for Rachel and all that was hers, he fixed evidence to point to her guilt and then spread unsavory rumors around the community, accusing Rachel of having a romantic assignment with the overseer and in a jealous rage killing him. He said she was perfectly capable of digging in the soft area devoid of the usual thick red clay, besides according to him, it was a shallow grave. Now Banks had aroused the community with his allegations and many pressed the sheriff to charge Rachel soon and threatened to go over the good man's head if he didn't.

The slaves refused to talk even to Andrew. He knew they feared for their lives. Banks had put the fear of retribution in the hearts of his people and somehow had managed to intimidate even the Sweetwater slaves until they were mute when Andrew or the Sheriff approached them.

He understood slave patrols. If a slave was captured and hung accidentally for a crime they hadn't committed, then who objected? Besides if there were objections, they were scant comfort for the one dangling by his neck, his life snuffed out by mistake. Walter Banks controlled the area patrols and so ruled the fears and minds of all the surrounding slaves. .

Andrew growled and lashed his mount, frustrated and angry at his inability to persuade anyone to come forward in Rachel's defense. When he questioned them, fear rolled their big ebony eyes and they denied seeing anything on that fateful summer day. Even Roger failed to allay their fears enough for them to come forward.

Now Andrew Meredith rode pell mell through the wet blackness in search of a community that was more myth than truth, its very existence threatened by exposure. If he found it, he would bodily drag the illusive Samuel back with him and squeeze the truth out of him. But if he didn't find it? He shuddered. Not even Andrew Meredith with all the wealth and contacts at his disposal could save Rachel from her certain fate.

Suddenly the ground beneath him turned downward and his horse stumbled, then righted itself and bolted straight down a steep embankment, beneath low hanging tree branches and a jumble of briars. Andrew fought to control the horse but something had spooked him and now the best he could do was to stay in the saddle. They ran like the wind, by this time he lost all sense of direction and the last hope of finding the village he wasn't sure existed. The horse thundered up a steep ridge and beneath the low branches of a large tree knocking Andrew from the saddle. As he flew through the air, pain gripped his heart with the realization that he had lost Rachel's cause before he hit the ground and a blanket of darkness wiped away all sorrow

---

Rachel sat white-knuckled, grasping the smooth mahogany chair arms in the front parlor, starring at the wall. Although she looked like a work of art carved in Carrara, cold and beyond feeling, a riot of emotions buffeted her heart.

Andrew had been gone four long days and tomorrow, unless he came with new evidence, Sheriff Holt would come to arrest her.

She knew when he left that his journey was more than likely a hope in futility, but she couldn't help the kernel of hope that had sprouted in her heart. Andrew had always been able to bring order out of chaos for her. Maybe he'd be able to pull off another miracle.

Unconsciously she sighed as reality settled in. Even if he did find Samuel and bring him back, saving her from jail, what then? Would Andrew still want her? She thought not. The angry lights in his eyes had frightened her the night he arrived. She thought she saw disgust in them and she withdrew from him emotionally moving beyond his reach. That had angered him even more, but it was her only line of defense and she took it.

Ever since that afternoon in the snow when Andrew had declared his love for her, she had battled her heart. After that brief vulnerable moment when she had confessed her love for him, she had rejected surrendering to the sweet agony that wanted to possess her. With stern resolve she had kept a tight rein on her emotions, choosing to concentrate on the advantage they made as a pair, focusing on the obstacles they could overcome and the challenges they could conquer if they worked together as a team. Thoughts of the miracles they could work at Sweetwater finally diverted her attention from the questions tearing her heart for which she had no answers.

She had seen the hurt and question in Andrew's eyes before he had left for Savannah, yet she remained emotionally paralyzed by some mysterious fear. When he returned to this disaster, she sensed even more misgivings in him and now she wondered if he partly believed the lies Banks was spreading.

She had to admit, it would be good enough for her. And her mind took her back to the morning they had breakfast together in the Fletcher House, a lifetime ago. He had pressed her to tell him the whole truth and she hadn't. How could he marry someone who had betrayed his trust? Rachel shivered in the gray twilight as her heart whispered what her mind had refused to consider, would even Sweetwater and all its glory be worth anything if she lost Andrew? And then she knew the secret that had immobilized her soul. She refused to surrender her heart to him without reserve because she was afraid she would lose him, like she had her mother and father, maybe even Randall. That fear had layered her heart, protecting her vulnerability and erecting a wall between her and the man she loved.

⊱──────────────⊰

Dawn cracked the eastern sky with fingers of pink and gold, caressing the sky and making a path for the sun's arrival. A light morning mist rose up from the earth, draping the lower part of the house. Roger O'Callahan impatiently paced the long porch that graced the front of the house. Every once in awhile he'd pause to look expectantly down the road, worry etched in the lines of his face. When he saw only the empty road, ignoring the dawn, he began his pacing again.

He'd slept little if at all the night before as he had tossed and turned thinking about Andrew. Trying to decide what was keeping him and not enjoying the dark implications that kept coming to mind.

Finally when he could take the bed and inactivity no longer he came here to pace. Usually his favorite place to meditate and read his Bible, today he found little comfort in either. He would be the last one to deny that his own faith was in the midst of a fiery trial. Every since he had challenged Rachel in her faith, his own had been tested.

He knew it was wrong to worry, his head fully accepted that truth, but his heart seemed reluctant to go along. Andrew Meredith was the son he never had and he loved him with all his heart. Today was the fourth day since he had gone off into no telling what kind of danger chasing a glimmer of hope. He'd flatly refused to take Roger with him, stating that his chances of being accepted were better if he were alone and commanding the preacher to see after Rachel. Reluctantly he had agreed and now he labored under the impatience only a man of action can know.

A mysterious hand scribbled note printed in a child's scrawl bearing simply one word, "Samuel" with an arrow and a crude map had lured Andrew. They both knew that it could very well be a trap, but Andrew insisted Rachel had no other hope. So he went, and Roger stayed. Now Roger paced, trying to make plans. In a few hours Sheriff Holt would be here to arrest Rachel. She seemed resolved to the inevitable, almost too calm. He'd feel better if she'd show some emotion, at least worry about Andrew. But she sat, stone like and cold in the same chair day after day. When he'd said her soul had a burr, he never realized it was one of such magnitude. He'd touched the edges of it the day her world caved-in, maybe if they'd had a little more time, but no, she'd been unmistakably resistant—.

Understanding battered his consciousness and he paused his pacing, "You're right, Lord. Sometimes resistance is worn down by adversity. Thank you for reminding me you're in control. But Lord, if it please you, do you have to take Andrew in the process? I love that boy and would be mighty lonely without him. Seems I really need him. But then, Lord, I yield to your judgment. I would be pleased if you'd be a showing me what I'm supposed to be doing. Do I need to form a search and rescue party?"

The heavens remained silent and only the sweet song of a mocking bird trilled across the fields but O'Callahan experienced peace where there had been only turmoil. He walked into the big house and toward the new kitchen, a spring in his step, a light in his eyes and his stomach rumbling for food. For the first time in three days he was hungry.

The blind fold chaffed Andrew's face and eyes but not nearly as bad as the snail's pace tested his patience. Physically weak and not in control of the situation, he felt threatened. Riding beside a towering black stranger, he made his way blindly through the briars and thickets toward Rachel, if she was still there. How long ago had he left Sweetwater in search of an elusive hope, a village only whispered about, suggested in a scribbled note and a crude map with an arrow pointing south?

He had seized the chance because he had run out of hope at Sweetwater and now he could remember very little about his wild ride into the darkness, only awaking later to black faces and wide eyes surrounding him, somewhere in a primitive village lost in the forest with only a small dim campfire for illumination.

The memory of that encounter was still etched in his mind. Startled, he had tried to sit up, when pain racked his head and ran down his body exiting out his very fingertips and toes, forcing him to fall back against the damp earth. He had placed a hand to his head, and felt a large lump swathed in a poultice, that smelled of turpentine and mint. Now the lump had diminished but a remnant of the pain remained, making him even more irritable.

An aging black woman, wide as she was tall, her head wrapped in a colorful turban had commanded, "White man, you be still. We thought you would be leaving this life." Then she cackled, "That's all we knowed, the Good Laud, it's all in His timing."

"Where am I?" Meredith asked through dry, cracking lips, his tongue thick.

"That's not for you to know, white man. We want to know what you're doing here. No white man comes this far in the forest less he's in deep trouble. Usually he don' live long enough to git out. We'll just have to see 'bout yu." She said, appointed spokesperson for the curious eyes that watched.

"I'm, I'm looking for Samuel," Andrew dragged out before his throat closed.

"Give him some of that tea and then try a drink of water," the old woman commanded.

Andrew drank, and then grimaced as the bitter dregs lodged against his tongue. Too weak to spit them out they lingered in his mouth. Soon they dissolved in trickling bitter streams. Surprised, Andrew felt his throat relax, ready to receive the water the young child held to his lips in a gourd dipper.

The water was sweet, cool spring water and he drank deeply. In the distance he could hear the tinkling of a cowbell and voices whispering to the night, but it was the musty odor of swamp and peat that assaulted his nostrils telling him he had reached his destination.

"O.K. white man, what do you want with this here Samuel and who is Rachel?" The spokesperson demanded.

"How did you know about Rachel?"

The old woman pressed three fingers commandingly against his lips, "Hush, we do the asking. This is our territory, you is an uninvited guest."

"Rachel Gregory is my fiancée. She is under suspicion for murder, a murder she did not commit. Samuel can clear her," Andrew explained, his voice miraculously stronger.

"Tell me about this here Rachel. What kind of woman be she?"

"What has that got to do with anything?" Andrew demanded, irritation constricting his throat again.

"I told you to hush, white man. You answer our question, if'n you want our help."

"You're going to help me?" Andrew asked, hope dawning for the first time.

"Never said we would, we just fer sho won't if'n you don't co operate,"

Knowing he'd lost, he told them about Rachel and as he talked the old woman got closer and closer to him, finally staring straight down into his eyes. Even in the darkness it would have been hard to miss the love that glowed in his eyes as he talked of the woman he was about to lose without their help.

When the old woman was satisfied he had told her all about the green-eyed beauty she stood up and merely commented, "Now you go to sleep."

Andrew clutched her ragged skirt, "Don't you understand, I've got to have your help. How long have I been here? It may already be too late."

"You go to sleep. Council will have to meet. No white man has ever been here and lived to go back."

"You've killed everyone who has come in here?" Andrew asked, disbelief widening his eyes.

The old woman shrugged, then grinned showing a mouthful of broken teeth, "We don't have to. The forest is our friend and takes care of unwanted guests, if'n the boggy peat don' git em, de cliff usually do. Lucky you landed whur you did, or we'd be funeralizing you, 'stead of listening to yo story 'bout dis here woman of yor'n."

Andrew shuddered and started to object, but suddenly he felt very sleepy and realized the last cool drink of water had been drugged. He slept deeply and dreamed of Rachel.

It was mid morning before the sun made its presence known in the dense forest. Virgin timber towered skyward, providing a thick canopy of protection. Andrew awoke and watched the activity through partly closed eyes, reluctant to let them know he had awakened.

Meredith felt as if he had been transported to Africa with a native village of thatched roofs and rudely constructed huts of sticks surrounding him. One hut, set apart from the others, appeared larger and better constructed with a chimney and a long front porch where the old woman from the night before sat in a crude rocking chair, smoking a corn cob pipe. She watched Andrew intently and when he moved his head, called out to him across the courtyard, "White man, you feel better this morning?"

He raised a finger in response, afraid to lift his head after last night's experience. She hoisted her broad frame out of the short chair and waddled toward him. When she reached him, she lifted the aromatic poultice binding his head and murmured under her breath.

"What did you say?" Andrew asked.

"Said you might live."

"You mean if you don't kill me?"

"If'n we'd wanted you dead, we'd left you where you lay on the edge of that cliff where your horse broke its neck."

"Oh," Andrew moaned, physical pain shot through him at the loss of his horse, "How will I ever get back in time without a horse?"

"Never you mind, we have our own ways of getting you back, if'n we decides to take you."

"What have you decided?"

"Council decided it's up to Samuel. His wife, dat sweet chile he brung here, is dead so's he won't be risking her if'n he goes back wid you."

Meredith's heart sank, "Dead?"

"Last week. She done died trying to birth a little one. Samuel lost both of 'em. Dat's whur he be now, off to mourn his loss."

"You mean he's not even here?" Andrew's voice rose as he jerked upright, unleashing a fresh onslaught of pain inside his head, then fell back on the soft pallet of leaves and branches.

"No, but I sent him word."

"Will he come?" Andrew asked, placing his hand over his throbbing eyes

"If I sent for him, he'll come," the old hag declared.

"But will he be willing to help me? Rachel?" Andrew turned his head toward the old woman his eyes capturing hers, pleading. "He has nothing to lose if he goes with me since his wife is dead. I will assure him of safe passage back."

"Some thangs are beyond yore assurance, Mr. Important White Man. If'n he goes back and gets caught, he puts our whole village in danger. But council decided, we're willing if'n he is."

Instinctively Andrew knew the council's decision was always synonymous with what the old woman decreed. The fact that she dictated the life and decisions of this renegade settlement was evident in her confidence as her distinctive housing reflected her standing and authority. Puzzled, he asked, "Why did you take that risk?"

"Cause we'd like to see Walter Banks get what's coming to him and because—Rachel's my girl! I be Agatha."

Andrew raised up on his elbow, ignoring the pain that coursed through his head, "You're Agatha? How, why, here?"

"Walter Banks. That's all you need to know, white man. What's yore name anyhows? I need to be knowing it if'n youse marry my sweet Rachel. And if'n you ain't good to her, I'm coming fer you and that won't be pleasant."

Andrew laughed, "Come home to her, Agatha. She longs to see you."

Agatha shrugged, "No, I wouldn't want my baby to see old Agatha like this."

"She wouldn't care how you look. She just needs you."

"No, she gonna have you to take kere of her, these people," she waved her hand toward the huts and the people quietly working beside them, "theys need me bad so I caint ever go home. Lak lil chil'ren, they be. Don' even tells her you seen me, cuz den she be pushin' you to finds me. I 'member her determination and you jest might giv in."

Andrew smiled, "Determination? That's an understatement."

Agatha chuckled, but a sadness touched her eyes, "Guess she ain't changed a bit. How I wud luv to see my little gal, but dis is de better way. I'm needed here, besides I ain't lost none of my pride, let her remember de other Agatha, tall and handsome. Memories are easier that way"

"What happened, Agatha?" Andrew countered, knowing it was

not Agatha's pride but her sense of responsibility that kept her here in the deep forest.

"Banks done ruint me, made me ugly with his cruelty cause I wuddn't gonna let him take my baby's furniture."

"So that's where the missing furniture is!"

"Da't's right. He done stole everything he could, saying it wuz his'n. I knew better. I's standing in the shadows and watched him cheat Mr. Gregory time after time, but wudden no use to say nothin', the mister done throwed away his life without considerin' my baby and whut she'd need when she come home from that fancy school. Then he sent her off'n to Europe and I thought I'd die if I couldn' see her, so I thought least I cud pertect her belongings. I blocked the door with my body. I knew when she cum home she'd want her bed. He kicked me out'n the way and then kicked me until they's give me up fer dead. I run away and here I is. Nearly kilt me, it did."

"Don't you worry, Agatha. I'll get everything that was hers back, I promise."

The old hag gave him a broken tooth cackle, "I believes you wud. Well here's Samuel."

Samuel had agreed to come, but only if Andrew was blindfolded so he wouldn't know the way back. Now they rode through the forest making their way back to Sweetwater, one mounted on a mule, the other blindfolded on a donkey his long legs barely missing the ground.

—the waters were made sweet— Exodus 15:25 _{KJV}

THIRTY

It was early afternoon and Rachel sat exactly where Andrew had left her four days ago. Now she watched through the window, her face a mask, as Sheriff Holt dismounted and walked toward the door. Only her white knuckles clutching the smooth ribboned mahogany arms of the chair gave evidence that she felt anything. Resignation dulled her eyes and, fleetingly, she wondered where the sheriff would find a suitable place to incarcerate a woman.

Roger met Holt on the porch steps, sympathy flaring in the evangelist's large, expressive eyes as he extended his hand. Creases of fatigue lined the sheriff's face with the strain of the last few days evident in the droop of his shoulders. "This is one of the hardest things I've ever had to do," he admitted to Roger.

"I'll be a knowing that, my man. But 'tis a real mistake you're a making. Our Rachel is as innocent as a babe in the cradle."

"Not quite, Roger. Even if she didn't do it, she knew about it and didn't report it. But the courts will have to decide her guilt or innocence. I have the evidence that demands I act. It tears my heart out. I've known her since she was a wee girl and knew her parents well. Tragic circumstances all around. I was hoping Meredith would turn up something, but I guess not. Have you heard from him?"

"Not a word, Sheriff. And I fear for him."

"Where was he going?"

"Ye've heard of the rumors concerning a renegade village deep in the forest near the treacherous bogs?"

"Hasn't everyone? Just a superstition—,"

"Drew went to find it, by now he'll be a knowing if it be truth or myth, that is if he's still alive."

"What a crazy thing to do. I thought he was investigating around here."

"When every avenue here proved a dead-end, he did the desperate thing to save our lassie and now I'm a worried about him, I am."

"And well you might be. Andrew Meredith has rubbed some feathers the wrong way around here, and if someone catches him off alone they might do him harm, thinking someone else could bear the blame."

"Do ye be a thinkin' the same as me, now do ye?" Roger asked, his brogue growing heavier by the moment.

"Now, Roger, I'm not naming any names, just saying Meredith needs to watch his step." Holt warned.

"That's my point, man. Would ye be interested in gettin' together a few men to search if'n he doesn't arrive soon?"

Sheriff Holt removed his hat and scratched his head, "Could be you might have a point there."

"And would ya be a doin' it a fore ye arrest our Rachel?"

Sheriff Holt smiled, relieved, "Seems this might be more pressing business. There are unsavory elements in the area with no reluctance to do violence. I do have my suspicion, but so far they've been too slick for me to apprehend. It might be just the chance to turn my hunch into hard evidence."

"Now you be thinking on the right track. You need to do all you can to rid our community of the threat."

"I guess Miz Rachel won't be a running off anywheres now will she?" Holt drawled, glad to delay his wearisome task, hoping to find some way of escape for the young woman he fondly remembered as a beautiful little girl.

A broad smile beamed from Roger's face, his generous mouth seemed to spread from ear to ear, "I'll give you my word on it."

"As a preacher?"

"As a man and a preacher."

The sheriff reached for Roger's hand, grasping his big paw, "A deal,—"

A young black boy ran through the front yard moaning loudly and calling for Roger, "Marse Roger, Marse Roger. Comma quick."

Roger whirled toward the demanding voice, "What's wrong, Jula? What's all the commotion about?"

"Them's bad men done come. I know'd dey wud, I know'd dey wud " He wailed, rolling his eyes wildly.

"Get hold of yourself and tell me what's happened," Roger demanded, grasping the boy by both shoulders.

"Dem bad men dey got Mr. Andrew and Samuel, deys got Mr. Andrew and Samuel, Deys got Mr. Andrew and Samuel," He moaned in sing song fashion.

Roger gave him a gentle shake, "Tell me, Jula, where they are, and what they plan to do to them."

"Way over t yonder by the hanging tree. Turrible, turrible. Deys got ropes and hanging fever. Deys whooping 'em, turrible, turrible."

"Can you show us, Jula?"

Jula's eyes widened, "Don' wanna go. Jula hide in the bushes so's dey don't hang Jula. Dey mought hangs Jula if he show'd ya, jes like dey wud if'n he told about Miz Rachel didn kilt yellow haired devil. "

Roger grabbed the dark, frail youngster, despite his protests, and hoisted him into the saddle of his horse tied to the hitching post then climbed in behind him, just as the sheriff leaped into his own saddle.

Jula's shouts stirred life in Rachel and propelled her toward the door in time to hear his message to Roger. Jula's words rang through her mind "They's got Mr. Andrew —and hanging ropes."

She rushed down the steps calling after them, demanding to go, but her requests vanished in a cloud of dust as the two horses thundered out of the yard leaving her behind.

Rachel's knees gave way and she sank to the ground, her whole body trembling. A pitiful moan ripped from her like a wounded animal as she buried her head in her lap, her voluminous—skirt forming a welcome tent of suffocating darkness around her head. So great was her sense of loss, that even light and air proved an intrusion.

In her agony, never once did she remember that Jula's very testimony had vindicated her, only the horror of life without Andrew penetrated her consciousness, forcing her to face the truth in her own heart as pain sliced it opened and spilled out its secrets. In blinding clarity she realized how much she loved him. He meant more to her than her dreams, more than her ambitions, more than her pride, more than Sweetwater, even more than life itself. But she'd failed to tell him and now perhaps death awaited him and he would never know.

Tears of repentance coursed down her cheeks as she faced the woman she was. Suddenly she saw the false gods she had created of her dreams and ambitions barricading her from Andrew's love and God's acceptance.

They toppled as she accepted and acknowledged she alone was responsible for the tragedy of this moment. When the remorse became unbearable, she confronted the blame she had placed at a loving God's door and cried out for mercy and forgiveness as her bitterness washed away in a sea of tears. When her well ran dry, she wracked with arid sobs.

Finally, she expended all her energy and Rachel was emptied of Rachel. Then through her misery, a gentle peace, like a light refreshing rain on a parched earth, invaded her heart. When it washed away the last remnants of the debris that had chained her, her tears renewed. But this time they healed, because the cleansing was complete.

With swollen eyes Rachel raised her head to face the light. Time had passed, yet she had no idea how long she had spent collapsed in the dirt. Although her journey to self-discovery had seemed like an eternity, in reality it took no more than a few minutes. Standing up, she brushed the dirt off her dress and Jula's words filtered into her remembrance. She whirled and stumbled up the porch steps, hindered by the wide hoops and crinolines beneath her dress.

Rushing through the front door, she finally picked up her skirt and ran down the hall and up the stairs, shouting as she went for someone to saddle Sundance. When she reached her room, she stepped out of her hoop and underskirts. As she grabbed her hat and dashed headlong back outside, her heart beat in rhythm to the prayer in her soul.

It was the 'hanging tree', she remembered and it was to the 'hanging tree' she rushed, fearing she would be too late, but needing to find Andrew, dead or alive, with every fiber of her being. If by some chance Roger had reached him in time, she could tell him of her love and if not, then—. She refused to consider his lifeless body. The tragedy of his energy and vitality expended at the end of a rope seemed impossible. Whatever happened, she determined to go to him. Her prayer that someway, somehow Andrew would know of her love, and in knowing, forgive her.

As she flew through the underbrush, she took every shortcut she remembered from her childhood. Since the 'hanging tree' was a place of intimidation and superstition for the slaves, it had proved the only place she could slip away from Agatha without discovery. Now she ran not away but toward her destiny, praying for a miracle.

The clearing was just ahead beyond the next rise in the crude, rarely used trail. Her short cut approached the tree from behind, opposite in direction from the main trail that Roger had taken, but she gave little heed to her route or what she might be riding into, because she heard the deep gravelly tones of Sheriff Holt ahead. She could scarcely make out what he said nor did she care, realization she had reached her goal propelled her on.

Rachel nudged Sundance in the ribs and she bolted into the edge of the clearing just as two hands grabbed the reins of her horse and two more jerked her to the ground.

"Now, sheriff, this kind of evens things up a bit, don't it?" an unfamiliar voice drawled as Rachel looked up wide-eyed into the barrel of a revolver pointed between her eyes.

"Let her go, you've got me." A familiar voice spoke from somewhere above her and joy flooded her being. Nothing mattered, not the gun pointed at her, not the prospects of jail, nothing but that voice. An angel choir would have paled in comparison. Andrew was Alive—Alive!

She cautiously peered around the pistol obstructing her view and her heart sank. Andrew Meredith sat on a fidgeting mule, a noose draped loosely over his neck, his hands tied behind his back. She shuddered realizing her unheralded arrival could have spooked the animal with disastrous results. Then she pushed the thought from her mind as her hungry eyes took in Andrew. He'd been hurt. His right eye was bruised and swollen, his cheek gashed open and bleeding while beneath his ripped shirt she could see stripes of purple whelps. She cringed, feeling his pain, then rejoiced realizing if they hadn't beat him, he'd already be dead.

Rachel's eyes found Samuel. He, too, had been beaten and waited his turn at the hangman's noose. He stood, his hands tied behind his back, while a tall, scrawny man held a gun to his head. Rachel straightened to get a better look and fearlessly pushed the pistol in her face aside. The rotund man objected and spat a dark stream of tobacco at her feet, "Now, pretty lady, you don't want to spook that mule, do you? You better behave." He crooned, leering at her.

"I do not want that gun in my face. I hardly think I'm a threat to you, unless you can't shoot straight," Rachel snapped and Andrew had to hide a smile.

"Leave her be, Dan." Walter Banks commanded as he crossed the open circle toward her.

Questions rioted Rachel's mind as she looked toward Banks and tried to get her bearings. Where was Roger? And Jula? Had they killed them? Only Sheriff Holt stood on the ground, disarmed, with angry sparks firing his usual placid blue eyes.

"What we gonna do with these new ones? You wan I jest shoot em?" Drawled the short man guarding Rachel.

"Shut up, I'm thinking. Sheriff, you kinda messed up my party. I was wondering what I was gonna do, but Miz Rachel's arrival has kinda put a new light on things. Don't think I'll hang Meredith after all. Take the noose off Meredith and put it on that darkie."

"You'd better let us go, Banks. Your future's not worth two cents now." Sheriff Holt exclaimed.

"It's worth less than that with Andrew Meredith alive. With him gone, I can recoup what I lost. I've been waitin' to get him out of my life. Course you're a different matter, Sheriff. Didn't have anything against you except you're too soft for my liking, course it wouldn't be anything I'd kill you for but now you're a witness. I can't let you escape, you know too much. So what am I to do with you?"

"If you know what's good for you you'll surrender."

"To what?" He asked, "Sorry, I've waited long and patiently to give these two their come-uppance. You were mighty thoughtful to come alone. What made you do a foolish thing like that?"

"Didn't expect any trouble," Holt explained, his eyes on Rachel. "Miss Rachel was worried because Meredith hadn't returned. I needed to arrest her and had promised him I'd wait until he came back so I went to find him. Guess I found him all right."

Some of the ragtag crew, lounging on the ground, grinned at his words while others, mounted and alert, looked worried. Banks walked across the clearing and kicked at the leg of one leaned back against a tree trunk with arms crossed behind his head and chewing on a twig. "Jack, I told you to put the noose on that boy . We came to see a hanging and we're goin' to have one. It'll put healthy fear in the heart of all the slaves here abouts. It's been too long since one of them got hung."

"What you gonna do 'bout them two?" The man asked as he got reluctantly to his feet and stretched insolently.

Walter Banks laughed, "That's easy. Take Meredith over there by her. Ya'll like to see the results of a lover's quarrel turned violent? That's what's gonna happen. Won't be hard to believe in town after the rumors I spread 'bout her and Pritchett." Banks leaned back against the tree pausing to enjoy his moment of triumph. "People like to believe the worst about people. And Miss High and Mighty shore helped them to do that."

Jack seemed pleased with Banks' explanation and motioned for Meredith to move toward Rachel, his hands tied behind him, then the tall, scrawny man spat on the ground, leaving a trail of tobacco juice trickling down his unshaven chin, "That's close enough for now. We'll put you together after you can't cause any more trouble."

Banks laughed at the man's joke, unaware of the unseen figure who waited patiently behind the tree he reclined on. Banks straightened up and stepped back beside the tree, propping his hand on the rough bark. Roger's powerful arm, swift as a lightning bolt, grabbed him from behind, pinning him beneath his chin with the tip of a large knife touching the skin covering his jugular vein. "Turn Samuel loose," Roger quietly commanded. "Andrew, you and Rachel come stand beside the sheriff. All you men throw your guns on the ground."

Stunned the men refused to move. Roger shouted, "Tell them to move or you'll not see the next tomorrow." One small drop of blood trickled down Banks neck where the sharp knife left a scratch.

"Do what he says. Turn him loose." Walter commanded.

"Why, boss, that preacher can't do nothing with a crowd this big, if'n we keep our guns." The tall scrawny guy argued, his cheek bulging from a new wad of tobacco as he cocked his pistol and put it to Andrew's head.

Roger jerked Banks, tightening his hold on him, the preacher's muscular forearm cutting off his windpipe, "Maybe I can't fight you all, but I can take your boss with me."

Banks gasped "Do as he says. Drop your guns."

"Naw, we don' wanna do that," the man called Jack complained. "What's gonna happen to us? We won't be able to get away."

Banks eyes bulged, his breath coming in gasps."Let 'em go."

Roger eyed Jack, recognizing resistance in him, warned, "My man has a large group of armed men on their way to this place. I am not acting alone."

"You're just bluffing."

Roger's green eyes burned, impaling the tall man's gaze, "I don't bluff," In the distance a rumble announced the approach of many horses. Jula had rallied re-enforcement.

Jack and the men on the ground scurried for their horses, the men mounted were already in flight. Andrew dived for the reins of the mule steadying him as Sheriff Holt lifted the noose from Samuel's neck.

Only the sound of the distant hoof beats broke the silence of the moment then one triumphant shout echoed through the forest as Rachel hurled herself into Andrew Meredith's arms, crying, "Drew, Drew, Drew! I thought I'd lost you."

THIRTY-ONE

The harpsichord mingled its sweet tones with the hum of conversation down below. Rachel waited in her room with Bertha Emory by her side. The older woman, her cornflower eyes bright with unshed tears, handed her a wreath of white rose buds and Rachel bowed her head, breathing in the sweet aroma

Today was her wedding day and Drew waited in the double parlor below along with Roger who would administer their vows. An indescribable joy bubbled within her and had since that day deep in the forest under the large oak hanging tree when, without reserve, she had surrendered her heart to Andrew Meredith. Today she would pledge her life to him.

Rachel attached an ivory lace veil to the wreath, and then paused to caress the rich fabric of the garment, tracing each intricate design with her index finger. A faraway look drifted into eyes as she thought of her mother, wishing she were here and wondering how she had felt when she wore this veil so many years before. Did she have the same breathless anticipation or was there a touch of anxiety marring her special day?

Rachel shivered. In her wildest dreams, she'd never imagined that she could experience such happiness, never knew she could love with such abandon. Now she could face the future without a trace of fear.

Lifting the delicate garment in her hands, she turned toward the large mirror that graced an ornate armoire, hand carved and especially built for her. It was her most recent gift from Drew. The person who smiled back at her seemed younger, with a new gentle vulnerability about her.

The bitterness that bound her had been released two weeks before when she collapsed in the dirt beneath a hot summer sun and faced what she'd become. With one touch of the Master's hand the bitter stream that had poisoned her soul had become sweet water, enabling her to give and receive love freely.

A tender smile lifted her full, pink lips and a radiance beamed from clear eyes that glowed as she nestled the wreath between the abundant loops of auburn locks. Her face flushed with youth and happiness above the tall lace collar of her mother's dress. The lace bodice hugged her feminine curves, accenting her tiny waist, before it fell in voluminous flounces over an underskirt of corded silk. Narrow silk sleeves overlaid with the same Maltese lace hugged her arms, ending in a point over her hand. On her left hand a large emerald surrounded in diamonds caught the candle light and glittered with their own fire and promise.

The veil in place, she turned from the mirror and toward the door. She made ready to leave her room and go on to her tomorrows where Andrew Meredith waited to share her life and love.

An uncustomary nervousness plagued Andrew as he greeted the hastily assembled guests. Surprised, he noted a broad community turnout. He realized that three quarters of them attended out of curiosity while the rest probably suspected they might need his business or maybe Bertha Emory had applied some pressure. But he didn't care what motivated their attendance, he was thankful Rachel would have guests at her wedding. The time had come to rebuild her relationship with her hometown community.

The whole affair occurred lightning fast. When she hurled herself into his arms, he knew he'd never let her go again. Discounting any obstacle, real or imagined, he insisted they wed immediately.

He wired Philip that he was extending his visit by two weeks and that he would be bringing his bride back to Savannah with him. Never mind that Aunt Tilde couldn't make the trip, that the house was not finished, or Laura was taking her final exams and couldn't attend. His patience had worn out somewhere between the noose around his neck and the sweet feel of Rachel in his arms sobbing out her love to him.

He'd learned one lesson in all that. Life was precarious at best so seize your opportunities while you can. Rachel surprised him by not offering one objection, only asked enough time to alter her mother's dress.

When Philip wired back that he insisted on being best man, Andrew was humbled at the man's generous spirit. He couldn't say that he wasn't alarmed when Philip arrived earlier in the week with Daphne by his side. He had explained she came to help Rachel with the festivities. Rather than resent it, Rachel appeared relieved. Now everything for the reception and ball was in order leaving Rachel free of any responsibility. He sighed.

Now where had that impulsive Philip disappeared to? He was the best man and Andrew had searched high and low for him without success. Glancing out the window one more time, Andrew spied him outside, standing beside Robert Goodman's carriage. Now what could he possibly be talking to Goodman about at a time like this? And Goodman was supposed to be upstairs, ready to give the bride away. The thought of the gruff Goodman doing the honors brought a brief chuckle to Andrew's tense face.

When Andrew elbowed through his guests and stepped outside ready to command his friends inside, his heart constricted. The two men bent over the opened door of the Goodman vehicle and lifted a frail, silver-haired man out, delicately placing him in a rolling chair that Daphne had waiting in the drive.

Could it possibly be? Randall? Here? Andrew rushed across the porch and down the steps, ignoring the curious guests who gathered around.

Randall's thin face, no longer so gaunt and with a flush of excitement coloring it, looked up into his and smiled, "I have to give the bride away, now, don't I?"

"How, when?" Andrew sputtered to Duval and Goodman's delight.

"I knew Randall was scheduled to go to Arizona. While you were gone, the doctor wired you that our friend needed the dry climate for the healing of his lungs. I'm afraid I opened your correspondence, fearing that something had happened to Randall. Having just learned of your plans, I immediately wired Boston, asking the doctor's permission to reroute him by here. He gave it and Goodman and his wife went to Savannah to meet him and escort him here," Philip explained.

Andrew grasped the older man's bony hand, "I couldn't be happier—."

Randall laughed, "That's evident, man and neither can I. This is what I have prayed for, to see my Rachel settled with a man who will love and care for her. Now I can die in peace. Course I'd rather live and have a passel of grandchildren running around my feet. But my future is in the Good Lord's hands."

"As all ours are." Andrew readily agreed. "Now get him in out of the sun. Does Rachel know? "

Philip explained, "I didn't let on for fear of disappointing her. Now we need to get inside, there's a wedding about to start and a bride waiting."

"Since I was supposed to give the bride away, I'll go upstairs and fetch her then bring her down to Randall." Goodman bossed, then added with a twinkle in his eye, " By the way Andrew didn't I tell you what you needed was a good north Georgia bride? Glad you followed my advice."

Rachel walked slowly down the delicately curved staircase clinging to Goodman's arm as Bertha followed; carrying her large bouquet of roses matching the rosebuds nestled in the bride's hair. Baby's breath and lilies of the valley rested on the broad silk streamers, cascading from the spray. Each step she took released a sweet, haunting fragrance that hung in the air, then enveloped Rachel.

Unexpected tears blinded her as she reached the bottom of the stairs and a longing for a member of her family with which to share this special moment of happiness overcame her. She tugged at Goodman's sleeve, wanting him to pause before they entered the parlor, not willing to face Andrew with tears in her eyes. Robert paused and looked at her, his eyes sympathetic beneath his craggy brows, "I think someone else wants to walk with you these last steps, my dear."

Startled, Rachel's mouth formed an "O" before he turned her away from the parlor and straight into the arms of Randall Wilkie who stood, gingerly supporting himself on a cane, "My dear, I had to come to give my girl away."

Tears of joy filled her eyes and cascaded down her cheeks, "Oh Uncle Randall, now my joy is complete."

The community buzzed for months about the beauty and radiance of the Sweetwater bride. Andrew and Philip stood side by side, two handsome giants, one dark and one golden. Both hearts beat wildly when she entered the room, one in ecstasy, the other in pain. One hid his emotion; the other could scarcely contain his. Andrew's journey had been long, his search diligent but his heart had finally found its treasure.

Another pair of eyes watched as the Irish evangelist pledged two lives into one and shed a tear of sorrow because this new beginning meant the end of old ways. But when Daphne saw the happiness in Andrew's eyes, she could hardly nurture the bitterness that threatened to taint her. She prayed that Rachel would prove worthy of him. By an act of her will she turned the caring of Andrew over to Rachel Gregory Meredith and stepped back into the shadows of the hall and of Andrew's life.

The house rang with music and laughter. The guests, who had come to stare, stayed and were charmed. Andrew hid his impatience well as he danced with every debutante and beauty, every wall flower and dowager. He knew the importance of winning Rachel's acceptance and his own, but he did his job too well. They all enjoyed themselves so much he feared they would stay the night and the party that had started when the sun was still high rambled on toward midnight. Couples relaxed and, enjoying themselves, requested tunes and dances, but he rarely got a dance with his bride. The same young blades who had whisked her away at the Dunbar ball claimed her; only tonight there was no Walter Banks to steal her away.

Banks languished in the Campbell County jail awaiting trial for kidnapping and attempted murder. Andrew also threatened to press charges for theft if he didn't return Rachel's furniture. Now it was safely back in her room along with the armoire he had ordered months before.

But from this night forward, it would no longer be her room, but reserved for a daughter of their own. This morning the servants moved Rachel's things to the new wing, where the grand master suite took up the entire location, providing solitude and privacy for the newlyweds. Tonight would be the first time anyone had occupied the rooms. Within the hallowed walls on this sacred night they would begin their life together. Already her shoes rested beside his, their garments mingled in the closet, and soon she would lay by his side in the oversized bed made especially for them. And then he would hold her in his arms and they would become one as God had intended.

The midnight hour approached and Andrew pushed his way through the crowded floor looking for his bride. He saw her across the room in Philip's arms and he paused, giving his friend a final moment with her.

Philip drank in Rachel's beauty. His eyes devoured her as if he wanted to catalogue each feature into his memory. He whirled her through the jib window and out into the cool night air and the beautiful waltz wafted through the light summer breeze following them. Rachel laughed, "Why Philip, I'm a married woman, people will gossip."

His mouth chuckled but his face didn't smile, "You never cared about that before."

"I'm going to try to change my habits so I won't be a liability to Drew." She answered without a smile.

Philip stopped dancing and captured both her hands between

his, "Rachel, you really love him?"

"More than I could ever tell you, Philip. Next to Andrew nothing else has meaning in my life,"

Philip's eyes brightened suspiciously, and then he expelled a long sigh.

"I've hurt you, Philip." She observed.

"The hurt would have been greater had you married me, loving him. Then we would have both been miserable. At least this way I can be comforted by knowing you're happy."

"I never knew I could experience such joy, Philip."

He gazed for a long moment into her eyes without speaking, battling his own emotions. He brought both of her hands to his lips and gently kissed them and replied, his voice husky, "Then your joy will be the source of my happiness. My love for you desires your happiness."

She leaned up on tiptoe and kissed his cheek, "Never has a woman been more blessed than me."

Philip mouth lifted in a half-smile, then resolution straightened his shoulders. With a hint of his former, jaunty confidence, he winked at her and offered his arm, "Mrs. Meredith, may I take you to your husband?"

Rachel's hands trembled as she fastened the last dome shaped pearl button. She had managed this ritual alone, refusing the help of a servant and not wanting even Bertha's intrusion into this private moment. Her friend had made the beautiful white nightgown of finest cotton that she wore. Rachel smiled as she fingered the lace that adorned it. Salvaged from her mother's gown, it comforted her, giving her a quiet confidence.

Outside the alcove door, she heard footsteps and knew that Andrew had returned from his own preparations and now waited for his bride. Her heart thumped wildly and she peered into the mirror for reassurance. The candlelight washed her in a soft radiance. Her eyes were large and luminous, the gown a perfect complement to her youth and beauty. Her hair pulled into a single loop formed a tiara around her head giving her a regal elegance. She sighed, satisfied that her husband would approve and moved toward the alcove door.

When she stepped into the room, Andrew caught his breath,

his eyes darkening with emotion as she walked toward him. Entranced with her loveliness and grace, he stood perfectly still, remembering a Savannah dock and the untamed beauty that had captured his heart. Without uttering a word, his gaze moved from her hair to the tips of her toes, admiring and claiming her for his own. Then he walked to meet her midway of the room, as the light of the candelabra spilled down on them. Touching her hair lightly, he pulled the pin that held it in place and her long tresses tumbled, wild and free, down her back and across her shoulders. His hand moved to cup her chin and, lifting it, he spoke, his voice husky, "I've been waiting all my life for you."

A radiant smile illumined her face as she stood on tiptoe and planted a whisper soft kiss on the lips of her husband. His arms enfolded her in a fierce embrace and suddenly Rachel Gregory Meredith knew she had come home at last.

EPILOGUE

The morning sun was high in the sky when Rachel stirred from her deep slumber. She smiled and snuggled into the soft white sheets, willing morning to go away, to leave her cocooned in this ethereal world of happiness. But the sounds of the day insisted so finally, she opened both eyes and stretched contentedly.

Andrew stepped inside the room enjoying the spectacle of his bride's awakening. The sweet languor of slumber still clung to her while her hair tumbled around her in profusion, framing her face. Her eyes like emeralds catching the morning light widened when she spied him staring at her. She patted the bed beside her and smiled. Walking over to her, he sat on the bed and gave her a long kiss, then asked, "Are you going to sleep all day?"

To which she responded, "Is my husband an early riser?"

He looked at her, mischief burning in his eyes, "Up to now I have been. Marriage may change my habits."

"Don't change a one, Andrew. I want you just as you are." She responded, suddenly serious.

"You think you'll keep me then?" he teased.

Her arms went around him and holding to him tightly; she wedged her head on his shoulder, "For the rest of my life."

"Or mine. Which brings me to another subject. I have something for you."

"Another gift? You shouldn't have!" she protested while her eyes grew bright with excitement.

Andrew handed her a small gaily-wrapped box, and she ripped the paper from it. A puzzled frown wrinkled her brow as she peered at a folded sheet of paper inside it, "What's this?"

"Open it, you'll see."

The crisp paper crackled as she opened it, the smell of ink still clinging to it. Curiosity changed to astonishment as she cried, "Andrew, this is a deed to Sweetwater—,"

"In its original size. I was able to buy it all back,"

"But it's made out to me—,"

"That's right, Rachel. Sweetwater is yours, free and clear. No one can ever take it from you."

"But, but," She stuttered.

"Don't you want it?" Andrew asked disappointment darkening his features.

"Of course, but don't you understand, Drew? I don't need Sweetwater anymore, I have you and you're all I need or want." She explained lifting her hands and bringing his face down to hers.

Andrew kissed the lips she offered to him then folded her in his arms. They sat thus for a long while, each relishing the joy of loving. Andrew finally stood up and handed her dressing gown to her, "Get up, Mrs. Meredith. We have hot tea, or it was hot, waiting for us on the balcony."

Rachel blushed, "You mean Sarah has been in here already this morning?"

Andrew laughed, "No, your husband went to the kitchen to fetch it. I didn't want anyone intruding in our world this morning. Are you going to join me or not?"

She leaped out of bed, "Wild horses couldn't stop me."

Minutes later they stood together, arms entwined as they looked over the broad expanse of fields. Andrew tightened his hold on Rachel as uninvited thoughts intruded, bringing a feeling of foreboding in the midst of their happiness. He spoke, "Rachel, I have set up an account for you in the Bank of England with enough funds for you to live comfortably on the rest of your life"

"But why? Drew?" Her heart fluttered.

"Because I want to protect your future, so that you need have no worry. With Sweetwater yours and enough money in a foreign bank to sustain you, you'll be safe."

"Drew, you're my future. I couldn't face it without you."

After a long silence, Andrew said hesitantly, reluctant to spoil their first morning as husband and wife, "Rachel, life as we know it will soon be over. Those fields in front of us may be strewn with the bodies of our people fighting for an existence that is doomed. I've taken an unpopular stand and am exposed to some danger because of it. My peace of mind requires that I make provisions for you while I can. The time may come when I am no longer able to."

Tentacles of fear gripped Rachel, "Then stop what you're doing. I need you, Andrew. Don't take any risk, I couldn't survive without you."

He gently shook her, "You are a survivor, Rachel; strong as a willow tree."

"I wouldn't want to survive without you, promise me you'll stop what you're doing." She pled.

"I can't. This conviction runs as deep in me as the love I have for you. If a man's not true to his conviction, he's no man at all. Rachel Gregory Meredith, would you require my manhood, my self-respect?"

Rachel dropped her head on his chest and clung to him as the dark, ominous clouds of change intruded, marring their golden promise of tomorrow.

Author's Biography

Doris English is a freelance author who resides, in Dallas, GA. Realizing that serenity nurtures creativity, Doris English and her husband, Bob, along with their three daughters, moved to a small farm in this community just outside metro Atlanta. The area which is steeped in civil war history along with her degree in history (emphasis in American history) from University of West Georgia ignited her imagination for times past thus the Sweetwater Legacy series was envisioned. Doris' work includes other novels, both contemporary and history, along with magazine and newspaper articles.

Don't miss the next exciting book in this series:

Follow Rachel and Andrew as they face the challenges of war as it draws ever nearer Sweetwater, threatening their dreams and plans. See how they handle the stress on their marriage as Daphne arrives without warning from Savannah bringing danger with her. Watch as a grownup Laura brings a new round of romance to Sweetwater.

From Dreams to Ashes

Sweetwater Legacy Series: Book II

available spring 2013

Join the discussion and stay up to date
on all the important announcements
by liking us on Facebook

Facebook.com/DorisStatonEnglish
and
Facebook.com/FromSavannahToSweetwater

CPSIA information can be obtained at www.ICGtesting.com
Printed in the USA
LVOW121152141012

302750LV00003B/1/P